ROYALS

Wed to the Prince

D0716594

ROYALS

COLLECTION

ROYALS

Wed to the Prince

Robyn
DONALD

Leanne
BANKS

Raye
MORGAN

Published in Great Britain 2017
By Mills & Boon, an imprint of HarperCollins*Publishers*
1 London Bridge Street, London, SE1 9GF

ROYALS: WED TO THE PRINCE © 2017 Harlequin Books S.A.

By Royal Command © 2004 Robyn Donald
The Princess and the Outlaw © 2012 Leanne Banks
The Prince's Secret Bride © 2008 Helen Conrad

ISBN: 978-0-263-93250-8

09-0218

Printed and bound in Spain
by CPI, Barcelona

BY ROYAL
COMMAND

ROBYN DONALD

Robyn Donald can't remember not being able to read and will be eternally grateful to the local farmers who carefully avoided her on a dusty country road as she read her way to and from school, transported to places and times far away from her small village in Northland, New Zealand. Growing up fed her habit. As well as training as a teacher, marrying and raising two children, she discovered the delights of romances and read them voraciously, especially enjoying the ones written by New Zealand writers. So much so that one day she decided to write one herself. Writing soon grew to be as much of a delight as reading – although infinitely more challenging – and when eventually her first book was accepted by Mills & Boon she felt she'd arrived home. She still lives in a small town in Northland, with her family close by, using the landscape as a setting for much of her work. Her life is enriched by the friends she's made among writers and readers, and complicated by a determined Corgi called Buster, who is convinced that blackbirds are evil entities. Her greatest hobby is still reading, with travelling a very close second.

PROLOGUE

WHEN the hair on the back of Guy Bagaton's neck lifted, he finished cracking a joke with the bartender before straightening to his full, impressive height and allowing his tawny gaze to drift casually across sand as white as talcum powder.

A woman was coming towards the bar, the fierce Pacific sun summoning blue flames from her hair as she emerged from the feathery shade of the coconut palms. Camouflaged by the woven side panels of the bar, Guy admired the way her crimson sarong set off bare white shoulders. On her the all-purpose cover-all looked coolly sophisticated, especially paired with frivolous sandals that emphasised long, elegant legs. Yet he'd be prepared to bet she hadn't come to the resort to lie in the sun; in spite of the sarong and the erotic sway of her hips, she walked with purpose.

Guy's body stirred in primal interest. 'Who is that?' he asked the bartender, pitching his voice so that it wouldn't travel.

The barman looked up. 'That's Ms Lauren Porter— got in on the plane from Atu a couple of hours ago. She's staying two nights.'

'I see,' Guy said without expression.

When the manager had rung Guy an hour previously, disturbed because their newest guest had broached her intention of visiting a mountain village, the name had rung bells somewhere in his mind. It hadn't taken him long to trace the thin thread of memory to its source—

a conversation a few months ago with one of his cousins, an elderly Bavarian princess who had a keen nose
for gossip and a connoisseur's eye for a good-looking
man.

'I noticed you talking to Marc Corbett and his charming wife,' she said after one of her famous dinner parties.
'I wonder if Paige knows that he keeps an English mistress.'

'I doubt it,' Guy said curtly. Paige Corbett had struck
him as straightforward and very much in love with her
husband, a magnate with varied interests and a reputation for honest dealing.

'Not many people do; they are very discreet and
never seen together, but of course you can't stop gossip—someone always knows. She is a Miss Lauren
Porter, who is long-legged and beautiful and English.
She works in his business. Very clever, I'm told. She
has been close to him for years now.'

Guy raised his brows but said nothing.

The elderly princess nodded. 'And now you don't
like him very much. Even as a child you had a rigid
sense of honour. I like that in a man—it's so rare.'

He'd smiled cynically down at her, but his respect
for Marc Corbett had lessened. When Guy made promises he kept them.

Now, narrowing his eyes against the tropical sun, he
watched Lauren Porter approach the bar. Her travel arrangements had been made by the Corbett organisation,
so this had to be the same woman.

What the hell was she doing here?

When she got close enough for him to see her face,
he blinked in something like shock and inhaled swiftly.
An enchantress—no wonder she kept Marc Corbett on

a leash! Skin like silk, large eyes so pale a grey they glinted uncannily like crystals, and a mouth sultry enough to set the world aflame, allied to a body that gave new meaning to the words sexual chemistry—Lauren Porter had all the necessary attributes for a mistress.

Why did she plan to visit a small, dirt-poor village in the mountains? It had to be business, and so it had to be connected to Marc Corbett, who had fingers in all sorts of industrial pies around the world.

Ignoring the reckless drumming of lust through his body, he frowned and watched her veer away from the bar and disappear into the reception area. He'd better go and find out what she was up to.

It shouldn't be too difficult to persuade her not to leave the resort; women who looked as though they'd just emerged from a fashion magazine scared easily. He'd mention that mountain cockroaches were huge, follow it up with an allusion to leeches, and she'd probably pass out.

Yet even as he grinned derisively, that sense of unease, of prospective danger, thickened around him. Although he had no information to back it up, the tenuous foreboding had been correct too often to dismiss; a couple of times it had saved his life.

He should have collected his mobile phone from the office before coming down to the resort.

'So you've heard nothing about any problems,' he said to the bartender.

The man shrugged. 'There's talk,' he said, 'but on Sant'Rosa we talk a lot.'

'Sit in the bush and drink grog and gossip,' Guy returned tolerantly. 'OK, forget I asked.'

The young man had been polishing glasses. He

stopped now and looked up, the concern in his dark eyes and dark face mirrored in his tone. 'What have you heard?'

'Nothing,' Guy told him truthfully. 'Not a single thing, but you know me— I like to gossip too.'

'War,' the bartender said wearily, picking up another glass. 'We hoped it had finished, but since this preacher started talking about John Frumm bringing in food and drink and cigarettes and all the good things from America, people are getting nervous.'

'I know. Just keep your eyes and ears open, will you?' Guy nodded towards the reception area. 'I think I'll go and make the acquaintance of Ms Porter.'

And once he'd convinced her a trip into the mountains wasn't feasible, he'd talk to the receptionist. She came from a village close by the border, so she might have heard something that would explain the elemental warning running down his spine like a cold finger.

The younger man grinned. 'That Ms Porter, she's pretty—skinny, though. Don't know why you Europeans like skinny women.' He shook his head over the weird tastes of western men, then added, 'She's nice—she smiles and talks to you when you carry her bags.'

She wasn't smiling when Guy stopped just outside the door to the entry lobby; she was talking so intently she hadn't noticed him arrive.

Recalling a fairy tale his English nanny had read to him, he thought, *Hair black as coal, skin white as snow, lips red as roses...*

Up close, she wasn't beautiful, but with a mouth that fuelled erotic dreams, who cared? His body certainly didn't; it was at full alert.

Yet in spite of that mouth and the high, small breasts

and slim waist beneath the sarong, Lauren Porter was all poised control, even though she wasn't getting what she wanted.

Time to bring on the cockroaches, Guy decided ironically, and stepped inside out of the sun.

CHAPTER ONE

LAUREN frowned. 'Do you mean it's *impossible* to get to this village?'

The receptionist hesitated before saying cautiously, 'It is not impossible, ma'am, but it is difficult.'

'Why?'

Anxious brown eyes avoided Lauren's in a respectful manner. 'The road is too dangerous, ma'am.'

On Sant'Rosa the word road was used loosely; the memory of the minibus juddering violently sent a reminiscent twinge through Lauren's body. And that was on the road from the airport to the resort.

The prospect of tackling an even worse route wasn't pleasant. So what, she thought grimly, was new? Nothing about this side trip had been easy.

Not for the first time, she wished she hadn't promised to check out Paige's favourite charity. In London it had seemed simple, a mere matter of breaking her journey to a New Zealand holiday with a couple of days on a tropical island.

Ha! Her flight to Singapore had been delayed so she'd missed the connection, and as she hadn't got to Sant'Rosa until after midnight she'd had to wait for the early-morning plane to the South Coast.

After only a couple of hours' sleep, her head was aching, her eyes were gritty, and her smile was hurting her lips. And now this! She pushed a stray strand of damp black hair back from her cheek. 'What about public transport?'

Still avoiding her gaze, the receptionist stopped shuffling papers to adjust the scarlet hibiscus behind one ear. 'Ma'am, there is nothing suitable for you.'

'I'm perfectly happy to go on the local bus,' Lauren said crisply.

The woman looked harried. 'It is not suitable,' she repeated. 'And that village is very alone—apart.'

The village had set up an export venture that involved a factory, so it couldn't be too isolated. A steely note running through her words, Lauren persisted, 'In that case, where can I hire a car?'

From behind a hard masculine voice drawled, 'You can't. There are no car-hire firms on the South Coast.'

Lauren stiffened, every sense sounding alarms. The new arrival's voice—deep, subtly infused with irony— oozed male confidence.

Slowly she turned. Although tall, she had to look up to meet half-closed topaz eyes between lashes as dark as her most forbidden desire. Her stomach—normally an obedient organ not given to independent action— lurched, then dropped into free fall.

Inanely she repeated, 'No car-hire firms?'

'Lady, the closest car-hire firm is in the capital, and that, as you already know, is an hour's flight away over a mountain range.'

He infused the word *lady* with a slow, purring sexuality that fanned over her skin like the warm breath of a lover. *And where did that thought come from?* Clutching her tattered dignity around her, she asked crisply, 'Then how can I get to this village?'

Because she couldn't pronounce the name she thrust out the slip of paper Paige had given her.

His expression altered in some subtle way as he examined it, but his tone didn't change. 'I doubt if you

can. The last rains brought down half a mountain onto
the road.'

'Surely they've fixed it.'

One dark brow—his left, she noticed—lifted in sardonic amusement. 'The locals walk it, and as you may
have noticed, Sant'Rosa hasn't yet flung itself headlong
into tourism. It's still trying to get over a civil war.'

'I know that.' Someone should tell him that the purpose of designer stubble was to emphasise boldly chiselled features, not blur them. And his black hair needed
cutting.

A second glance convinced her that the shadow
across his jaws and cheeks wasn't for effect—this man
hadn't shaved because he didn't care what people
thought of him. From the corner of her eye she catalogued the rest of his assets, admitting reluctantly that
the overlong black hair had been well cut, and stubble
couldn't hide strong bones and a mouth that combined
sculpted beauty with a suggestion of ruthlessness.

An elusive flash of memory teased her brain.
Somewhere she had seen him…or someone who looked
like him?

Startled, she pinned a brief, dismissive curve to her
lips. Of course she didn't recognise him! An unkempt
expatriate on an island in the middle of the Pacific
Ocean was as far out of her ken as an alien. The men
she met as a junior executive wore suits and strove for
worldliness. This beachcomber, clad in an old black
T-shirt and trousers, looked as though neither the word
sophistication nor the concept existed for him.

She took a deep breath and spoke clearly and carefully. 'Can I fly in? Ms Musi—' she indicated the receptionist, who was gazing at the newcomer as though

he'd saved her from a shark '—tells me that the local public transport isn't suitable.'

'She's right.'

'Why?'

His eyes glinted. 'Would you be happy to travel on the back of an elderly, bullet-holed truck with no shelter from the sun and no seats?'

'If I had to,' she said curtly.

'And cockroaches.' No malice coloured the words as he said, 'Big, black ones. If you go to sleep they chew your toenails.'

Hoping he couldn't see her skin crawl, she snapped, 'I can cope with the local fauna.'

'I doubt it,' he drawled. 'If you're really determined to get there, you could try walking.' He inspected her without haste before adding gravely, 'But if you go like that you'd better invest in some sunscreen.'

Who was this sarcastic newcomer with mocking eyes and far too much presence? The manager? Hardly, but it was typical of this trip into the wilds of the Pacific Ocean that she should be confronted by a scruffy dead-beat with an attitude—and a bewildering, raw sex appeal that set every treacherous nerve in her body jangling into awareness.

Her composure evaporating under the impact of his lazily appreciative smile, Lauren stiffened. All right, so the pretty sarong in her favourite shade of crimson revealed an uncomfortable amount of white skin, but she wasn't an idiot! Forcing her voice into its usual confident tone, she asked, 'How long would that take me?'

'It depends how fast you walk. Don't stop for long or leeches will bite you. Do you know how to take a leech off your skin? Remove the small end first—'

The receptionist broke in. 'Mr Guy is making a joke,

ma'am, because it is too far for you to walk.' She gave him a shocked look, as though this wasn't what she expected from him. 'It takes two days to come by walking, ma'am.'

Mr Guy didn't exactly tell her who this man was, but at least his name gave her a handle.

In a voice that blended satire with long-suffering, he said, 'Your travel agent should have warned you that this region is pretty much without civilisation.' He paused a fraction of a second before finishing, 'As you'd know it, anyway.'

'As you know nothing about me, I'm going to ignore that remark!' Furious with herself for letting him get to her, she reined in her temper.

Fortunately the receptionist burst into the local language and the newcomer turned to listen, obviously understanding every word.

Skimming a cold grey glance over the T-shirt and trousers moulded lovingly to long, powerful legs and lean hips, Lauren was forced to revise her first impression. This was no loser. His thrusting bone structure—high cheekbones and a chin that took on the world—spoke of a total lack of compromise.

And now that he'd dropped the mocking veneer, neither old clothes nor villainous stubble could hide his formidable authority. Beneath the beachcomber persona was pure alpha male, testosterone and arrogance smoking off his bronzed hide like an aura. Untamed, certainly, but—intriguing, if you fancied men who looked as though they could deal with anything up to and including marauding Martians.

In other words, she thought hollowly, just the sort of man to take her to Paige's pet village—if she could ignore the instincts that warned her to run like crazy in the opposite direction.

He looked up, meeting her sideways glance with a coolly speculative survey.

Lauren's self-possession crumbled under an awareness as steamy and ruthless as the tropical heat. Not my type! she thought fiercely. She preferred men with at least basic social skills. More colour stung her skin, fading swiftly at the note of desperation in the receptionist's tone.

Black brows meeting above a nose that hinted at Roman gladiators, the newcomer posed several staccato questions, to which the woman responded with increasing reluctance.

Feeling like an eavesdropper, Lauren examined a rack of postcards. Fans hummed softly overhead, sending waves of sultry air over her bare arms. The small resort promised total relaxation, and what it lacked in modern luxuries it made up for in exquisite beauty and peace. Until this man appeared she hadn't missed air-conditioning a bit.

Now, in spite of the heat, she wished she'd slung a shirt over her shoulders before leaving her cabin.

Eventually the receptionist's lengthy explanation— punctuated by worried glances at Lauren—wound down to a conclusion.

Something was clearly amiss; a chilly emptiness congealed beneath Lauren's ribs, but she hadn't come all this way to be fobbed off.

The man turned to inspect her. 'Why do you want to go to this village? It has no accommodation for tourists, nothing to do. The only bathroom is a pool in the river. They are not geared for sightseers.'

He had a faint trace of an accent, so elusive Lauren

wasn't sure it existed. Exasperated by the beads of moisture gathering across her brow and top lip, she evaded his question. 'I know that, but I'm not planning to stay. All I want is to spend an afternoon there. In fact, that's why I came to Sant'Rosa—specifically to go there.'

'Why?'

'I don't see that it's any concern of yours.' Lauren didn't try to hide the frosty undertone to her words.

He shrugged broad shoulders. 'Whatever your reason is, it's not good enough,' he said flatly, and forestalled her instant objection. 'Come and have a drink with me and I'll explain why.'

Was this merely a pick-up? Obscurely disappointed, Lauren glanced at the receptionist, who hurried into speech with an air of relief. 'Mr Guy will help you,' she promised, indicating the man with a wave of one beautiful hand and a smile that paid tribute to his potent male magnetism.

OK, so he wasn't a rapist or serial killer. Not here, anyway.

'In that case, I will have a drink, thank you,' Lauren said calmly, wishing that she'd worn something cool and well-cut and sharply classical—and a lot less revealing.

And it would help to have some make-up to shelter behind; sunscreen and a film of coloured lip gloss were flimsy shields against the hard intimidation of his gaze.

The man beside her walked as silently and easily as a panther, his controlled grace hinting subtly of menace. Lauren resented the way he towered above her, especially as each inch of powerful, honed male exuded a potent sensuality.

So his name was Mr Someone Guy. Or Mr Guy

Someone. And she wasn't going to tell him who she was; if he didn't have the manners to properly introduce himself, she certainly wasn't going to make the effort.

As though he felt her survey, he shafted a glance her way. A high-voltage charge sizzled between them, part antagonism, part heady chemistry. Tension jolted her heart into overcompensation.

Turning her face resolutely towards the small bar, she decided wildly that he was wasted here. A man who gave off enough electricity to melt half the world's ice caps should head for some place where his talents could be really appreciated.

The North Pole, for instance.

Who was he? The local layabout, angling for a wild holiday fling? Or perhaps looking out for a rich, lonely woman to rescue him from all this tropical heat?

No. Disturbingly sexy he might be, but instinct warned her he was more buccaneer than gigolo.

In the voice her half-brother, for whom she worked, referred to as Patient but Friendly Executive, she asked, 'Do you own the resort, Mr Guy?'

Winged black brows lifted. 'No,' he said briefly. 'It belongs to the local tribe.' Without touching her, he steered her across to a table beneath a large thatched umbrella. 'This is probably the coolest spot around, and it's got a good view of the lagoon.'

Grateful for the shade, she lowered herself into a chair and persevered, 'But you live here? In this particular area of Sant'Rosa?' she amended, when his brows lifted in saturnine enquiry.

'Off and on.' He nodded to a waiter. 'What would you like to drink?'

'Papaya and pineapple juice, thank you.'

He ordered it for her, and a beer for himself. A tiny

gecko scuttled across the table; smiling, Lauren watched it disappear over the edge. When she looked up, Guy was watching her.

'You're not afraid of them?' he asked.

A subtle intonation convinced her that he wasn't English. 'Not the little ones, although some of the big ones have a nasty predatory gleam in their eyes.'

He laughed outright at that—another slow, sexy laugh that brushed her taut nerves with velvety insinuation.

'They won't bite, not even in self-defence,' he said, stressing the first word just enough for Lauren to immediately wonder if he bit—and when...

He finished, 'But you'd be surprised at the number of women who are terrified of even the tiny ones.'

'Men too, I'll bet. It makes you wonder why some people come to the tropics.' Was the stubble soft to touch—or bristly? She'd never kissed a man with that much—

Whoa!

He leaned back in the chair, his pose utterly relaxed, but his level, cool gaze held her prisoner. 'So why are you here? More specifically, why are you determined to find your way to one of the more untamed spots on Sant'Rosa?'

She parried, 'Is that untamed as in dangerous?'

'As in without conveniences,' he told her, his keen gaze steady and intimidating. 'But it's in the border area, and the border between Sant'Rosa and the Republic has always been tense.'

'I thought the treaty after the civil war stopped the threat of an invasion by the Republic.'

Wide shoulders lifted in a slight shrug. 'A new player—a charismatic preacher—seems to have got together a ragtag following on both sides of the border. He's preaching part religious revival, part cargo cult. Which is—'

'I know what a cargo cult is,' she said crisply. 'Its followers expect a saviour to bring them the benefits of western civilisation. I'd not realised they could be violent.'

'So far they're not, but over the past couple of days there have been rumours that someone is supplying them with weapons.'

Not that anyone had actually seen the rifles and explosives that were being talked about. Guy suspected they didn't exist. However, every islander was taught to use a machete from a very early age, and he'd seen the damage the long blades could inflict. If—and it was a big if—any hyped-up converts decided to go on the rampage, they could kill.

He watched her slender black brows draw together. What the hell was she doing here? And why was she so evasive? Women like her—sleekly elegant from the shiny top of her black head to the polished nails on her toes—demanded more from their holidays than a tiny resort with little social life and a heavy emphasis on family groups.

She looked up sharply, the eyes that had been ice-clear now silvery and impossible to read. 'Only rumours?'

'Almost certainly. Rumours—most of them false—run hot through Sant'Rosa. The people are barely coping with the aftermath of a bloody ten years of civil war, and in spite of the peace treaty they still don't trust the Republic over the border.' He paused. 'The receptionist comes from the village you want to visit, and she's just told me that the preacher has disappeared.'

'And that's bad?'

'Almost certainly not,' he said, hoping he was right.

Because it was too easy to watch her face, he switched his gaze to a family, parents shepherding two small children. Armed with beach toys and a couple of inflatable rings, the children dashed into the improbably turquoise lagoon, yelling and laughing as they splashed each other and their parents.

That itch at the back of his neck sharpened his senses to primitive alertness, a fierce, feral reaction to stimuli his rational brain couldn't process.

Which was why he was resisting the compulsion to bundle up these helpless family groups—and the woman opposite with her cool touch-me-not air—and get them out of here on the next plane.

He didn't dare follow his impulse because the local tribe had sunk every bit of cash they had into the resort; a false alarm, with the resultant bad publicity, could see them lose it all.

The woman opposite was watching the group too, her mouth curving as one of the children shrieked with delight. Grimly, he cursed his unruly loins for responding to that smile with piercing hunger.

Lauren Porter frowned. 'So are this preacher's followers likely to turn violent when no saviour turns up with all the blessings of western civilisation free for the taking?'

'I doubt it. They've seen what fighting does, so they'll almost certainly drift off through the bush to their native villages.'

But they were edgy and frustrated. Peace hadn't brought the people the benefits they'd longed for, and many were ripe for unscrupulous manipulation. When the promised saviour didn't eventuate the preacher might try to salvage his slipping authority by suggesting they collect the material benefits from the nearest place that had them.

They wouldn't go to the mine, which had its own private security force; they'd choose easy pickings. In other words, the resort.

All ifs and buts, with absolutely nothing to base it on. Guy shrugged, trying to banish that needling premonition.

'But they might not,' she said shrewdly, and echoed his thoughts with uncanny accuracy. 'Perhaps they might decide to come and get the goodies for themselves.'

'It's unlikely, and even if they did, the police are watching the situation very closely. The resort would be notified in time to get you out.'

'And everyone else too, I hope.'

'Trust me,' he said with a smile he hoped was reassuring.

The arrival of the bartender with their drinks silenced her; Guy eyed her from beneath his lashes, controlling the sharp appetite her presence roused. The combination of thoroughbred lines and the gentle curves of her breasts and hips packed an explosive impact. Mix all that with silky black hair and eyes of cool, translucent grey, and you had trouble.

He wasn't even going to think about her mouth; it did serious damage to his objectivity.

Lifting his beer in silent salute, he said, 'At the moment it wouldn't be sensible to go into the mountains.'

'What about you?' she asked abruptly.

'What about me?'

'Would you go there?'

'If I had to,' he said warily, watching her.

'So you could take me with you to the village?'

Even softened by femininity, her jaw was combative. God save him from stubborn women, and this one in particular. 'I'm not taking you there,' he said curtly.

'Of course I'd pay you.'

'Lady,' he said, angry in a way he'd never experienced before, 'I am not going, and neither are you. If you want to see how the third world lives, the resort will organise a tour to the local village.' His voice was scathing.

Colour swept along those high cheekbones and her teeth clamped down on her bottom lip.

Guy resisted the urge to lean forward and put a hand over her mouth to stop the ravaging of that ripe bow. He'd take much better care of it than she did…

It was no better when she drank some of her juice; how the hell did she make a simple act like that signal a prelude to sex?

Get over it! he ordered savagely.

Putting the glass down, she fixed him with a determined gaze. 'I want to visit that particular village and tribe because a—a friend of mine has helped them set up an oil industry from *sali* nuts. I'm on my way to New Zealand on holiday, and I promised my friend I'd see how things were going.'

Marc Corbett, of course. Guy nodded, watching her from beneath drooping lashes. 'Then you'll have to tell *your friend* that I wouldn't let you go.'

He wasn't disappointed by her reaction to this deliberate provocation. Her smile froze, but she let it linger as she reached for her glass and lifted it once more to her mouth, keeping her gaze on his face while she drank the juice slowly and delicately.

Although he knew exactly what she was doing—using her female appeal as a weapon—his pulses jumped, and a carnal urgency heated his blood. When lust hit inconveniently he could usually kill it without too much effort, but this time he had to wrestle it back into its lair.

'Well, that's a moot point,' she said sweetly, putting the glass back down. 'I don't know that you have any authority to stop me.'

She didn't lick the juice from her lips; she wasn't so obvious. Guy counted to ten before saying bluntly, 'I'll stop you if I have to handcuff you to my side until I can put you on a plane out. Going into the mountains might well be dangerous; if you pay enough you'll probably get someone to take you, but you'll be putting them in danger too.'

Her eyes were translucent, the grey soft as a dove's breast, but intelligent and searching. She scrutinised him for several long seconds before nodding. 'Yes, you really do mean it. All right, I won't go.'

Surprised by relief, Guy picked up his beer and took another long swallow, welcoming the cool bitterness before realising that she hadn't actually said she wouldn't try to go. 'Give me your promise that you won't leave the resort.'

She looked at him with stony dignity. 'You have no right to demand any promise from me, but I'm not stupid; I don't want to put anyone in jeopardy and neither would my friend. I wish I could get in touch with the headman, though, just to ask how the scheme is going.'

That he could give her. 'As far as I'm aware, it's doing very well, but if you want to contact him, I have a mobile phone in my office,' he offered.

She sent him a glance, cold as moonlight, from beneath her lashes. 'Thank you, but I'll ring from here,' she said politely.

'You can't.'

When her brows shot up he explained, 'After the civil war each village chief in this area was supplied with a mobile phone. Their link isn't connected to the ordinary telephone system, which doesn't extend much beyond the towns.'

After a moment's pause she said, 'I see.' And added on a sigh, 'It's so beautiful here, like paradise. Why can't it be peaceful too?'

'There's always a serpent,' he told her laconically, getting to his feet. 'And usually what it wants is power and money.'

'Do you think this has anything to do with the fact that there's a huge copper mine in this part of Sant'Rosa—and that the area has been under claim by the Republic for fifty years or so?'

'You've done some research.'

'I always research,' she said calmly, thick lashes hiding her thoughts.

When they flicked up again she gazed at him with a limpid innocence that sent suspicion bristling through him.

He jibed, 'And now you know its limitations.'

She ignored that. 'It seems interesting that the preacher started destabilising the border area just after the international peacekeeping force left. If I were cynical, I might wonder whether the Republic hopes that perhaps they can use the cargo cult to foment trouble, then invade under the excuse of preventing yet another civil war.'

He nodded. 'I'd call that realistic rather than cynical. Especially as the Sant'Rosan army is very small, and made up of units that still don't trust each other after fighting on opposite sides in the war. How they'd fare in battle no one is prepared to say.'

'Do you expect war?'

'No.' He drained his beer and set the bottle down on the table with a sharp clink. 'Come on, we'll go into town.'

'Town?' Lauren asked foolishly.

His brows lifted. 'You wanted to use the telephone, didn't you? It's in my office in town.'

When she didn't immediately answer he added with mocking amusement, 'You'll be perfectly safe with me. I have a reputation to uphold.'

And because she didn't suspect him of anything more than an overdose of testosterone, she shrugged slightly and got up to go with him—although not before stopping at the reception desk to tell the woman where she was going.

That done, she hitched her bag over her shoulder. 'I'd better go and get some money,' she said brightly. And after she'd extracted her money from the safe that held her papers, she'd sling a shirt over her shoulders.

With an amused glance he opened the door for her. 'Why? I don't expect payment, and the shops aren't open so late in the day. Even if they were, I doubt very much whether you would find anything to buy in them.'

Bother. She summoned her most dazzling smile, recklessly glad when she saw his eyes darken. 'You'd be surprised,' she said sweetly, going through the door ahead of him.

CHAPTER TWO

GUY'S vehicle could probably take the terrain on Mars in its stride. An elderly Land Rover, it possessed only the most basic conveniences and had never had air-conditioning, but that was all right; it didn't have any windows either.

'At least it doesn't have bullet holes,' Lauren observed with a kind smile that might have been overdone.

'Only because I had them taken out,' he said blandly, opening the passenger door for her. 'It probably has cockroaches, though.'

She gave him a repeat of her smile, and forced herself not to search for insects while she waited for him to get in. Because her father, a motoring enthusiast, had taught her to recognise a well-tuned engine, she was surprised when he switched on the key; the battered, dusty vehicle ran like a dream.

Guy Whoever—or Whoever Guy, she reminded herself scrupulously—was familiar to the locals; most waved cheerfully at him, flashing smiles as he tooted in return.

She turned around to gaze at two small boys, hand in hand on the side of the road. 'Are they born with machetes over their shoulders? They look far too young to be carrying such dangerous implements around with them.'

'They call them bush knives here, and yes, they learn to use them almost as soon as they can walk.'

Rebuffed by his indifferent tone, she concentrated on

admiring the jungle and the range of mountains ahead, purple-blue in the distant haze that indicated the approach of dusk. When they arrived at the little town, some miles along the road to the mine and the airport, the empty streets gave it a disturbing, almost sinister atmosphere.

'Dinner time,' Guy said laconically, stopping outside the only block of shops in the scruffy main street. He cast her an enigmatic glance. 'The women prepare the food while the men wind down.'

Refusing to rise to the bait, she shrugged and opened the door to get out.

'My office is on the first floor.' Guy indicated a flight of stark concrete steps rising from the street.

Noting the casually efficient way he examined the street and the stairs, Lauren decided that he'd know how to deal with any threat. His seamless air of confidence placated fears she hadn't allowed herself to recognise.

A large, anonymous room, his office was at least clean and tidy, with everything locked away in steel cabinets.

'To keep the insects and vermin out,' Guy said when he saw her looking around.

When eventually they got in touch with the headman of the village, Lauren spoke to him for some minutes, straining to follow his heavily accented English. The *sali* nut scheme was coming along well; the chief told her proudly of the oil-extraction process, and the amount sent to be turned into soap and other toiletries in New Zealand, and the teacher who had come to live in the village once they'd built the school.

'I'll tell the person who sent me,' she said. 'I've been told it might not be a good idea to travel to the village just now.'

'Not good, ma'am,' he said somberly. 'There are too many rascals around now. Come back next year, when it is quiet again.'

'If I can,' she promised.

From beside her Guy said, 'I'd like to speak to him, please.'

Lauren handed over the receiver and walked to the window to peer down at the dirt road, still eerily vacant except for two small dogs glowering and posturing in a show of dominance. The buildings and trees were rapidly losing substance in the swift tropical dusk. Deep and thick and velvety, it softened the raw intrusion of the buildings on the timeless tropical landscape.

Covertly eyeing Guy as he rattled off what sounded like a set of questions, she learned nothing from his face. He was, she thought warily, big in every way— tall and lithe and powerfully muscled, his wide shoulders and long legs backed up by an overpowering air of strength, both mental and physical.

Conversation concluded, he put the phone in his pocket and said in his almost perfectly accented English, 'Everything seems quiet there. The headman says the preacher is with his family high in the mountains—there has been a death.'

'So we can breathe again,' she said frivolously, shocked to realise how tense she'd been.

'I hadn't stopped,' he returned on a dry note, and opened the door.

Unclenching her teeth, Lauren preceded Guy out into the darkness, tossing words over her shoulder like hand grenades.

'I'm glad I can tell my friend that the nut-oil scheme seems to be working. It's great that the villagers get a reliable income from their land without having to fell the forests for lumber.' A little more steadily she added, 'I wish I could have seen what they're doing, though.'

Locking the door behind them, Guy responded with brutal frankness, 'They've got enough to worry about without trying to keep you safe. What are your plans now?'

Lauren looked at the single naked bulb that lit the stairwell. Fighting back a highly suspect—and dangerous—temptation to linger a few days at the resort, she said too promptly, 'I'll leave for New Zealand as soon as I can. Tomorrow, if I can get a seat on an outgoing plane.'

Guy startled her by unlocking the door again. 'You might, but don't bank on it. There are only two a day, not counting the twice-a-week flight to Valanu.'

'Where's Valanu? I've never heard of it. Is it another town on Sant'Rosa?'

'No.' Back in the office he picked up a telephone and punched in a few numbers. 'It's a scatter of islands to the south, part of another small Pacific nation.'

'The back of beyond, in other words.'

'Or paradise, depending on your outlook. It's a fair way off the beaten track,' he conceded, a disconcerting thread of mockery running through each word as he surveyed her with unreadable eyes and a tilted smile. 'But incredibly beautiful.' His voice lingered half a beat too long on the final word.

Colour tinged the skin along her cheekbones and an odd sensation twisted fiercely in the pit of her stomach. Swallowing, she switched her mind to her half-brother's holiday home in New Zealand, remote and lovely and utterly peaceful. Until she'd seen—until a short time ago, she amended swiftly, she'd been aching to get there.

And she still was. Jet lag had clouded her mind. As soon as she had some sleep she'd be her usual self. 'Who are you ringing?'

'The last flight to Atu will have just left, but someone should still be at the airfield. I'll book you a seat on the first plane out.'

Oddly piqued that he was so eager to get rid of her, she said lightly, 'Thank you so much.'

Someone *was* at the airfield, someone called Josef, with whom Guy conducted a conversation in the local language. When he hung up Lauren lifted her brows enquiringly.

'You've a seat reserved on tomorrow afternoon's flight,' he told her.

Formally, her smile set, she murmured, 'You've been very kind.'

His white teeth flashed in a grin. 'My pleasure,' he returned easily. 'Now, as the Chinese restaurant seems to be closed, we can go back to the resort and have dinner or I can take you home and feed you.'

'The resort,' Lauren said instantly, stopping when she realised that he'd tricked her. She met his amused eyes and thought with an entirely uncharacteristic rashness, Well, why not?

She was leaving tomorrow, so why shouldn't she share dinner with the most intriguing man she'd met for a long time? Utterly infuriating, of course—far too macho and high-handed and dominating—but since she'd seen him that dragging tiredness had been replaced by a swift, intoxicating excitement.

They had absolutely nothing in common, and when she was back home she'd wonder what it was about him that arced through her like an electrical charge, but for one night—one evening, she corrected herself hastily—she'd veer slightly towards the wild side. Every woman probably deserved a buccaneer experience once in her life.

But to make sure he didn't think he could lure her into his bed, she said, 'It won't be a late night, though— I've had two hours' sleep in the last twenty-four, and I'm running on empty.'

He understood the implication. Irony tinged his smile as he held open the door. 'I'll deliver you to your door within two minutes of the first yawn. Watch where you put your feet.'

The single bulb over the stairs flickered ominously as a huge moth came to rest on it. To the sound of their footsteps echoing on the bare concrete, Lauren gripped the pipe handrail and negotiated the stairs.

'Now that it's dark the air is fresher, even though it hasn't cooled down much,' she remarked sedately as they walked towards the Land Rover. 'I can smell the scent of the flowers without any underlying taint of decay.'

'That's the tropics—ravishing beauty and rotting vegetation,' Guy said unromantically, opening the vehicle door.

Lauren slid in, watching him walk around the front of the vehicle, tall and powerful in the weak light of the only street lamp. She felt exposed and tingling, as though meeting him had stripped away several skins to reveal a world of unsuspected excitement and anticipation.

Calm down, she warned herself. Heady recklessness is so *not* your thing.

She'd built a successful and satisfying life on discretion and discipline; she wasn't going to allow the tropics to cast any magic spell on her!

Halfway back to the resort, Guy said, 'It seems a pity to leave the South Coast without seeing our main claim to fame.'

'Which is?' she asked cautiously.

'A waterfall.'

Lauren paused. Maybe it was the soft radiance in the sky that proclaimed the imminent arrival of a full moon, but another rash impulse overrode common sense.

'All right,' she said, regretting the words the moment they left her mouth.

Guy swung the vehicle between two dark walls of trees; within seconds the unmarked road deteriorated into teeth-jolting ruts. Nevertheless, he skirted potholes with a nonchalant skill she envied. Clinging to the seat, she looked around uneasily; nightfall had transformed the lush vegetation into an alien, menacing entity that edged onto the track.

Watching large leaves whip by, she decided she'd been crazy to accept Guy's challenge—because challenge it had definitely been.

He pulled up beneath a huge tree, its heavy foliage drooping to the ground to make a kind of tent around the Land Rover. As he switched off the engine, Lauren groped for the handle and jumped out.

'This way,' he said crisply.

After a few yards the oppressive growth pulled back to reveal a swathe of coarse grass. Lauren's eyes grew accustomed to the darkness as they walked towards a steady soft murmur, infinitely refreshing, that whispered through the sticky air.

'Look,' Guy said, stopping.

Water fell from on high, a shimmering veil under the stars. Down the rock face clustered palms, their fronds edged with the promise of moonlight.

'It's beautiful,' she said softly. 'Oh— I didn't realise we were so close to the coast.'

The wide pool emptied over another lip of rock into a small stream that wound its way a few hundred yards to the sea. Through the feathery tops of the coconut palms she could see the white crescent of a beach and the oily stillness of a wide bay.

'I'm surprised there's no coral reef around the island,' she said, uncomfortably moved by the exquisite allure of the scene. It roused a wild longing she'd never experienced before—an urge to shuck off the trappings of civilisation and surrender to the potent seduction of the Pacific.

Guy told her, 'Not all South Sea islands have them. Right, it's just about time for the show. Look at the waterfall.'

The moon soared above the horizon, its light transforming the fall of water into a shimmering gold radiance.

'Oh!' she breathed. 'Oh, that is exquisite—like a fall of firelit silk! Thank you for bringing me here.'

When he didn't answer she looked up.

He was watching her, the bold structure of his face picked out by the moonlight. His mouth was compressed, and his high, faintly Slavic cheekbones gave him a half-wild, exotic air. He looked, she thought feverishly, like the buccaneer she'd likened him to before—merciless and utterly compelling. Tension flamed through her, driven by a rush of adrenaline that took her breath away.

Dry-mouthed and desperate, she swivelled away to fix her gaze on the quietly falling water, glowing with an iridescent mingling of gold and silver and copper, and tried to defuse the situation with words. 'It's such a familiar glory, isn't it, moonrise, and yet I get carried away by it each time. But I've never seen anything like this—it looks like cloth of gold, almost as though the light is coming through the water from the back.'

'As you say, a familiar miracle.' He took her arm and walked her across to the bank. The moonlight hadn't yet reached the pool; it gleamed before them, a shimmering circle of obsidian.

His touch cut through her defences, bypassing willpower, smashing her hard-won control to kindle fires in her flesh.

Dark magic, she thought despairingly. She ached to surrender to its terrifying temptation so much she could taste the craving, sweet and potent and desperate.

Staring into the smooth black water, she clenched her muscles against desire, forcing herself to freeze, not to turn into his arms and lift her face in mute invitation. He said nothing, but she heard his breathing alter, and tension spiralled between them, glittering and seductive. All it would take was one movement from her, and she'd know the power of his kiss and shiver at the warmth of his hands on her breasts...

'The stream comes from springs in the mountains, so the water is cold.' His voice was steady, yet a raw note grated beneath the matter-of-fact tone.

Heat spread from the pit of her stomach, a sweet, piercing flame that took no prisoners.

Cold water, she thought feverishly, just might do the trick, because this instant arousal had never happened to her before, and one-night stands were not her style. Stooping, she dipped her hand in, whipping it back with shock as it numbed her fingers. 'It's freezing!'

Something in his stillness alerted her; he seemed to loom over her, almost threatening. She scrambled up

again and took a couple of hasty steps away, turning to
watch the transient radiance of the waterfall fade as the
moon leapt higher in the sky. Her blood pulsed heavily,
filling her with this strange, exotic madness.

The tropics, she thought feverishly, were notorious
for this sort of thing. *Get over it.*

'That is utterly beautiful,' she said, striving for a
briskly practical tone. 'Thank you for bringing me here.'

'My pleasure,' he told her without expression. 'Shall
we go?'

She nodded and they started back towards the tree
that hid the Land Rover. A few steps beneath the overhanging branches, Guy stopped and listened, an intimidating shadow in the darkness of the canopy. Startled
and uneasy, Lauren opened her mouth to ask what was
going on, but the hard impact of his hand across her
mouth stopped the words.

Oh God, she thought, struggling violently, you utter
moron, Lauren Porter!

Hand still across her mouth, he hauled her into the
thicker darkness and slammed her against the trunk,
judging his strength so that although she was crushed
breathless between his body and the unforgiving tree,
she wasn't hurt. Imprisoned by his strength, she felt the
iron strength of muscles flexed for action.

Think! she adjured herself, fighting the terror that
tried to freeze her brain. Buying time and hoping to take
him by surprise, she slumped against him and sucked
in air, visualising just what she'd do to disable him.

His words pitched only for her ear, he said, 'I can
hear voices, and I don't know who they are.'

Lauren strained to listen, but apart from the sweet
singing of the waterfall she could hear nothing.

Eventually, still in that same chilling monotone, he said, 'Stay still and don't make a noise.'

Eyes enormous above the ruthless hand that compelled her silence, she nodded.

His grip relaxed. Instantly, fingers curving into claws, Lauren reached for his genitals and opened her mouth to scream.

His cruel hand stifled any sound. With lethal strength Guy quelled her struggles and pulled her against him, locking his other arm around her.

'Shut up!' he said in a low, fierce thread of a voice that terrified her anew.

When she tried to fight with her teeth and her nails, he shook her hard enough to jar her, then muttered, 'Listen, damn you! What can you hear?'

Above the softly lyrical music of the waterfall came voices. Male voices chanting something—the guttural rhythms becoming louder. Tension dried Lauren's mouth and drove more adrenaline into every cell. The primitive fear of assault and rape was replaced by an even more basic one—that of death.

Yet possibly they were just villagers out on a fishing trip, and Guy was making sure there'd be no witnesses to—to whatever he wanted to do.

She had an instant to make up her mind whether or not to trust him. Later she'd convince herself that her decision was based on sheer pragmatism—she'd have a better chance of survival if she had to deal with only one man.

Yet it was instinct that convinced her, not common sense or good judgement.

In her ear he murmured, 'Don't move, don't say anything.'

She nodded. Stealthily, slowly, he eased his hand

away from her mouth. In spite of his size he moved as
silently as a cat, positioning himself with his back to
her, shielding her, she realised, with his body from
whatever danger lurked out there. Terrified for his
safety, she took comfort from the steady pounding of
his heart as her apprehension condensed into ice.

The voices receded, but still Guy stayed motionless.
She was stiff and shaking when at last he stepped
away.

'Who—?' she whispered.

Guy's lethal, slashing gesture stopped the words in
her throat. He was looking towards the sea; as she
watched he moved with a fluid lack of noise to part the
leaves on one of the branches that sheltered them.

Beneath his breath he said, 'There—yes. Can you see
them?'

They were some distance away, but the moon shone
on lithe oiled bodies, already almost on the beach.
About twenty men, carrying what appeared to be spears.

'Out to sea,' Guy said quietly.

Narrowing her eyes, she squinted into the glare of the
moon. Small black shapes seemed to be skipping across
its path over the sea.

'Canoes?' she whispered.

'Dugouts. Banana boats, which have outboards, but
they're not using them tonight. And they're coming
from the wrong direction—heading towards the resort.'
He made up his mind. 'Come on, we need to get out of
here. Get into the Land Rover, but don't slam the door
until I turn the engine on. Then lock it and keep down.'

Numbly, Lauren obeyed. As the vehicle burst from
beneath the tree, she locked the door and prayed that
no one lay in wait along that narrow, treacherous track.

Guy had the night sight of a predator; without head-lights, he drove at high speed through the thick darkness, confidently following the track Lauren couldn't see. On the way to the waterfall she'd enjoyed the difference between the exotic vegetation and the woods she was accustomed to; now the jungle threatened, hiding who knew what danger.

'Do you think they were going to join the canoeists, or fight them?' she asked once they had left the waterfall and its black pool behind.

'I don't know, but that was a war chant,' he said curtly.

Fighting a sickening knot of fear, she swayed as the vehicle swung around corners and surged through potholes and ruts. A sense of danger—palpable and chillingly pervasive—settled around them. Once, in a small clearing, she caught a glimpse of Guy's profile against the moon, and a memory teased her mind with fugitive recognition.

She'd seen a photograph—and then the tantalising image vanished, wiped from her brain.

Where—and how—would she have seen a photograph of a beachcomber from Sant'Rosa?

He glanced at her and suddenly swore in a liquid language that sounded vaguely Italian before ordering, 'Pull my shirt out of my trousers.'

'*What?*'

He flashed her a feral grin. 'Contain yourself. You're showing far too much gleaming skin—far too obvious. Cover it with my shirt.'

'But that leaves you exposed.'

'I'm much darker than you, so I'm harder to see.' The amusement was gone; this time it was an order. 'Pull the shirt out from my waistband and haul it up over the arm furthest from you; I'll tell you when to drag it over my head.'

'Surely stopping—'

'I'm not stopping,' he said quietly. 'I don't know who else might be around. Get the shirt off.'

Lauren gritted her teeth as her questing fingers skidded over sleek skin padded with muscle. Once his arm had been freed she waited, the material gathered in her hand.

'There's a straight length of road— OK, haul it over my head. *Now!*'

She jerked the soft, warm garment over his head in one smooth movement.

'Get it off my other arm—now!' he barked.

He made it easy for her, lithely shrugging free of the shirt. 'Now cover yourself,' he ordered in a tone that lifted every tiny hair on her body upright.

Silently she hauled it over her head, shivering as the material settled around her shoulders. The faint scent of his skin—vital, potent—almost banished the metallic taste of fear in her mouth.

Guy commanded, 'Crouch down on the floor and stay there until I tell you to get out. Cover your face and your hands. If we stop, don't move unless I tell you to. If we get stopped, don't say anything—try not to breathe.'

The ice beneath her ribs expanding, she obeyed, folding herself into the foot well and praying that the maverick instinct to trust him hadn't played her false. 'Those men were aiming for the resort, weren't they?'

He didn't try to evade the truth. 'That was the direction they were heading towards.'

'Do you think there might be violence?'

When he didn't answer immediately she said with

sharp emphasis, 'I'm not going to faint or scream or panic.'

The swift flash of his grin reassured her. 'I believe you.' But the momentary spark of humour dissolved into grimness as he swerved to avoid some small animal scurrying across the road.

Lauren braced herself, wincing as her elbow hit the floor.

He went on calmly, 'What their leader—or leaders— plan, I have no idea. If they find the resort empty, they'll probably take what they want, get drunk on the contents of the bar, then go back home.'

She nodded. 'How long will it take us to get to the resort?'

'We're not going there,' he said, changing gear.

CHAPTER THREE

'WHAT?' When he didn't answer she demanded, 'Why not?'

'Because I'm taking you straight to the airport,' he said above the snarl of the engine.

Lauren peered up at an angular jaw harshly outlined against the radiant moonlight. She pitched her voice louder. 'But we have to warn them.'

'They'll have been warned. The jungle might look empty, but there are eyes everywhere, which is why you're sitting on the floor now.' He shot a swift glance at her shocked face. 'Worrying about them isn't going to achieve anything; I'm not going back to the resort.'

Appalled, she demanded, 'But—what about the children?'

'Leave it,' he bit back, his voice coldly adamant. 'The resort's in direct contact with the police—the staff will have evacuated the tourists as soon as they got the word.'

'And if it isn't just a ragtag and bobtail group of cargo cultists who want European-style beds and television sets?' she almost shouted. 'If they're armed and they mean mayhem, what then?'

He concentrated on steering at heart-shocking speed around a tight corner. 'Once we've got you all out of the way, we'll deal with whatever happens.'

Lauren huddled uncomfortably against the seat, wondering if people were crouching in ambush with rifles and machetes. She was, she realised, afraid, but not terrified; somehow Guy exuded an aura of such authority that she trusted him to get them out of whatever situation they were in.

Something he'd said clicked. She blurted, 'You're planning to stay and fight, aren't you?' When he didn't answer she persisted, 'Why? Are you Sant'Rosan?'

'No,' he said curtly, a total lack of compromise in his tone. 'But I know the people and I've got a lot invested in Sant'Rosa— *Get right down!*'

Before she could react, he swore and thrust her forcefully beneath the dash as he applied the brakes. The vehicle slammed to a stop.

Crouched in a heap, her heart jumping so noisily she was sure it could be heard above the noise of the engine, Lauren heard rough, angry male voices. In spite of the thick heat, she shivered and tried to slow down the quick, shallow pants of her breathing.

Calmly Guy answered, his voice level and without fear. When someone laughed Lauren relaxed slightly, glancing up as Guy asked a question. Harsh yellow light—a spotlight?—traced the sweep of his cheekbones; she recalled the Slavic horsemen who had ridden into Europe over a millennium ago, and wondered just what his ancestry was.

Someone said something that made him frown and fire another question. He looked so confident and completely in charge of the situation that she was startled when she saw his lean fingers tighten on the steering wheel. His next remark produced much more laughter; he grinned and added a few words that brought a babble of comment.

Oh, how she wished she understood the language! Fluency in French and German amounted to nothing in this turbulent part of the world.

Although her body soon began to complain, she didn't dare move a muscle, not even when the vehicle started and they drove off to a chorus of deep farewells.

'All right,' Guy said a few minutes later, 'we're out of sight. You can sit up, but keep your head down.'

Stiffly she uncurled, stretching her arms. 'Who were they?'

'A police patrol, but they warned that there are roving bands of possible looters in the bush so we won't take any chances. The resort's been cleared—the guests are at the airport.'

Well, at least they'd be safe there, and she'd be able to resume her journey to New Zealand.

She said, 'I'm so glad they're all right.' And then remembered something. 'But you said there are no flights until tomorrow morning.'

'Josef, the manager, has managed to radio a pilot who's doing a chartered freight trip to Valanu from the Republic,' Guy said briefly. 'He's prepared to take everyone. You'll be sitting in the aisles, but you'll get there.' The note of the engine deepened as the vehicle picked up speed. 'The only problem is, he wants to leave as soon as possible, so brace yourself. I've got twenty minutes to get you to the airport.'

Valanu? She frowned, then remembered what he'd called the place. *A scatter of islands...*

Her breath hissed out. 'But why Valanu? Can't he fly us to the capital?'

'Communication with the rest of Sant'Rosa has been cut.'

'Why?'

'I don't know, but it's almost certainly nothing to do with this business.' His voice was reassuring. 'Communications here are erratic at the best of times—it's probably a coincidence.'

Lauren digested this. 'Will the mine be safe?'

'Against anything smaller than an army, yes. They have their own security, but they're too far away to help us.'

He swung the vehicle around a corner, and after that there was no further chance to talk. Lauren was un-clenching her jaw muscles for about the fifth time when above the sound of the engine she heard something else—a sudden outbreak of loud pops.

Guy said something under his breath in the language she didn't recognise.

'What was that?' she asked, afraid she knew the an-swer.

'Gunfire,' he said laconically. 'And that means seri-ous trouble.'

Lauren's stomach dropped endlessly.

He glanced briefly down. 'Relax, I'll keep you safe.'

Lauren didn't doubt that; what frightened her was the possibility of him being hurt. And that was strange, be-cause she barely knew the man. OK, so he had a be-wildering effect on her, but she didn't even like him much, although he'd been kind in his arrogant way. Apart from common humanity, why should she care about his safety?

'Here we are,' he said at last. He killed the engine and looked around with the curiously still intentness of a predator sensing prey, before ordering curtly, 'Stay there.'

A swift, silent rush took him out of the Land Rover and around to her door. When it opened Lauren pulled herself onto the seat, groaning beneath her breath when her cramped legs protested painfully.

Strong hands caught her by the waist; as he lifted her out and set her down, Guy said, 'You did well. I'm sorry you got caught up in this.'

Her legs refused to carry her; when she staggered, he lifted her and strode off towards the dim figure waiting outside the small terminal building.

From here the gunfire seemed harmless, more like fireworks. Locked in Guy's safe, strong arms with the moon silvering his bare shoulders, Lauren hoped fervently that no one was dying out there—and desperately that the raiders would be repelled by the time Guy left the airport.

The waiting man gestured, saying something urgently. Lauren felt Guy tense, before he rattled out a question.

The answer didn't please him. He replied in a quiet, deadly voice and put Lauren down, supporting her with an arm around her shoulders. The man stepped back swiftly to usher them both into the reception area.

Tiny, it was almost filled with the resort guests, several carrying children who cried or stared around with bewildered eyes. Suitcases were being shuffled onto an elderly cart, and everyone looked strained and serious.

The man who had met them glanced at Lauren and switched to English. 'Passport, please, ma'am.'

Lauren said shakily, 'It's back at the resort. In the safe with my ID—with all my papers.'

The solid, middle-aged man whose glossy dark hair was greying at the temples looked shocked. 'I'm sorry, ma'am, but—'

'Josef, this is no time for formalities,' Guy interrupted, his deep voice harsh. 'You know she can't stay here.'

A uniformed man—the pilot, Lauren realised—strode

swiftly in from the other side of the building. 'Guy!' he said, grinning largely, 'I might have guessed you'd be here! No show without Punch, eh?' He examined Lauren with interest.

Guy acknowledged the greeting and concisely told him what had happened.

The pilot frowned. 'Man, I can't take her to Valanu without papers! You know they won't let her in— they've been paranoid ever since that drug syndicate tried to infiltrate.'

'You'll take her,' Guy said curtly. 'There's no alternative.'

Frowning, his voice tight with concern, Josef interposed, 'She cannot travel to Valanu without papers.'

In a voice that could have splintered granite, Guy said, 'She'll leave Sant'Rosa if I have to hijack Brian's plane.'

The pilot looked at Lauren's startled face and away again. 'You know what they'll do with her, Guy. They'll chuck her in prison with the prostitutes and the addicts, and she won't get out until someone vouches for her or she gets new papers. In Valanu that could take weeks—everything goes through Fiji. Now, if it was you, Guy, it would be OK. They know you—they'd let you in without a passport.'

Lauren said, 'Look, it's all right. Don't worry about me.'

All three men stared at her with identical expressions, and then at each other.

'Don't be stupid,' Guy said brusquely.

Naked from the waist up, with light gleaming gold on his broad, tanned shoulders and strongly muscled arms, he looked like a barbaric warrior, his unshaven face only emphasising his formidable presence.

Between his teeth he said, 'Josef, you're a pastor in your church, aren't you?'

Josef glanced at him with astonishment. 'I am,' he agreed.

'Very well, then. You can marry us and I'll vouch for her.'

The pilot gave a crack of laughter. 'Yep, that'd do it. Trust you, Guy, to come up with the goods.' He glanced at his watch. 'But you'd better tie that knot as soon as you can. I'm leaving in ten minutes. That gunfire's getting closer.'

Stunned, Lauren gasped, 'That's utterly impossible. I don't even know your name.'

'Guy Bagaton,' Guy said indifferently, adding with brutal candour, 'And you don't have a choice.' He nodded at the airport manager. 'All right, Josef, let's get it over and done with.'

A ragged salvo of popping noises silenced everyone in the terminus. It faded away, to be followed by a heavy *whoomph* that seemed to lift the ground beneath their feet. One of the women stifled a scream and a child started to whimper. With a muffled oath, the pilot raced out of the building.

The harassed Sant'Rosan marshalling the passengers had jumped along with everyone else, but recovered himself quickly. 'Please, board in a line. Women and children first, please.'

The small crowd clumped into a disorderly file and began to follow the pilot across the grass airstrip.

Guy said shortly, 'Josef, get going! We don't have time to waste.' He took Lauren's elbow in a grip that meant business and urged her after the manager, already heading into a small office.

Once there, Josef said, 'I am a minister in my church

here, but perhaps such a marriage will not be legal anywhere but on Sant'Rosa. However, ma'am, it will mean
that you will get out of here and they will not put you
in prison in Valanu.'

Lauren protested, 'No! Look, prison can't be that
bad—and it shouldn't take long to get another passport
from Britain. Anyway, how do you know they'll let me
in even if I do go ahead with this?'

'Trust me,' Guy answered, his expression grimly determined, 'they will. And trust me again—tropical pris-
ons are more than unhygienic, and it could take weeks
to replace your papers—always assuming the Valanuan
authorities let you contact the British representative in
Fiji.' The hard authority in his tone and the granite cast
of his features silenced her objection. 'Just say yes in
all the right places, otherwise you'll be caught in a war
zone. If that happens, you'll endanger anyone who has
to look after you.'

It was that final truth that convinced her. White-
lipped, she said, 'What are you going to do?'

'Don't worry about me.'

Nightmarish images from television screens clouded
her mind so that she couldn't think beyond a silent,
urgent plea that he stay safe.

'Don't worry,' he said, a cynical edge to the words.
'The marriage will satisfy the bureaucracy on Valanu
that you're not a beachcomber intent on drinking and
drugging the rest of your life away at their expense.'
He drew the gold signet ring from his little finger and
turned her to face Josef.

Numbly, Lauren went through with the brief ceremony, backed by the sound of the plane's engines and
punctuated by the ominous sound of gunfire and a couple more of those heavy explosions.

She responded like an automaton, shivering when Guy slid the ring onto her finger, holding it there because it was too big. Warm from his body heat, it felt like a shackle, but she relaxed a little as he gripped her hand in his strong one.

At last Josef said, 'You may kiss the bride,' and tactfully busied himself with the papers.

A marauder's smile played across Guy's sensual mouth. Eyes gleaming, he murmured, 'If I'd known I was going to get married today, I'd have shaved.'

Then he kissed her—not a swift, parting kiss, nor a clumsy, unsubtle expression of lust. His mouth took hers in complete mastery, replacing every fear with poignant delight and a swift, fierce longing that lodged in her heart.

And because she didn't know whether he'd survive, whether she'd ever see him again, she kissed him back with everything she had to give.

Too soon, he released her with an odd half-smile to scribble a name on a piece of paper. 'My agent on Valanu,' he said, handing it to her. 'Get in touch with him straight away and show him the papers Josef's making out now—he'll find you a place to stay. You have no money?'

'No,' she said wretchedly, feeling empty and oddly weepy.

He wrenched a wallet from his pocket and took out the notes in it. 'This will cover your costs for tonight.' He handed them over, adding with wry humour, 'And there's enough there to buy you another sarong from the market.'

'Your shirt!'

One hand clenched around the notes and his ring, she

began to jerk his T-shirt upwards, but he said, 'Keep it on. It gives you that authentic refugee look.'

She hesitated, then let the material fall. 'What will you wear?'

'I will lend him one of mine,' Josef said sombrely.

Guy's intent, uncompromising scrutiny drowned her in tawny fire. 'I'll contact you as soon as I can.'

'P-promises,' she said, sudden tears blinding her.

He laughed and picked up her free hand, kissing the back and then the palm, folding her fingers over to keep the kiss there. 'I always keep my promises.' It sounded like a vow.

'Come, ma'am,' Josef said earnestly. 'The plane is ready.'

'Go now,' Guy said, and strode out into the darkness without a backward glance.

An hour later, as the engines droned above the dark, empty ocean, Lauren twisted the gold signet ring on her finger, and wondered what was happening back on Sant'Rosa.

'Keep him safe,' she whispered.

And with the stars swallowed up by the moon's light, and the white circle of Valanu's biggest atoll on the horizon, she tried to forget that somewhere behind her a stranger, a man she had only met that day, might be fighting for his life.

And tried very hard to convince herself that she hadn't fallen in love in three short hours.

The ceiling fan whirred, wafting a sluggish wave of clammy air over Lauren's head. Gathering her dignity, she said, 'So I can't leave Valanu yet.'

Regretfully the immigration official shook his head. 'I am afraid not,' he agreed. 'It is complicated, you see.

You came here without papers; we let you in as a favour because you are married to a man who has a good name in this place.' He tapped the file on his desk. 'But it is taking longer than we expected to get replacement papers from Britain, and until then you cannot leave Valanu because our only air link to the outside world is Sant'Rosa, and they say they will not allow you to land there without a passport.'

'My parents said my passport had been sent by courier two days ago.'

They had had variations on the same conversation for the past six afternoons. Tension plucked Lauren's nerves, but screaming wouldn't achieve anything. Everyone had been utterly polite, very helpful—and determined to stick to the rules.

Guy had been right. With no British consulate, all official matters had to go through the distant island nation that ruled Valanu, so she was stuck on this lovely, isolated atoll until proof of her identity and citizenship arrived.

Guy's agent might have been able to speed things up, but he'd flown to Singapore the day before she'd arrived on Valanu and wasn't expected back for several more days.

Fortunately the clerk at Valanu's airport who'd converted Guy's notes to the local currency had asked her where she was staying. When she'd admitted she had nowhere, he'd recommended his cousin's place, and half an hour later she'd rented a one-room bungalow standing on a coral platform in a tangle of foliage and sweet-smelling flowers.

She pasted a smile to her face and got to her feet. 'Thank you very much for all your help.'

'I'm sorry I can't make things happen more quickly

for you, but I hope you are enjoying our little island.' He paused, before saying carefully, 'It is a possibility that if you spoke to one of the journalists trying to get to Sant'Rosa, they might be able to help you contact your family in England.'

God, no! Lauren had been carefully avoiding them for the past few days. Not that she was interesting to the media, except for the fact that she was Marc Corbett's half-sister, and Marc was a player on the world stage. She didn't want anyone poking around in the past and discovering the secret of her mother's long-ago affair with Marc's father. Apart from humiliating her mother, any publication of that indiscretion would stress her father, whose health was precarious.

She held out her hand. 'I'm enjoying my time on Valanu, and you've been most kind,' she told the official truthfully. 'I'm just worried about what's happening on Sant'Rosa.'

Sombre-faced, he shook her hand. 'Yes,' he said heavily. 'War is a terrible thing, and it is so sad to see the Sant'Rosans suffering again. However, if what we are hearing is correct, the invaders are already being pushed back beyond the border and their ringleader is dead.'

Rumour or truth? 'I hope so,' she said in a flat voice.

Slowly, because the late-afternoon sun beat down with unmitigated ferocity, she walked to her bungalow. Once in its blessed coolness, she poured a glass of water from the jug in the tiny refrigerator and stood slowly sipping it in the minuscule kitchen.

Beneath the high, thatched roof, a huge bed draped in mosquito netting dominated the room; although Lauren slept with only a sheet over her, the coverlet was a work of art, brilliantly quilted in a pattern of hibiscus flowers. With a table and chairs, the only other furniture was a wardrobe that held Guy's shirt—washed and pressed and awaiting his arrival—and the spare sarong she'd bought the morning after she'd been decanted from the plane.

During the day the woven mats that made the walls were rolled up so that sea breezes cooled the building; at night, they provided privacy.

Spartan, she thought, draining the glass with relief, but clean and comfortable; more importantly, it was cheap. The call she'd made to her parents in England had used so much of Guy's money that she'd had to watch every penny, haggling for fish and fruit in the market. With funds from home apparently wending their way via outer space, she'd soon be forced to borrow from Guy's agent when he returned from Singapore.

Apart from her daily trek to report to the immigration officer, she swam, prepared meals and chatted to her landlady's teenage daughters, trying to satisfy their curiosity about life outside their idyllic island. Unfortunately, such a lazy life gave her too much time to imagine Guy Bagaton dead...

Even though death was no respecter of persons, it was impossible to imagine all that vibrant power cut down by a bullet—or worse.

'He'll be fine,' she said aloud. She had the oddest feeling that if he died she'd know.

'You don't even know *him*,' she scoffed, and went down to the lagoon to swim off the dust and the sweat of the walk home.

The water lapped against her like liquid silk, soothing and lukewarm, but a blood-red sky to the west heralded the sunset, turning her white skin copper as she strolled back along the beach. It seemed ominous, a bad omen.

'Grow up,' she chided, slipping off her sandals at the door. 'You are not superstitious.'

Once inside she showered and washed her salt-laden hair before changing into her other sarong, a splashy print of gorgeous, improbably coloured frangipani blooms. Thanks to the landlady's daughters, she now knew three ways of tying the garment. This time she settled for a simple knot above her breasts before sitting on the side of the bed to comb her hair. As the teeth smoothed through each strand, a feather of awareness stroked along her skin.

Several times she looked around, but the tangle of growth that surrounded the bungalow was empty of prying eyes. Anyway, it wasn't the sort of sensation that whispered of danger. More a feeling of languorous expectancy, as though something good was going to happen...

'Perhaps your new passport will arrive tomorrow,' she murmured, looking down at her clenched hand; because she wasn't married, she'd taken to wearing Guy's signet ring on her middle finger. It was still too big, but it didn't slip off.

It was made of heavy gold, and the engraving almost worn away; not for the first time, she turned her hand in the red light of the dying sun, trying to make out its form. Some sort of crest, she thought—a bird? Were those wings? The outline danced in the smoky light and she blinked hard to clear her sight, but had to give up again.

Whatever, he clearly valued it, so when she finally got off Valanu she'd leave it with the agent.

Driven by restlessness, she let down the woven sides

of the room and loosened the knot on her sarong, walking out onto the coral platform to enjoy the cooler air of evening on her bare shoulders and arms. A yawn took her by surprise.

'What the *hell* are you doing here?' a familiar voice enquired from behind.

CHAPTER FOUR

ONE hand holding back her heartbeats, Lauren swung around. A large dark silhouette against the violent crimson of the sky, Guy Bagaton stood a few feet away.

Relief and incandescent joy rioted through her, shocking her with their intensity.

Guy demanded, 'Why aren't you staying at the resort?'

'I didn't have enough money,' she told him, fighting to keep her voice level. Although he stood about ten feet away, his awareness rested like a blade against her sensitised skin. 'Your agent is in Singapore—he's expected back tomorrow.'

Guy said something that made her brows shoot up. 'So what have you been using for money? The amount I gave you wouldn't have kept you for a week.'

'It has,' she said.

Then her eyes adjusted to the rapidly fading light, and she gasped and raced towards him. *'What happened?'*

He ignored the bandage around his upper arm. 'It's nothing—a crease from a bullet,' he said curtly. 'How are you?'

'I'm fine.' Brows drawn together, she examined him closely.

He was still villainously unshaven, his autocratic features were more deeply carved, and something in his eyes—a kind of bitter determination, as though he'd kept going through events that no one should ever see—had dimmed his tremendous vitality.

Empathy twisted her heart into a hard knot in her chest. No man should look like that. 'How did you know I was here?'

He sent her a stabbing glance. 'It took me a while. In the end I called in a favour from someone who works in the immigration service.' He looked around. 'This is no place for you.'

'Has a doctor looked at that bullet crease?'

'Yes. She jabbed me and provided me with antibiotics. It's barely a scratch.' He held out a plastic bag and, when Lauren automatically took it without stopping her anxious scrutiny of his face, commented drily, 'You can open it. Your passport is in there.'

'My passport!' Hastily she pulled the bag open and saw the familiar cover. She looked up again sharply. 'Did you go back to the resort?'

His lashes drooped. 'Briefly. It had been looted, but they hadn't been able to get into the safe.'

The hairs on the back of Lauren's neck lifted. 'How—was everybody all right?'

'There was no one there, but as far as I know, the staff survived.' He finished, 'The passport's intact and unblemished.'

Gratefully she said, 'Thank you so much. It was terribly kind of you to take the trouble.'

Yet all she could think was that it meant she could now leave Valanu—when he had just arrived. A dangerously heady enchantment wrapped her with silken energy.

Lust, she thought, yet knew she was wrong. At the beginning, yes—it had been stark, undiluted animal attraction—but now she knew much more about Guy

Bagaton, and that physical chemistry had transmuted into something she didn't dare examine. He had saved her from what could have been her death; she wished she could help him with the cocktail of emotions simmering beneath his granite façade.

She put her passport on the table, its familiar formality incongruous amongst the scarlet taffeta of a cluster of hibiscus flowers. 'Come in—no, let's sit outside; it's slightly cooler.'

True, but it was also less intimate. Babbling slightly, she continued, 'You look as though you could do with a drink—a previous guest left behind a couple of cans of beer if you want some. They're still in the fridge.'

He said on a harsh half-laugh, 'You're a woman out of every man's fantasy.'

A rill of pleasure ran through her, hotly disturbing. Getting a can, she said lightly, 'Because I offered you a beer? You've got remarkably low standards if that's all a woman has to do.'

He took it from her, broke the seal, and drank half the contents in one swallow. Lauren busied herself pouring a long glass of tangy fruit juice before turning to find him watching her with a narrow-eyed intensity that almost sent her swaying into his arms.

'Nothing like a can of beer after a few days' fighting in the jungle,' he said after a second so taut she could feel its impact twanging along her nerves.

Lauren let her breath go on a noiseless sigh. 'Let's sit on the terrace.'

He sank into one of the chairs with a sigh that hinted of bone-deep weariness. 'Did you have any problems getting into Valanu?'

'At first they didn't want to let me off the plane.' She drank the juice, taste buds purring at its acidic tang, every sense honed and on tiptoe. 'The fake marriage papers—and the pilot—persuaded them to relent. He stayed long enough to convince them that I was truly married to you.'

'Beachcombers are a damned nuisance in the Pacific. Without tough policies for keeping them out, the islands would have freeloaders from all over the world preying on the locals. Who have little enough for themselves, most of the time.'

'Your name did the trick.' She wanted very much to know what had happened on Sant'Rosa, but instinct warned her not to probe. 'And you can't believe how grateful I am to you for thinking of it. I walked past the prison the other day, and you were right, it didn't look like a place I'd enjoy staying in.' Remembering how he'd tried to put her off going up to the village in the mountains, she finished with a hint of humour, 'I'll bet the cockroaches there are truly outstanding specimens.'

'No toenail is safe,' he agreed gravely and swallowed another mouthful of beer. The warm light of the lamp emphasised the lines engraved down his cheeks and the dark fans of the lashes hiding his eyes.

Fighting a disturbing urge to cradle his head against her breasts, Lauren averted her gaze to a sky so deeply black it was like staring into the heart of darkness. Stars began to wink into life, huge, impersonal, the pure air cutting the familiar cheerful twinkle.

Pitching her words just above the soft murmur of the waves, she asked, 'How long are you here for?'

The silence stretched so long she thought he'd gone to sleep.

Finally, in a voice completely without emotion, he said, 'It's over; there's a bit of mopping up still to do, but the preacher's followers have slunk back to their villages and the invaders have either been killed or fled back across the border. Sant'Rosan forces are in control.'

Not exactly an answer. 'It must have been bad,' she ventured.

He lifted the can and took another deep swallow of its contents. 'Bad enough,' he said flatly. 'About eighty people died—mostly villagers who got in the way. Crops destroyed and villages burned down, the bodies of dead children—the usual aftermath of war.'

'I'm sorry,' she said inadequately, her heart contracting.

'Why? It wasn't your fault.'

After a short silence she drawled, 'Are you looking for someone to blame?'

His quiet, mirthless laugh chilled her. He drained the rest of his beer, then stood up. 'Probably,' he said roughly. 'I'd better go; I'm in no fit state to discuss life and its unfairness with a gently brought-up Englishwoman.'

'Have you a place to go to?' She was teetering on the brink of something that would change her life, but she couldn't let him take his memories back to an impersonal hotel room.

'I'll get a room at the resort,' he said indifferently.

'And face a pack of ravening journalists who haven't been able to get anywhere near the fighting?' she returned, keeping her tone light. 'Although if the fighting's over, I suppose they've all left for Sant'Rosa. When did you eat last?'

He didn't answer straight away, and she suspected that her question had startled him. It had startled her too.

His broad shoulders lifted. 'God knows.'

'I'll get you something.' She got to her feet, strangely unsurprised to realise she'd made a decision—one, she thought with a flare of panic, that was totally unlike her. But her voice remained steady when she added, 'And while I'm doing that, why don't you have a shower?'

He didn't move. Although her eyes were attuned to the night, she couldn't see enough of his face to discern any expression, but his stance and his silence were intimidating.

Not so intimidating as his voice. Deep and raw, almost menacing, it sent a cold sliver of sensation down her spine. 'Not a good idea, Lauren.'

The darkness wasn't a barrier to him. When she flinched in humiliation, he cupped a lean hand around her chin. Applying the slightest pressure, he said without apology, 'I'm not fit company. I probably need to get drunk.'

His hand was warm, the long fingers rough as though he'd been working hard, the strength of it palpable against her skin. She said crisply, 'Then you'd regret it less tomorrow if you start out clean, and with some food in your stomach.'

'Indeed, a woman out of every man's fantasy,' he said in a voice like rough velvet.

His thumb stroked across her lips in a caress that melted her bones so that when he dropped his hand she had to grab the back of her chair.

But there was nothing caressing in the gaze that held hers. It was hot and dark and devouring; it reached into the hidden depths of thoughts and emotions she'd never recognised, never experienced before, and made her face them. 'But I'm not staying unless you're sure.'

Sure that she wanted to be with him? Utterly. Sure that she was ready for what might happen? No, but

certain that if she sent him to the resort she'd regret it.
'I'm sure.'

He nodded and stepped back, letting her go first into
the bungalow. Lauren switched on the light at the door,
and opened the wardrobe door to hand him the shirt
he'd lent her so many days ago. Tawny eyes quizzical,
he took it.

But when she drew the ring from her finger, his gaze
darkened. Her finger felt cold, abandoned, but her hand
didn't shake as she held out the gold trinket. 'Thank
you.'

'Is that what your offer is? Gratitude for getting your
passport? Or for getting you out of Sant'Rosa?' His tone
was softly aggressive, and he watched her so narrowly
she felt that her every thought was being catalogued by
that keen mind.

'No,' she said.

Guy slid the ring onto his little finger and went into
the bathroom.

He stayed for so long that Lauren, preparing a meal
of fish and salad in the kitchen, wondered whether he
was indulging in a ritual of cleaning war's filthy detritus
from his body.

It wouldn't be so easy or so quick to rid his mind of
the horrendous images.

She listened to the soft swish of the tiny waves brush-
ing the sand a few feet away and tried to sort out her
emotions. Send him off to the resort, common sense
urged. Now—before it's too late.

But it was too late. He'd issued a challenge and she'd
accepted it. Beneath Guy's tight control she sensed a
darkly primitive hunger; remember the traditional rec-
reation of the warrior, she thought—banishing unbearable memories in the pleasure of a woman's body.

But she didn't fear him; instinct told her that he wouldn't hurt her. And she wanted him with a heated desperation that fogged her mind, turning the unthinkable into the inevitable.

Oh, she could blame the heat and danger of the tropics—the perfume floating on the moist air, a sultry, sinful fragrance breathed out from the hearts of the crimson flowers on the vine wreathing the terrace. But the tropics hadn't produced the smouldering intensity that sent the blood singing through her veins.

Her teeth gnawed her lip as she went on with the dinner preparations. She wanted Guy, but even more important than that, she suspected that tonight he needed her.

When he emerged, clad in the clean shirt and his trousers, she was sitting on the terrace with the second can of beer and a plate of sliced fruit. She didn't hear him come up behind her, but some instinct switched her gaze from the geckos creeping ever closer to the lamp, intent on picking off the moths that danced in dazzled swirls around the dangerous, alluring light.

Her heart blocked her throat. He'd shaved, and in the soft light he was beautiful, the boldly carved framework of his face a miraculous, exotic blend of Mediterranean machismo and the northern-European angularity that nagged at her memory.

'That food looks good.' His voice was cool and noncommittal.

He didn't fall on it like a starving man, but by the time he'd told her of the situation in Sant'Rosa he'd almost cleared the platter.

When he finished she observed, 'So the Republic *was* behind it. Are they likely to try again?'

'I don't think so. They lost too many men.'

She said quietly, 'And if they don't know by now that they can't ignore world opinion, they will once the Press gets there.'

'I'm surprised that a local fracas, however bloody and determined, was interesting enough to attract the attention of foreign correspondents.' His tone was satiric. 'There can't be much happening in the rest of the world.'

'A meeting of heads of state has just finished in Australia.' She looked up as a plane flew overhead.

'Ah, so that's it,' Guy said sardonically. 'And Sant'Rosa is an interesting detour on the way home. As for waking the world up to what's happening here—it'll be relegated to obscurity once the next flashpoint explodes.'

Unfortunately he was right. She said, 'I'd like to be sure that the hotel staff on Sant'Rosa survived. And how did the village in the mountains fare? It was right in the thick of things, surely?'

'No. As far as I know they didn't come off any worse than any other village. You're not going back,' Guy responded in a flat, lethal tone.

A cold shiver scudded down her spine. 'But—'

'No buts,' he said implacably. 'You won't be allowed anywhere near the South Coast. It's still a sensitive area. Civilians and sightseers—even well-intentioned ones—are nothing but a damned nuisance in a post-war zone unless they've got skills to help the victims.'

'Are you going back?' She held her breath until he answered.

'Yes.'

Something about his intonation and the formidable expression made her say, 'Why? What skills do you have to help?'

His left brow rose, as mocking as the smile that curved his mouth. 'I have contacts—I know who to apply to for the kind of aid that's needed, and I can act as go-between.'

An odd, aching foreboding clutched her with a cold grip. Ignoring it, she got to her feet and said, 'Dinner's ready. I'll go and get it.'

Over the meal Lauren set herself to switch Guy's mind away from the horrors of the past few days. She filled him in on the latest headlines, culled from the newspaper stand outside the immigration office, then skimmed over a couple of juicy financial scandals and the spectacularly spicy meltdown of a singer's marriage.

He knew what she was doing, but he went along with her and by the end of the meal he was laughing and the lines of tension scoring his lean face were slightly less deep.

Whereas she was now racked by taut expectancy.

'Coffee?' she asked, shielding herself with the banal little rituals of everyday life. 'It's only instant, I'm afraid.'

'It'll be fine.' He yawned and rubbed the back of his neck, the easy flexion of his big body sending a shivering little ripple of anticipation through her. 'But before you make it, I'll go and collect the other parcel I have for you.'

'What—'

'You'll see,' he said coolly.

It took him about twenty minutes, the longest twenty minutes of Lauren's life. When he came back she was sitting out on the terrace waiting for him, the friendly darkness pressing against her.

'Here,' he said, tossing a parcel onto the table.

'Oh.' Another plastic bag. 'What is it?'

'Clothes.'

Her clothes from Sant'Rosa. She said, 'Thank you. I thought they'd have been looted.'

'They're new.' He paused, then said, 'I should go.' He spoke abruptly, the words falling stark and curt in the heavy air.

Lauren got up and walked across to the tiny kitchen. With her back to him she filled the battered electric kettle and plugged it in, then set two cups on a tray with sugar and milk. Only when she'd made the coffee and picked up the tray did she ask coolly, 'Why?'

Guy watched her carry the tray across to the table. She walked as he'd dreamed of her in the hot, foetid jungle nights—with the lithe, easy grace that set off her long, lovely legs and the sensuous little sway of her hips that had dragged him temporarily out of hell.

He waited until she'd sat down and picked up the milk jug before saying in a deliberately prosaic voice, 'Because if I stay it will be in your bed, and I doubt if either of us will sleep much.'

Guy regretted the words as soon as they left his mouth. Pragmatism was doing its best to convince him that making love to a woman he'd forced into a temporary marriage was a stupid thing to do.

For once, pragmatism could go bury itself.

Her hand shook so much she had to set the milk jug down. She kept her head down too so that all he could see was the lovely curve of her cheekbone. After a moment she poured the milk in, then got up and turned off the lights.

In the soft half-darkness, illuminated only by the stars, she said quietly, 'I wouldn't have asked you to stay if I hadn't wanted that.'

Damn it, he could taste the need, hot as sin, dangerously heady as any drug; wanting Lauren was an ache in his guts, a reckless loss of control that both excited and infuriated him.

And for the first time in his life he was being propositioned by a woman who had no idea who he was. Here in Valanu they knew him only as Guy Bagaton. Combined with the heated sexual appetite raging through him, Lauren's offer was damned near irresistible.

'Neither reward nor gratitude,' Lauren said.

Was there a hint of nervousness beneath the polished surface? When she stopped a step away, Guy refused to reach out, although the muscles in his shoulders and arms bunched with the effort to keep them still. Leaping on her with famished savagery was not the way to endear yourself to a woman, he thought derisively.

He asked, 'So what is it?'

The taut seconds that followed his question didn't give him enough time to impose control on his more primitive instincts. He could die wanting her, he thought, grimly fighting the physical longing that undermined his will-power, but he hadn't come here for this.

Then she bent and fitted her mouth to his. Against his lips she said, 'This.'

And kissed him.

She tasted of mystery and delight, of sex and truth, of daring and intensity and grace. An exultant, desperate need roared through him, and he said too harshly, 'Good, because that's what I want too.'

When Lauren began to straighten, he came up with her in a silent, purposeful movement that sent shudders through her.

'Like this,' he said.

He caught her against him, his mouth taking hers in a kiss that gave no quarter. Dimly, Lauren realised that it was a signal of dominant masculinity, and she gloried in it, demanding as much from him as he asked from her, her eager body thrumming with need.

He kissed her as though she was the only woman he'd ever wanted, as though they shared infinitely more than this transitory passion, this time out of time in the empty blue reaches of the Pacific.

Shuddering, she opened her mouth to his, and relished the wild kick of passion inside her—and the fierce hardness of his body against hers.

'When I first saw you,' he said, reluctantly giving her air, 'I wanted you.' That faint trace of accent flavoured each word, intriguing and different.

'Mmm,' she murmured. 'You looked like a pirate. A very sexy pirate.'

His heavy eyelids almost covered his eyes, but she could see a gleam of laughter in their golden depths. 'You have a thing for pirates?'

'Stubble suits some people,' she said demurely, nipping her way along his jawbone.

He laughed again, deep and low and triumphant, and kissed the spot where her neck joined her shoulders, and then the warm swell of her breasts above her sarong. Pleasure raced through her in a dizzying flood; as he deftly untied the knot she knew that nothing in her previous life had prepared her for the ardent, honeyed recklessness of making love with Guy.

When the sarong fell away, he froze. Lauren gazed into his stunned face, and her heart tumbled into free-fall. She hadn't known a man could look like that—a mixture of conqueror and supplicant, eyes glittering in a darkly drawn face while he gazed at the slender white curves and lines of her body.

And then he lifted his head, and there was no supplication in his expression now—he was all conqueror. Her breath locked deliciously in her chest when he cupped a small, high breast, tanned fingers shaping the pale curves with erotic confidence as his thumb brushed the tight pink bud at the centre, slowly, back and forth, back and forth, until she moaned deep in her throat.

Needles of pure desire ran along her nerves; she couldn't speak, couldn't tell him that he was killing her with sensation. Even her breath died when he bent his head and kissed the nipple his thumb had tantalised. Carnal sensation sparked an inferno inside her when the tight little nub peaked in a silent, evocative plea for more.

He gave it to her, his dark head drawing close. Lauren swallowed, and when he drew the nipple into his mouth her knees buckled.

Guy caught her before she fell, lifting her into his arms and stepping over the fallen sarong to carry her across to the bed. As her feet touched the floor, his free hand jerked aside the bright quilted coverlet and he put her down gently on her back.

'Are you sure?' he asked deeply, his gaze caressing her body, exposed now for his delight with only a scrap of cotton hiding her most secret parts.

They had so little time, Lauren thought desperately. Soon she'd be leaving for New Zealand.

And Guy? He'd go back to Sant'Rosa, and she had no right to ask him to stay away.

A smile trembled along her lips. 'Utterly sure,' she said like a vow.

Guy stood very still, then said, 'So am I,' and without haste he shrugged out of his shirt.

Her pulses drummed faster as she feasted her eyes on the clean, perfect symmetry of his body. But when he stood naked before her, her breath locked in her throat. He was, she realised on a note of primitive panic, big all over, and it had been a long time since she'd done this…

'Relax,' he said softly, and ran a deliberate forefinger from the centre of her breast to the soft, warm nest between her thighs. 'I won't hurt you.'

The path of that finger burned like a streak of fire, and her confidence returned in a rush. Her first glance had told her that he was an experienced lover. 'I know.'

Solemnly she watched the play of powerful muscles beneath his sleek bronze skin as he untied the mosquito netting so that it fell around the bed in a billow of white, shutting them off from the rest of the world.

Then he came down beside her, dark to her light, sun to her moon, strength to her grace.

CHAPTER FIVE

LAUREN had expected a slow, sophisticated wooing. Perhaps Guy had planned that, but when she smoothed her hand over his shoulder and down the flexible line of his spine, her fingers tracing out the vertebrae beneath the hot skin, he muttered a word she couldn't discern. And followed it with another devouring kiss that set her afire with heady, primal intoxication.

A ferocious intensity wiped away the last pathetic shreds of her self-control. When she gasped and arched beneath him, her hips grinding into his, he took an importunate, demanding nipple into his mouth and suckled strongly.

Delicious arrows blazed through her body; groaning, she tightened her fingers around his head, holding him close to her breast while the craving intensified, burning hotter and hotter until she thought she might die of need.

'Now,' she muttered. 'Now, for heaven's sake... Guy, please—'

He kissed her again, and a second later he was buried to the hilt in her, his big body so rigid she thought he might not be able to control himself any longer.

But he dragged a quick, impeded breath into his lungs, and slowly, deliciously eased out of the slick passage until she gasped his name again, and once more her hips jerked in involuntary provocation.

On a harsh, feral sound, he thrust even deeper inside her, and she met the powerful rhythm and matched it

71

until every thought fled her brain, lost in the sensual tidal wave of Guy's mastery.

It was like drowning in rapture, and for a sudden moment she fought it, wondering where it would lead, what it would take from her.

'Relax,' he said, the words purring roughly into her ear. 'Let go, Lauren—it won't hurt. It can't hurt.'

Yes, it can, she thought wildly, her head tossing back and forth on the pillow, but it was too late. She could no more resist this blatant bewitchment of her senses than she could push him off; she had never before felt so much a woman, so much herself, as she did when Guy made love to her.

Anyway, she couldn't speak. The pleasure that had been threatening her since her first sight of him boosted her into some stratosphere of sensation. Her lashes flew up and she stared into his face. Lean and dark, every arrogant bone prominent, eyes glittering like the heart of the sun, he looked like a corsair intent on plunder.

And she was it, and she wanted it as much as he did. Lauren abandoned every last inhibition and surrendered to passion, rocking herself against him and tightening her inner muscles in an ancient, provocative rhythm every time he pushed into her.

She saw the moment his control cracked and shattered, registered the split-second of understanding in his aristocratic face, and then the torrent of ecstasy rolled over and through her in waves from the centre of her body.

Savage, merciless, exquisitely arousing, they hurled her into an alternate universe where all she saw was the golden gleam of Guy's eyes and all she felt was an ineffable rapture that lasted too long and not long enough, where its slow fading was at once a tragedy and a glory.

And then Guy followed her into that secret, bewildering place, a low, hoarse sound torn from his throat as he fought for that peak, his beautiful body like steel against her and in her.

As the savage physical longing ebbed into sweet sorrow, Lauren linked her arms around his neck and pulled his head down to kiss him. Yielding to her conviction that he needed her had brought her wild ecstasy, but she'd chosen to break through an invisible barrier into another world where invisible chains linked her to him.

How would she ever forget him?

Mouth still holding hers captive, Guy rolled onto his back, scooping her with him so that she was lying on him.

When they could both breathe again, both speak, he asked, 'When are you leaving Valanu?'

Her heart wept, but she answered steadily, 'When funds come through for a plane ticket.'

'I'm returning to Sant'Rosa three days from now,' he said. 'Would you like to spend those days with me?'

Lauren lifted her head to stare into his eyes; she saw the pupils dilate, and the fracture in her heart widened as she pulled back. Although the residual heat of passion still smouldered in the golden depths, she realised that once she left Valanu she'd never see Guy again. At least, she thought painfully, he made no promises, offered no inducements. 'Here?'

'A little further along the coast.'

'On a desert island?' she asked, putting off the moment of decision.

His smile was a sensual challenge. 'Deserted,' he said. 'Not exactly an island.'

Although she hesitated, she knew what answer she'd give him. 'Yes. But I'll have to ring my parents and tell them what's happening.'

He kissed her collar-bone. 'Everything?' he asked wickedly.

And although it hurt, she smiled. 'Not everything,' she admitted, and yawned.

'You can tell them when we get there.'

'You've got a telephone on your deserted not-island?'

He tucked her against his shoulder. 'Yes. Now, go to sleep. We'll leave at dawn tomorrow morning.'

But he woke her once more, and towards dawn she woke him, and both times they made love with slow, sweet passion that culminated in white-hot savagery, leaving them sensually replete.

Sputtering across the lagoon in a banana boat, Lauren turned to look at Guy. Something about his stance, his expression as he frowned into the sun and steered, sent a shiver across her nerve ends. Dismissing the momentary unease, she said lightly, 'Where did you learn to run a departure like a military exercise?'

The canoe met the oncoming wave a little clumsily, splashing a sparkling cascade of water over the bow. 'I did army training for a couple of years,' he said. 'It's a tradition in my family. Look, can you see the frigate birds?' He pointed to a pair of long-tailed birds that swooped above the lagoon.

In other words, she thought bleakly, do not go there, Lauren.

That morning she'd woken in his arms, and for a few seconds she'd allowed herself to feel at home there—until common sense took over, reminding her that Guy belonged in some way to Sant'Rosa, and she was a rising executive in her half-brother's large organisation. Apart from the passion that blazed between them, they just didn't connect—something Guy clearly understood, and something she had to accept.

Although the house he took her to sprawled alone beneath the coconut palms lining another white beach, there was nothing primitive about it. 'Does this lovely place belong to you?' she asked after she'd rung her parents using the latest in communications technology.

'No. The resort,' Guy told her. 'The owner wanted to build a dozen or so along the lagoon, but his plans fell through. Do you like it?'

She gazed around the open, airy room, decorated in the blue of the lagoon, the soft green of the palm leaves and the white of the sand, and smiled a little ironically. Of course a buccaneer wouldn't have a home.

'It's beautiful,' she said, her voice dying as he kissed her.

During the next few days Lauren learned how lost in desire she could become; this new capacity for sensation both overwhelmed and scared her. But because these precious days were all that she'd have of Guy, she surrendered to erotic fantasy—and the arms and body of a man who set himself to satisfy appetites she hadn't known existed.

Time enough to consider the implications when she returned to the workaday world.

He was the perfect lover—intelligent, intriguing, and he could cook. He made her laugh and he talked about anything she wanted to discuss, although by mutual consent neither spoke of their ordinary lives.

And he seemed to know by instinct when she wanted tenderness, when she wanted to walk on the wild side, and when she wanted to sleep. She soon lost any inhibitions about swimming naked in water as warm as her blood, walking back to the house over sand like powdered sugar to shower with him in the huge bathroom.

Sun-warmed, star-silvered, threaded with passion, the days and nights slid through her fingers like pearls on a silken cord, perfect, irretrievable, until at last it was the morning they were due back in Valanu. Just before they left Lauren spoke to her parents again.

Guy left her to check that everything was ready, coming back in the brightening light to hear her say, 'I thought I might come straight back home instead of going on to New Zealand.'

He'd heard her voice in so many moods—sultry, playful, sophisticated, determined, and the way he liked best, shaken by craving—but never the warmly affectionate tone she used for her parents.

So? he thought restlessly.

She listened, then said, 'Well—are you sure?'

A long silence followed, during which her soft mouth tilted at the corners in a smile she'd never bestowed on him. He watched a graceful hand trace a pattern on the table and responded to the familiar heaviness in his loins with tight anger. He didn't want to feel like this. They had made love so many times he'd lost count; with Lauren he was insatiable and her response was equally reckless, but she had been careful to avoid any reference to the future.

Perhaps she was that rare thing, a woman who treated her lovers with affection, then let them go without any emotional strings.

Until that moment he'd deliberately pushed the shadow of Marc Corbett to the furthest reaches of his mind, but now a jagged pang of jealousy, barbaric in its intensity, thrust through his iron control. Guy had always considered himself a sophisticated man, one who didn't expect anything more from his lovers than he was prepared to give them—affection, respect and good sex.

Yet the thought of Lauren going from his bed to another man's summoned a primitive possessiveness that infuriated him.

'Well, all right,' she said cheerfully into the telephone. 'I'm leaving today, but I have a few hours' stopover in Fiji so I won't get to New Zealand until late. I'll spend the night at an airport hotel in Auckland and fly up to the Bay of Islands tomorrow morning.'

She listened again, then laughed. 'Fusspot. Yes, I'll ring you as soon as I get to Marc's house. Goodbye.' She put the telephone down.

A fierce, elemental anger almost consumed Guy; unlike his normal coldly disciplined response to provocation, this hot outrage seethed under such pressure that it took his entire stock of will-power to restrain it.

'Everything under control?' It was all he could trust himself to say, and even then his voice sounded guttural and aggressive.

Grey eyes wary, she looked up. Clearly, she hadn't heard him come in. 'Yes, thank you. I wondered if I should go home to reassure them that their darling daughter is safe and healthy, but my father wouldn't hear of it.'

Guy wrestled his simmering rage into enough of a strait-jacket to say curtly, 'A thoughtful father.'

So she was going to Marc Corbett's house. It could mean nothing more than that they were on good terms even though their relationship had ended. It wasn't so unusual; he prided himself on staying good friends with his previous lovers. He'd have offered a holiday house to any of them.

But it might also mean that the time they'd spent together meant nothing more to her than an exotic interlude.

He tried for a mental shrug, wondering coldly why his usual practical logic had abandoned him. So what? They'd made no commitment; Lauren might be every man's dream lover, but their idyll was over. She could go wherever she wanted, sleep with whomever she wanted. And so could he.

Her tone deepened. 'My father's a darling.' She joined him on the tiled terrace outside the airy sitting room and said carefully, 'Guy, it's been magic. Thank you so much.'

'You sound like a small child at the end of a party,' he said, exasperated by the rasping undertone in his voice.

Her face went still. Without moving she met his eyes, her own now as opaque as burnished silver, but her withdrawal hit him, palpable as a blow.

Steadily she said, 'Probably because that's what I feel like. It's been a lovely, lovely party, but like all good times, it's come to an end.'

Hiding his astonishing anger with the disciplined control he'd fought to acquire, Guy relaxed hands that were curling into fists by his sides. 'You'd better give me an address so I can contact you if I need to.'

At first he thought she was going to refuse, but she nodded and reached into her bag for a small notebook. He watched her write down the address, tear the page out and hand it over. 'I'll be there for three weeks,' she told him, that seamless poise firmly in place.

Guy wanted to smash it into splinters. Get a grip, he

told himself roughly. A few days making love to a woman gave you no claims to her.

'Right, we'd better go,' he said, and picked up the bags.

They got back to Valanu not too long before her plane was due to leave. As the banana boat sputtered across the brilliant blues of the lagoon, Lauren gazed around, pretending that nothing had changed, that Guy wasn't steering with an expression of such concentrated authority it shut her out as effectively as a barred door.

A car was waiting at the docks; Guy must have organised it. He walked her towards it, and as the driver slung her bag into the boot she held out her hand in farewell and said steadily, 'Goodbye. Thank you for everything.'

Equally formal, his golden eyes dark and unreadable in his handsome face, he bowed over her hand. But there was nothing formal about the way he lifted it to his mouth; his kiss burned against her skin like a brand, quickening her heart and tightening inner muscles accustomed now to enclosing him in their subtle grip.

'It was,' he said with silken distinctness, 'my complete and utter pleasure.'

Colour scorched along her cheekbones; she looked away, blinking at the figure of a man in the distance. 'Mine too,' she said uncertainly.

He held open the door and she slid into the back of the car. It drew away and she didn't look back; she didn't even notice the man who stared into the vehicle as it passed him, then straightened to examine Guy, a big figure striding into the distance.

During the flight to Sant'Rosa's capital and then on to Fiji, she fought a savage, unrelenting emptiness, refusing food and anything to drink except water and fruit juice. Once aboard the big jet for New Zealand, she watched the jewel that was Fiji's main island drop away from beneath the plane's wings and forced herself to eat something that tasted like a mixture of plastic and sawdust in her mouth.

Afterwards she saw the sun go down in a splendour of blood-red and scarlet, and blamed the sight for eyes that felt heavy and dry, as though if she relaxed they might sting with tears.

Stop that right now, she told herself roundly. You knew right from the start that once you left you'd never see Guy again. You knew, and you accepted it—you can't renege on the deal now.

She was not in love with Guy Bagaton.

But halfway to New Zealand she finally accepted something she'd been refusing to acknowledge. She had done the exact same thing as her mother—without considering anything other than her own desires, she'd embarked on a wild, defiant, unrestrained affair with a man she didn't know.

At least, she thought tiredly, she wasn't married, as her mother had been. And there would be no pregnancy—Guy had seen to that. A hollow sadness took her by surprise, and was hastily banished.

But Isabel Porter had known more about her lover than Lauren knew about hers. The genetic father Lauren shared with Marc Corbett had been a businessman of note, a lover of beautiful women and a rampantly unfaithful husband notorious for his affairs. Although her mother had known he was married—and been married herself—she'd been unable to resist his powerful magnetism.

Just like me, Lauren thought, hands tensely locking together in her lap. I am truly my mother's daughter.

And my father's!

Well, her *genetic* father's. Her *true* father was Hugh Porter, who discovered that the daughter he had considered his own was the result of his wife's adultery only when Lauren was in her early twenties. As he was already fighting heart disease, the shock had almost killed him, but he had forgiven Isabel and reassured Lauren of a love that had never faltered.

Her mouth setting into a straight line, she steered her thoughts away from that period. Guy could be a planter of some sort; rice, or indigo or copra—whatever planters produced on tropical islands. He could be a scout for one of the forestry companies that were buying tropical hardwoods; he'd been scathing enough about the *sali* nut scheme to make this possible.

Half-pirate, half-warrior, he lived on an island marooned in the endless blue waves of the Pacific Ocean. Apart from sharing a blazing sexual attraction, they had nothing in common. She lived and worked in London. She loved her career, and her favourite city was Paris— about as different from the steamy heat of Sant'Rosa as any place could be.

Her lips formed the words *nothing in common* as they echoed in her mind with cold resonance. A giant fist squeezed her heart into a painful knot.

Of course she had to repay the money he'd lent her, but that wouldn't need personal contact. She didn't have his address, but she'd soon find one; everyone was traceable on the Internet. And even if he wasn't, any letter addressed to him in Sant'Rosa would find its way to him. Everyone there seemed to know him.

And he had her address...

For the rest of the journey to New Zealand she stared

unseeingly ahead while her treacherous mind replayed images of the time she'd spent in Guy's arms.

Once she got to Marc's house in New Zealand she'd be fine. She'd recover from this inconvenient and heady rush of blood to the loins, and be her normal self again.

Well, she thought drearily, I now know what happens when you hit the tropics—madness.

Lauren stroked the elderly golden retriever's insistent head.

'No, Fancy,' she said patiently, 'I don't want to go for a walk along the beach, and no, I don't want to row you around to Cabbage Tree Bay, and no, I don't want to climb the hill either. Nor do I want to throw your ball or feed you treats.'

All I want to do, she finished silently, is lie here in the sun and mourn a man I won't see again.

Tail wagging, Fancy sighed, gave her a forgiving lick on the fingers, and flopped down in the sun beside the lounger. Lauren's eyes narrowed against the glare as she gazed out across the bay; although this was a distant reach of the huge Pacific Ocean, it was much cooler and more green than the warm tropical seas surrounding Valanu and Sant'Rosa.

'But just as beautiful,' she said sternly.

Fancy's tail thumped agreement. Now and forever, Lauren knew, she'd measure every island against Valanu, where Guy had taught her the exquisite pleasures of sex.

For long forbidden minutes she lay still and remembered—as she'd been remembering for the past two days. Two days and four hours, actually. At least, she thought drearily, she wasn't counting the minutes...

Fancy sat up, ears pricked and alert as she stared into the sky.

'What is it, girl?' But Lauren too had heard it by now—a helicopter, coming fast and low.

Her half-brother, Marc? No, he and Paige were still enjoying a second honeymoon in the Seychelles, having left their adorable twin daughters with Marc's doting mother in Paris.

Some secret instinct shortened Lauren's breath. Telling herself not to be an idiot, she sprinted inside to change her brief shorts and top for linen trousers and a silk shirt.

'Just in case,' she murmured, and gave a dreary little laugh. Of course it wouldn't be Guy.

And if by some miracle it was Guy, she'd send him away. Even if he wanted her to, she couldn't see herself spending the rest of her life on a tropical island.

'Oh, you idiot,' she muttered, hastily masking her face with a discreet film of cosmetics. 'When did you start thinking in terms of the rest of your life? He certainly wasn't considering permanence.'

Combing her hair into place, she wondered what on earth had happened to her normally disciplined brain.

'You let yourself be ambushed by temptation. You blatantly let him know you were available, and you didn't put up even a minor objection when he carried you off for days of hot sex and wild passion,' she muttered.

OK, so other people did things like that all the time, but she'd been utterly irresponsible. She should have fled to New Zealand the minute he handed over her passport on Valanu.

Even then, it was too late. That hasty fake marriage conducted under gunfire was just the sort of human-interest story a journalist would love. To save her mother humiliation and her father the stress that worsened his precarious health, she and Marc had always been careful not to attract attention to their relationship.

Frowning, she slid on small gold earrings as the chopper eased down towards the pad behind the house.

She'd been lucky because it didn't seem that her recklessness had compromised the old, hidden scandal of her conception. Surely, if any journalist had got a sniff of her time with Guy—or of that fake marriage— it would have turned up in the papers by now. They'd been having a great time with the heroic, unknown 'Englishman' who'd fought side by side with the Sant'Rosan forces.

A knock on the door announced the housekeeper. 'Lauren, it's a Mr Bagaton,' she said, looking both intrigued and slightly put out. 'He insists on seeing you.'

Lauren's stomach clenched, a chaotic surge of joy wiping everything but anticipation from her mind. Trying hard not to beam, she said, 'Thanks, Mrs Oliver. I know him.'

He was waiting in the morning room, completely relaxed in casual trousers that clung to his long, muscular legs. The rolled sleeves of his shirt revealed tanned forearms. He had shaved.

Yet there was nothing casual in the way he watched her come across the room; narrowed, intent eyes in an impassive face examined her as though she was some rare specimen he'd been searching a lifetime for.

Sensation slammed through her, hot and unashamedly primeval.

This was a different man from the one on Sant'Rosa, the beachcomber, the man of action, the lover. He was harder, his control an icy cloak around him, and there was something about his dark gaze that sent tremors scudding the length of her spine.

Yet her body had sprung to life at the first glimpse of him; that consuming hunger surged through every cell, ran molten along her nerves, fired synapses all through her body until she burned with elemental urgency.

She'd never thought to meet anyone to match her half-brother, Marc, yet now another man stood in his house clothed in the same ruthless authority, exerting the same effortless dominance.

Calling on every shred of restraint, she said, 'Good morning, Guy. This is an unexpected pleasure.'

Her composed, measured greeting brought a swift, taunting smile. Before she realised what he intended he covered the distance between them in three long strides and dropped a stinging kiss on her startled mouth, before stepping back. 'I'm glad it's a pleasure.'

'Of course,' she said, hiding the uncertainty in her tone with a quick, abrupt delivery. 'What brings you here?'

'You look pale—are you all right?'

'I'm fine.' Oh, *fine* was such an inadequate word! She was terrified at how alive she felt now, reborn by his presence.

Still frowning, he said, 'Sit down.'

An icy bubble suddenly expanded beneath her ribs. She searched his face, but the hard angles and planes revealed nothing. 'Why?'

'I'm not a bearer of good news.'

Shaking her head, she unconsciously stiffened her shoulders. 'Tell me.'

But it wasn't until another rapid, unsparing survey apparently reassured him she had the stamina to deal with what he had to say that he told her bluntly, 'The marriage we contracted in Sant'Rosa might be legal.'

CHAPTER SIX

'IT'S legal?' Ashen-faced, Lauren stared at him.

'According to my lawyer we could be on shaky ground if we assume it's not binding.' He spoke levelly, no emotions showing in either tone or expression.

Rallying, she exploded, 'But there was no licence, no identification—nothing but the form that—that—'

'Josef,' Guy supplied helpfully.

'That Josef had with him.' She unclenched the fists at her sides. 'It cannot possibly be legal.'

Guy's broad shoulders lifted in a negligent shrug. 'On Sant'Rosa, it seems, the ceremony and Josef's form might be enough.'

Numbly Lauren walked across to the window, staring out at the picture-perfect garden, lushly subtropical, familiar and safe. The dog, Fancy, wandered across the lawn and spread herself out on the terrace in the sun, yawning prodigiously before curling up for another of her interminable naps.

Panic hollowed out her stomach, brought her brain skidding to a halt. *Married to Guy Bagaton?*

'No,' she said starkly. 'I won't accept it.'

'Accepting it or not isn't going to make a blind bit of difference,' Guy stated with brutal frankness. 'And it's not certain; my solicitors are working on it. I thought you should know so that you can be prepared.'

'Thank you.' She took a deep breath and forced her brain into action.

Even if the marriage was valid, it would only be a

nuisance. It would take time and money she couldn't afford to sort out, but that was all. That had to be all; she couldn't let memories of the time they'd spent together affect her—they certainly weren't affecting him.

But if a journalist got to hear about it, there was a chance that someone might dig deeper to discover the secret at the heart of her life. She'd cope—but her parents had to be protected.

Taking a deep breath, she asked, 'When will you know?'

'Things are still confused in Sant'Rosa, but my solicitor is confident that he'll get an answer within two weeks. I shall, of course, let you know immediately.'

She nodded stiffly. 'Thank you,' she said again.

Eyes narrowed golden slivers beneath heavy eyelids, Guy scrutinised her face. 'However, if this gets out you may find journalists contacting you to ask about your escape from Sant'Rosa.'

Lauren's stomach dropped. Before she could stop herself, she said, 'Oh, God no! The last thing I want is the media poking around in my life!'

Black brows lifting, he scanned her like a predator assessing prey, yet his voice was idly enquiring when he asked, 'Any particular reason?'

Careful, she cautioned herself. 'Just an innate dislike of figuring in headlines.'

He observed casually, 'Which is why I warned you. Don't answer the phone—tell the housekeeper to say you're not here.'

Logic kicked in just in time to stop her from panicking. 'But surely public interest in a small war on a tiny island nation is already waning? I noticed there wasn't much in this morning's paper.' She added with a smile that was a bit lopsided, 'I'm sure they'd like to discover the identity of "the mysterious Englishman" who fought for the Sant'Rosans, although that must be stale news now too.'

'Unfortunately some fools tried to shoot down a plane leaving the airport,' he said bluntly. 'It's stirred up the whole hornet's nest again.'

Lauren bit her lip. 'I can't imagine Josef will tell anyone what happened.'

'It's unlikely,' he agreed, angular features hard and determined, 'but there were other people in the terminal building that night.'

'They wouldn't have seen anything,' she said evenly, thoughts milling uselessly around in her mind. Trying to convince herself, she added, 'And the journalists will be war correspondents. Surely they won't be interested.'

'A reporter is always a reporter. Curiosity is their trade.' When she stayed silent he went on, 'It's not exactly a death sentence if you appear in a headline or two.'

His choice of words startled her, but she told herself not to overreact. Even if someone found out about the marriage ceremony, it didn't mean that they'd pry any deeper into her life. Even if they did—

'If you're worried about anyone discovering that we spent several days together on Valanu—'

'No,' she said too quickly. 'Well, I'd sooner it didn't star in a media frenzy, of course, but I'm sure they won't be interested in that.'

Resisting a gaze that frightened her with its probing intelligence, she finished on what she fervently hoped was a throwaway note, 'Of course you'll look even more of a hero than you already are.' She indicated a newspaper on the table.

Ignoring it, he shrugged. 'It means nothing.'

That maddening flash of memory resurfaced, only to vanish, leaving her to stare into the face of a stranger—a stranger she knew more intimately than any other man.

'I know,' she said stiffly. 'It's just that I value my privacy.'

'As do we all.' He looked around the elegant, civilised room and said, 'This house is a far cry from Valanu. Are you going to show me the beach?'

Baffled and hurt by the whip-flick of contempt in his words, she said, 'Yes, of course.'

They went out into the mellow autumn sunlight, Fancy joining them with a frisk of her head. Guy crouched down to stroke the golden head with a skill that indicated familiarity with dogs.

Fancy, of course, adored him, wriggling with delight when he scratched in exactly the right place behind her ears. Well, the dog was female, Lauren thought with a queer twist in her heart. Acquaintance made, he stood up in a lithe movement, tall and strong against the green of the garden, and looked around him with an expressionless face.

Lauren scanned the bold, autocratic bone structure, skin tingling as though she'd brushed up against an electric fence. 'If we are married—if the ceremony was legal—what can we do?'

'Annulment on the grounds of non-consummation being out of the question,' he said curtly, 'I presume it will mean divorce.'

A pang of—bitterness?—ripped through her. Trying to regain some sense of control, she dragged in a deep breath and led the way down to the beach. She bent sideways to take off her sandals and dropped them on the grassy bank beneath one of the huge pohutukawa trees. 'Surely it will be invalid everywhere but Sant'Rosa?'

Despising the pleading note in her voice, she clamped her mouth on more words. When Guy didn't answer she swung around to face him.

He said coolly, 'A marriage contracted legally in one country is usually legal in any other, unless it's polygamous. Even underage marriages are not necessarily invalid.'

Lauren concentrated on relaxing her taut muscles as she walked beside him along the sand, pleasantly warm beneath the soles of her feet. A gull soared up in front of them with a shriek that sounded too much like derisive laughter.

'Thanks for warning me,' she said slowly.

Fancy pushed into her, offering comfort for an emotion she'd never understand—one even Lauren didn't recognise.

Guy's face was a handsome mask over his thoughts. 'If anyone contacts you, simply refuse to comment.' He waited before adding with exquisite suavity, 'You needn't, of course, be concerned that I plan to claim any marital rights.'

Colour scorched along her cheekbones. 'I'm not,' she said shortly. 'Why didn't Josef tell us it might be valid?'

Guy's mouth thinned. 'If you remember, he warned us that it might be valid only on Sant'Rosa. But what else was he to do? He's a good bureaucrat—even with his world falling to pieces around him, he wouldn't send you to another country without papers.'

Lauren's teeth savaged her lower lip for a second. Faced with the horror of war, Josef had done what he could to save her from a similar fate.

She said on a sigh, 'If you wanted to make me feel like a heel, you've succeeded. Is he all right?'

'As all right as a man can be who has lost his oldest son,' he said brusquely.

Lauren's eyes filled with sudden tears. 'I'm sorry,' she said again, groping for a handkerchief to wipe her eyes and blow her nose. 'Against that, I haven't got much to complain about.'

'Not a lot.' His tone was so dry it could have soaked up a minor lake or two. 'It's not a disaster, Lauren; inconvenient, certainly, and with the prospect of some rather fulsome and irritating publicity if it gets out, but nothing to panic about.'

Head held high, Lauren said, 'Of course. But I don't consider myself married to you!'

'That,' he said calmly, 'is entirely mutual. On reflection, our charming idyll on Valanu was rash, but hindsight is always wiser than foresight.' He turned and examined the house, a sprawling white place mellow with many years of love and care. 'If the ceremony turns out to be legal, I'll contact you so that we can apply to whatever court has the power to have the marriage dissolved.'

'Thank you,' she said automatically.

Still with his gaze on the house, he said, 'You have a very indulgent employer. Does he allow all his executives to take their holidays in his private hideaway?'

How did he know that Marc was her employer?

Then she realised what he was implying.

Cool distaste coloured her tone. 'You'll have to ask him that.'

'I assume your fear of the media is in case your lover hears about your indiscretion on Valanu,' he said, his pleasant tone failing to hide the steely edge in the words.

'What?'

He said contemptuously, 'Don't lie to me. I know you are his mistress, since even before he married his lovely New Zealander.'

One of the first things Marc taught her was that losing her temper put her at an immediate disadvantage. With his advice in mind, Lauren had kept her cool when facing down unfriendly meetings, rejecting sexual harassment and dealing with carpet sellers in Middle Eastern markets.

Pain clawed her so sharply that she lost control. 'My life is none of your business,' she said in a voice that should have turned the ground beneath them to permafrost.

Black brows climbed just enough to indicate Guy's total and scornful disbelief. 'When you invited me into your bed and your arms, it became my business,' he said silkily.

Stabbed by a searing mixture of anguish and outrage, she said thinly, 'That was an—an aberration.'

He laughed. 'A very pleasurable one for me,' he drawled.

'I am not Marc Corbett's mistress,' she ground out.

'It is an old-fashioned term, I agree. Do you prefer lover?'

Her lips tightened. 'Neither.' Trying to regain control of the situation, she went on, 'Before I decide what to do, I'll consult my solicitor. He might be able to find out something yours hasn't.'

Guy stopped and looked down at her, narrowed golden eyes uncompromising in the stark framework of his face. 'Get this straight,' he said flatly. '*You* don't decide—we're in this together.'

Her mouth dried. 'I didn't mean that I'd make a unilateral decision.'

After a pause he said abruptly, 'Tell me about your relationship with Marc Corbett.'

Guy watched the familiar blankness shut down her expression. When her tongue stole out to wet her lips, he had to rein in the lash of desire that cut through him.

She said quietly, 'I don't know whether I can trust you.'

Cold fury stirred beneath the desire. 'I can't, of course, force your confidence.'

She glanced up, pale eyes glinting and intelligent. After a long moment she said abruptly, 'He saved my life.'

Astonishment replaced his anger. Whatever he'd expected to hear, it wasn't that. 'How?'

Muscles moved beneath the silken skin of her throat as she swallowed. 'Just after I graduated from university I developed leukaemia.'

His blood ran cold. 'Go on.'

'I needed a bone marrow transplant, but they couldn't find one to suit.' She spoke dispassionately, as though it had happened to some other woman. 'In the end we discovered that Marc was a perfect match. If he hadn't been, I'd have died.'

The ugly clutch of fear fading, Guy said slowly, 'I see.' It was outrageous, unbelievable that this lovely, vital woman had been threatened by death.

Lauren stopped to pick up a shell. Keeping her gaze on its pearly sheen and intricate spirals, she said, 'After that, I hero-worshipped him a bit.'

'I can understand that.' The crispness of his tone hid, he hoped, the questions seething through his mind.

How had her doctors found that Marc Corbett was a bone marrow match? Common sense told him that the man had probably enrolled on the worldwide register— but why? And surely donors' names were kept secret?

Lauren looked at him with eyes so translucent it seemed impossible for her to hide a thought. 'He told me that when I got better he'd give me a job if I wanted one and if I was suitable; of course I was delighted, and when I got the all-clear I fronted up. I had to go through the same process as anyone else, but I got in, and ever since then we've had a sort of—well, closeness. I try not to impose on it, but he's a darling, and so is his wife, Paige.'

Guy's mouth curved in an ironic smile. He liked Marc Corbett and respected him, but *darling* wasn't a word he'd have used to describe the man.

Once again she lifted limpid eyes to his. Her voice rang true, she was looking him straight in the face, but instincts honed in the cutthroat world he'd made his own told him she was lying. Or at the very least, only revealing part of the truth.

Coldly, clinically, he decided that if her story was a front for an affair, it had the advantage of originality. Even if it was true, she could still be Marc Corbett's lover.

As for her obvious affection for Paige Corbett, it wouldn't be the first—or the last—time a woman had an ongoing relationship with the husband of a friend.

Lauren wondered uneasily what was going on behind those fabulous features, gilded by sunlight. Did he believe her? And had it been enough to satisfy him?

She found herself wishing she could trust him with

the whole truth. If it had just been herself she might have, but in the end it wasn't her secret.

She said brightly, 'It's an old story, and not one I'd like to get around. Some people say that if you save someone's life you're responsible for them forever afterwards; I'd hate people to believe Marc gave me a job because of some quirk of genetic good fortune.'

'I can understand that,' Guy said with a smile that blended irony with a hint of self-derision.

Sunlight conjured a shimmer of mahogany fire from his black hair. He dragged out a wallet from his pocket, scribbled something on a page of a small diary, and tore it out to hand to her. 'In case you need me,' he said.

Their fingers touched, and Lauren's heart jumped.

'And just to remind you how it was with us—' he said through his teeth, and covered the three paces that separated them, drawing her into his arms.

Every nerve speared by forbidden delight, Lauren froze. He looked down into her face, his own angrily intent. 'No, you haven't forgotten,' he said in a raw voice.

And then he kissed her eyelids closed, his breath warm on her skin.

Pierced by erotic poignancy, Lauren's defences crumbled into sand. This was what she'd been waiting for—this sense of rightness, of completeness...

His lips crushed hers in a kiss that obliterated all sense of time and space. Helplessly she melted into his arms and gave him everything he asked for, responding with feverish passion to his sensuous onslaught.

But although she wanted nothing more than to let this go on to its inevitable conclusion, she finally fought free of the consuming hunger to shake her head and drag her mouth from his, gasping hoarsely, 'No!'

A fierce, possessive gleam fired his eyes. 'But you were saying yes a moment ago.'

Even then she hovered on the brink of surrender until hard common sense forced its way through the mists of desire.

'No,' she repeated quietly, uncompromisingly, because she knew that she'd never be safe, that the only way to stop herself from falling headlong into infatuation was to end it now.

But oh, it was hard to say, with his strength and his heat seducing her, with the sexy, evocative aroma of his skin scrambling her brain, and his taste on her lips, in her mouth—when every cell in her body screamed for the release only he could give her.

His mouth hardened. 'Why?'

'Because I don't want this.' The lie hurt, and it hurt more that he knew it was a lie. 'I find you very attractive,' she hurried on, surprised at the clarity of each word, 'but the idea of being married to you—if that's what I am—is ridiculous. And I certainly don't want an affair with you.'

She invested the final word with a flick of scorn, and saw it register on his face. He smiled, and as she shivered he freed her and stepped back.

'Really?' he said politely. 'I can think of plenty of words to describe such a marriage, but ridiculous doesn't come to mind. As for the affair— I thought we'd already had it.'

'We spent a few days together,' she corrected, gripped by intolerable anguish. Yet she had to send him out of her life. 'I'm sorry, but a tropical fling is not expected to last beyond the tropics. I'll always be grateful to you for saving my life, because I suspect that's what you did.'

'Stop right there,' he advised with an inflection so deadly it chilled her into temporary paralysis. 'If you're telling me that you slept with me out of gratitude, I'll just have to show you that you're wrong. We made love because we wanted each other.'

'Of course I did—we did!' She struggled to clear her mind. 'You know very well that I—that we—that it was mutual.' She stopped and dragged in a jerky breath before finishing defiantly, 'But it's over.'

For a charged moment he surveyed her, his beautiful mouth hard against the chiselled angles of his face. Finally he drawled, 'Then there's nothing more to say,' and turned away. 'Goodbye, Lauren.'

Aching with a bleak sense of loss and pain, she watched him stride towards the thick row of trees that hid the helicopter pad. Fate and war had shackled them together until they could get free of this marriage.

Whatever she felt for Guy Bagaton couldn't possibly be love; that involved much more than gratitude and great sex.

Only a loser would love a man who thought she was another man's mistress, and she wasn't a loser. She didn't even know him.

Not really.

The sound of the helicopter's rotor blades drove her to shelter beneath the overhanging branches of one of the great trees bordering the champagne curve of the beach. As she listened to the machine carry Guy away from her, she found herself thinking of all the ways she did know him...

Perhaps when people had forgotten about the war in Sant'Rosa, it might be safe to see him again. Without all this other baggage cluttering up their relationship, they could perhaps meet as ordinary people.

No. She'd sent him away.

And she'd do it again. When she'd asked her mother why, of all the people in the world, Marc's bone marrow matched hers, Isabel's admission of adultery had been shattering enough, but what had appalled her was her mother's response when Lauren began to ask if her father knew.

After the first two tentative words her mother had interrupted fiercely, 'He does now. Don't ever speak to him about it. The stress could kill him.'

Lauren didn't know how her parents had worked through this rough patch, but their love had held them together through the trauma.

When the steady thump-thump-thump of the rotors had died away, she went back inside and rang London.

'How's Dad?'

'He's fine,' her mother said reassuringly. 'How are you, darling?'

'Fine too, but I've had an unsettling visit from the man who got me out of Sant'Rosa.'

Censoring heavily, she told her mother why Guy had come, ending with, 'I think I'll come home as soon as I can.'

'No,' Isabel said firmly. 'You need that holiday, Lauren—your health isn't anything to take lightly.'

'I feel perfectly normal again,' Lauren assured her. Well, apart from worrying about journalists, the marriage, and obsessing about Guy. 'But if some reporter finds out about this wretched marriage they'll probably come looking for you.'

After a silence in which her mother absorbed the implications, Isabel responded with even more firmness, 'So we will just ignore them.'

Lauren said bleakly, 'They might start digging around.'

The hesitation at the other end of the line revealed that her mother had already thought of that. 'They won't find anything,' Isabel said finally, her voice taut but confident. 'If this false marriage does come to light, it will be a three days' wonder. Ah, darling—your father's just come in.'

Lauren waited tensely, smiling as her father's voice echoed across the world. 'Stay there,' he commanded. 'By the way, what's the man who got you off Sant'Rosa like?'

'Forceful and formidable,' Lauren said lightly. And judgemental.

'Would I like him?'

She laughed. 'Yes, I think you would. You like Marc, don't you?'

'Very much,' he said gruffly. 'Mind you, Marc saved your life, but then, this man might have too. When this bit of a fuss is over, I'd like to shake his hand. Stay there and finish your holiday, Lauren. I want to see colour in your cheeks when you come back.'

'Yes, Daddy,' she said in mock obedience, and heard him guffaw and say goodbye.

He endured his condition like a soldier, gallantly fighting the limitations it put on his life. She said her goodbyes to her mother, and with stinging eyes rang through to the person who handled her travel arrangements. Whatever her parents said, if the marriage ceremony with Guy ended up in the media she wanted to be at home, not stuck on the other side of the world.

Frowning at the skyline of Singapore through the hotel window, Guy swore succinctly under his breath.

The man on the other end of the telephone said drily, 'At school I used to envy you the ability to swear in five languages. Now I can swear in twenty. But I still can't pull the birds like you.'

In a level, cold voice Guy said, 'Bloody tabloids.'

'They have a place in life.'

'Bottom feeders. Any idea when it's due to break?'

He could almost hear his friend shrug. 'Tomorrow,' he said succinctly. 'They've got a tasty little piece—the dramatic circumstances of the marriage and that it might turn out to be legal, as well as the insinuation she might be Corbett's mistress. He's always good for copy, and it's always a coup to get the sights on someone as newsworthy and cunning at avoiding we poor hacks as you are. Naturally they want to make the most of it.'

'Naturally,' Guy said lethally, fighting back the urge to kill someone. 'How did you find this out?'

'I have friends in high places,' his friend the war corespondent said airily, adding with a muffled snort of laughter, 'Or low places.'

'OK, Sean, thanks a lot. I owe you.'

'Don't worry, I owe you more. After all, you once saved my miserable life.'

'Forget it,' Guy said briefly, and hung up.

He stood for a long time frowning into space before reaching for the telephone again. With the time distance it would be eight in the evening in New Zealand.

As he dialled a number he recalled the way the sun had shone through the window of Marc Corbett's house, collecting in Lauren's hair so that it fell like a river of molten obsidian around her face, somehow giving a soft, pearly glow to her milk-white skin.

Skin like satin against his hand...

As Mrs Oliver wasn't in the house, Lauren picked up

the receiver. 'Hello,' she said carefully above the noisy thud of her heart.

'Can anyone overhear what we're saying?'

Guy! 'No.' Marc had made sure the communications system was incapable of being bugged. Cold foreboding knotted her inside. 'What's happened?'

'I have it on good authority that the news of our marriage is about to explode onto the front pages.' He waited while her hand clenched on the receiver, then asked sharply, 'Are you there?'

'Yes.' She said crisply, 'Thank you for telling me. I'll ring my parents straight away and let them know.'

'Do they know about the marriage?'

'Yes.'

'Sensible of you to tell them,' he said calmly. 'When do you go home?'

'I'm leaving tomorrow.'

He asked for the details of her airline and arrival time, then said, 'I suggest you change your booking to get off the flight in Rome.'

'That's being paranoid,' she said brusquely. 'I'll be fine. No one will be expecting me anyway—the airline won't tell anyone when I'm due in, and my parents are the only other people who know. They're certainly not going to confide in any nice, inquisitive journalist.'

'Fair enough,' he said calmly. 'Have a safe flight home.'

And he hung up.

Blinking back stupid, unnecessary tears, Lauren put down the receiver. She felt like an animal in hiding, every sense strained to the point of pain while wolves closed in on her.

CHAPTER SEVEN

BUT even though Lauren had prepared herself mentally and emotionally on the long flight, the pack of photographers and reporters that greeted her at Heathrow both shocked and scared her. Light exploded in her face as they bayed her name and took photographs.

'Look this way, Lauren!' 'Hi, Lauren—can you tell us about this marriage to—?' 'Lauren, Lauren, over here!' until command and shouted comment blended into a din that mercifully blocked out individual yells.

Shaking inwardly, she clamped her lips together, tuning them out while she searched for the quickest route through the milling mass. And then salvation arrived, in the form of two burly men stamped with the indefinable mark of security personnel.

'This way, please, Ms Porter,' the largest and most solid one said in her ear while the other commandeered her luggage trolley as a shield.

Locking every muscle against a cowardly impulse to run, she allowed herself to be escorted away from the hordes and along a corridor. They stopped outside a door and the one in front held it open.

Bewildered, Lauren went through.

And stopped as the door closed behind her and Guy Bagaton rose to his feet, big and vital and ablaze with raw power. Her heart jumping in incredulous joy, she managed to say in a brittle voice, 'Oh—hello. I gather that the news has broken?'

'This morning.' He sounded as fed up as he looked,

but his size and that indefinable air of competence and authority was hugely reassuring.

Shivering, she rubbed her arms; the impersonal room reminded her sharply of that other room a world away when she and this man had exchanged the vows that now bound them in a false relationship.

'I see,' she said unevenly. 'I expected interest, but nothing like that pandemonium. How did they know I was coming in today?'

With cold contempt he said, 'There's always someone who'll spill the beans.' Eyes as bright and burnished as fool's gold narrowed. 'You look tired. Didn't you get any sleep on the flight?'

'Not a lot.' And now her head was pounding, excitement and shock producing a wild mixture of sensations: intense relief, because she trusted him to deal with any situation, and a fierce sensual charge honed by absence. 'The plane was seething with high school students embarking on a year's exchange in Europe. They settled down for an hour here and there.'

'I see. Come on, let's go.' Still frowning, he took her arm and steered her towards a boarding bridge.

Although a debilitating combination of exhaustion and astonishment tempted her to let him take over, she croaked, 'What's happening? Where are we going?'

'Dacia.'

Blinking, she wondered where Dacia was, before remembering a small princedom in the Mediterranean Sea. She balked, trying to stop. 'Why?'

With an expression as grim as his voice, Guy exerted just enough strength to urge her on. 'Your parents are already there.'

What on earth was going on? Her mind spun stupidly

so that all she could say was, 'But my father can't travel by air.'

'He can if he has a nurse with him,' Guy told her, escorting her along the bridge. 'He's fine; I've just been speaking to your mother. I'm sorry you had to run the gauntlet back there.'

Summoning the last remnants of common sense, Lauren dug her heels in. 'Wait. I'm not sure this is a good idea. What's going on? Why Dacia, for heaven's sake?'

'Because it's quiet and peaceful and you wanted to be out of the limelight,' Guy said evenly. 'A few days there will see the media frenzy die—there's nothing so stale as last week's news.'

'But I—'

'Your parents agreed that this would be the best idea.'

'But I don't understand—'

He rasped, 'It's all I can do to protect you from the sort of gossip that could destroy your life.'

'What? In this day and age? You've got a very naïve attitude to modern society if you think that a marriage of convenience is going to do more than mildly titillate readers.'

Flint-hard and formidable, Guy said brusquely, 'You're the one who's completely naïve. To start off with, you might as well kiss your career goodbye.'

The pain in her breast solidified into a rock, so big she couldn't breathe properly. 'Don't be ridiculous—'

'Don't be an idiot,' he ground out, eyes cold as frozen fire. 'Unless you've got enough incriminating evidence to blackmail him, Corbett's not going to keep you once he knows that you and I were lovers. And with journalists combing through Sant'Rosa and Valanu, it won't be long before he does know.'

'It won't matter,' she said dully. It hurt that he should still believe that ancient piece of gossip.

And that was dangerous, because she shouldn't care what he thought of her.

Guy said harshly, 'He doesn't strike me as a man who's happy sharing his women, and I doubt if he'd surrender to blackmail.' Contempt darkened his face and thinned his mouth.

'No,' she said, her voice muted. 'He wouldn't.'

They were facing each other like enemies, eyes duelling, tense with antagonism. He despised her. 'So you'll be notorious; no one will take you seriously. You might get offers for television or some sort of modelling, but your career's gone. Face that now. If you lie low on Dacia for a week or so, the fuss will die down and you can regroup.'

Taking her numb silence for consent, he urged her into the cabin. Later, she was convinced that jet lag had scrambled her brain and sapped her will-power; surely that had been why she'd surrendered so meekly to his authoritative handling!

Once inside, a harried glance revealed that the plane was a private one, and they were the only passengers.

'You'll get an excellent view from this window,' Guy said, standing back to let her sink into a superbly comfortable leather seat.

When he leaned down, sensations rioted through her in a delirious mixture of fire and honey and aching need. She swallowed to ease an unbearably dry throat and closed her eyes against the arrogantly angular jaw and the bold male curves of his beautiful mouth.

But as he clicked her seat-belt into place, she couldn't block out the subtle, spicy scent that was his alone. Memories rushed back, of heat and long tropical nights when the evocative, erotic perfume of frangipani blossoms and the drowsy sound of the sea on the reef provided the perfect setting for passion. And of Guy, taking her to heaven with his lean, skilled hands and experienced understanding of what a woman's body needed to drive it to unbearable ecstasy...

He straightened, his hard-edged face shutting her out as effectively as a mask. 'I'm going up to the cockpit. Try to get some sleep.'

With gritty eyes, Lauren watched him walk away, big body moving with a fluid, controlled confidence that came close to arrogance.

What she and Guy had shared was nothing more— nor less—than transcendental sex. Neither then nor in New Zealand had either of them thought about love.

When the door closed behind him she transferred her gaze to the window, not taking in the minor bustle of getting a plane into the air. Surely he couldn't be the pilot?

But why not? He'd known the man who'd evacuated the resort guests from Sant'Rosa. When he wasn't fighting wars did he fly charter planes?

A movement from behind called her attention to a steward, who smiled and offered her a drink.

'Water, please,' she said thickly.

Once he'd brought it and explained the safety features, the plane taxied out onto the runway. She sank back into the seat and let the cool liquid slide down her parched throat until she'd finished the glass.

At cruising height the steward reappeared, offering food and more drinks.

'Just a pot of tea, thank you,' she told him with real gratitude.

She'd occasionally flown in private jets chartered by Marc to get him and his family quickly and privately between New Zealand, where they spent many of their holidays, and Paris, where they lived.

This one, she thought dreamily, had a personal touch that meant someone had cared about its decoration. Elegantly serene, it invited relaxation. She decided she'd like whoever had decided on the colour scheme and the carpet.

Her roving gaze settled on the bulkhead between the cabin and the kitchen. Frowning, she discerned a crest that seemed familiar—a leopard fiercely clawing the air. Something about the outline nagged at her tired mind. She closed her eyes and set about capturing the elusive memory.

The ring! Her lashes flew up. Guy's ring, the one he'd put on her finger at that mockery of a wedding ceremony. Narrowing her eyes, she stared at the crest, superimposing the remembered lines over the leopard.

It fitted exactly.

Brain working furiously, she recalled a faint note of pride in his voice when he spoke of Dacia. Did this plane belong to a Dacian airline?

'Would you like something to read?' the steward murmured after he'd delivered a tray of tea.

'Yes, thank you.'

He arrived back with a couple of extremely expensive-looking fashion magazines.

Just what she needed—something light and cheerful. With stubborn determination she eyed models in what appeared to be designer shrouds before turning the page to read her horoscope, which announced that she'd met the only man she'd ever love.

Lauren shut the magazine with a snap and stared unseeingly out of the window.

Was Guy Dacian? Part Dacian, anyway; he was built on too impressive a scale to be wholly of Mediterranean stock, but genes inherited from that area would explain his olive skin and beautiful mouth.

And a different first language would be the source of the faint, intriguing hint of an accent that intensified when he was making love...

More dangerously bittersweet memories burned through her. Hastily she picked up the magazine again. Nothing on the pages could banish flashbacks of days and nights on Valanu—the rich gleam of sunlight on Guy's wet skin, the quick flash of white teeth when he'd laughed, and the note in his voice when he'd spoken her name...

She dreamed about him every night now.

Swift excitement pulsed through her when the door into the cockpit slid back to let him through. So he was part of the crew.

When he stopped to speak to the steward, Lauren watched him uneasily. He looked different—much less of the beachcomber, much more a sophisticated European. And it wasn't just the removal of that stubble. She'd always been aware of his bred-in-the-bone authority, but in the hothouse situation on Sant'Rosa and Valanu she hadn't noticed this cool, urbane detachment.

Now, filling her hungry eyes with the sight of him, she finally accepted something she'd been trying to repress since their first meeting. Some time during their idyll in Valanu she'd slipped over the invisible dividing line between attraction and love.

The knowledge hit with heady impact, sending a tidal

wave of adrenaline rushing through her. For a precious few seconds she allowed herself to savour the exquisite thrill of loving Guy. Then she forced herself to lock that love in her heart and throw the key away.

Because Guy didn't love her. Everything he'd done had been because he was chivalrous and protective. Twice he'd rescued her from unpleasant situations; he'd lent her money and bought her clothes, and he'd made sure she didn't get pregnant. He'd made love to her with heart-shaking tenderness and raw desire, but all that meant was that for those days he'd wanted her—even though he'd believed her to be Marc's mistress.

But lust chose without discrimination and died swiftly. The father she shared with Marc had wanted her mother too—for a week—although he'd been married.

She couldn't let herself love Guy.

He said something that brought a white grin to the steward's face, then turned. Just in time, Lauren fixed her gaze on the magazine in her lap, every sense strung as tight as piano wire. When he was a couple of paces away she forced herself to glance up enquiringly, because ignoring him would be as much a giveaway as gazing at him with her heart in her eyes.

He sat down beside her with a flash of the reckless grin she remembered from Sant'Rosa. 'You English and your tea!'

'Don't Dacians drink tea?'

His smile disappeared. After a taut second he said, 'Not a lot—we mostly drink coffee.'

'You have excellent English.' It was an inane remark, but it was all her scrambled brain could come up with.

'I spent some years at school in England, and I'm fortunate enough to be a good linguist.'

She nodded, thinking of his mastery of the Sant'Rosan language, then donned her coolest composure and looked up into his face. 'Thank you for getting my parents out of that feeding frenzy. I had no idea a media pack in full cry would be so—' she abandoned *frightening* to substitute '—so intimidating.'

'Your parents are sensible enough to see when retreat is the best decision,' he said with a casual lack of emphasis. 'And you still have holiday time, I believe.'

The aloof enquiry in his tone slammed up more barriers. 'Another couple of weeks.'

'You parents said you'd been ill.'

She shrugged. 'A bout of pneumonia. It wasn't very serious, and it's over now.'

'You're still pale.' His voice was deliberate, but an unsettling note in it made her acutely aware of his closeness.

'I'm always pale, and at the moment I'm jet lagged,' she admitted with a wry smile. 'I'll be fine after a good night's sleep.' And to convince him, she finished brightly, 'I've never been to Dacia, but I believe it's beautiful.'

'Every bit as much as Sant'Rosa or New Zealand,' he said ironically, 'although in an entirely different way.'

She relaxed a little while he told her of its blood-stained history and eventual conquest four hundred years previously by a pirate. 'He sailed into the harbour and imposed a rule that was ruthless and autocratic, but surprisingly enlightened for the time.'

'He sounds familiar,' she murmured dulcetly.

He directed an enigmatic glance her way. Her heart-beat shot into overdrive, a wild counterpoint to the drugging sweetness of desire that washed through her, merciless and compelling.

'Are you calling me ruthless and autocratic?' he drawled, eyes gleaming with tawny fire.

Laughter bubbled through her. 'How intuitive of you to guess! Of course you are—you think nothing of ploughing roughshod over anyone who gets in your way.'

'Admit that I always try to convince with sweet reason before I bring in the heavy artillery,' he returned virtuously, the lazy note in his voice belying his words.

'I'll admit no such thing,' she retorted. 'Within a few hours of meeting you I found myself married to you, and I don't recollect any sweetly reasonably discussion then.'

And a few days later she'd been in his bed, willing prisoner of a reckless, desperate passion that overthrew years of restraint and self-discipline.

Yet she couldn't regret it, although the aftermath seemed likely to cause endless complications and heartache. Hastily she finished, 'And now I've been hijacked to Dacia!'

'Some situations call for action,' he observed, straight-faced.

Lauren went very still. 'Yes,' she said, remembering the all-pervasive smell of fear on Sant'Rosa. 'I don't remember whether I actually thanked you for getting me off Sant'Rosa.' She looked up as far as his chin. 'I am very grateful. I know what could have happened if I'd been stuck there.'

'I'd have taken care of you.'

Startled, she took in a face carved of granite, coldly determined, so implacable that a cold finger of foreboding ran down her spine. She'd known him as a beachcomber, as a man of action, as a lover, but her first impression had been of a pirate.

Now she suspected that the pirate persona revealed his true nature.

God, she thought, what have you got yourself into? You should have stuck it out in London...

She said sombrely, 'I'd have been a nuisance, and as you pointed out then, I'd have put you in even more danger than you were already in.'

'It's over now; don't worry about it.' He stood up and smiled down at her, although his eyes were unreadable. 'Drink up your tea, then try to catnap. I'll see you once we land.'

Throat aching and tight with repressed emotion, Lauren watched him go, remembering moments when she'd lain on the bed in that house in Valanu and watched him walk towards the glass doors onto the terrace. Sunlight had gilded every powerful curve and line of his body, the smooth play of muscles, the lean strength of legs and arms. Unbearably stirred, she had closed her eyes against him, but that bronze image was burned into her retina and her heart.

She dragged her mind back to the present with relief. Both the china and the silverware had the same crest, the Dacian leopard, she'd noticed as she had poured tea.

If she'd had any sense she'd have asked Guy about the owner of the plane. Unfortunately her mind shut down when he came near.

She drank some tea and ate one of the small, delicious sandwiches, then leaned back in the seat and tried to sleep. It didn't work. Thoughts of Guy tossed through her mind, so to give her restless brain something else to chew on, she reached for the discarded magazine and began leafing desultorily through its pages.

After several moments she realised she'd been staring at one page. Blinking, she focused. Beefcake, she thought as several handsome male faces gazed back at her with varying degrees of interest.

One of them was Guy.

Unable to believe what she was seeing, she shook her head, then gazed again at the photograph. Yes, it was Guy.

He was a *model?*

Stunned, she began to read the text beneath the photograph.

'And the most gorgeous,' it burbled, *'if you like your royalty moody, magnificent and hard to catch, is Prince Guy of Dacia, billionaire...'*

Lauren blinked again, her heart contracting into a cold, hard ball in her chest. Royalty? *Prince* Guy?

...and at thirty-two still unmarried and breaking hearts all over the world. We wonder if he'll follow the footsteps of his cousins, Prince Luka, the ruler of Dacia, and Princess Lucia, Mrs Hunt Radcliffe, who both fell in love with New Zealanders.

Prince Guy of Dacia, Lauren thought woodenly, jettisoning hopes she'd barely recognised.

Oh, she knew that name; prince, hugely successful businessman, lover of beautiful women, and reclusive object of intense media interest. She closed her eyes, but when she opened them he was still frowning out from the page.

She'd heard of him, seen photographs—why hadn't she recognised him when she'd met him in Sant'Rosa?

Because stubble had blurred the aristocratic features, and because—well, because you simply didn't expect to find a European prince on an island in the middle of the Pacific Ocean.

And because she'd been so aware of him that she'd temporarily lost her mind!

Why hadn't he told her? She bit her lip. Presumably he expected her to know that Bagaton was the family name of the Dacian royal family. Well, she hadn't.

A turbulent mix of emotions—a stark, wholly irrational sense of betrayal, fury and dark desolation—razed every thought but one from her brain. She had been a complete and utter fool, wilfully ignoring anything that didn't fit her first impression of him.

No wonder the Press had met her with such avid determination at the airport! This jet, with its luxurious seats and its atmosphere of privilege and power, its crested china and silver, was either his or his cousin's—the reigning prince.

The distance between Lauren Porter and their world of birth and privilege loomed like a cliff face, dangerous and insurmountable.

How long would it be before someone started digging into her background? Her stomach tightened as fear kicked in. If they hadn't already begun. She was already linked to Marc; would someone pursue that link and find out that she and her boss were half-siblings?

If anyone made the connections, she'd be revealed as the bastard daughter of Marc Corbett's father, the cuckoo in her father's nest. She could cope with that, but her parents would be exposed to sly, sniggering insinuations that would hurt them unbearably and strain her father's precarious health.

All to sell a few more newspapers...

Trying to swallow the lump in her throat, Lauren stared down at the photograph of Guy. By the forbidding expression of his angular face he'd been furious at being snapped. Setting her jaw, she forced herself to read the rest of the blurb.

Prince Guy is probably the richest of the playboy princes; he inherited millions from his mother, a Russian heiress and great beauty, and he set up his own software firm after leaving university. It now earns him millions each year. Fiercely protective of his privacy, he's also a humanitarian who is interested in ecology.

Lauren closed the magazine and fought back despair. If she'd known who he was, she'd have taken her chances on Sant'Rosa.

As for making love with him—never!

Somewhere deep inside her, a mocking voice laughed. Oh, yes, you would, it mocked. You wanted him desperately. You still do. And you're angry with him because not telling you means he didn't trust you.

Which was ridiculous, because she hadn't trusted him with the entire truth about herself.

Her ears popped as the plane banked and turned. Lauren stared stonily ahead, trying to convince herself that no one would be able to find out that Marc was her half-brother.

It was extremely unlikely that they'd discover that he had donated his bone marrow to her. And why should they search twenty-nine years in the past to discover that her mother and Marc's father had been on the same cruise through the Caribbean?

No, her parents were safe from media prying—and

even if they weren't, Guy had pulled them out of the vortex and into temporary safety.

When the seat-belt sign flashed on with a melodious chime, she relaxed her hands from their death grip on each other in her lap and began to breathe deeply, and out, in and out, until the wild turbulence of her emotions abated. If it killed her she'd be calm, because she didn't dare be anything else.

CHAPTER EIGHT

AT THE Dacian airport the steward escorted Lauren into a private room, empty except for flowers and some comfortable lounge furniture, then went off to get her luggage. She waited tensely until Guy came into the room.

Her heart clenched. You can do this, she told herself with ice-cold resolve, determined not to wilt under his keen scrutiny. You'll be polite and crisp and very, very restrained. You are infatuated with this man, but it won't last, because you won't let it.

She took another deep breath.

Guy said, 'Your luggage will be here in a few minutes. Did you manage a nap?'

'No,' she said, adding with a smile that hurt the muscles in her cheeks, 'I'm fine, thank you.'

He didn't seem to notice anything different about her attitude, but she didn't fool herself. Like every predator, he was acutely tuned to his surroundings.

Neither spoke as they went down in a lift and walked out of the building into heat that sucked the breath from her lungs. Ahead, a limousine purred softly, like a waiting cat. Apart from that and the sound of a jet in the distance, it was blessedly silent. No hounds of the Press yapped around her, no lights flashed in her eyes. A uniformed man gave a short salute to Guy and held the back door open. Behind the wheel she made out the form of a driver.

Sliding into the seat, she commented in a voice with

no expression at all, 'It's every bit as hot as the tropics, but not at all humid.' And because she could no longer hold the question back, she asked with a cool lack of emphasis, 'What exactly were you doing on Sant'Rosa?'

'I have interests there. And friends.' He glanced down at her, thick lashes veiling the glimmering depths of his eyes. His tone told her nothing as he went on, 'Several years ago I spent a few weeks there as a hostage.'

A *hostage?*

Horrified, she asked unevenly, 'How on earth did that happen?'

'I delivered medical supplies during the civil war, and the government of Sant'Rosa saw a way of using me.' He shrugged, looking straight ahead as the car drew smoothly away. 'They kidnapped me to persuade my cousin to act as intermediary between them and the rebels.'

She stared at him. 'What happened?'

'I escaped the second night,' he said nonchalantly. A swift grin reminded her again of the buccaneer she'd first met, as did the wry note in his voice when he added, 'It wasn't difficult; they were pretty half-hearted gaolers.'

She closed her eyes. 'You escaped, but you stayed on the island? In the middle of a civil war?'

'They were desperate,' he said briefly. 'And I liked them. They knew the Republic was ready to move troops across the border if there was any chance of a truce between the warring sides. In fact, we fought off an incursion while I was there.'

Appalled at the risks he'd taken, she demanded, '*We* fought off?'

His broad shoulders lifted. 'I was involved in a very minor way,' he said casually. 'They were much better bush fighters than I was, but terror makes fast learners.'

'Or dead ones,' she said tightly.

'Life's for living; it's not worth much if you're forever looking over your shoulder.'

The car purred quietly down a road shared with an occasional donkey and many more motor-scooters, all ridden by young men with very white teeth who waved insouciantly at the limousine as it eased past them.

Lauren clamped her lips together to stop herself from raging at Guy for valuing his life so cheaply.

'We're heading inland to a villa up in the hills; I thought your parents would prefer it to the coast because it's cooler there,' he told her.

'Thank you.' She had to fight back a heavy thud of disappointment. For some reason she'd thought they'd be at the same place...

Fool! A sensible woman would want as much distance between them as possible.

But she wasn't sensible about Guy. From the moment she'd seen him, villainously unshaven on Sant'Rosa, she'd battled a ferocious, elemental appetite that had nothing, she reminded herself stringently, to do with love or respect.

He said, 'My cousin, Luka, and his wife would like to meet you, but they're sure that you and your father need to rest today, so it will probably be tomorrow.'

'I'll look forward to that,' she said untruthfully.

He lifted a lean hand to acknowledge a wave from a donkey rider. Olive trees shimmered in the slow breeze, their leaves gleaming silver against a sky as blue as heaven. Small plants and wild flowers grew against the bases of ancient stone walls that bordered the road.

Guy surveyed her, his eyes cool and intent. 'What's the matter?'

Lauren gathered her composure around like cling film, leaned back and showed her teeth.

'Nothing,' she said coolly. 'Well, nothing apart from a dodgy marriage to a man who neglected to tell me he was a prince.'

His brows lifted. Wielding courtesy like a weapon, he said with suave distinctness, 'It didn't seem relevant at the time.'

'Most people would consider it very relevant. I had no idea that you were a member of the Dacian royal family until—' she glanced at her watch '—about half an hour ago, when I saw an article about you in a magazine. When we went through that ceremony on Sant'Rosa I did think Bagaton sounded vaguely familiar, but not enough to ring alarm bells.'

'Alarm bells?' he said softly. 'Why should you be alarmed?'

She lifted her head and met his glinting gaze full on. 'I'm not in the habit of marrying princes, even to get out of a bad situation.'

'I didn't tell you because you didn't ask,' he returned with cutting urbanity. 'You found me useful, so you sensibly used me. Besides, it didn't matter—it's merely an accident of birth. The important thing on Sant'Rosa was to get you to safety.' He flicked her a glance edged with satire. 'You didn't ask who I was when I came to you in Valanu.'

Lauren bit back the rash words threatening to tumble from her tongue but couldn't stop herself from snapping, 'I thought I knew who you were.'

'Perhaps,' he said softly, 'I should ask you the real question.'

'Which is?' Although her voice was crisp with hauteur, she knew the moment she said the words that they should never have been spoken.

'Why did you offer yourself to me in Valanu?'

Humiliation burned in her throat. Without thinking she flashed, 'I felt sorry for you.'

His eyelashes drooped and for a frightening second she flinched at the very real menace she saw in the hooded eyes.

But when he said, 'You have a charming—and very effective—way of feeling sorry for men,' his voice was insultingly indifferent. 'Not that it matters. The title is completely irrelevant—apart from affection for my cousins and the islanders, I have only sentimental ties to Dacia. Prince Luka has a very promising four-year-old son, and the prospect of another arriving before the end of the year, so Dacia is well set up without me, a situation I'm more than happy with.'

'Lucky you,' she said, her voice as wooden as her expression. 'All of the deference and no responsibility.'

He shrugged. 'I assume you're blaming me for the Press frenzy at the airport.'

She said quietly, 'No. You could have told me who you were when you came to New Zealand to warn me the marriage might be valid, but I suppose there was always the chance that I might have charged you a handsome sum for a quick divorce.'

'I can deal with blackmailers,' he said on a ruthless note. 'Perhaps I should have told you, but it seems pretentious to announce that I'm a prince to people who couldn't care less.'

'I suppose it is.'

'As for the media—' His voice hardened even more. 'Yes, if I hadn't been who I am I doubt very much if there'd have been any reporters to meet you in London. I'm sorry you got caught up in it, but I'm not answerable for people who like to season their breakfasts with highly suspect gossip about princes and pop stars and sportsmen.'

'Of course you're not,' she said in a toneless voice, feeling small and petty.

He covered her rigid hands with his warm, strong one. 'But knowing who I am wouldn't have made any difference on Sant'Rosa—you'd have married me if I'd had to hold a pistol to your head.'

Her heart picked up speed, the pulse at her wrist fluttering under his fingers.

Of course he noticed. After a charged second he said on a raw note, 'I promised myself I wouldn't touch you.'

Lauren had to force herself to return, 'Then don't. It's not necessary.'

He lifted his hand, but as the car left the main road and began to climb, he said deliberately, 'I don't seem to be able to forget that for a few days we were lovers. Can you?'

Her bones melted as images from those few days flashed across her mind with full sensory impact. Attacked by a bitter regret, she said doggedly, 'It was a time out of time—a lovely tropical fantasy, but now we're in the real world, and it's over.'

His ironic laughter stunned her. She flashed a sideways glance and shivered at the compelling determination of his expression. 'Liar,' he said calmly.

When Lauren opened her mouth to object he sealed her indignant response with his fingertip. Mutely, her body struggling with an overload of sensation, she stared at his arrogant, handsome face.

With that fascinating hint of an accent underlying each forceful word, he said, 'No matter how hard we try to pretend, when I touch you we both feel that electricity. Don't try to convince me—or yourself—that it doesn't exist. What we need to talk about is how we're going to deal with it.'

He removed his finger from her lips and sat back in the seat, his profile an angular, uncompromising statement against the silver-grey foliage of the olive trees lining the road.

With stubborn precision Lauren said, 'We don't do anything about it.'

Still quivering inside, she dragged her head around to stare blindly out of the window, fuming when Guy made no answer. Instead she heard him speak in Dacian through the intercom to the driver. His voice, easy and relaxed, told her that he wasn't suffering any inner turmoil.

Lauren clawed back the tattered remnants of her control. Her father had once told her that the tone of a man's servants told much about the master; listening to the driver, she decided that his respectful reply was entirely free from servility, and that he liked Guy.

Who said no more about the attraction that smouldered between them. Instead, with infuriating self-possession he turned into a tour guide, explaining the age and the reason for various interesting ruins along the way, and discoursing on his cousin's plans for the island.

The villa in the hills was a tall, square house, redeemed from severity by blush-pink walls and shutters in a muted dark green. Gardens stretched around it, the trees and arbours melding inconspicuously into olive groves.

Delighted by its faded charm, Lauren leaned forward a little as the car swung up the drive.

From beside her Guy observed, 'According to family tradition the house was built for the Venetian mistress of one of the nineteenth-century princes. She had an embarrassment of children, but he spent most of his time here.'

Lauren stiffened. 'Why didn't he marry her?'

'He was already married to a very stern woman who never, so the story goes, smiled.'

'I wouldn't smile either if my husband flaunted a mistress in my face,' Lauren said astringently, reaching for her bag as the car slowed down.

The second the words left her mouth she realised she'd made a mistake. Guy's brow lifted and he surveyed her with a twisted smile. 'Is it the infidelity or the flaunting that you disapprove of?'

'Both,' she said shortly, wishing that she could tell him about her relationship with Marc. She couldn't, of course, because it wasn't her secret.

Her mother came out of the shadows beneath the portico, graceful and composed as always, the grey eyes she'd bestowed on her daughter serene and limpid. Nevertheless her smile was a little too set, her movements too careful to be natural.

Hurrying out of the car, Lauren gave her a quick hug. 'How's Dad?'

Isabel smiled at Guy. 'Fine. He's waiting inside for you.'

As Lauren ran up the steps she heard her mother say, 'Guy, thank you so much for organising this— I don't know what we'd have done without you.'

Her tone revealed that she liked him. So did every other woman, Lauren thought with crisp cynicism as she

walked into the coolness of the house and found her
father waiting in a big drawing room decorated in a
subdued palette of cream and ochre and the same silvery
green as the olive leaves.

Nothing lushly tropical about this place!

'Hello,' she said and hugged him tightly. He returned
it with vigour. Relieved, she pulled back and regarded
him. 'So now we know that you can travel by air without any problems,' she observed severely, 'you've no
excuse to stay at home in future.'

He smiled at her. 'It seems I need a nurse to keep an
eye on me, but I got here in one piece. How are you,
darling?'

'A bit groggy from lack of sleep.' Her rapid descrip-
tion of the exchange students' antics made him laugh.

When she finished Guy said from behind, 'I have an
appointment in a few minutes, so I must leave now. I
hope you enjoy your stay here.'

Flushing, Lauren remembered her manners. 'I'll
come out with you.'

He stood back to let her through the door. Once it
had closed behind them he said, 'Walk in the garden
with me for a few minutes.'

'Why?'

His brow lifted. 'Because it's cooler than standing
out on the gravel in the sun. Dacia is not as hot as
Sant'Rosa or Valanu, but the sun will burn your white
skin.'

Feeling foolish, she said, 'Oh. Yes, all right.'

The garden, throbbing with cicadas, was certainly
cooler. In the shade of a dark, dome-shaped tree, Guy
remarked with disconcerting shrewdness, 'Satisfied that
your father hasn't taken any harm from flying?'

She blinked back tears and gave him a strained smile.

'He looks great. They both do. Guy—oh, in public, should I call you Your Highness?'

'No,' he said tersely, his voice quick and hard and cold.

'I don't want to break any rules,' she said.

He showed his teeth in a smile that held little humour. 'Between us,' he said sardonically, 'we've broken so many that it doesn't matter. The first time you meet Luka, call him Your Royal Highness. After that it's sir, until he tells you not to bother with formality. The same applies to Alexa, although she has a tendency to giggle when anyone calls her ma'am.'

He sounded fed up. Lauren said, 'Thanks. In fact, thank you for everything. I imagine that between us we've made a huge mess of your schedule, and I'm sorry—'

He interrupted with curt impatience, 'Don't be foolish. Naturally I feel responsible for this situation; I shall do what I can to make it easier for you. Now go inside, have a meal, talk to your parents and go to bed as soon as it gets dark. Do you ride?'

She blinked. 'Yes, I do. Well, Pony Club level.'

'Then I'll call for you after breakfast tomorrow morning with a suitable mount,' he said and flicked her cheek with a casual finger. 'Sleep well.'

'No— Guy—that's not a good idea.'

His black brows lifted. 'What? Sleeping? I think it's an excellent idea.'

The lazy, caressing note in his voice set fires smouldering deep inside her. Gritting her teeth, she said, 'I don't want to fuel more media furore. Shouldn't we keep as far away from each other as possible in case the marriage has to be annulled?'

'Discovering that the marriage might be valid hasn't

turned me into a serial rapist,' he drawled in a voice like chipped ice.

Her eyes widened as she searched his hard face. 'I know that, but—'

He cut her off with a total lack of finesse. Every word sharp-edged, he said, 'My cousin Luka is as close to being an absolute ruler as you can get nowadays without aspiring to dictatorship. He's slowly organising a democratic system of government—against the wishes of most of his subjects so far—but at the moment he can ban anyone he doesn't want on the island, and if anyone does sneak in, he can see that they get shown politely off.' He frowned, but his voice softened as he said, 'Why do you think I brought you here?'

Lauren said doubtfully, 'I hope you're right,' then made the mistake of smiling at him.

Her heart kicked into high gear when he smiled back. Experienced and wicked, that killer smile promised untold delights—delights that figured largely in her dreams each night, so that she woke hot and aching with frustration.

How long would it take for the Press to forget them? If she had to stay here for more than a week she'd be in real trouble…

He bent his head and kissed her cheek, a touch so light there was no reason for her bones to melt.

The heat in his eyes transformed into cynicism. 'As for the Sant'Rosans, don't worry about them. Believe me, they're not in the habit of reading gossip columns. They've got more important concerns to worry about.'

He took her arm and steered her back to the house. At the door he said, 'Get a good night's rest. Shadows under your eyes don't suit you.'

*   *   *

Towards morning Lauren opened her eyes, only slowly realising that she was staring at the tester of a massive four-poster bed. The fabric was arranged like the roof of a tent, fastened in the centre with a medallion carved in high relief.

A leopard.

She was in Dacia, and she was in love with a prince.

No, she was not in love—she was besotted, infatuated, in lust, smitten by the man, but never in love! As soon as she got back to work she'd see it for what it was—a temporary sexual bewitchment, so fierce it would burn out in the routine of ordinary life.

In other words, exactly what her mother had felt for the man she'd taken as a lover for one crazy week. Isabel had always loved Hugh Porter; when she'd come to her senses she'd gone back to him.

Lauren frowned and wondered why it was so hard to convince herself that all she felt for Guy was that temporary flash and dazzle.

Because he'd shown himself to be brave and chivalrous? Or something so simple as being able to make her laugh?

Whatever, she couldn't let it affect her. Fairy stories were for children; she wasn't a Sleeping Beauty and Guy was too tough and autocratic to be a fairy prince, and there'd be no happily-ever-after for them.

The bleak truth hurt, but not facing it would lead to greater pain; better to accept it, ignore the heartache and get on with her life. But oh, it would have been so much easier to deal with if she'd been able to go cold turkey. This stay on Dacia was going to be refined and subtle torture.

Thank heaven the media's voracious appetite for stories soon burned out!

Yet she couldn't regret meeting Guy. As for making love with him—the thought of never knowing that extreme pleasure made her shudder.

A wistful fantasy drifted across her mind; for a few minutes she indulged herself in the tormenting memories, but self-preservation forced the dangerously seductive images from her mind. Instead, she wondered what had happened to her laptop computer in Sant'Rosa; if she had it here she'd be able to contact Marc in the Seychelles. She should warn him that their relationship might become public knowledge. Besides, she'd like the benefit of his ability to cut concisely through to the heart of any matter.

Eventually she drifted off to sleep again, to wake with a thick head and a sombre mood.

In contrast, her father had never looked better across the breakfast table. Any pain, she thought with renewed determination when she ran upstairs to change into the jeans and cotton jersey she'd bought in New Zealand, would be endurable if it kept him safe.

A knock on the door heralded her mother. 'You look much better,' Isabel said with a smile that faded too quickly.

'So does Dad.'

Her mother's voice softened. 'He loves this weather. In fact, he seems to have taken a great liking to Dacia itself. Darling, I'm so glad you're here. I'll never be able to thank the prince enough for rescuing you both times, from Sant'Rosa and then from those journalists.' Her gaze lingered on Lauren's face. 'He was wonderful yesterday—just took over and organised us so smoothly onto the plane and over here. Your father likes him very much, and so do I. What do you think of him?' she finished casually.

Lauren's heart contracted. Infusing her tone with wry briskness, she said, 'I'm very grateful to him, but he's too much like Marc—inclined to take over.'

Another knock on the door produced one of the maids, to tell her with a broad, significant smile that Prince Guy had arrived to take her riding.

'Make sure you put on sunscreen,' her mother said automatically, then laughed. 'I know, I know—modern cosmetics have sunscreen in them. I suppose I'll stop being an over protective mother when you marry. Really marry, I mean.'

The taut note in her voice made Lauren say steadily, 'That's not on the agenda at the moment.'

After a second's hesitation Isabel returned, 'I hope that when you meet a man you can love, you won't let any considerations weigh on you but your chances of a happy life with him.'

Their eyes met. 'When I meet him,' Lauren said quietly, 'I'll let you know.'

Her mother nodded.

Guy was mounted on a chestnut gelding; he rode, Lauren thought for one dazzled moment, like a centaur, at home on the animal in a way she'd never achieve. As she came out into the sunlight a groom dismounted from another gelding with an amiable face and two white socks.

After greeting them both, Lauren swung into the saddle and spent the next few minutes concentrating on staying in the saddle. Guy monitored her carefully, riding close enough to help if things went wrong, and proffering only advice she needed.

She had never felt so safe, she thought despairingly.

At last, confident she could cope, she gazed around. She felt reborn, her worries temporarily allayed by the sheer delight of riding with Guy through a morning all gold and blue and freshly flower-scented, the sea a swathe of purple silk stretching away from the coast.

When the silence grew too intimidating, she could think of nothing more intelligent to say than, 'This horse has a lovely temperament.'

'He's the nursery horse.' Effortlessly Guy controlled his mount, which was trying to take evasive action against the shocking pink flowers of a cyclamen.

Lauren gave a wry grin. 'Entirely suitable.'

'Next time we'll find you something better than old Carlos here—you ride well enough to try something less like a slug.'

Ridiculous that a simple compliment should make her colour like a schoolgirl! She hadn't blushed for years, yet Guy had only to look at her and she went as scarlet as any tomato. 'That's unkind to Carlos—he's a very sweet-tempered slug,' she said, adding, 'I'm nowhere near as expert as you.'

'In our family,' Guy told her drily, 'we're expected to ride before we can walk.'

Indeed. Her pleasure plummeted. His world of high society and the upper echelons of business didn't connect in any meaningful way with hers; although Marc was perfectly at home in that rarefied atmosphere, she'd never socialised publicly with him in case it gave rise to speculation—a precaution that had clearly failed.

Her eyes skimmed Guy's arrogant profile; he was all aristocrat today, and she sensed an aloofness that hadn't been there before. Had the villa, the love nest, been an indication of what he wanted from her? No, she thought grimly, not with her parents in residence!

Yet in spite of the icy splash of down-to-earth practicality, she looked around at a world more sharply experienced, so brightly coloured, the soft ruffle of breeze on her skin so perfumed, the birdcalls so lyrical, that until then she might have been living under a shroud.

'Is all of Dacia as lovely as this?' she asked.

'*I* think so,' Guy said. 'But then, I'm biased. What's your favourite place?'

'A bluebell wood in spring,' she told him promptly, adding without guile, 'But I love Paris in all seasons.'

'Sentimental memories?' he drawled, each word sharp and lethal as a blade of steel.

Was he jealous? No, that was probably too strong a word, but he might be possessive; he'd know Marc lived in Paris.

CHAPTER NINE

LAUREN said coolly, 'My parents took me there for a holiday when I was eight. We arrived at the Arc de Triomphe on Bastille Day, and I lost my heart. Whenever I've gone back I've always found something new and wonderful to love.'

The horse jogged placidly beneath her, ears turning back every so often. Beneath the olive trees the grass was starred with flowers, blue, white, crimson and scarlet, some she recognised and many she'd never seen before.

In a neutral voice Guy said, 'Your—employer—is half-French, I believe.'

'Indeed he is.' The maternal half; their mutual father had been a New Zealander. She straightened her back and said brightly, 'I love riding through a flowery meadow like this, but it seems a shame that the horses crush the flowers.'

'They're resilient. Would you like to canter?'

'If I remember how.'

To her pleasure it came easily. 'It's like riding a bicycle—you truly don't forget,' she said, delighted and glowing when they'd arrived at their destination, a rocky meadow, its grass eaten short by goats, with a magnificent view out over the coast. Distant and dim on the horizon sprawled the indigo shadow that was the mainland of Europe.

After they'd dismounted to tether the horses in the shade of a clump of cypresses, she walked beside Guy across the sweet-scented grass and remarked, 'There's something special about islands— I wonder what it is.'

'Freedom,' Guy stated, turning to point out a couple of smaller islets off the coast of Dacia. 'Islands represent some hidden mystery, places out of time and ordinary life. Almost anything might happen on an island—why do you think Pacific nations spend so much effort repelling would-be beachcombers?'

Lauren's gaze lingered on the powerful male triangle of shoulders sloping down to narrow hips, and the strong curves of his muscled thighs. Sensation pulsed through her like lightning—dangerously beautiful and so powerful she was helpless before it.

Speaking quickly, she said, 'You're probably right. Perhaps it's the beaches that bring out the adventurer in all of us.'

'Are you suggesting that it was the sand and coconut palms on Valanu that persuaded you into my bed?' he drawled, steel underlying the lazy words.

Lauren kept her gaze fixed on the white line of the distant coast while she sat down on a sun-warmed rock. 'You know it wasn't.'

He said brusquely, 'I spoke to my solicitor last night.'

Lauren swallowed. 'And?'

'It's not good news. The marriage is legal, and an annulment is not possible as we've already consummated it.'

A bewildering mixture of regret and chagrin lent an edge to her involuntary response. 'I wish none of this had happened!'

'No more than I do, believe me.' His voice was flat and judicial.

Lauren looked down at her hands. Although he'd

agreed with her, his reply had hurt. 'So what do we do now?'

'We accept it,' he said crisply. He overrode her outraged protest with forceful authority. 'And we announce a date for the formalisation of our marriage in the cathedral here.'

She jumped to her feet and advanced on him, hands clenched at her sides. 'No! I won't accept—'

His regard, cold as frozen sunlight, silenced her. 'Yesterday while we were flying here one of the more noisome English tabloids splashed details of the days we spent together in Valanu across its front page.' His impersonal voice made his next words all the more outrageous. 'The only way to protect you from the gossip and innuendo that's already building is for us to acknowledge the marriage.'

Images of the days and nights spent in his arms jostled through her mind, bringing bright, fleeting colour to her pale skin. She snatched a glance, noting with savage anguish that he'd lost none of his trademark self-assurance.

Pain splintering inside her, she shook her head. 'I can tough this out, and I'm sure you can. After all, this is not the first time you've taken a lover and been outed in the Press.'

'It's the first time my lover had no idea what she was getting into,' he said abrasively. 'If you'd known who I was it wouldn't matter so much.'

So he believed that, even if he believed nothing else. Relief lightened her mood for a second, but his next words darkened it again.

'We'll play it whichever way you choose, but I suggest we stay married for a couple of years. After that you can have a divorce. Of course, I'll make sure that you'd never have to worry about money again.'

'Pay me off, you mean? No, thank you.' Lauren had to articulate each word carefully, gauging her tone to hide how much his pragmatic suggestion hurt. 'Marrying you is out of the question.'

His expression hardened. 'Lauren, we are already married. Nothing is going to change that but a divorce, either now or in two years' time. Before you say any more, you'd better have a look at a sample of the sort of garbage that's being printed.'

He pulled a folded newspaper from his back pocket and handed it over to her.

'Is This Marriage For Real?' it demanded, beside photographs, the one of her a startled mask snapped at the airport.

Appalled, Lauren scanned the page.

'Exclusive details. Tropical Love Nest for Prince and His Commoner Bride.'

Nausea gripping her, she closed her eyes, but cold courage forced her to open them again and read on. Someone had interviewed the charming family who owned the beach shack, and from their replies had cobbled together a tissue of vulgar innuendoes and speculation.

Once she trusted her voice enough to speak, she said distastefully, 'I suppose it could have been worse.'

'Not much.' Anger ran like a rapier blade through the two words.

She shrugged and handed the newspaper back to him. 'It makes no difference,' she said in her most distant tone.

'To what?'

'To my answer to your pro—proposition.'

'It was a proposal,' he snarled.

'For all the wrong reasons.'

Of course he picked her up on that. 'So are there right reasons?'

Although it hurt so much she had to dredge every word from deep inside her, she said tensely, 'I don't want a marriage that means nothing and is programmed to destruct in a couple of years.'

'You weren't so fussy on Sant'Rosa,' he pointed out brutally.

She lifted her hands as though to ward off a blow, then let them drop. 'I know,' she admitted. 'I am truly grateful—'

'I don't want your gratitude!' Guy said between his teeth.

Stiffly she continued, 'I didn't foresee such repercussions. I just want this to be over so I can go back to my real life.'

A line of colour darkened the exotic sweep of his cheekbones. 'And forget that I ever met you? Can you do that?' he asked silkily.

He didn't touch her—didn't even make a movement towards her—but she felt the compelling force of his will-power lock around her like fetters. The temptation to give in was so strong she almost took a step towards him.

That was when she accepted that if she stayed in this marriage she'd fall irrevocably in love with a man who didn't love her. This fierce passion would drive them into each other's arms, and at the end of the two years she would walk away with a shredded heart into a future without hope.

She didn't dare risk such a death of the spirit. 'I can try,' she said tautly. She gripped her shaking hands behind her back and stared at him, eyes darkly desperate. 'Guy, I *can't* do this. I don't know how to behave in your world.'

His brows drew together. 'Alexa is extremely popular, yet she was not brought up to be a princess. She learned; so will you.'

To the sound of her heart splintering, Lauren said childishly, 'You can't force me to.'

He grinned, darkly dominating, dangerous and fiercely attractive. 'I think I could,' he said slowly, 'but it won't be necessary.'

Taking the biggest gamble in her life, she said abruptly, 'I am not who you think I am. Marc Corbett is my half-brother as well as my employer. My mother had a week-long affair with his father, and I'm the result.'

With shoulders held so rigidly they hurt, she scanned his impassive face while seconds ticked by, broken only by a whicker from one of the horses, and the cry of some bird, haunting and lyrically tragic in the warm air.

By the time Guy spoke her nerves were wound so tautly she jumped at the sound of his inflexible words. 'I see. However, it makes no difference. It's common knowledge that Luka's wife, Alexa, is the result of an affair between the then Crown Prince of Illyria and her grandmother.'

'I'm sure it helps if the product of a liaison can claim royal blood,' she said quietly. 'I can't.'

His next words astounded her. 'Does your father—Porter—know?'

She bit her lip, but she'd started this. 'He found out after I had leukaemia.'

At his silence Lauren glanced up. The boldly chiselled angles and planes of his face revealed neither condemnation nor interest—nothing but a concentration that sent a swift scurry of foreboding down her spine.

'So she kept quiet and let your father think you were his child.' Although Guy's tone was neutral, she picked up the note of contempt.

'I'm not going to judge my mother—' she retorted, her voice forbidding him to go any further.

Guy cut her off. 'It is a terrible thing—to deceive a man into believing that the child he loves and cherishes and protects is blood of his blood, bone of his bone, breath of his body.'

She looked at him pleadingly, and then sighed. 'Yes, but in every way that counts, I am his daughter. He convinced me of that after I'd recovered.'

'That is obvious. Thank you for telling me, but it makes no difference.' He smiled without humour and came over to her, taking her cold hands in his.

Her fingers trembled. 'But if anyone finds out—'

His broad shoulders moved in a shrug. 'I will protect your parents as much as I am able,' he said indifferently, and lifted her hands to his mouth, kissing the palm of one, the wrist of the other, smiling with cool satisfaction when she flinched at the sudden thunder in her blood.

Wounded by the calculation in the kisses, she protested, 'Don't you dare try to use sex to influence me.'

'Could I?' he asked in a low, dangerous tone that lifted the hairs on the back of her neck.

'No,' she said untruthfully. Her body was ready for him now; if he wanted, she'd lie down in the flowery meadow and let him take her.

'Liar,' he said, but he let her go. In a level, uncompromising voice he said, 'Luka spoke to me this morning. Last night he was visited by a deputation of islanders. They think the whole affair hugely romantic, but they were adamant that they want our marriage formalised here on Dacia.'

Lauren walked across to where the horses were tethered in the shade. When the gelding lifted his head she stroked the soft nose, desperately fighting a darkness that threatened to overwhelm her. 'I thought your cousin could keep the media under control.'

'He has no power over the airwaves, and the television sets on the island can be tuned into Italian stations, which are full of the news.' He paused, then said deliberately, the faint intonation of his native language in his accent suddenly stronger, 'I would lose respect—and so would Luka—if the people here believed that I used the excuse of a marriage ceremony to take a lover and then dump her. It would be seen as a deliberate flouting of the sacredness of marriage vows.'

Lauren swallowed to ease a mouth suddenly gone dry. 'I can understand the personal aspect of this, but why would your cousin lose any respect?'

'Because he is my cousin, and he is the head of the family. On Dacia, that matters; he would be seen as not wielding proper authority over me, and if a man cannot control his own family, why should his people trust him to rule them fairly?'

'But that's mediaeval!' she protested.

Guy said austerely, 'They haven't had the benefit of democracy. Luka hopes very much that he or his son will eventually be able to relinquish the sole responsibility for the future of Dacia, but of course he wishes to make sure a democratic system is in place first. For that he needs time and the confidence of the people.'

Lauren closed her eyes. She thought raggedly, I can't fight this.

For Guy to lose his reputation like this would scar the part of him that had been brought up to feel an inherited duty towards the islanders.

All she had to weigh against that duty was her heart, and that was far too light to balance the scales. She couldn't allow the personal misery of unrequited love to stand against his hopes for the future of the islanders, made more poignant because they both had firsthand experience of the terror that could inflict people unprepared for independence.

But because she was a fighter, she drew in a ragged breath and made one last effort. 'So he's leaning on you to ratify a marriage of state convenience?'

Guy's broad shoulders lifted in a shrug. 'I am not easily leant on, and Luka would not do so, but I understand the situation and I agree with him.'

The iron jaws of a trap edged closer. 'This is important for you, isn't it.' It wasn't a question.

He was silent so long she turned her head to look at him. With painful honesty, Lauren thought he had never looked so forbidding—a man accustomed to wielding authority and power faced with a distasteful decision.

A man who'd accept a fake marriage out of a sense of duty. Would he take a mistress, as his distant ancestor had done?

No, she thought, her heart a stone in her chest. His honour wouldn't allow that.

Sunlight conjured fire from his dark hair as he gave a short nod. 'I owe my family and the people of Dacia my best efforts.'

It hurt so much her breath locked in her throat, but she managed a humourless smile. 'So I was wrong when I said you got the deference without the responsibility. Why is this so important to the Dacians?'

'They are a conservative, religious people; they hold marriage vows in high esteem.'

He didn't say that none of this would be happening if she hadn't seduced him on Valanu. He didn't have to, just as he didn't have to say that her parents would hate the speculation her continued refusal would have caused.

Defeat bitter in her mouth, Lauren swung around and walked away to look out over the rocky hillside to the settled lands below, rows of olive trees and grapevines making patterns across the countryside.

Like her mother, she had followed her heart to danger. If she'd kept her head she wouldn't be in this situation, heading knowingly into a love that could only hurt and humiliate her.

Because it was important to him, she would agree. She said in a muted voice, 'Then it seems that I have no choice. It isn't fair that you should pay for something I did.'

'What?'

She lifted her chin. 'Seducing you on Valanu.'

The sudden glitter in his eyes surprised her, but not as much as his uncompromising inflection when he said, 'You gave me passion and warmth and tenderness; you showed me that there is more to the world than the casual brutality I'd seen on Sant'Rosa. Although I knew it intellectually, I found that knowledge in your arms.'

Lauren said quietly, 'And I didn't make love to you because I felt sorry for you.'

His smile was ambiguous. 'It doesn't matter. I could have walked away from you, so we are in this together, Lauren. This marriage is not something you made happen because you got carried away by the tropical moonlight and the scent of frangipani.' He turned and said abruptly, 'Luka's Press secretary can announce the date tomorrow.'

She said bleakly, 'And afterwards? What then?'

'That,' he said calmly, 'is entirely up to you. If you desire to live here, I own a house on the coast that will be yours for as long as you wish, but I also have houses in London and New York.'

And one in Valanu, she thought. But he still hadn't answered the real question. *What sort of marriage will it be?*

In his eyes glinting gold and amber and tawny shades mingled into heat and fire. 'If the story of your birth is uncovered marriage with me will give you the position to fight anyone who dares slander your parents. I have power, and I will use it on your behalf.'

Lauren tried to form the words she should say, but her tongue wouldn't utter them and her throat wouldn't let them past the lump lodged halfway down it. She knew she was going to agree, because she loved him and this was important to him.

Eventually she said quietly, 'All right.'

Guy gave a low laugh and kissed her, and she kissed him back, even as her heart wept.

When he released her she shivered, but held her head high.

'Don't look so tragic, Lauren.' He sounded sardonic. 'I suggest we go back to the villa now. We'll leave other decisions to a time when both of us are more relaxed.'

He was a fantastic lover and a man with more charisma in his little finger than most other men had in their whole bodies. Her parents liked him very much. Lauren knew he was brilliant, and a hard but fair businessman, but she hadn't known he was a prince until yesterday.

Presumably he had other secrets. And she had just agreed to marry him.

Back at the villa he refused her mother's offer of lunch, but asked if his cousin's wife, Princess Alexa, might call on a short, private visit the next afternoon.

'How very kind of her,' Isabel Porter said. 'We'd love to meet her and thank her for offering us sanctuary.'

'She'll probably want to photograph you,' he warned, amusement glimmering in the topaz depths of his eyes. 'She's brilliant.'

'I saw her exhibition in London—absolutely superb.' Isabel was excited.

Guy nodded, smiling at her with such blatant, unbarred charm that Lauren didn't blame her mother for blinking and going under.

He said, 'You'll like her—she's entertaining and intelligent with the kindest heart in the world. She wishes very much to meet you.'

He looked past her mother to Lauren, still and quiet and very composed. Sunlight pouring through the windows lent warmth to her white skin. She smiled at him, yet he sensed tension beneath her confident exterior, something defiant about the way she met his eyes.

Because they both knew that his touch brought swift colour to her skin, and that when he kissed her that delectable mouth softened and gave him everything he wanted.

And he'd better get the hell out of here, because he wanted her now, warm and willing and eager, lost in ecstasy in his arms.

But first, he had to make the decision he'd forced from her irrevocably.

He said bluntly, 'Mr and Mrs Porter, Lauren and I

have something to tell you. We plan another ceremony in the cathedral to regularise the marriage that took place on Sant'Rosa. I hope you will give us your blessing.'

Hugh Porter said, 'It seems the most sensible decision.' He gave Guy a look that made Lauren's spine snap straight, and finished grimly, 'It saves me from borrowing a shotgun.'

As Lauren choked on the coffee her mother exclaimed, 'Hugh!'

Guy said coolly, 'I don't blame you, sir. I shall look after Lauren to the best of my ability.'

Lauren glared at her unrepentant father, heart twisting at the effort with which he was holding himself together.

Guy stood up. 'Alexa's visit will be the first of a round of social engagements for you,' he said. He didn't look at Hugh Porter as he went on, 'It will be a busy month, but not too exhausting, I hope.'

'I can manage,' Hugh said abruptly.

After a keen glance, Guy nodded. Formally, he said, 'I have to fly to America this afternoon, so I will see you again in about three days. Until I get back, enjoy Dacia in the spring.'

CHAPTER TEN

THE visit from the princess went off well; warm and lively, she talked photography with Isabel, Italian literature with Lauren's father, and exchanged reminiscences of New Zealand with Lauren.

But Lauren knew that behind the charming façade the princess was summing her up, and when she suggested casually that they might like to come to the Little Palace for lunch in a couple of days' time, Lauren wished there were some way of refusing.

Of course they had to go, so it was arranged.

That night, when they were alone together, her mother said in a tone she tried hard to make casual, 'Lauren, are you sure you want to marry Guy?'

'Utterly sure!' Lauren told her, glad it was the truth. She met her mother's scrutiny and added with a wry smile, 'With all my heart. Just not this way.'

Concern glimmering in her eyes, Isabel said quietly, 'I guessed as much. How does Guy feel?'

'That it's his duty to do this.' In a steady voice she sketched in the conversation she and Guy had had.

'And that hurts?'

Lauren bit her lip. 'Yes.'

'Swift passions often die as quickly as they flare up.'

Lauren knew her mother was remembering the long-ago affair that had led to her own conception. 'At first I thought that's all it was,' she said steadily. 'But I—well, it's not just the sex.'

'Oh, darling.' Isabel got to her feet and came over,

147

giving her a swift hug. 'You must not feel you have to marry him just because you have been lovers. Gossip is unpleasant, but it invariably fades. And no one ever died of embarrassment.'

'I know the difference between sex and love,' Lauren said simply. She drew in a deep breath and at last admitted it to herself as well as to her mother. 'I do love him. I feel for him what Paige feels for Marc—what you feel for Dad.' A smile trembled on her lips because it was the first time she'd said it out loud. 'It's real, I promise. Beneath that formidable exterior he's kind and brave and honourable.'

Isabel frowned, saying drily, 'I know about the brave and honourable parts of his character. They're wonderful qualities, but a husband needs a little more than that.'

'I think we can take his intelligence for granted,' Lauren said, brows knitting as she tried to find the right words, 'and he can laugh at himself. He makes my bones melt and my blood sizzle. I want to spend the rest of my life with him.'

But it wasn't going to happen. Not many people, she thought, had married with the date of the divorce already set.

For Guy it was a winning situation. He'd keep his honour in the eyes of his countrymen, he'd have great sex on tap, and in a couple of years he could wash his hands of her and find himself someone with the right bloodlines to be a suitable bride.

Her mother got to her feet and smoothed down her skirt. 'In that case, there's nothing to be said. Whatever you do, your father and I will back you.' She paused until Lauren nodded. 'Have you let Marc know?'

'Yes,' Lauren said, summoning a smile. 'He was like

you, not at all convinced I know what I'm doing, but Paige and I managed to talk him out of flying here to see what was going on. He settled for coming to Dacia as soon as they get back from the Seychelles.'

That night, in her lovely, subtly decadent room, Lauren tried to relax the tension that gripped her. A bath didn't work, and neither did a surprisingly pleasant herbal tea one of the maids offered.

'For a sore heart,' she said, with a smile that indicated she knew why Lauren had been restlessly pacing around the garden in the darkness. 'It will help you sleep.'

But after drinking it to its dregs, Lauren still felt wired, every cell in her body filled with frustrated longing. In the end she stood at the window and stared out across the gardens and the olive-furred hills.

Owls called in the perfumed dusk beneath stars that burned with a hard white fire. A mile or so away stood the Little Palace, so named because Dacia's other palace, now part museum, part administrative and ceremonial centre, was a huge mediaeval pile built on an ancient Roman fortress that protected the harbour.

It was from the Old Palace that the bald Press statement of the marriage had been issued the previous day. Newspapers had garnished the announcement with speculation, but she and her parents had been protected from any direct contact.

Her painful craving for Guy, so dark and urgent it ached in the core of her heart, produced an instantly muffled sob.

When exhaustion at last closed her eyes in brief, unsatisfying slumber, she fell prey to erotic dreams, all of them starring Guy as he'd been on Valanu, and woke the next morning with heavy eyes that mimicked the state of her spirits.

Action would clear her head and lighten her spirits. And she knew where to go. A few minutes later she slipped through the silent house, her bathing suit covered by one of her sarongs. Early though it was, the first cicadas of the day were already tuning their small zithers.

Halfway down the garden a swimming pool was sheltered behind thick conifer hedges. Elegant and formal with a fountain trickling into one side, it had been built many years before, perhaps for that long-ago prince who'd disported in the villa with his mistress and their large brood.

Ironic, really—the mistress had probably yearned for the security of marriage, whereas Lauren would gladly swap marriage for Guy's love.

The water was still cool, but she dived in and swam methodically, counting out the laps until self-preservation forced her out.

Well, action hadn't worked; drying herself in the tiled bathing cubicle, she accepted that only going cold turkey on Guy Bagaton would exorcise him from her mind and her heart.

'And because of a nation of people you don't know, whose language and culture you don't understand, you can't do that. You're trapped!' she told herself, fastening the sarong above her breasts.

But this ceremony with Guy wasn't for the Dacians; she'd do it because she loved him, and because it was important to him, part of the commitment to honour and duty she admired in his character.

She picked up her hat and towel and walked out into the sunlight, the cold emptiness of her heart a painful contrast to the sensuous heat that caressed her bare shoulders. Emerging into the wider sweep of the garden, she stopped to admire the acrobatics of a pair of tiny birds with gold crests foraging upside down in the dense branches.

Smiling, she watched for a few seconds before a creeping sense of being overlooked tightened her skin; she straightened and turned, and there was Guy striding along beneath the trees, his big, powerful body striped by the sun in tiger shades of amber and black.

Joy burst into life inside her, incandescent and overpowering; she had to bite the corners of her mouth to stop herself from smiling with sheer delight.

He didn't kiss her; instead he examined her with a deliberation that sent little shivers of sensation scudding the length of her spine. 'You don't seem to be making a good job of shifting those shadows under your eyes,' he finally said.

'Whereas you look fine.'

The brilliant tawny eyes softened. 'Do you want to call it off?'

For a moment she didn't believe she'd heard what he said. She stared blankly at him, and his beautiful mouth twisted into a mirthless smile.

'If this business is going to drive you into a decline we'll finish it now.'

Lauren fought with herself before saying tonelessly, 'And what about the Dacian sensibilities you waxed so eloquent about only a few days ago?'

Although he shrugged broad shoulders, his eyes were hard. 'They'll be hurt.'

She said something in French, and he laughed softly and caught her and kissed the word from her lips, and said against them in the same language, 'You have a superb accent.'

'So do you,' she muttered. Words jostled in her head,

but none made the trip from brain to tongue; sickened and humiliated, she closed her eyes.

And then warmth enveloped her, and his strength supported her.

'Please—no,' she whispered, but it was too late. He kissed her forehead and then a vulnerable temple, and she—oh, she surrendered shamefully, without protest, to the unexpected tenderness of his embrace, her heart surging into overdrive in response to the thunder of his.

He said harshly, 'I don't blame you for never wanting to see me again—because of me you've had your life turned upside down.' He cupped her chin and tilted it so that he could look down into her face. 'But I'm no sadist. I hate to see the shadows under your eyes.'

'I don't go back on my promises.' Lauren swallowed. 'And if we cancel now, there'll be an orgy of speculation. My father won't care for himself if the truth about my parentage is discovered, but he'll hate for my mother to face the humiliation. I'm not prepared to put him through that stress.'

Guy released her. 'If you've made up your mind,' he said crisply, 'stop drooping, or people are going to wonder if I beat you.'

She said between her teeth, 'Has anyone told you that you're an arrogant swine?'

He gave a lazy, cynical grin. 'Join the club.'

Of course her mother asked him to breakfast, and of course he agreed. By pasting a thin skin over her emotions and drinking twice as much coffee as usual, Lauren managed to get through the meal, until Guy said, 'I'd like to take you to meet my cousin.'

It was not a request.

Lauren bristled as he went on. 'He is the Prince of

Dacia and the titular head of the family, so it will be tactful to visit him now.'

Her father forestalled Lauren's acid rejoinder. 'Excellent idea.' He added austerely, 'As your relationship has been so unconventional, a little propriety won't do any harm.'

Balked, Lauren wrinkled her nose at him. 'You sound like a Victorian great-aunt,' she teased.

'At the moment,' he said, but with a dry smile, 'I feel very much like a Victorian father.'

So it was arranged, but on the way to the Little Palace Lauren said evenly, 'From now on I'd like you to discuss things with me, not present me with a *fait accompli* in front of my parents, who, as you well know, think you're wonderful.'

'Not your father,' Guy said with a sardonic glance.

'You've redeemed yourself.' She didn't trust her voice enough to say any more.

Thinking about her future filled her with a tearing mixture of anguish and elation; she swung wildly from bleak despair to hoping that sharing Guy's bed would lead to physical satiation and eventual indifference.

Guy turned the car into a gateway, nodding to the guards, who presented arms and saluted. Lauren froze, realising for the first time how utterly alien his life was from hers.

She blurted, 'Will I be a princess?' And could have bitten out her tongue at the childish naïvety of the question.

'I'm afraid you will,' he said calmly. 'Do you like emeralds?'

The abrupt change of subject startled her. 'Of course I like emeralds. They're beautiful.'

'It's a family tradition that each Bagaton bride

chooses an emerald from the treasure house for her engagement ring, but if you prefer another stone, we'll do that.' When she didn't answer he said, 'Crimson suits you superbly, so if you prefer a ruby then that is what you will have.'

'I don't want—'

'An engagement ring is traditional.' A steely note in his voice warned her there would be no compromise. 'Think of it as a costume in a play—it helps to set the mood.'

'An emerald will be fine.' Angry pain drove her to finish, 'I will, of course, return it when the marriage is over.'

His face hardened, but before he could answer she hurried into speech again. 'I'm sorry, that was rude, even though it's true. I'm jittery. What if your cousin hates me?'

Guy sent her a sideways look. 'He'll like you,' he said calmly, and dropped one lean hand over hers, holding them for a second before putting his back on the wheel.

'I'm wondering what I'll do after the—once things settle down,' she said. 'I'm used to working.'

'There is plenty you can do. Charities are always looking for a titled patroness.'

She said restlessly, 'I don't want to just lend my name to things. I need to do something or I'll go mad.'

'Lauren, relax.'

Stiffening her jaw, she looked down at her hands, imagining one of the fabled Bagaton emeralds on her ring finger. If he put it there with love she would wear it with such happiness…

But it wasn't going to happen. Abruptly she asked,

'Do we tell your cousin the real reason for this marriage?'

His jaw tightened into a formidable line. 'No,' he said uncompromisingly. 'Luka and I are great friends, but our relationship, as opposed to our marriage, is none of his business.' He braked, steering the car to the side of the road. 'To anyone who asks, we met on Sant'Rosa, fell instantly in love, and sealed that love during the days we spent together on Valanu.'

Colour drained from her skin, then came flooding back. 'It sounds very romantic,' she said, trying to conceal the misery in her tone with a note of cynicism.

He leaned over and pushed her door open. 'Get out,' he said, straightening up.

Eyes enormous, she stared at him. 'What?'

'Get out,' he said pleasantly. 'You're wound up tighter than a screw. We'll walk a bit so you can use up some of that excess energy.'

It seemed a good idea, so she unfolded herself and pretended to look around at the flowers pushing joyously through the grass.

'And just to make sure we present a convincing face to Luka,' Guy said conversationally, coming up behind her, 'we should do this.'

Hands on her shoulders turned her around; Lauren's gaze flew to a face she didn't recognise, hard with purpose, an implacable will bent on subduing.

'I don't—' she started to say, but the last word was crushed to nothing on her lips and she was lost in a fierce passion that had been starved for too long.

How long they kissed she didn't know, but when he lifted his head she felt bereft and angry and afire with sharp frustration—a turbulent combination of emotions, each fighting for mastery.

And beneath them, the honeyed urgency of sexual anticipation, of need.

Of love.

'Yes,' Guy said, his accent deepening as he scanned her face, 'that looks better.'

She closed her eyes. 'I hate lying!'

His laughter was close to a taunt, but there was a sombre note in his voice. 'You want me—that's no lie. Lack of control is always frightening. I wonder what it is, this strange mixture of need and desire.'

'I read somewhere that it's a cocktail of chemicals in our brains.' If that was so, why did her heart hurt, not her brain?

'I felt it the first moment I saw you.' His hooded eyes were slivers of polished gold, unreadable, compelling.

Shivers of excitement raced down her spine and exploded in the pit of her stomach, but Lauren wasn't ready to admit anything. 'I thought you were a beachcomber.'

Dark brows shooting up, he glanced at his watch. 'We'd better get going.'

But in the car, as she was checking her appearance in her tiny mirror, he remarked, 'A beachcomber?'

Horrified by the feverish glitter in her eyes and the full ripeness his kisses had given her lips, Lauren stroked on lipstick and closed the tube with a fierce turn of her wrist. 'You were arrogant, abrupt and dismissive,' she said with relish.

'So were you.'

She swivelled to stare at his angular profile. The crease in his cheek indicated that he was hiding a smile, but she said indignantly, 'I was just determined to get to that village.'

'You took one look at me and your eyes went dark, and I knew I could have you.'

The lazy satisfaction in his tone catapulted her back to that steamy little resort with the threat of death hanging over it, and the man who'd crossed swords with her there.

'As I said, arrogant,' she retorted. 'And conceited. I wondered if you were there to entertain any single women.'

'A gigolo? What changed your mind?' When she refused to answer, he laughed softly. 'As for who was the most arrogant—that is a question we can discuss at greater length later. For the time being we should leave it, because here is the Little Palace.'

Of course it was huge, a splendid champagne-coloured building, both dignified and appropriate for the Mediterranean landscape.

Swallowing a hard lump in her throat, Lauren eyed the flight of steps that led up to a pillared portico like something out of Rome, and said thinly, 'I don't know what to say to your cousin.'

His swift glance took in her set face. 'You enjoyed talking to Alexa, didn't you?'

She swallowed again. 'Yes, of course—very much.'

'Then you'll like Luka. And it will be mutual. After all, he married a woman with spirit and flair and strength, and fell in love with her when he thought she was what he hated most—paparazzi. Theirs is a true love match.'

Was he wishing this was? His words gave nothing away, and neither did his hard, handsome face. Stubborn pride kept Lauren's spine erect and her shoulders straight as they were shown into the private apartments of the royal family. Only when a delicious small boy came running through the door did she manage to relax a little.

The princess and her son, the grand duke, made any attempt at formality impossible, but Guy's pleasant, inordinately good-looking cousin observed her with a cool interest that missed nothing. He was, Lauren thought unhappily, reserving judgement.

It seemed he might have made up his mind when, just before they left, he said, 'If your parents approve, we will have the formal ceremony at the cathedral, not in the palace chapel, so there will be a parade of carriages through the streets. Dacians love to celebrate, and after this there will be no more royal weddings until the next generation grow up.'

Lauren's expression must have revealed more than she wanted, because Alexa laughed.

'A formal occasion in Dacia isn't like formal occasions anywhere else, Lauren—you'll be fine. I can help you make the arrangements.' She patted her still slender waist and added, 'It will give me something to do while this baby grows.'

Lauren produced a smile that hurt her cheeks. 'I have to admit that a private ceremony is more my style, but if you think it's a good idea, we'll do it.'

On the way back to the villa Guy observed, 'That wasn't so bad, was it?'

'No,' she said on a silent sigh. 'Thank you.'

He lifted an ironic eyebrow. 'For what?'

'Your support.' She had felt it all the time, a solid, reassuring stability that could become addictive.

'You didn't need any support,' he said with an assurance she had to envy. 'You did very well—and in case you're wondering, yes, Luka likes you.'

What Lauren had noticed during that royal inspection

was the power of the love between the prince and his wife. They didn't show it in obvious ways, but it was like a chain of gold linking them, subtle, pervasive and unbreakable.

That was what she wanted. And while she was about it, she might as well reach for the moon too. She gazed out of the window at the glowing countryside slipping by.

When, back at the villa, Guy told her parents of Luka's plans for the wedding, Isabel's elegant brows drew together.

'Hugh, how do you feel about this?'

He answered firmly, 'I have no intention of dying, I can assure you, until I have held my grandchildren in my arms.'

Lauren turned her head and stared out of the window to hide eyes that stung. She would never carry a child of Guy's under her heart.

Very smoothly, apparently not at all concerned by the unsubtle reference to children, Guy said, 'In that case, unless there is a reason for you to return to England, we would be delighted if you stayed here until then.'

Isabel said thoughtfully, 'What about clothes for the wedding?'

'The local couturier is excellent,' Guy told her. 'She is Paris-trained. Alexa buys her clothes from her, and it helps the local economy. Tourists flock to buy clothes from the woman who dresses the princess.'

'Oh, yes, of course.' Isabel looked suddenly startled as though she'd just realised that her daughter's life was going to change irrevocably.

'And Alexa asked me to tell you that she is more than happy to help with anything. My cousin Lucia, Mrs Hunt Radcliffe, was a great source of support to her when she came to Dacia to marry, so Alexa is delighted to be able to do this for another princess of Dacia.'

Guy's urbane charm set Lauren's teeth on edge. He was completely convincing in his role as lover and fiancé. He acted, she thought wretchedly as he let his gaze linger on her face, like a man who was truly in love with her.

He left soon after that, but not before making an appointment to collect Lauren in an hour. 'We need a ring,' he said at her startled glance. 'I've organised the jeweller to assemble a few stones that you might like, but as they're in the Old Palace vaults we'll have to go there.'

They were now outside the door. 'I see,' she said numbly.

He gave her a swift, ironic smile. 'Cheer up, my heart—it won't be as bad as it seems at the moment.'

'Is that a promise?'

'Enough, Lauren.' He looked very uncompromising and remote. 'I am sorry if the idea horrifies you, but it is going to happen. Now, try to think about the design of the ring you wish to wear.'

Unable to put her unhappiness into words, she gestured vaguely. 'I don't have any ideas, I'm afraid.'

'I know this isn't what you expected, or wanted. It is not for me, either,' he said with relentless honesty, 'but as we are the two who caused the whole situation, it is only fair that we be the ones who suffer for it.'

She wouldn't let him see how much his words cut. Pasting a smile onto stiff lips, she said brightly, 'You are absolutely right. Guy, I've been thinking. I can use the time we're married to do a master's degree, something I've been planning to do anyway.'

He nodded and slowed down to negotiate an intersection with the main road. 'An excellent idea. We will have to entertain,' he said calmly, 'but there should be plenty of time to work as well.'

The road took them into the heart of the island's port and main city, a bustling little town that had struck a clever balance between catering for tourists and the needs of its own people.

'The treasure house is in the Old Palace,' Guy told her.

Once there, he escorted her to a small room inside the thick walls of the ancient fortress. Someone had arrayed a collection of emeralds on white velvet—glorious stones that condensed every existing green into a glowing intensity. Guy introduced the jeweller, a stocky middle-aged man with patent-leather hair, who glanced professionally at Lauren's hands.

'Beautiful,' he said approvingly. 'I suggest perhaps a classic setting, without too much ornamentation?'

'I'd like that.' Lauren sketched a quick look across the intense fire of the stones, her gaze stopping on one.

Guy picked it up and held it against her hand. 'That one?'

The stone felt cold against her skin, a violent contrast to the warmth of his fingers. Her heart contracted into a knot. 'Yes, that one.'

The jeweller beamed. 'An excellent choice. A glorious stone almost free of flaws. You know that almost all emeralds have flaws? We call them the *jardin,* or garden, because when you look into the stone it looks like a pattern of foliage.' He put a portfolio of sketches onto the table and flicked through them. 'This one, I suggest,' he said fussily, pointing to one sketch. 'In platinum, not gold, to suit your colouring, and with trillion diamonds on either side to point up the magnificent colour of the stone. It would suit your hand very well.'

Lauren looked at it and then at the stone. Guy had said nothing, but when she glanced up he was watching her with tawny, half-closed eyes, and she coloured and glanced back at the stone she'd chosen.

It was utterly beautiful; perhaps, she thought as Guy and the jeweller went into technicalities, it was a symbol. Nothing was ever perfect; if she could be satisfied with a flawed stone, surely she could settle for a flawed marriage? She loved Guy, and even if he didn't love her, he wanted her.

It might not be enough, but shielding her emotions to protect herself was a coward's way, and she had never been a coward. She'd fought for her life when she'd been ill; she'd relished the chance to prove herself in her career.

If she didn't fight for this man she'd never be able to look herself in the face again.

'Still sure that that's the one?' Guy asked. 'This one is flawless, if you'd prefer that.'

'No,' she said, shaking her head. 'The colour is breathtaking, and I like the idea of having my own garden on my finger.'

She met the quizzical gleam of his gaze with head high, relaxing only when he turned to the jeweller.

'In that case, we'll have it. Thank you.'

CHAPTER ELEVEN

THE choosing of the ring and the Press release signalled a month of intense—almost frenzied—activity.

The day before the ceremony, Lauren sank into a chair in the small parlour at the villa and slid her shoes from her aching feet.

'By now I must have met every person on the island who has the least interest in this marriage,' she told her mother drily. 'There were over five hundred people at the garden party, and they all wanted to tell me how much they liked Guy, and how lucky I am. Especially the women.'

Her mother nodded. 'He's also very popular with the men, which is so important, isn't it? Your father likes him very much.'

When Guy came strolling through with her father, Lauren leaned back and fixed him with a steely gaze. 'I seem to remember you saying once that apart from a sentimental affection for the island, you had little to do with it. Clearly the Dacians don't feel anything as mild as a sentimental affection for you—adulation describes it better.'

He grinned and put a long glass of fruit juice on the table beside her. 'I told you they loved weddings.'

'That's not it,' she said, grateful for the glossy, seamless façade she'd developed over the past hectic weeks. 'They love you. Someone told me today that you had given the government of Sant'Rosa the mobile-telephone network that connects the village chiefs.'

He shrugged. 'Good advertising,' he said calmly.

Her brows shot up. 'On Sant'Rosa? He said that you also fund an air ambulance that's already cut the death rate there.'

'Even better advertising.'

His bored tone effectively silenced her. Picking up the glass of juice, she sipped it while he spoke to her parents.

In this past hectic month she'd learned a lot about the man she loved—always from others. Guy himself had transmuted into a sophisticated stranger who wore power and position like an extension of himself. As they went about their duties she sensed beneath his consideration and courtesy an inner withdrawal that hurt her as much as her unrequited love.

In twenty-four hours he would be her husband, but she still had no idea whether he intended it to be a real marriage, or one in name only. Their public duties and her parents' constant presence meant that they hadn't had a chance to discuss anything beyond arrangements for the wedding.

He'd made no move to secure them some private moments.

He had only touched her when it was necessary, and although he'd kissed her hand—even lightly kissed her on occasion—it had been for the benefit of the family and close friends who'd gathered to celebrate.

The panic that had been building over the weeks clogged her throat; she sipped more juice, gratefully letting the tangy sweetness ease the blockage, but it did nothing for the deep, unfathomable sadness that coloured every waking moment.

As though he felt her tension, Guy said, 'Come for a walk in the garden.'

Surprised, she went with him out onto the terrace and down the shady length of the garden, saying nothing while her heart and mind and body sang with forbidden delight.

'Is everything all right?' he asked.

'Yes, of course.'

He stopped in the heavy shade of a tree and scrutinised her face. Lauren held his regard without flinching.

A hard smile curved his mouth. 'Arrogant,' he said, not without satisfaction. 'I like it when your eyes flash diamond fire at me. Your mother is worried about you.'

Feeling her way, she said, 'It's just a hangover from when I was ill. If I look a bit tired it's because I'm not used to playing princess.'

'You do it brilliantly.' But he didn't look convinced.

Standing her ground against his intense golden scrutiny, she admitted, 'I watch Alexa and follow her example.'

'And she learnt from my cousin Lucia,' he said, still watching her with hooded eyes.

Lauren nodded. She didn't know whether the beautiful Princess Lucia, Mrs Hunt Radcliffe, liked her or not; she suspected not. She even understood why. Sensible, intelligent women, both fond of Guy, Alexa and Lucia must sense that all was not normal in the relationship.

'What do we need to discuss?' she asked politely.

He put a hand in his pocket and pulled out a river of emerald fire. 'I want to give you this.' He dropped the necklace with its pendant stone over her head. 'I know that most brides wear pearls, but not royal brides in Dacia,' he said with a hard twist of his lips as he stepped back to examine the necklace on her. 'Emeralds are supposed to endow their wearers with the power to predict the future.'

'Very useful.' If only…

Her hand came up to touch the cool stone. 'I—thank you. I've got you something too, but it's not—'

'I don't need any more cuff-links,' he said laconically.

'So it's just as well I didn't buy you any,' she snapped.

Tension drummed between them, dark and heavy as the shade of the tree, eventually broken by Guy's rueful voice. 'I'm sorry, that was uncalled for. I know that whatever you give me will be as unusual—and as beautiful—as you are.'

The practised compliment grated. 'Unusual?' she asked with a lift of her brows.

'Didn't you know?' He leaned back against the trunk of the tree, the dappled shade that played across the aquiline features hiding any nuances of expression. 'On the outside you're the epitome of cool sophistication, yet you've won the hearts of these conservative islanders with your grace and your laughter and your interest in them. I suspect that glossy exterior is only a veneer.'

'No one reveals themselves openly to strangers,' she said uncertainly.

He was silent for a heartbeat, before saying tonelessly, 'Of course you're right.'

Summoning a smile, she touched the glowing green gems on her breast. 'Thank you for this. It's magnificent, and I'll wear it with pride in the tradition.' Her smile fading, she added steadily, 'And I believe it's also traditional to quarrel the day before the wedding.'

Laughing softly, he straightened. The sounds of the birds dwindled into nothingness; eyes widening, Lauren watched him come towards her, so big he blocked everything from her sight.

'So perhaps,' he said deliberately, 'we should end this very minor quarrel the traditional way.'

Excitement beat high within her and she lifted her face in instinctive invitation. With an odd, raw sound he caught her in his arms.

Her lashes fluttered down, but lifted within a few seconds when the kiss she expected didn't eventuate. He was looking at her with scorching intensity, tawny eyes narrowed and piercing.

Through lips that scarcely moved, he said, 'But I don't think this can be the traditional kiss of peace. There is nothing peaceful about the way I want you. It eats into my guts and steals my mind and shatters my sleep and shoots holes in my control. You are a torment to me.'

Lauren's lips trembled. Nothing about love, but it was enough—for the moment. Oh, she might regret this, but for now she needed him.

She reached up and pulled his head down and opened her mouth to him without dissembling or holding back.

Hunger, fire, need, the aching demand for completion, sharp and sweet and fiery, the longing for something more than this physical flash and glamour—and a potent glory in the taste and feel and scent of him—all combined to hurl her into waters that closed over her head.

It was Guy who pulled back, Guy who muttered something outrageous beneath his breath in three languages, one of which she knew, and Guy who said on a half-laugh that held both satisfaction and regret, 'Darling heart, someone is coming—several someones, in fact, talking loudly enough to warn us.'

Only then did Lauren hear the voices; crashing back to earth, she groaned.

'I so agree,' Guy said, irony glimmering in the depths of his eyes, and dropped a swift kiss on the tip of her nose before letting her go and running a hand through his hair—hair she'd disarranged with her fingers.

For a second she saw the man she'd fallen in love with on Sant'Rosa, but in the space of a breath he donned the mask again, replacing the buccaneer with the worldly prince and tycoon.

The intruders were her parents, followed by Marc and his wife, Paige, with their two children, twin girls of three, who'd arrived a few hours previously and were staying in another house owned by Prince Luka.

Introductions performed, Lauren gave in to the appeals of the two small girls and sank to her knees, hugging them to her. 'Darlings,' she said extravagantly, 'how are my two favourite girls in all the world?'

They babbled happily in a mixture of French and English, one in each ear as they pressed soft, moist kisses to her cheeks. Heart overflowing, she gathered both for another big hug. When she looked up it was to see Guy watching her, his expression totally devoid of expression. A cold chill of disappointment whispered through her, but she smiled and laughed and chattered for an hour until they left.

Marc managed a word with her. A small frown drawing his brows together, he said, 'Is everything all right?'

Deliberately misunderstanding him she bestowed her sunniest smile on him. 'Not you too! My mother has been watching me like a hawk, and I'm surprised Guy doesn't take my pulse every hour. I only had pneumonia, for heaven's sake, and I'm well over it now.'

His frown deepened. 'I know you too well. You look fragile.'

Aware that Guy was watching them, she said brightly, 'All brides totter up the aisle in an exhausted state—it's tradition! Your bone marrow is still doing excellent work.'

He didn't pursue it. 'If you ever need me,' he said in a voice she'd heard only a couple of times, 'contact me or Paige.'

'Thank you, but I won't need you,' she said, hoping her voice didn't sound as brittle as her emotions.

Later, after what Alexa had referred to somewhat wryly as, 'Just a family dinner for eighty people in the Little Palace,' Lauren watched Guy charm them all— the rich, the successful, the titled and the beautiful, she thought sardonically.

Her mother laughed at a witticism from an elderly Austrian duke, and her father obviously enjoyed the company of a younger woman whose face was so familiar she had to be famous.

'That's a somewhat *triste* expression,' Guy commented from behind.

She turned, bracing herself to meet his burnished eyes. At least the kiss had told her that behind his unreadable façade was the man who wanted her. She clung to that knowledge with passionate intensity, because it warmed her; inside she might be dying, but at least Guy desired her as much as she did him.

It would have to be enough.

'All right,' she said softly, 'I admit that I am just the tiniest bit tired. Everything's gone like a dream, and no one could have been nicer to me and my family than your cousins and the Dacians and everyone I've met, but I am really looking forward to all this being over.'

'This time tomorrow,' he promised, 'you'll be able to relax.'

They had decided to spend the first night in his house on Dacia; Guy had refused to take her there so that it would be a surprise. After that they'd fly to a small Caribbean island that belonged to a friend of his.

He took her hand, feeling it tremble in his, and fought back a pang of lust so potent it almost unmanned him then and there. He'd spent a wretched month grinding down the temptation to take her, and the kiss they'd exchanged that afternoon had been small solace. Whatever she felt for him, she had no control over this physical craving. Like him she was inextricably bound to it, barely able to control it, completely unable to overcome it.

Once the decision had been made she'd thrown herself into learning to do as good a job as Alexa and Lucia, succeeding brilliantly, but the shadows darkening her clear eyes worried him.

Something compelled him to say, 'Do you trust me, Lauren?'

She gave him a startled look that refused to engage with his eyes. 'Of course— I wouldn't be going through with this if I mistrusted you.'

Her words didn't satisfy him, but as he didn't know what answer he wanted this wasn't surprising. Perhaps he too was tired, he thought ironically, nodding as Luka glanced across the room.

'It's time to go,' he said. 'Sleep well tonight, my heart.'

A clouded glance and a tight smile were her only response, and he wondered what was going on in the sleek black head behind those deceptively translucent eyes. Other women had always been easy to read.

Lauren kept her thoughts and her emotions to herself; only in his arms could he tell what she was feeling, and even then, her mind was closed against him.

From his lovers he'd never asked anything more than companionship and the willing and enthusiastic sharing of their bodies, but with Lauren he faced the compulsion to storm her guarded heart.

CHAPTER TWELVE

FOR Lauren, the next day passed in a daze: thousands of Dacians cheering as the open coach passed through the streets, its white horses decked in a panoply of silver and white; the solemnity of the service, the flickering lights of candles and the glorious singing; the poignant moments when Guy slid her ring onto her finger and after she had done the same for him they were pronounced man and wife; the wild, jubilant clangour of the bells as they turned to face the congregation.

Together, they were pelted with flower petals on the short trip in an open carriage back to the Old Palace. They floated on the air, some settling like coloured snowflakes on the skirt of Lauren's gorgeous dress. The couturier, a small, determined despot in her mid-sixties, had searched the world for silk in exactly the right shade.

'With the faintest hint of pink,' she'd explained, contemptuously tossing discarded samples onto the bench. 'Otherwise with that white, white skin you will look like a marble statue, not a living, breathing bride for our prince!'

She had found what she wanted in India, and transformed it into a dress that took the breath away. Now, with a bouquet of moon-coloured roses on the seat beside the coachman, and the excited roar of the crowds in her ears, Lauren smiled until her cheeks ached, and then smiled some more, waving as she'd been taught.

They were almost at the Old Palace when she turned

to Guy and said, 'I see what you mean when you told me Dacians adore a good wedding! This is overwhelming.'

He laughed and looked down into her face with kindling eyes. 'They love you too,' he said. His voice deepened. 'Can you hear what they're calling? *Beautiful lady—*'

Dazzled, she caught a glitter of metal from the corner of her eye. Time froze—a silver blade splashed with scarlet flamed under the hot sun, aiming straight for Guy's chest.

People screamed as she tried to fling herself across him; he pushed her away, twisting his big body to shield her, and the object hit his shoulder before rolling harmlessly in the drifts of flower petals on the floor.

Grey-faced, he gave it one searing glance, then turned and said her name on a note of raw pain as he pulled her upright with exquisite tenderness.

Against a cry of people and the sharp clatter of the horses' hooves as the postilions fought to control them, she gasped, 'Are you hurt? God, are you hurt?'

'No. It's all right, it's not a bomb.' Locking her against him, he barked out an order to the security man who appeared from nowhere to scoop up the object, a roll of paper with an incongruous red rose tied on to it by silver ribbons.

'I'm fine,' she said against the cries of the crowd. 'It didn't even touch me. What is it?'

The crowd noise changed from panic to vengefulness, and Guy released her, setting her back on the seat, such cold fury hardening his face that she had to stop herself from shrinking back.

He called out another order, and the man who'd thrown the object was shoved unceremoniously towards them, some of the outraged people striking at him as he was pushed up to the carriage.

Only young, about eighteen, he looked terrified. Adrenaline pumping through her in devastating surges, Lauren listened without comprehension to the rapid-fire conversation that took place between Guy and the youth. When the crowd, so ugly a moment ago, began to laugh, she caught her breath.

Although Guy was frowning when he turned to her, the black anger had faded. 'It is a petition,' he said softly, grasping her cold hands. 'He wishes to apologise for frightening you—see, he tied a rose to it so that you would know it wasn't dangerous.'

Shock had set her teeth chattering, but she gritted them and said, 'Tell him that if he ever throws anything at you again—no, you'd better not. What should I say?'

'That you forgive him this time but suggest he uses more conventional methods to present a petition?' he suggested, and when she nodded he dropped a fleeting kiss on her hand and turned to the youth. Crisply he conveyed Lauren's words.

From behind the living barriers of soldiers people called out to Lauren. Straightening her spine, she saw concern and affection and lingering shock in their faces. One woman was weeping silently.

Still shaking, Lauren managed a smile and a wave, and the Dacians cheered and blew kisses, and cheered again as the youth was hurried off and the horses urged on their way.

Guy's hand closed around hers, warm and firm and reassuring. 'I could kill him, the fool,' he ground out.

She shivered, but maintained that smile. 'I thought—I feel an utter idiot. I thought it was a dagger or something like that.'

'You have fast reactions,' he said quietly. 'If it had been a dagger it could have killed you.'

If it had been a bomb it would have killed them both. At least, she thought, reaction leading to something perilously close to hysteria, they'd have died together.

'Thank God it wasn't,' she said devoutly. 'What on earth made him think of such a thing?'

Guy gave her an unreadable glance. 'He wishes to marry, but his mother doesn't want it,' he said gravely. 'He was sure we'd be able to talk her into a better frame of mind, so he chose this way to dramatise his situation. He thought we would understand from the rose that we shouldn't be afraid.'

Lauren stared at him, then said in a voice that trembled uncontrollably, 'If I start laughing now I'm going to end up with full-blown hysterics, so I'll save it for later.'

'A wise decision,' her husband agreed solemnly, and they waved and smiled to the cheering crowd. But Lauren's hand remained in Guy's until they reached the Old Palace.

Much later, after a banquet and farewells to her parents and Paige and Marc, they drove out from the palace as dusk was falling. Guy was behind the wheel, and soon they left the partying islanders behind for the narrow roads to the other side of Dacia.

Neither spoke for a long time, until Guy said, 'How do you feel?'

'Still a bit hyped,' she admitted. 'And I probably drank a glass too much of that delicious champagne. How about you?'

'I alternate between wanting to dismember the kid slowly, and being grateful that's all it was. Luka is furious; the security service will be going to bed with a flea in its collective ear.' He turned off the road onto a private one, and a few minutes later they stopped outside his house.

Her first glimpse startled her. 'I thought it would be old,' she exclaimed, tension thinning her tone into a travesty of her normal voice. Lights blazed all along the double-storeyed modern building, and a man was running out to meet the car.

'Are you disappointed?'

'No,' she said quietly, looking around her at the gracious lines and ambience of the building. 'This is beautiful, and it suits you.'

Inside it was spacious and airy, the scent of the sea mingling with those from the gardens. Someone had gone crazy with roses—not the red blooms of passion, but old-fashioned flowers in milky colours, their scent overpowering on the warm, dry air.

And candles—tall white candles bloomed with golden tips amidst the flowers.

'This is so beautiful,' Lauren breathed, looking around her with astonishment. She glanced up at Guy's angular face, then away again. 'Will you thank whoever thought of it and the ones who did it?'

'I will.' He introduced a housekeeper and two maids, conveying her thanks in rapid Dacian.

They beamed at her, and then the housekeeper showed her to a huge bedroom, indicating a sumptuous bathroom and the wide glass doors that opened out onto a tiled terrace. More flowers hazed the room with perfume, more candles glowed softly on the dresser, and she saw with a pang that the bed had been covered with rose petals in the same shades of white and dusky pink and subtle, old-fashioned reds.

Her clothes had been delivered that morning; no

doubt Guy's had been too, but they weren't hanging with hers in the room-sized wardrobe.

So she would be the only one to sleep in that beautiful bed. Guy probably planned to make love with her there, but afterwards he would go back to his own room.

Gripped by acute, devastating disappointment, she walked out onto the terrace and stood for a long, lonely time while the stars bloomed above her and waves purred onto a white beach not far below. A faint whisper of sound, soft as satin, came from a fountain somewhere, and the air was fragrant and silky on her bare arms.

Eventually she set her jaw and went back inside to change from her exquisite going-away outfit in pale silk to something more suitable for an evening with the husband who didn't want anything more from her than the temporary use of her body.

If he wanted that. The empty wardrobe indicated that he didn't plan to share his life with her.

Guy showed her around the austerely beautiful house, showed her how the security system worked, and then said, 'You look exhausted. The garden can wait for tomorrow. Why don't you have an early night?'

'Yes, I'll do that,' she said evenly, pain slicing through her.

Half an hour later, ready for bed in a pair of sleeveless cotton pyjamas, she looked at the enormous bed with its counterpane of petals, and shivered.

A knock on the door to the terrace whirled her around, and joy possessed her in a white-hot sunburst when she saw Guy there, only to fade when she realised he was still wearing the casually tailored trousers and fine cotton shirt he'd changed into after they'd got there.

She had to clear her throat to say, 'Come in.'

One step into the room made it his own; he dominated it with bold, unleashed power. Her heart began to beat faster.

Eyes narrowing, he said harshly, 'You've been bruised.'

'It's nothing,' she returned quickly, because his fingers had done the damage when he'd flung her out of the way of the missile.

But he came across and lightly touched the purpling blotches. 'I'm sorry—I wanted to get you out of the way. I thought it might have been a bomb. Have you anything to put on them?'

'They've already been anointed with arnica.' Her voice sounded distant, robbed of colour and texture.

He bent his head and kissed each bruise, his mouth lingering and tender. Little rills of sensation purled through her, sweet as love, sensuous as rapture...

Guy let her go, his face set in the distant expression she'd come to know so well during the past month. 'We have to talk.'

'I—all right.'

But he walked across to the open doors and with his back to her said, 'When I came to New Zealand, I told myself that it was to visit Lucia and Hunt—they live not far from the Bay of Islands—but I wanted to see how you fitted into Corbett's world.'

Something clicked into place. 'Did Lucia tell you I was Marc's mistress?'

'No. I'd already been told by a cousin.' He paused, then finished deliberately, 'Before I met you.'

So he'd known who she was when she'd turned up on Sant'Rosa.

He resumed, 'Lucia said there was a link between you and Corbett, but she didn't know what it was.

Everything seemed to back it up—you were staying in his house, you were terrified that the media would find out about our marriage...'

She angled her chin at him. 'Even if I had been his lover, what business would it have been of yours?'

'You can say that after the time we spent together in Valanu?'

'Oh, the sex was wonderful,' she agreed bleakly. 'But we made no commitment to each other.'

He swung around and directed a shaft of searing gold fire at her. 'I wanted you the second I saw you. When it seemed you were his mistress I despised myself for not being able to chisel that hunger from my body— but I knew right from the start that I wasn't going to give you up.'

Lauren breathed in sharply. 'But why—when you found out I wasn't Marc's lover, when you understood the reason I was so afraid of the media—why did you pull away? The minute we decided to marry again on Dacia you got colder and colder and harder and harder and more and more distant.'

'Because by then,' he said deliberately, 'and without acknowledging it, not even to myself—*especially* not to myself—I was head over heels in love with you. And you were not in love with me. You made it obvious— frequently!—that the last thing you wanted was the marriage I'd forced on you.'

Lauren's pulses jumped, but she shook her head in disbelief. 'You might have railroaded me, but I was the one who gained. That first marriage saved me from— at the least—a nasty experience in a very unsavoury gaol. And the second time you offered—insisted!—on formalising our marriage, partly it was to protect me and my family if our private lives and sins were hung out to dry.'

His mouth curved sardonically. 'That was partly the truth. Just as the way the Dacians feel is part of the truth. But only part. When I came back from the States I saw that you hadn't been sleeping, and I knew then that I had to offer you your freedom because I couldn't bear to chain you to me. And that's when I knew I loved you.'

Too shocked to be able to believe him, she breathed, 'And I turned you down.'

'Yes, you were very stiff about keeping your promises. I started to hope then.'

'But you didn't—'

'Didn't woo you?' he said when she fell silent. 'When did we have the opportunity? The decision had to be yours—it is still yours. If you ask me to go back to my room, I will do that.' His grin briefly illuminated his face. 'Of course, I won't promise to stop trying to make you fall in love with me.'

'For a man of your experience,' she said, so quietly she could barely hear her words above the singing of her heart, 'you've been awfully obtuse. Of course I love you. Not that I admitted it—I kept trying to convince myself that I was just like my mother, I'd jumped head-long into a sizzling infatuation—but I wouldn't have made love with you on Valanu if I hadn't loved you. But when I arrived here and found out who you were, I knew that it had just been a dream of love, a fantasy.'

'Why?' he demanded. And when she didn't answer he said, 'Surely not because of your family history? That won't wash, Lauren. It's not as though anyone else cares—everyone knows about Alexa's father.'

'Her grandfather was a prince,' she said quietly.

He gave a hard laugh. 'All right, if it's bloodlines you're concerned about— Hunt, Lucia's husband, fought his way up from a foster home with nothing but his guts and intelligence and determination.'

'Yes,' she said simply, 'but he's rich.'

'Lucia didn't marry him for his money.'

She wanted him to convince her with his kisses, with his love, but he stayed three paces distant. 'I know, but there's no scandal in his past, only poverty. And you know perfectly well that old scandals cast long shadows.'

'Lauren, it doesn't matter. It will never matter. You have courage and a brain as well as a warm heart and a charm that has everyone on their knees in minutes— from little Nico to Luka, who is a much tougher nut than his son.' With an exasperated shake of his head he finished, 'I would never have thought you lacked self-esteem!'

Lauren looked at him, saw the truth naked in his eyes and his face, and a huge weight she hadn't been conscious of rolled away, leaving her so light and carefree she almost laughed with the joy of it.

Speaking carefully, groping for her own particular truth, she said, 'I think I convinced myself that my past was utterly shameful partly because I didn't want people to sneer at my mother, but also because it kept me safe. Love had to be terrifying if my mother could almost throw away a good marriage.' She hesitated before continuing, 'But it wasn't like that. My birth father met her at a particularly vulnerable time in her life, when she'd just discovered that she wasn't likely to ever have children. She said she felt like a failure as a woman. He was kind, he made her feel feminine and desired. But she soon came to her senses—only to find that she was pregnant with his child.'

'Does that hurt you?'

'No. My *real* father— Hugh—has never stopped loving her, and she loves him too. I'm not perfect, so why should I expect my mother to be?'

'I'm not perfect either,' Guy said. He paused, and she heard the fountain outside whispering softly in the darkness.

He said deeply, 'But I will love you until the day I die, and I will never be unfaithful to you.'

Tears ached behind her eyes. 'I love you. I might kill you if you even think of being unfaithful to me, but I will be true to you, I promise.'

He flung his head back and laughed, the angry tension of the past weeks dissolving like sugar in the mouth, so that he was free and younger than he had ever been. 'Killing me would certainly put a stop to any unfaithfulness,' he agreed. He sobered quickly, and said, 'But it is not something you will ever need to contemplate. I mean what I say. You are all that I want.' He looked more closely at her, and said in a shaken voice, 'Tears, my heart?'

She blinked them back; they could not be allowed to sully this precious moment. 'These past weeks have been hideous. I felt as though I was living two lives, and both of them were false. I could feel you pulling away and I didn't know what to do about it because you said you didn't want to marry me—'

'Only after you'd said flatly that you hated this whole business,' he cut in. 'I wanted you to feel safe—to know that I wouldn't force myself on you once we were married—although I had every intention of seducing you!'

Lauren gave him a glimmering smile. 'Idiots, both of

us. Utter and complete idiots. I'm surprised you didn't understand what was happening to me—after all, I'm not your first lover. And I've seen your effect on women. You catch everyone's eyes just by walking into the room!'

He ignored the faint note of bitterness. 'But you're the only woman I've ever loved,' he said, and at last he reached out for her and they came together and exchanged their first kiss without barriers.

'And the only woman I will ever love. It's so different,' he said quietly, stroking her hair back from her face. 'Loving you makes me vulnerable and at first I hated that. Then I kept remembering you as you were on Valanu, warm and loving and passionate, and despising myself because something I'd done had changed you.'

'Falling in love has that effect on people,' she said into his neck.

He glanced down at her pyjamas. 'I forbid you ever to wear anything like this again,' he said sternly. 'You look far too young and sweet in them. From now on you must wear silk when you come to bed with me.'

Suddenly radiant, Lauren laughed. 'Everyone has been telling me that a good marriage involves compromise, so because I love you I'll wear silk, but you have to make a concession too.'

'Certainly.'

She kissed the fine-grained skin of his shoulder, relishing the way the muscle hardened and flexed beneath her questing lips. 'No clothes,' she said succinctly, and ran her hand down to the waist of his trousers, pushing them down.

Laughing, Guy let her strip him, and then he did the same for her before carrying her across to the bed, where the laughter faded into passion and at last they made love with no defences, no inhibitions, nothing to spoil the complete union both had longed for.

Eventually, when she was lying against him, listening to the solid drumming of his heart as it eased into a normal beat, she said, 'I thought you were going to leave me alone tonight.'

His chest lifted. 'I'd planned to, but when that young idiot hurled his ridiculous petition, you tried to fling yourself in front of me.' Stone faced, he looked at her. 'The only thing that stopped me from killing him without mercy there and then was that it seemed to mean you had some feelings for me.'

'I see,' she said shakily.

'It gave me hope.' He rolled her on top of him and in the darkness she caught the white flash of his smile. 'The pretty wedding Alexa put on for us wasn't necessary, but I have to admit that I am glad. Once in his life, every man should feel as I did when you walked down the aisle towards me in that exquisite dress, with my ring on your finger and flowers in your arms. Until then I felt that perhaps I could let you go if you wanted to leave after a couple of years. But when I saw you then, I knew that I would do anything to make you love me.'

Unbearably moved, she dropped a kiss on the point of his chin. 'You could have told me,' she said indignantly. 'You must have known how I felt about you!'

'I didn't want to use the sexual charge between us to dazzle you into thinking you loved me,' he said, a sombre note intensifying his meaning. 'I need more than the unwilling response of your body, no matter how magnificent that is for us both.'

She shivered, because magnificent described exactly

how she felt when they made love—as though the world and everything in it had been made for them.

'You hid it well,' she complained, but with a note of understanding in her voice.

'So did you,' he returned. 'Shall we make a vow never to hide big things from each other again? I don't want to bore you with details of business—'

'Now that, I'd find very interesting!'

'So that was a poor example,' he said, laughing softly. 'But if you are sad I want to know why, and if you are happy I want to share your happiness.'

'And the same applies to you. No shutting me out again. I thought I'd wither away.'

He kissed her softly, and then not quite so softly, and then said, 'We must find work for you to do—you are not going to be happy organising charity events.'

'No,' she said instantly. 'Where are we going to live?'

'Wherever you want to.' When she didn't answer he said, 'Paris, if that would please you.'

'I'd love to live there,' she told him, 'but my parents are already in love with Dacia. Yesterday Dad said something about buying a house here. Would it be too inconvenient if we lived here too?'

'They won't be able to buy a house. Dacian property belongs to Dacians, but they can rent. And I'd be very happy to stay on the island; when our children come along it will be good for them to have their only set of grandparents living close by, and to play with the island children as I did, and with Luka and Alexa's brood. I think it will be good for your father's health, also.'

She kissed him and after a long, passionate interlude, confessed, 'When we make love, I feel as though I might die of pleasure.'

Guy laughed softly. 'No one ever died of pleasure, my sweet one.'

Snuggling against him, she murmured, 'And if I did, one kiss from you would bring me back to life.' She jackknifed upright. 'Your present!'

Golden eyes gleaming, he said deeply, 'I have already had it.'

She laughed and groped under the pillow. 'Your *wedding* present,' she said, hauling out a small jeweller's box.

He looked at it in surprise. Long tanned fingers flicked it open, and he saw the ring she'd had made for him, a signet ring with the leopard of Dacia carved into the face. Jauntily, wickedly, a tiny emerald eye glittered in the heraldic beast's head.

Suddenly uncertain, Lauren watched as he slid it onto his finger. 'I know your other one is precious to you,' she began.

'Doubly precious because you wore it. This is more precious because you gave it to me,' he said.

He laughed, rich and deep and satisfied, and pulled her down beside him. 'Lauren, I love you,' he said on a raw note. 'With all my heart, with everything I have, everything I am, more and more each day. I will love you until I die.'

Joy expanded to fill her completely. From now on, she thought happily as she drifted off to sleep in his arms, and no matter what happened, they would be safe together, she and her prince.

THE PRINCESS AND
THE OUTLAW

LEANNE BANKS

Leanne Banks is a *New York Times* bestselling author with over sixty books to her credit. A book lover and romance fan from even before she learned to read, Leanne has always treasured the way that books allow us to go to new places and experience the lives of wonderful characters. Always ready for a trip to the beach, Leanne lives in Virginia with her family and her Pomeranian muse.

Prologue

"What is *he* doing here?"

Phillipa was wondering the same thing. At her sister Bridget's gasp, her other sister, Tina, leaned toward Bridget. "Zach says he's a huge contributor here. Everyone loves him," Tina said distastefully.

"They clearly don't know him," Bridget said and nudged Phillipa. "Why can't we escape him?" she whispered. "Maybe it's because he's the devil and that means he can be everywhere at once."

At that moment, Phillipa almost agreed with Bridget. Nic certainly seemed to have some kind of dark power over her.

Phillipa had tried to slow things down with Nic Lafitte, but persuading the man to move at anything other than warp speed had proven impossible. He was a force of nature with a will that rivaled every kind of powerful destructive weather. Typhoons and tornadoes had nothing on him. She'd successfully avoided him for the past three weeks and she had been certain that fleeing her home country of Chantaine to visit her sisters in Texas would buy her even more time.

Who would have ever thought she would be caught staring at him at a charity social ball in Texas as he accepted an award for philanthropy? Phillipa knew that Nic had ties to Texas, but with his extensive business dealings, he had ties to many places.

The ballroom suddenly felt as if it was shrinking. Panic squeezed her chest. She had to get out. She had to catch her breath. Feeling her sister's curious gaze, she swallowed hard over the lump in her throat. "I'm not feeling well," she said. "Please excuse me."

When Bridget offered to come with her, Phillipa had to remain firm. "I'll be back in a little bit."

Sticking to the perimeter of the room as she fled, she kept her head down, hoping she wasn't drawing attention to herself. If she could just get out of this room, she would be fine, she told herself. Out of the room and away from Nic. Away from how he affected her.

She stepped out of the ballroom and held the door so it would catch softly as it closed, then took a few more steps away and leaned against the wall, which felt cool against her skin. Her sisters hadn't been exaggerating when they'd told her Texas summers were hell.

Phillipa took several deep breaths, willing her heart and mind to calm. How had she gotten herself into this? Why? Among her siblings, she'd done her best to maintain a low profile. As number five out of six strong personalities, it hadn't been that difficult. Her oldest brother, Stefan, had been born and bred to rule—everyone except his siblings anyway. Phillipa had found refuge in academia. It was much easier pleasing a few professors than being a princess and constantly making public appearances and dealing with the media. By nature, she'd always been an introvert. She'd never enjoyed crowded gatherings, hated posing for photographs and had little patience for all the effort it seemed to take to make her presentable.

When her first two sisters began to focus on their new husbands instead of royal duties, Phillipa had plunged herself into graduate studies to avoid being in the public eye. Her sister Bridget had seen through her plan and it had clearly irritated her, although Bridget had bucked up and done a fantastic job. The trouble now was that Bridget was determined to get a break and she had earned it. Phillipa cringed at the prospect of all the public appearances she would be forced to make.

"I'll be damned," a familiar male voice said, making her eyes pop open. "If it isn't the missing Her Highness Phillipa of Chantaine."

Phillipa stared into the dark gaze of Nic Lafitte and her lungs seemed to completely shut down. "I didn't know you would be here."

His mouth twisted in a half smile. "Why doesn't that surprise me?" he asked and slipped his hand around her arm. "Lucky for both of us that I am. We have unfinished business. You're coming with me. I can have my car delivered in seconds."

Her heart pounded. "I can't. My sisters expect me back for the rest of the event. They'll call the authorities if I go missing," she said.

"It wouldn't be the first time your family has tried

to get me in trouble with the law." He glanced around and tugged her down the hallway. "If you won't leave with me, then I'll take my moment somewhere else."

"Where are you taking me?" she asked. "This is crazy. I need to go back to my table. I need—" She broke off as he pushed open the door to a room marked Coat Closet and dragged her inside.

He pulled her to the back of the small room and gently, but firmly gripped her shoulders. "Tell me what you really need, Pippa. What do you really want?" he asked her in that dark, sexy voice that made her feel as if she were turning upside down.

A half-dozen images from the stolen moments they'd shared shot through her brain. The time they'd gone swimming at night. The afternoon she'd spent on his yacht. The walk they'd taken on the opposite side of the island when she'd learned so much about him and he'd made it so easy for her to talk about herself. Despite the bad blood between her family and his, Phillipa had never felt so drawn to another man in her life.

He lowered his head, holding her gaze until his mouth took hers. His kiss set off a riot of reaction and emotion inside her. He made her feel alive and out of control. She pulled back and whispered. "This is insane. It will never work. That's what I tried to tell you before."

"Why not?" he challenged her. Nic was always challenging her. Sometimes gently, sometimes with more strength. "If I want you and you want me, what is most important?"

Pippa bit her lip and struggled to remain rational. Members of her family had caused a lot of trouble by giving in to their emotions. She didn't want the same kind of trouble. "Want is a temporary emotion. There are more important things than temporary emotions."

"If that's true, why did you kiss me back? Why are you here with me right now?"

Pippa heard a gasp from the doorway and terror rushed through her. "Someone is here," she said. "We've got to get out of here," she said, stumbling toward the door. Nic helped to steady her as they stepped outside the closet.

Her sisters Bridget and Tina greeted them with furious disapproval stamped on their faces. Pippa inwardly cringed.

"Get away from my sister," Bridget said.

"That's for her to say, not you," Nic said.

"You're just using her," Tina said. "You only want her because she can redeem your terrible family name."

"Not everyone finds my family name reprehensible. Some even respect it," he said.

"That's respect you've bought with money," Tina said. "Leave Phillipa alone. You can never be good enough for her. If you have any compassion, you'll at least protect her reputation by leaving now."

Nic tightened his jaw. "I'll leave, but Phillipa will make the ultimate decision about the future of our relationship." He glanced behind him and met Phillipa's shocked, pale face. "*Ciao,* darling. Call me when you get some courage. Some things are meant to be," he said and strode away.

Chapter One

Seven Months Later

She'd started running for exercise. That was what Pippa told her security detail anyway. She knew the truth. She was running from memories. Memories and the possibility that there was only one man for her and he was the one man she couldn't have.

"Stop it," she told herself, staring at the empty beach in front of her. Azure waves dappled onto white sands. By noon, there would be quite a few more bodies enjoying the beach. At six in the morning, however, she was the only one around. She debated turning on some music via her smartphone. She usually welcomed the noise, hoping it would drown out some of her thoughts. Today, she was searching for a little peace. Maybe the sound of the waves would help, she thought, and started out.

One foot in front of the other, she ran for two min-

utes, then walked for three. It was called interval training and the different paces suited her. Pippa had never
been athletic. From the time she'd learned to read, she'd
always been happiest with her nose stuck in a book.
Her nanny had been relieved because her brothers and
most of her sisters had been more demanding in one
way or another.

Running again, she inhaled the scent of the salt air.
The humidity was low today and she could feel the
moisture on her skin begin to evaporate. Slowing after
three minutes of running, she took a swig of her water
and trudged onward.

Along the shore, in the distance, she spotted a long
figure walking. She would wave and be friendly. Pippa
was a royal and Chantaine royals were not allowed to be
snooty. Other runners might be able to put their blinders
and zip past everyone in their path, but not a Devereaux.

As she drew closer, she saw that the figure was that
of a woman. Short white hair crowned her head, and a
sundress that resembled a nightgown covered her pe-
tite frame.

Pippa nodded. "Good morning," she said.

The woman looked away and stumbled.

Curious, Pippa vacillated as to whether to approach
her. Perhaps she was longing for solitude just as Pippa
was. The woman stumbled again and Pippa felt a twist
of concern. She walked toward the woman. "Pardon
me, may I help you?"

The woman shook her head. "No, no. I'm fine. It's so
beautiful here," she said in a lilting voice that contrasted
with the lines on her face and the frailness of her frame.

Something about her seemed familiar, but Pippa

couldn't quite identify it. The woman stumbled again, and Pippa's concern grew. Was she ill?

"Yes, the beach is lovely. Are you sure I can't help you? I could walk you back to where you started," she said. "Or perhaps you would like some water."

The woman's face crumpled. "No, no. Please don't make me go back. Please don't—" She broke off and collapsed right in front of Pippa.

Alarm shot through her. "Oh, my God!" she exclaimed and bent over the woman. This was *one* time when she would have loved to have had her security detail close by. Pippa put her arms around the woman and lifted her, surprised by her light weight. Glancing around, she pulled her toward a small stand of palm trees.

Frantic, she held the woman and gently shook her. "Please. Miss. Please." She spilled water from her bottle onto one of her hands and gently patted the woman's face. "Please wake up. Please."

Terrified that the woman was dying, she reached for her cell phone. The woman clearly needed emergency medical attention. Just as she put her finger over the speed dial for her security, the woman blinked her eyes. Huge and full of emotion, her eyes captivated Pippa.

She held her breath. "Are you all right? Please take a few sips of my water. It's clearly too hot out here for you. I'll call for help and—"

"No," the woman said with a strength that surprised Pippa. "Please don't do that." Then the woman closed her amazing, mesermizing eyes and began to sob.

The sound wrenched at Pippa. "You must let me help you."

"There's only one thing I want," she said and met Pippa's gaze again. "I just want to die in Chantaine."

Pippa gasped. Then a lightning flash of realization rocked through her. She looked at the woman and saw the resemblance of Nic in her eyes. His bone structure was a stronger, more masculine version, but his eyes were all Amelie. "Amelie," she whispered. "You're Amelie Lafitte."

The woman reluctantly nodded. "How do you know?"

"I know your son Nic." Pippa also knew that Amelie was in the final stages of cancer. Her time was drawing painfully close.

Amelie looked away. "I just wanted a little walk on the beach. I bet he's quite peeved that I left the yacht."

Peeved wasn't the word that came to Pippa's mind. "I'll call him for you," she said.

"Then all my fun will be over," she said with a cute pout. "He's such a worrywart."

Stunned at how quickly Amelie's spirit had returned, she hesitated a half beat, then dialed his cell. Despite the fact that she'd deleted it from her phone records months ago, every digit was engraved on her brain.

Five minutes later, a black Mercedes came to screeching halt on the curb of the road above the beach. Pippa immediately identified the dark figure exiting the driver's side of the vehicle. Nic. As he strode swiftly toward her and Amelie, she could see the tension in his frame. Seeing him after all these months set off a visceral response inside her. Her stomach clenched. Her heart beat unevenly.

"Hi, darling," Amelie said, remaining seated on the sand under the tree as she sipped Pippa's water. Pippa was still surprised at how quickly the woman had recovered after fainting. "Sorry to be a bother, but I woke up early and I just couldn't resist the chance to go for a walk on the beach."

"I would have been happy to walk with you," Nic said and turned to Pippa. What she wouldn't give to get a peek behind his dark sunglasses. "Thank you for calling me. I'll take her back to the yacht now and you can continue your run. I didn't know you were a runner."

She felt her face heat with self-consciousness. "I'm more of a combination walker and runner."

He nodded and glanced back at his mother. "Dad's beside himself with worry. It was all I could do to keep him from tearing after you."

"Paul can't hobble with crutches let alone tear after me with that broken foot of his. The doctor said it will be ten more weeks before he can put any weight on it at all," she said, then turned her head thoughtfully to the side. "You know what I'm in the mood for? Crepes. There used to be a wonderful café on the edge of town. They made the most delicious crepes."

"Bebe's on Oleander," Pippa said. "It's still there, and Bebe's granddaughter helps makes the crepes."

"Oh," Amelie said, clasping her hands together. "It's still there. We must go. And we can bring one back for Paul." She turned to Pippa. "You must come, too."

Pippa blinked at the invitation and slid a quick helpless glance at Nic.

"Mother, do you know who Pippa is?" he asked as he extended his hand to help her rise to her feet.

Amelie studied her for a long moment and frowned. "She looks a bit familiar. I can't quite." Her eyes widened. "Oh, dear. You're a Devereaux. I can see it in your eyes and your chin. Oh, dear. This could get a bit messy."

"Just a little," Nic said in a wry tone. "But let's give her the choice. Would you like to join us for crepes, Your Highness?"

Pippa heard the hint of goading challenge in Nic's voice. She'd heard it before, but it seemed to hold more of an edge than ever. The truth was she didn't want her photo taken with Nic and his mother. To say it could cause problems was a huge understatement.

"That's okay," he said before she could respond. "Thanks again for looking out for my mother. Ci—"

"I'm coming," Pippa said impulsively. "Unless you're rescinding the invitation," she tossed back at him in her own challenging voice.

He paused a half beat and tilted his head as if she'd taken him off guard. The possibility thrilled her. "Not at all. Would you like to ride with us in my vehicle?"

"Thank you, but no. I'll drive myself and meet you in about fifteen minutes," Pippa said and turned her gaze to Amelie. "I'll see you soon. Please drink some more fluids."

"Thank you, darling. Isn't she delightful?" she said to Nic. "She fusses just like you do."

"Yes," he said in a dry tone. "Delightful."

Fifteen minutes later as Pippa put a ball cap on her head and adjusted her large pair of sunglasses, she wondered if she'd lost her mind agreeing to join Nic and his mother, the notorious Amelie, for crepes. Glancing in the rearview mirror, she could easily imagine the horror on the face of the royal advisers. Running on the beach at 6:00 a.m. in her current state was one thing, but walking into a public place of business was quite another. She thought of Nic's goading attitude and made a face at the mirror. Well, she couldn't back down now. Stepping from her car, she could only hope she wouldn't be recognized.

Because she'd spent far less time in the public eye than her siblings, that was on her side. Her hair, however, was very distinctive and not in a good way. Wavy and brown with a tendency to frizz, she hoped she'd concealed it adequately by pulling it back in a ponytail and covering it with a cap.

She walked into the old but elegant eating establishment that featured every kind of crepe one could imagine. As soon as she stepped inside, she spotted Amelie, who also saw her and lifted her hand in a wave. Nic, sitting opposite Amelia, turned his head around to look at her and also waved. His gaze said he was surprised she'd shown up, which irritated Pippa.

She walked to the booth where Amelia and Nic sat and sank onto the red vinyl seat.

"Lovely that you joined us," Amelie said and smiled as she lifted a menu. "How shall I choose? I want one of everything."

Enchanted, Pippa picked up the menu. The array of choices was vast and mind-boggling. "What are you in the mood for?"

"Something sweet," Amelie said. "Sweet, fruity. Oh, no, chocolate, too." She shrugged helplessly.

The waitress approached. "*Bonjour.* How can I help you? Coffee?"

"Yes," Amelie said. "Café au lait."

"Tea," Pippa said.

"Coffee, black," Nic said. "Ladies, any idea what you want to order?"

"Apricot crepes. Strawberries and cream. Chocolate hazelnut. Banana cream." Amelie paused.

Wondering how the woman could possibly consume that many crepes, she exchanged a quick glance with Nic, who shook his head and rubbed his jaw. She glanced back at Amelie. "Do you want anything with protein?"

"Not particularly," Nic's mother said.

"And you?" Pippa asked Nic.

He shrugged. "I'm here for the ride."

"Can you please also bring us the crepe suzette and some carryout boxes?" Pippa asked the server.

"No problem, ma'am," she said and stared at Pippa for a long moment. "Pardon me, you look familiar."

Pippa fought a sliver of panic and held her breath. *Please don't recognize me.*

"Are you a newscaster?"

Relief rushed through her, making her almost giddy. She shook her head and smiled. "Nope, I'm just a university student. Thanks for the compliment, though."

The server's face was sheepish. "No trouble. I'll have your order up as soon as possible."

"Thank you so very much," Pippa said and after the server left, she felt the gazes of both Nic and Amelie.

Amelie sighed, lifting her shoulders and smiling with a charm that lit up the room and Pippa suddenly realized who the woman resembled. Gamin with super-expressive eyes, Amelie could have been a white-haired twin of Audrey Hepburn. "It's so wonderful to be here again. Magic. The smell is divine. I should have come back sooner, so I'll just make up for it today."

"You don't want to make yourself sick," Nic said.

"Of course not. I'll just take a bite of each, and we can take the rest back to Paul." Amelie's smile fell and she made a tsking sound. "Poor Paul. He's in such pain with his foot."

She said it as if she suffered no pain herself, but Pippa knew she did. She took a quick glance at Nic and caught the tightening of his jaw. She was struck by Amelie's determination to grab at every experience in life and Nic's struggle to hide a myriad of the emotions he was experiencing.

"I've heard the recovery from a broken foot can be a bear," Pippa said.

"Oh, and trust me, Paul is a being a complete bear," Amelie said. "He doesn't like being restrained. Never has." Amelie glanced at Nic. "It runs in the family." She turned back to Pippa with an expressive, interested gaze. "But enough about us. Tell me about you, your interests, your life. Over the years, I've read a few stories in the news about the Devereauxs, and I must confess I wondered about Edward's children. I'm sure he must have been proud of all of you."

Pippa paused. The truth was her father hadn't been very involved with any of his children. He'd given the most attention to her brother Stefan because he would be the heir, but her father was mostly pleased that he had enough children to do the work, so he could spend more time playing on his yacht. Often with women other than his wife.

"I've always been a bit of a bookworm. I'm working on my doctorate in genealogy with a specialization on the medical impact on the citizens of Chantaine. My brother Stefan is determined to improve the health care of our people, so he has approved my path of studies."

"That's fascinating," Amelie said. "What have you learned so far?"

"Like many countries, our people are more susceptible to some diseases and conditions than others. These can be traced back hundreds of years to the introduction of different immigrants, new foods and changes in our environment. The neurological disease that struck down my father can be traced back to his great-great-grandmother's family. There are also certain cancers that became more common such as when Chantaine experienced a large immigration from Iceland."

Amelie gave a slow nod. "I wonder if—" She glanced up and broke off with a smile. "The crepes are here."

Just as she'd said, Amelie only took a bite of each crepe. She savored each bite, closing her eyes and making a *mmm* sound. "I'm tempted to eat more, but I know it would be a mistake." She leaned toward Pippa and extended her hand. "Dear, I must tell you that even though I couldn't marry your father all those years ago, I wished him only the very best after we parted. I hope he was happy."

Pippa tried to think of how to respond to Amelie's words. The story about Edward and Amelie's courtship was the stuff of tabloids. Before he'd taken the throne, Prince Edward had fallen for Amelie and Amelie had been entranced by him for a short while. When she'd met Paul Lafitte, from the States, however, she'd fallen for the tall, dark Texan hook, line and sinker. The Lafittes descended from pirates and even Pippa had to agree the Lafitte men held a dark, irresistible charm.

When Amelie tried to break off her engagement, Prince Edward had refused. Paul had intervened on her behalf and there'd been a terrible brawl. Her father the prince had been humiliated and Pippa wasn't certain he'd ever truly given his heart away again.

"I think he enjoyed his life," Pippa finally said. "He loved his yacht and the sea and we always felt glad that he was able to indulge his passion."

Amelie patted Pippa's hand. "You're a lovely girl. As they say in Texas, you do him proud. Now, if you'll both excuse me while I powder my nose," she said and stood.

Nic also stood. "Need an escort?" he asked.

"Not this time, darling. Maybe you can talk Pippa into nibbling on some of those crepes," she said and walked away.

"Is she okay?" Pippa asked when he sat down.

He shrugged. "For the moment. The next moment could bring something totally different. She knows her time is short and she's decided to make the most of it. The only problem is she's turned into an eight-year-old. Impulsive, runs off without thinking. With my father down due to his broken foot, I've become her keeper."

Pippa swallowed over the knot of emotion in her throat and began to put the crepes in the carryout boxes. "I'm sure it's difficult. On the one hand, you want to give her everything she wants. On the other, you want to keep her safe. It's an impossible situation. She told me," she said, biting her lip, "that she wants to die in Chantaine."

His gaze narrowed. "That's going to be a tough wish to fulfill given the fact that my father isn't allowed to set foot on Chantaine."

Cold realization rushed through her. "I forgot all about that. I can't believe that would be enforced after all these years."

He gave a rough chuckle. "After all these years, your family still hates me. I can't take the chance that your family would lock him up in prison."

"It wouldn't be my family. It's a silly law," she said.

"Same result. It sucks, but Amelie can't have every wish on her bucket list. I'll do my damn best to make sure she gets as many as I can," he said and stood as his mother arrived at the table.

Amelie met his gaze and sighed. "We should leave, shouldn't we?"

He nodded and placed the boxes in a bag.

"Let me look around just one more moment," she said, surveying the room as if she wanted to savor each detail, the same way she'd savored each bite of the crepes. "I've already spoken to Bebe. She's lovely as is her granddaughter. *Ciao,*" she whispered and picked up the bag, then led the way to the door.

A terrible helplessness tore at Pippa as she followed Amelie out the door. She felt Nic's presence behind her and tried to tamp down the painful knot in her chest. Seeing him again had been like ripping off a bandage before the wound was healed. She'd thought the longing she'd felt for him before was awful, but now it was even worse. Knowing that he was facing some of his darkest days and that she shouldn't, couldn't, help him, was untenable. Meeting his magical mother face-to-face and seeing her courage and joy made her feel like a wimp. Her biggest challenge to date was writing her dissertation.

Amelie stopped beside Nic's Mercedes and turned to Pippa. "I hope we meet again, Your Highness. You're the nicest princess I've ever met. I'm sorry I frightened you with my annoying fainting spell. But then you gave me water and helped me remember Bebe's. I certainly came out the winner in this situation."

"I beg to differ," Pippa said. "It was my great pleasure to meet you."

"*Ciao,* darling princess," she said and Nic opened the door for her.

Pippa should have turned away, but she couldn't resist one more look at his face. It was the worst kind of craving imaginable.

He turned and met her gaze for a heart-stopping moment that took her breath away. "*Ciao,* Princess."

Still distracted by her encounter with Nic and his mother after she'd returned to the palace, Pippa started down the hallway to her living quarters. She would need to set the Lafittes' situation aside if she was going to make any progress on her research today, and heaven knows, progress had been very slow coming since she'd made the insane mistake of getting involved with Nic. The problem was that even after she'd broken off with him, he still haunted her so much that she struggled to get her work done.

Just as she turned the corner toward her quarters,

she heard a shrill scream from the other wing. *Tyler,* she thought, easily identifying one her sister's toddler stepsons. He was going through a screaming stage.

"Tyler, darling, you're not dressed," her sister Bridget called, her voice echoing down the marble hallways. "Don't—"

Pippa heard Tyler cackle with glee. She also heard the sound of her sister's heels as she ran after him. Chuckling to herself, she wondered when Bridget would learn that toddlers and high heels didn't go together. She rushed down the hall and turned another corner, spotting Tyler running toward her in all his naked glory. Bridget followed with Travis in her arms.

"Oh, Pippa, you saved my life. Can you grab him? The little beast thinks it's funny to run all over the palace bloody naked."

Tyler shrieked when he saw Pippa and skidded to a stop. Glancing over his shoulder at Bridget bearing down on him, he knew he was caught. Pippa scooped him up in her arms before he had a chance to get away.

"What are you doing? Did you just get a bath?" Pippa asked and buried her nose in his shoulder, making him laugh. "You smell like a deliciously clean little boy."

"Thank you so much," Bridget said breathlessly. "At least I got a diaper on Travis."

As soon as she stepped within touching distance, Tyler flung himself at her. "Mumma," he said and pressed an open mouth kiss against Bridget's cheek.

Bridget squeezed him against her and shifted Travis on her hip. "Now, you get all lovey-dovey," she said and gave him a kiss in return.

"Where are the nannies?" Pippa asked and held out

her hands to Travis. He fell into her arms, then stuck his thumb in his mouth.

"I gave Claire the morning off and Maria had to take care of an emergency with her mother," she said. "I had planned to check on the ranch Ryder and I are having built." Bridget rolled her eyes and laughed. "I never dreamed Stefan would permit a ranch to be built on Chantaine."

"I never would have dreamed you would live on a ranch with twin stepchildren."

"They're not steppies to me," Bridget said. "Ryder and I are in the process of making it all legal. The little perfect, gorgeous beasties will be mine just as much as they are his."

"Would you like me to watch the boys while you go check on the new house?" Pippa offered. Because Chantaine was an island, new construction was a long process and she knew both Bridget and Ryder were eager for their own place.

"I feel like I take advantage of you far too often. I know I'm not helping you get caught up on your studies...."

Pippa felt a sinking sensation in her stomach. Bridget and the boys weren't the real reason she'd had a difficult time focusing on her studies. "It's not as if you'll be gone all day," she said.

"True," Bridget said. "Only an hour or two. You're the perfect sister," Bridget said, leaning forward to give Pippa a kiss on the cheek. "Let's go back to my quarters so I can at least get my little nudist dressed before I leave."

Pippa smiled as she followed Bridget down the hall

and into her family's suite of rooms. "I think it's your outlook that has changed. Since you got married to Ryder, everything's close to perfection."

"That just goes to show the power of having a good man in your life," Bridget said. "As soon as I have more than half a moment, I must get to work on finding one for you."

Alarm shot through Pippa. "Oh, so not necessary. I still have to finish my work for my PhD."

"That won't be forever," Bridget said as she dressed wiggly Tyler.

"I can only hope," Pippa muttered.

"It won't be," Bridget said emphatically. "Besides, you can't wait forever to move on, romantically speaking. I can help with that."

"You seem to forget that our family is dreadful when it comes to matchmaking," Pippa said. "How much did you enjoy Stefan's attempts at matchmaking?"

Bridget waved her hand in a dismissive gesture. "That's different. I won't be trying to match you up with someone who can contribute to Chantaine. I'll find someone hot and entertaining."

"Lovely intentions," Pippa said. "Don't strain yourself. The boys and I will have some fun in the playroom."

"Perfect. If I'm late they can have lunch in an hour."

"Will do," Pippa said. "Are you truly going to have cattle at this ranch?"

"If Ryder has his way," Bridget said with a sigh. "If we have to take the man out of Texas, we'll just bring Texas to him. *Ciao.* I'll be back soon," she said and kissed both of the boys.

As soon as Bridget left, the twin toddlers looked at her with pouty faces. Travis's lower lip protruded and he began to whimper. Tyler joined in.

"Absolutely none of that. She'll be back before you know it." Bridget set both of them on their feet and took them by the hand. "To the playroom," she said and marched them into the small backroom. If there was one thing she'd learned about caring for toddlers, it was that it helped to be willing to make a bloody fool of herself. She immediately turned on the animal sounds CD and followed the instructions to make honking sounds. The boys dried up and joined her.

Just over an hour later, Bridget returned and Pippa could no longer escape her studies. She retreated to her room with a half sandwich for lunch. She thought of the crepes and her stomach clenched. Her mind kept wandering to the time she'd spent with Nic and his mother.

She told herself not to think about it. It wasn't her responsibility. These genealogy charts required her complete and immediate attention. She'd used every possible device to procrastinate doing her work entirely too long. Inputting her second cousin's name to the chart, she forced herself to focus. Whenever she conducted her research on people whom she knew, she often thought about their personal stories. Her second cousin Harold had moved to Tibet and his sister, Georgina, had married a man from England and was raising her children in the countryside. Pippa had always liked Georgina because she'd been such a down-to-earth sort of woman. It was a shame she didn't see her more often.

Harold and Georgina's deceased parents had owned a lovely cottage on the other side of Chantaine that was now left vacant because neither Harold nor Georgina visited Chantaine very often. Why, in fact, Pippa was certain it had been nearly eight years since either of her second cousins had set foot on Chantaine.

Pippa stopped dead, staring at the cursor on her laptop. *Vacant lovely cottage. Nic's parents.*

"Stop it," she hissed to herself. It would be incredibly disloyal. If her brother Stefan ever found out, he would never forgive her. And there was no way he wouldn't find out. Not with her security haunting her. She was lucky she'd escaped discovery today.

Back to work, she told herself sternly and worked past midnight. She finally crawled into bed, hopeful she would fall into deep sleep. Thank goodness, she did. Sometime during the night, she sank into a dream where a black limo crawled through a beautiful cemetery. Cars and people dressed in black but carrying flowers followed the limo. Everything inside her clinched with pain. A white butterfly fluttered over the black limo, capturing her attention. It could have been the spirit of…

Pippa suddenly awakened, disoriented, the images of the limo and the butterfly mingling in her mind. She sat up in bed, her heart slamming into her chest. Images of her brother Stefan, Nic, his mother, Amelie.

This wasn't her business, she told herself. Her heart ached for Nic and his mother, but she couldn't go against her family to make his mother's dream come true. She just couldn't. It wouldn't be right. It would be a terrible betrayal.

She tried to catch her breath and closed her eyes.

She tried to make her brain stop spinning. How could she possibly deceive her family for Nic? For Amelie?

But how could she not?

Chapter Two

It took most of the rest of the day to catch up with her cousin to get permission to use the cottage. Georgina was so gracious that it made Pippa feel guilty. Oh, well, if she was going to go through with providing the cottage for Nic's mother and father, then her web of deception was just getting started. The choice to deceive her family was unforgivable, but the choice to turn her back on Amelie was more unacceptable. Her stomach churned because she wasn't a dishonest person. The prospect of all the lies she would have to tell put a bad taste in her mouth.

She would normally try to reason with Stefan, but Pippa knew her entire family was unreasonable about the Lafitte matter. She would have to learn to push aside her slimy feelings about this and press on. The first task was to call Nic.

* * *

Nic studied the recent reports from his and his father's business on his tablet PC while he drank a glass of Scotch. He took a deep breath of the Mediterranean night air as he sat on the deck of his yacht anchored close enough to shore for his mother to catch a glimpse of her precious Chantaine whenever she liked. He just hoped she didn't do anything impulsive like jump overboard and swim to shore. Rubbing his chin, he shuddered at what a nightmare that would be. He couldn't put it past her, though, especially after she'd sneaked off the other morning.

Nic was caught somewhere between genie and parent, and he wasn't equipped to be either. The reports on both his father's businesses and his own looked okay for the moment, but he knew he would have to go back to the States soon for his father's company. With Amelie's illness, Paul Lafitte had understandably been distracted. Despite the fact that they'd separated on two different occasions, Amelie was the light of Paul's life and Nic wasn't sure how his father would survive after his mother… Nic didn't even want to think the word, let alone say it, even though he knew the time was coming.

Sighing, he took another sip of his Scotch and heard the vibrating buzz of his cell phone. The number on the caller ID surprised him. After his surprise meeting with Princess Pippa the other morning, he figured he'd never see her again except for public affairs.

He picked up the phone and punched the call button. "Nic Lafitte. Your Highness, what a surprise," he said, unable to keep the bite from his voice. Pippa had turned out to be the tease of his life.

"Hello. I hope I'm not interrupting anything," she said, her voice tense with nerves, which made him curious.

"Just a perfect glass of Scotch and rare solitude," he said.

A short silence followed. "Well, pardon the interruption, but I have some news that may be of interest to you."

"You called to tell me you missed me," he said, unable to resist the urge to bother her. During and after their little interlude last year, the woman had bothered the hell out of him.

He heard her sharp intake of breath and realized he'd scored. "I called about your mother."

His pleasure immediately diminished. "What about her? Have you discussed the situation with your family, and now they won't even allow her and my father in the harbor?"

"No, of course not," Pippa said. "If you would just let me finish—"

"Go ahead," he said, the semi-peacefulness of the evening now ruined.

"I found a cottage for your parents where they can stay," she said.

Nic blinked in sudden, silent surprise.

"Nic, did you hear me?"

"Yes. Repeat that please."

"I found a cottage for your parents on Chantaine," she said.

"Why?" he demanded.

Another gap of silence followed. "Um, well, I have these cousins Georgina and Harry and neither of them live in Chantaine anymore. They haven't even visited in years, and they inherited a cottage from their parents. It's been vacant, again for years, so I thought, why not?"

"Exactly," Nic said. "Why not? Except for the fact that my father has been banned from setting foot on Chantaine. I don't suppose your brother experienced a sudden wave of compassion, or just a rational moment and has decided to pardon Paul Lafitte."

"You don't need to insult Stefan," she said. "My brother is just defending my father's honor."

"Even though Stefan wouldn't have been born if your father had married Amelie," Nic said.

"Yes, I know it's not particularly logical, but the point is I have found this house. Your mother wants more time in Chantaine. Staying there can make it happen."

"You still haven't addressed the issue about my father," Nic said.

"Well, I thought we could work around that. Your mother mentioned that he broke his foot, so it's not as if he'll be able to tour much. When he does, perhaps he could wear a hat and glasses."

"And a fake mustache?" he added, rolling his eyes. It was a ludicrous plan.

"I know it's not perfect," she said.

"Far from it," he said.

"But it's better than nothing."

"I can't take the chance that my father will end up in jail."

"Perhaps that's not your decision to make," she countered, surprising him.

"What do you mean by that?"

"I mean shouldn't he be given the choice?" she asked. "Besides, your father's presence may never be discovered. It's not as if there are copies of his photo posted everywhere the way you do in the States."

"It's called a Wanted Poster, and they're mostly just displayed in post offices and convenience stores these days. We've progressed since the Wild West days," he said.

"Exactly," she said. "And so have we. No one has been beheaded in over one hundred and fifty years, and we haven't used the dungeon as a prison for nearly a hundred."

"Why don't I feel better? I know that Chantaine doesn't operate under the policy of innocent until proven guilty. Your judicial system, and I use the term loosely, moves slower than the process of turning coal into diamonds."

"I didn't call to debate my country's judicial system. I called to offer a place to stay for your mother and father. If you want it, I shall arrange to have it cleaned and prepared for them. Otherwise…" She paused and he heard her take a breath.

"Otherwise?" he prompted.

"Otherwise, *ciao,*" she said and hung up on him.

Nic blinked again. Princess Pippa wasn't the rollover he'd thought she was. He downed the rest of his exquisite Scotch, barely tasting it. What the hell. She had surprised him. Now he had to make a decision. Although his father had caused trouble for the entire family, Nic felt protective of him, especially in his father's current state with his broken foot and his grief over Amelie.

Nic closed his eyes and swore under his breath. He

already knew how his father would respond if given the choice of risking prosecution in Chantaine. Paul Lafitte was a blustering bear and bull. He would love the challenge…even if he was in traction and confined to the house.

Raking his hand through his hair, he knew what he had to do. He walked inside to the stateroom lounge where his father dozed in front of the television. A baseball game was playing and his father was propped in an easy chair snoring.

Maybe he should wait until tomorrow, Nic thought and turned off the television.

His father gave a loud snort and his eyes snapped open. "What happened? Who's ahead?"

"Rangers," Nic lied. The Rangers were having a terrible season.

"Yeah, and I'm the Easter bunny," his father said.

Nic gave a dry laugh. His father was selective with the use of denial, and apparently he wasn't going to exercise that muscle with the Rangers tonight. "Good luck hopping," he said. "You need anything to drink?"

"Nah. Take a seat. What's on your mind? I can tell something's going on," he said, waving his hand as if the yacht belonged to him instead of Nic.

Nic sank onto the sofa next to his father. "I got an interesting call tonight."

"Must have been a woman. Was she pregnant?" his father asked.

Nic gave a short laugh. "Nothing like that. I've been offered a cottage where you and Mom can stay. On Chantaine."

His dad gave a low whistle. "How did you manage that?"

Nic shrugged. "Lucky, I guess. The problem is you still have legal issues in Chantaine."

His dad smiled and rubbed his mouth. "So I do, and punching Prince Edward in the face after he insulted your mother was worth it ten times over."

"Easy to say, but if you stay in Chantaine, there's a possibility that you could get caught." Nic shook his head. "Dad, with their legal system, you could be stuck in jail for a while."

"So?" he asked.

"So, it's a risk. You're not the young buck you once were. You could end up stuck there while Mom is..." He didn't want to say the rest.

His father narrowed his eyes. It was an expression Nic had seen several times on his father's face. The dare a pirate couldn't deny. He descended from wily pirates. His father was no different, although his father had gotten caught a few times. "Your mother wants to rest in Chantaine. We'll accept the kind offer of your friend. To hell with the Devereauxs."

"Might not want to go that far," Nic said, thinking another glass of Scotch was in order. "A Devereaux is giving you the cottage."

"Well, now that sounds like quite the story," his father said, his shaggy eyebrows lifted high on his forehead.

"Another time," Nic said. "You need to rest up for your next voyage."

His father gave a mysterious smile. "If my great-

great-grandfather escaped the authorities on a peg leg,
I can do it with a cast."

Nic groaned. "No need to push it, Dad."

The next morning, he dialed the princess.

"Hello," she said in a sleep-sexy voice that did weird
things to his gut.

"This is Nic. We'll accept your kind offer. Meet me
at the cottage and I'll clean it. The less people involved,
the better."

Silence followed. "I didn't think of that," she confessed. "I'm accustomed to staff taking oaths of silence."

He smiled at her naïveté. "This is a different game.
Too many people need to be protected. You, my mother
and father. We need to keep this as quiet and low-profile
as possible."

"Okay. I'll meet you at the cottage mid-morning,"
she said.

"What about your security?" he asked.

"I'll tell them I'm going to the library," she said.

"Won't they follow you?"

"I'll go to the library first. They'll get bored. They
always do."

"Who are these idiots on your security detail?" he
asked.

"Are you complaining?"

"No," he said. "And yes."

She laughed, and the breathless sound made his chest
expand. He suddenly felt lighter. "How do you end up
with the light end of the security detail?"

"I'm boring. I don't go clubbing. I've never been on

drugs. I babysit my nieces and nephews. I study genealogy, for bloody's sake."

He nodded, approving her M.O. "Well done, but does
that fence ever feel a little too tall for you? Ever want
to climb out?"

"I climb out when I want," she said in a cool voice.
"I'll see you this afternoon around 1:00 p.m. The address is 307 Sea Breeze. *Ciao,*" she said and hung up
before he could reply.

Nic pulled the phone away from his ear and stared
at it. He was unaccustomed to having anyone hang up
on him, let alone a woman. He must have really gotten
under Pippa's skin to affect her manners that way. The
possibility brought him pleasure. Again, he liked the
idea of *bothering* her.

Just before one, he pulled past the overgrown hedges
of the driveway leading to an expansive bungalow.
Looked like there was a separate guest bedroom. Dibs,
he thought. He could sleep there and keep track of his
parents while keeping on top of the businesses.

He stopped his car behind another—Pippa's. He recognized it from the other day. Curious, he stepped from
his vehicle and walked to the front door and knocked.
He waited. No answer. He knocked again.

No answer again, so he looked at the doorknob and
picked the lock. Pirates had their skills. He opened the
door and was shocked speechless at the sight in front of
him. Pippa, dressed in shorts and a T-shirt with her wild
hair pulled back in a ponytail, was vacuuming the den.

The princess had a very nice backside, which he enjoyed watching for a full moment…okay, two.

Pippa turned and spotted him, screaming and dropping the vacuum handle. She clutched her throat with her hands. The appliance made a loud groan of protest.

"Did you consider knocking?" she demanded.

He lifted two fingers, then pulled up the vacuum cleaner handle and turned it off. "Twice. You didn't answer. I would have never dreamed you could be a cleaning fairy. This is a stretch."

"I spent a couple summers in a rustic camp in Norway. Cleaning was compulsory. We also cleaned the homes of several of the camp leaders."

"You didn't mention this to your parents?" he asked.

She laughed. "I didn't speak to my parents very often. I mentioned something about it to my nanny after the second summer and was never sent back after that. The cleaning wasn't that bad. The camp had a fabulous library and no one edited my reading choices. Heaven for me," she said.

"Will clean for books?" he said.

She smiled and met his gaze. "Something like that."

He held her gaze for a long moment and saw the second that her awareness of him hit her. Breaking the visual connection, she cleared her throat. "Well, I should get back to work."

"Anything special you want me to do?"

"Mop the floors if you don't mind. I've already dusted the entire house, but haven't touched the guest quarters outside. I think it would also be a good idea for you to assess the arrangement of the furniture throughout the house for any special needs your parents may have, such as your father's foot problem. We don't want him tripping and prolonging his recovery."

"I don't know. It might be a good thing if my father is immobile. He could cause trouble when he's full strength," Nic said. "He's always been a rebellious, impulsive man. I hate to say it, but he might just take a trip out of the house so he can feel like he's flying in the face of your family."

Pippa winced. "He wouldn't admit his name, would he?"

"I hope not. That's part of the reason I wasn't sure this was a good idea," he said.

"What made you change your mind?"

"You did. My father will be okay if he's reminded that his responsibility is to make this time for my mother as trouble-free as possible. I'll make sure he gets that message in multiple modalities every day."

"Thank you very much," she said.

"If you're so terrified that your family will find out, why did you take this risk for yourself? Your relationship with your brothers and sisters will never be the same if they know you did this."

She took a deep breath and closed her eyes for a half beat as if to bolster her determination. "I hate the idea of disappointing my brothers and sisters. I hate it more than you can imagine, but I wouldn't be able to live with myself if I could help your mother with this one wish if I had the ability. And I have the ability."

"I'll do what I can to make sure the rest of the Devereauxs don't find out. I haven't told my mother yet about the cottage. She's going to be very excited."

Pippa smiled. "I hope so."

"Thanks," he said. "I'll go check out the bedrooms."

An hour later, after Pippa finished vacuuming and tackled the kitchen, she found Nic cleaning the hall

bathroom. It was an ironic sight. Hot six-foot-four international businessman scrubbing the tub. Just as he
wouldn't expect to find her turn into a cleaning machine, she wouldn't expect the same of him, either. She
couldn't help admiring the way his broad shoulders followed the shape of a V to his waist. Even in a T-shirt,
the man looked great from behind. Bloody shame for
her. *Get your mind out of the gutter.*

He turned around before she had a chance to clear
her throat or utter a syllable. She stared at him speechless for a second, fearing he could read her mind. *Not
possible,* she told herself as she felt her cheeks heat with
embarrassment.

"Can I help you?" he asked.

In too many ways, she thought, but refused to dwell
on them. "I'm almost finished with the kitchen, and it
occurred to me that it might be a good idea to arrange
for some groceries to be picked up for your parents before they arrive."

"Groceries?" he echoed.

"Yes, I was hoping you could help with a list."

He made a face. "I don't do a lot of grocery shopping. My housekeeper takes care of that."

"I have less experience with grocery shopping that
I do with cleaning. That's why I thought we could send
someone."

"Who can we trust?" he asked.

She winced. "Excellent point."

"After we move them in, I'll just arrange for a member of my staff from the yacht to take care of house and
shopping duties," he said. "But unless we want to delay

their move-in, it looks like we'll need to do the initial run ourselves."

"We?" she squeaked.

"I didn't think it would be nice to ask you to do it by yourself," he said.

But it had clearly crossed his mind. She frowned.

"Will that put you a little close for comfort to the plebeians?"

"No," she told him, detesting the superior challenging expression on his face. "I was just trying to remember if I'd left my cap in my vehicle."

"I have an extra," he said. "I'll take you in my car."

"What about the list?"

"We'll wing it," he said.

Moments later, she grabbed her cap from her car and perched her oversize sunglasses on her nose. She didn't bother to look at her reflection. After spending the afternoon cleaning, she knew she didn't look like anyone's idea of a princess. Nic opened the passenger door for her and she slid into his car.

After he climbed into the driver's side, the space inside his Mercedes seemed to shrink. She inhaled to compensate for the way her lungs seemed to narrow at Nic's proximity, but only succeeded in drawing in a draft of the combination of his masculine scent and subtle but sexy cologne. He pulled out of the driveway.

"Which way to the nearest market?" he asked.

Pippa blinked. She had no idea.

"Here," he said, handing her his phone. "Find one on my smartphone."

It took a couple moments, and Nic had to backtrack, but they were moving in the right direction.

"I'm thinking eggs, milk, bread and perhaps some fruit," she said, associating each item with one of her fingers. It was a memory trick she'd taught herself when she was young. The only problem was when she ran out of fingers.

"Chocolate, cookies and wine," Nic added. "A bakery cake if we can find it. My mother's priority for eating healthy went down the tubes after her last appointment with the doctor. My dad will want booze and carbs. His idea of health food is a pork roast with a loaded baked potato."

"Oh, my," she said, trying to wrap her head around Nic's list versus hers. "I hope we can find—"

"They'll be happy with whatever we get for the first twenty-four hours," Nic said as he pulled into the parking lot. "Let's just do this fast," he added and pulled on a ball cap of his own. "The faster we move, the less chance you have of being discovered."

"I think I'm well-disguised," she said as he opened the door and helped her out of the car.

"Until you open your mouth," he said.

"What do you mean by that?"

He led her toward the door of the market. "I mean you have a refined, distinctive voice, PD. A combination of husky sweet and so proper you could have been in Regency England."

"PD," she echoed, then realized PD stood for Pippa Devereaux. "Well, at least I *look* ordinary," she huffed.

He stopped beside her. "And I don't," he said, tugging on his ball cap.

She allowed herself a forbidden moment of looking at him from head to toe. He could have been dressed in rags and he would be sexy. She swallowed an oath. "You don't know the meaning of ordinary," she said and walked in front of him.

Hearing Nic grab a cart behind her, she moved toward the produce. "Surely, they'd enjoy some fruit. Your mother seemed to favor fruit crepes the other day."

"They were wrapped in sugar," he said as she picked up a bunch of bananas and studied them. "In the basket," he instructed. "We have a need for speed, PD."

"I'm not sure I like being called PD," she said, fighting a scowl as she put the bananas in the cart.

He pressed his mouth against her ear. "Would you prefer PP instead? For Princess Pippa?"

A shiver of awareness raced through her and she quickly stepped away. "Not at all," she said and picked up an apricot. "Does this look ripe?"

"It's perfect," he said, swiping it from her hand and added two more to the cart. "Now, move along."

She shot him an affronted look but began to walk. "No one except my brothers or sisters would dream of speaking to me that way."

"One of my many charms, PD," he said and tossed a loaf of bread into the cart.

Moments later, after throwing several items into the cart, they arrived at the register. Pippa picked up a bag of marshmallows.

"Good job," he said.

"I thought they could make that camping dessert you Americans eat," Pippa said. She'd read about it in a book.

"Camping treat?" he echoed.

"Some More of something," she said.

His eyes widened. "S'mores," he said. "We need chocolate bars and graham crackers. Get him to hold you," he said and strode away.

"Hold me?" she said at the unfamiliar expression and caught the cashier studying her. He was several years younger than she was with rings and piercing in places that made her think *ouch*.

He leaned toward her. "If you need holding, I can help you after I finish my shift," he said in a low voice.

Embarrassment flooded through her. She was rarely in a position for a man to flirt with her. Her brother usually set her up with men at least twenty years older, who wouldn't dare make an improper advance, so she wasn't experienced with giving a proper response. "The grocery order," she finally managed. "I was repeating what my, uh, friend said. He misspoke, as he often does. The grocery order need holding."

The cashier looked disappointed. "The customer behind you is ready."

Pippa considered pulling royal rank, but knew it would only hurt her in the end, so she stepped aside and allowed the person behind her with a mammoth order go first.

Less than a moment later, Nic appeared with chocolate bars and graham crackers. He glanced at the person in front of her and frowned. "How did that happen? I told you to hold the cashier."

"There was a mix-up and he thought I wanted, uh, him for reasons other than his professional duties. When I refused his kind invitation, he felt spurned and allowed the customer behind me to proceed." She sighed. "Do all men have such delicate egos?"

Nic lifted a dark brow before he pulled his sunglasses over his eyes. "Depends on how many mixed messages we get. Poor guy."

Chapter Three

"Are you sure you want to read to Stephenia tonight?" Eve Jackson Devereaux, the wife to the crown prince of Chantaine, asked in her Texas twang as she walked with Pippa to her stepdaughter's room inside the royal master suite. "You look a little tired."

"I wouldn't dream of missing it. You and Stefan enjoy a few extra moments this evening. You deserve it."

"You are a dream sister," Eve said.

Pippa felt her heart squeeze at how Eve left off at the in-law. "As are you," she said and studied her sister-in-law. "You look like you could use a long night's rest yourself."

Eve frowned and pressed her hands to her cheeks. "Oh, no. Maybe I need one of those spa boosts Bridget is always talking about."

"Or just rest," Pippa said. "You may be Texan, but you're not superhuman."

Eve laughed. "If you say so. I didn't want to ask, but I have a routine medical appointment tomorrow. Can you backup for the nanny?"

It wasn't convenient, but Eve so rarely asked that she couldn't refuse. "No problem. You're sure it's just routine?" she asked.

Eve smiled. "Nothing else. Thank you. I knew I could count on you. But Stefan and I were talking the other night and we both realized how much you do for all the nieces and nephews. You're due some happy times of your own and we're going to work on that."

"Work?" Pippa echoed, fighting a sliver of panic. She definitely did not want to become the object of her family's attention. Especially now. "How?"

Eve shot her a sly look that frightened her. "You'll find out soon enough."

"There's no need to work that hard," Pippa said. "I'm busy with my dissertation and—"

"Don't worry. Just enjoy," Eve said.

"Right," Pippa said nervously. "Don't work too hard."

Eve opened the door to Stephenia's room where the three-year-old sat playing with her toys. "Steffie, I thought you wanted Pippa to read to you tonight. You're not in bed."

Stephenia immediately crawled into bed with an innocent expression on her face, her ringlet curls bouncing against her flushed cheeks. "I'm in bed," she said in her tiny voice, which never failed to make Pippa's heart twist.

Eve tossed a sideways glance at Pippa and whispered, "She's such a heart stealer. We're so screwed."

Pippa laughed under her breath. "Thank goodness Stefan has you. I'm lucky. She'll fall asleep by the time I finish the second book."

"Or first," Eve said in a low voice. "She's been a Tazmanian devil today. I have to believe she's spent some of her energy."

Stephenia lifted her arms. "Mamaeve."

Pippa knew Eve had felt reluctant to take on the name of Stephenia's mother even though the woman had perished in a boating accident. Out of respect, Eve had taught the child *Mamaeve*. Eve rushed toward the child and enveloped her in a loving hug.

"Daddy?" Stephenia asked.

"In the shower," Eve said. "He'll kiss you good-night, but you may already be asleep."

Steffie sighed and gave Eve an extra hug. The sight was heartwarming to Pippa because she'd mostly been raised by hired nannies. She knew it could have been much worse, but it gave her such relief to know that her nieces and nephews would have such a different life than she'd experienced.

"Pippa," Stephenia said, extending her arms, and it occurred to Pippa that she would fight an army to get to her niece.

"I'll let you two go to *Where the Wild Things Are*," Eve said, backing toward the door and giving a little wave. "Sweet dreams."

"Good night," Pippa said.

"'Night Mamaeve."

Eve smiled and left the room closing the door behind her.

Pippa sank onto Stephenia's twin bed and pulled the child against her. *Where the Wild Things Are* was especially appropriate for Stephenia because the child had been such a bloody screamer when she'd first arrived at the palace. Stephenia was the product of a relationship between her brother Stefan and a model who'd never bothered to tell Stefan about his child. He'd only learned about Stephenia after the mother's death. It had been a shock to the family and the country of Chantaine, but everyone had taken Stephenia into their hearts. How could they not? She had Stefan's eyes and spirit and she was beautiful.

Pippa began to read the book and before she was halfway through, Stephenia was slumped against her, sleeping. She felt the warmth of sleepy drool on her shirt underneath the child's face. Pippa chuckled to herself and carefully situated Stephenia onto the bed. She brushed a kiss onto her niece's head and slid out of the bed, leaving the book on the nightstand. Pippa turned off the light and kissed Stephenia once more, then quietly left the room.

As she walked down the hall, she wondered, not for the first time, if or when she would have children of her own. Pippa knew she'd been shielded from normal relationships with the opposite sex. Every date, and there'd been few, had to be vetted by Stefan, the advisers and of course, security. The only relationship she'd had that approached normality had been her brief *thing* with Nic. She supposed she couldn't really call it an affair because they hadn't done the deed, but Nic hadn't bowed to her unless he'd been joking. He'd treated her like a desirable woman. Pippa couldn't remember another time when she'd felt genuinely desirable.

She rolled her eyes at herself as she entered her small suite. She had far more important things to do than worry about feeling desirable. Thinking back to what Eve had said about how she and Stefan were planning to work on her happiness, she cringed. This was *not* the time.

Nic moved his parents into the cottage. The activity exhausted both of them, so they were taking naps, his mom using her oxygen. She'd begun to use it every night. Nic had adjusted the bed so that her head would be elevated. Many days his mother hid her illness well, but lately he could tell she'd had a harder time of it. She resisted taking too much pain medication, complaining that it made her sleepy. Amelie was determined to get every drop of life she could, and she was giving Nic a few lessons he hadn't expected along the way.

He'd brought over a few members of his crew to clean the pool and jacuzzi and get them operational as soon as possible. He dug into the labor with his men, hoping that expending physical energy would help relieve some of his frustration. Even though he mentally knew that he couldn't make his mother well, he had a bunch of crazy feelings that he spent a lot of effort denying. It was important that he continue that denial because his parents sure as hell had enough on their own plates without his crap.

As he cleaned the side of the pool wall with a brush, he spotted Pippa coming through the gate carrying a bag. She was wearing a skirt that fluttered around her knees and a lacy cotton blouse. As usual, her wild hair was pulled into a topknot. He'd always thought her hair was a sign that she wasn't nearly as proper as she seemed. He knew she considered herself the plainest of the Devereaux sisters, but during that brief period they'd spent time together, he sure had enjoyed making her fair skin blush with embarrassment or pleasure. She was the most sincere and sweetest woman he'd ever met.

Appearing intent on her plan, whatever that was, she walked right past him as if she didn't see him. Just as she lifted her hand to the door to knock, he gave a loud wolf whistle.

His men stopped their work and gaped at him. Pippa stood stock-still, then lifted her hand again to knock. "Hey, PD," he called, climbing out of the pool. "What's the rush?"

Hearing his voice, she whirled around to look at him. "I didn't see you." She glanced at the pool. "You were working?" she said as if such a thought was impossible.

"Yes, I pitch in with manual labor every now and then. It's good for the soul, if I have one, and it usually helps me get a good night's sleep." He liked the way her gaze skimmed over his shoulders and chest, then as if she realized, she was looking where she shouldn't, her gaze fastened on his nose. "My parents are both taking naps. They're worn out from the move."

"It's already done," she said. "You move quickly."

"When it's necessary," he said, thinking perhaps he'd given Pippa too much wiggle room all those months ago.

The door suddenly opened and his mother, wiping

sleep from her eyes, blinked at the sunlight. "What—"
She broke off when she saw Pippa and her lips lifted in
a smile. "Well, hello, fairy princess," she said.

"Mom," Nic said. "Don't use the P word. Remember
this is all on the down low."

"Oh, sorry," she said with a delicate wince. "I'm
just so grateful and you made it happen with the snap
of your fingers."

"My cousins made it easy," Pippa said.

"But you made the call," Nic's mother said. "I must
leave them something in my will."

Pippa bit her lip.

"TMI, Mom," Nic said. "What's in the bag?" he
asked Pippa.

"Gelato," she said. "I know we got ice cream yesterday, but this is from one of our favorite gelaterias."

"Let me think of the name," his mother said. "It's on
the tip of my tongue."

Pippa opened her mouth, then closed it.

His mother's eyes widened. "Henri's."

"Yes," Pippa said, clearly thrilled. "You have a great
memory."

"Bet you brought hazelnut chocolate," his mother
said.

"Yes, and a new flavor from the States. Rocky Road.
It has marshmallows, chocolate and nuts. Worth a try,"
Pippa said with a shrug.

"I'll say," his mom said. "Let's taste it now or I'll
have to fight the mister for that one."

Nic chuckled at the interchange between his mother
and Pippa.

"What are you laughing at?" his mother asked. "Be careful or you'll get no gelato."

"No gelato for me. Water now and beer later," he said.

"Spoil sport," his mother said and he guided Pippa and his mother inside the house.

"I didn't know you were going to fill the pool," his mother said. "Could be a waste," she warned.

"If you enjoy it once, it won't be," he said, heading toward the kitchen. "If you enjoy thinking about taking a dip in the pool or Jacuzzi, then that's enough, Mom," he called over his shoulder as he went to the kitchen and grabbed a bottle of water.

"You're such a good son," she said.

"Does that mean I get some of that gelato?" he asked as he reentered the room.

"And you are the very devil," she said. "Just like your father."

He glanced at both his mother and Pippa. "And you know I'm not anyone but me," he reminded her.

"True," she said. "But he is a scoundrel," she said to Pippa.

"I agree," Pippa said, her eyes swimming with emotions that reflected the drama of the moment. "Well, I can't stay, and I must confess I thought you might not even move in until tomorrow, but I clearly underestimated your son."

"It's not the first time I've been underestimated," he said, meeting Pippa's gaze.

She gnawed on her lower lip and he felt a tug toward her. He'd made a mistake with that before, but something about her got under his skin. He'd known a few women. Some as beautiful as beauty queens and world-class models. Why did she affect him this way?

"I'll try not to do the same thing again," she said.

He shrugged. "We'll see."

"I want gelato," his mother said.

"Then you shall have gelato," Nic said.

Pippa met his gaze, then looked away and walked to the kitchen. "Let me scoop it for you, Mrs. Lafitte. I hope I didn't overdo the chocolate."

"Call me Amelie," she said as she followed Pippa into the kitchen. "And you can never overdo chocolate."

"That's good to know," Pippa said and searched through several drawers for a scoop. "There we go," she said and dipped a scoop of both flavors into a bowl. "Enjoy," she said with a smile on her face.

She shot an uncertain glance at Nic. "Would you like some?"

"I'll wait until later," he said, noting the way Pippa pressed her lips together.

She nodded. "I should go," Pippa said.

"Oh, no," his mother said. "You just arrived."

"You need to rest. You've had a busy day," Pippa said.

His mother frowned. "Promise you'll return."

"Of course I will," Pippa said. "Don't let your gelato melt."

"You're so right," his mother said and dipped her spoon into the treat.

"I'll walk you to your car," Nic said.

"I can do that myself," she said.

"No," he said and escorted her to the driveway. "You need to know," he told her. "It's going to go down from here. She was good just now, but she's struggling and it's just going to get worse. A lot of people wouldn't be able to handle it...."

She stopped and turned, looking offended. "I'm not a lot of people. I'm not the type of person to abandon someone when—" She broke off and realization crossed her face. "You said that because I broke off our relationship."

He shrugged. "If the shoe fits."

"That was a totally different situation," she said. "It was a temporary flirtation. You and I are not at all well-suited."

"Because your family hates mine," Nic said, feeling a twist of impatience.

"That's part of it. There's no good reason for us to continue a relationship when we know there's no future. It was sheer craziness on my part."

He laughed. "Good to know. You're saying you weren't really attracted to me. You were just temporarily insane."

"I—I didn't say that," she said.

Nic watched the color bloom in her cheeks with entirely too much pleasure.

"And what if my last name was not Lafitte?" he had to ask because the question had dug at him at odd moments.

Her expression changed and a hint of vulnerability deepened her eyes. She opened her mouth, then closed it and looked away. "I can't let my mind consider that because you are who you are. I am who I am." She shook her head and turned toward her vehicle. "I need to leave. I'll check on your mother la—"

Nic saw her foot catch on a tree root and instinctively caught her as she tripped. He pulled her against him and inhaled her soft, feminine scent and felt her body cling to him. For about three seconds. Then she pushed at his arm and moved away from him.

"I should have been watching. Sorry," she said and met his gaze.

"No big deal. You're okay. That's what matters," he said.

In that moment, in her gaze, he saw the same tug and pull of feelings that he had inside him about her, about them. There was so much she wasn't saying that she looked as if she could nearly pop from it. "Thank you," she finally said.

"Ciao," he said and watched her as she got into her car and drove away. There was unfinished business here for both of them, he thought. He'd tried to leave Pippa behind, but something about her nagged at him like a fly in the room he couldn't catch. He needed to find a way to get her out of his system.

That night Pippa dressed for the family dinner her brother Stefan had called. With her youngest brother playing soccer in Spain, and her oldest two sisters and their families out of the country, that left Bridget, her husband, Ryder, the twins and Stefan and Eve and Stephenia. She was extremely bothered from her visit with Nic and his mother this afternoon. Amazing how such a brief time in the man's presence could disrupt her so much. She'd suspected he would get over her in no time. He was far more experienced than she was. There must have been a dozen women ready and willing to soothe his ego.

Yet, he acted as if he was still irritated by the fact that she'd ended things. It wasn't as if she'd truly dumped him. They had never had a public relationship, just a few furtive meetings. She couldn't deny he'd made her knees melt with the way he'd looked at her, and the connection she'd felt with him had made her breathless. She also couldn't deny that he'd acted as if he were attracted to her, as if she meant something to him.

The truth was part of the reason she'd refused to see him again was because her out-of-control feelings frightened her. If ever a man was unsafe, it was Nic Lafitte. Yet she'd found him irresistible which only proved that she must have some sort of self-destructive tendency inside her that she hadn't known existed. Now that she knew she had this tendency, she had to beware of it and fight it if it ever reared its head again.

Pippa looked into the mirror and adjusted her topknot of out-of-control hair. She called it her curse. Every once in a while, the humidity lowered and her hair was almost controllable. Not today, though. Putting on a little lip gloss, she dismissed it and her other thoughts and headed toward the royal dining room.

Stefan had instigated the "family dinners" a couple years ago. Ever since Bridget had gotten married, she'd felt the odd man out at the dinners. She'd worked around those feelings by focusing on her nephews and niece. But still…

Entering the dining room, she spotted Bridget and Ryder holding the twins while Eve chased Stephenia.

With the three high chairs, the palace looked far different from last year.

"Stefan will be here any minute. No need to put the darlings in the high chairs until then. How was your day?" Eve asked Pippa.

"Good," Pippa lied. "Made a little progress on my research."

"Good," Ryder said as he held Tyler and shifted from foot to foot. "Your genealogy studies could really help me with medical plans for Chantaine. I'm working on health prevention at the moment, and I'd like to see a better developed hospice plan in space."

Pippa's stomach clenched at the mention of hospice, although she wished Amelie could have access to such a program. "Both of those are vital. We're very fortunate Bridget brought you to us."

Bridget held Travis and smiled up at Ryder. "I can't agree with you more," she said as she jiggled the boy. "I hope Stefan doesn't take much longer or this family dinner is going to turn into a family scream-in."

Eve winced. "He said it would be just a moment."

"Yes, but we all know it's tough being crown prince and we're glad he's doing it and not us."

Seconds later, Stefan entered the small room with a broad smile. "You're all here. And healthy. This is good."

"And rare," Bridget added. "Given the twins' on-and-off sniffles. We'd better get on with the family dinner. I can't promise how long they'll last."

"No problem," Stefan said. "Sit down and relax. The food will arrive immediately. My assistant advised the chef."

The small group situated the children and sank into their chairs as staff poured water and wine for the adults and juice for the young ones. Before too much fussing, a server brought Cheerios for the babies.

"Takes them longer to pick up," Eve said with a smile.

"Well done," Bridget said.

"The main course will arrive in just a moment. I'd like to take this moment to share some good news. Eve and I are expecting our first child."

"Second, including Stephenia," Eve added.

"Oh, how wonderful. Another baby," Bridget crowed. "Takes the pressure off me."

Pippa laughed at her sister's reaction. "And me."

Bridget and Eve gasped at the same time. "You wouldn't dare. You're the good sister."

"Oh, no," Bridget corrected herself. "That's what we said about Valentina and she got pregnant before she was married."

"I was just joking," Pippa said.

"Thank you," Stefan said as he lifted his glass of wine and took a hefty sip. "One heart attack at a time, please."

"Besides," Bridget said as the staff served filet of sole. "We have plans for you."

Pippa felt a sliver of nervousness and took a sip of her own wine. "You and Eve keep talking about plans. You're making me uneasy."

"They're good plans," Bridget said as she set a plate of cheese, chicken and vegetables on Tyler's tray.

"We know you've been cooped up working on your degree," Eve added.

"Chantaine has several celebratory events scheduled during the next few weeks," Stefan said.

Pippa took a bite of the perfectly prepared fish.

"And we're going to set you up with some of the most eligible bachelors on the planet," Bridget said gleefully. "How exciting is that?"

Pippa's bite of fish stuck in her throat. "What?"

"It will be fun," Bridget said.

"No pressure," Eve said. "We just want you to enjoy yourself. You work hard with your nephews and niece and your studies."

"It's occurred to me," Stefan said, "that you haven't had many opportunities to form relationships with men. You've been protected. Perhaps overprotected."

Pippa's stomach tightened. "How lovely of you all to decide it's time for me to have a relationship. Without consulting me, of course."

Silence descended over the room. Even the children were silent as they munched on their food.

"We thought this would make you happy," Bridget said. "You work so hard. We wanted you to have some fun."

"Would you want your sisters and brother to make decisions about men you would date?" Pippa challenged.

Bridget winced. "When you put it that way..." she said.

"I am," Pippa said. "I don't need or want you to find dates for me. It's embarrassing," she said, her appetite completely gone.

"We don't intend it to be embarrassing," Stefan said. "Your position in the royal family makes it difficult for you to socialize with men. We'd like to make that easier."

"The same way the advisers tried to make it easy for you," Pippa said, setting down her fork.

"There's no call for that," Stefan said.

"And there's no call for matchmaking for me," Pippa said.

"Pippa, you haven't been the same since the incident with—" Bridget cleared her throat and lowered her voice. "That horrible Nic Lafitte. We just want to help you get over it."

"I'm completely over it. I know he was only interested in me to make a point with his ego." Even as she said the words she knew her family wanted to hear, she felt as if she were stabbing herself. "I may be naive, but I'm not a complete fool." She debated leaving the table, but knew her family would only worry more about her. She lifted her drink. "We have more important things to celebrate. Cheers to Stefan and Eve's new baby. May your pregnancy be smooth and may your child sparkle with the best of both of you."

Ryder lifted his glass. "Here, here."

"Here, here," Bridget said.

Tyler let out a blood-curdling scream, and the tension was broken. Soon enough, Travis joined. Stephenia followed.

Most important the focus was no longer on Pippa. She took another big sip of wine and knew she wouldn't be able to eat one more bite of food. With the children providing a welcome distraction, she gave a discreet signal to one of the servers, who immediately removed her plate. As she looked at each face of her family, she felt a combination of love and sheer and total frustration. She wished she could scream just like Tyler did.

Chapter Four

Two days later, Pippa mustered the time and courage to visit the Lafittes. The name Lafitte was like pyrotechnics as far as her family was concerned. Perhaps she should mentally give them another name so her stomach didn't clench every time she even thought it. Instead of Lafitte, she could think of them as the LaLas. Much less threatening. No unnecessary baggage with LaLa.

The idea appealed to her and Pippa smiled to herself when she thought about it, which was entirely too often. It was difficult not to become impatient with her sisters and brothers over the feud with the Lafittes. After all, the Lafittes were human, too. Look at their current situation with Amelie trying to make it through her dying days and poor Paul with his broken foot. And poor Nic trying to manage all of it.

Sighing, she pulled into the driveway and stopped the car. She glanced over her shoulder even though she was certain her security guy had been dozing when she'd left. That was Pippa. She knew well how to bore a man to sleep. She glanced in the mirror and bared her teeth at herself.

Grabbing the flowers from the passenger seat, she got out of the car and braced herself for the possibility of seeing Nic in workman mode in a tight T-shirt and slim-fitting jeans. Walking into the courtyard, however, she saw no workers around and the pool and Jacuzzi were full of fresh clean water. The sunlight glinting on the water made it all the more enticing, but she suspected the water was frigid.

The house was so quiet and peaceful she wondered if Amelie and Paul might be napping again. She hesitated as she stood in front of the door, not wanting to disturb their rest.

"Hey."

Pippa turned at the sound of Nic's voice as he walked from the guest quarters closer to the driveway. "Hello," she said. "I was afraid to interrupt. It's so quiet."

"I heard your car in the driveway," he said. "Last I checked both my parents are napping again, although I think my mom is getting restless. She'll need a field trip soon. Nice flowers. Come on inside," he said and opened the door to the cottage. He paused, cocking his head to one side. "I'll check to see if the bedroom door is still closed. Just a minute."

She watched him walk down the hallway. Seconds later, he returned, his face creased with concern. "She's gone."

Pippa bit her lip, feeling a quick spurt of apprehension. She couldn't help remembering how Amelie had fainted the last time she'd gone out on her own. "Are you sure she's not somewhere else in the house? Taking a nice long bath. Maybe she's in the kitchen."

He shook his head as he walked toward the kitchen. "I could see the open door of the bathroom." He glanced in the kitchen. "Not there. This isn't good."

"Maybe she went for a little walk in the neighborhood," Pippa suggested hopefully.

"The problem with my mother is that she doesn't take little walks. She probably escaped when I was working and the new house staff went to the market. I thought she was sleeping," he said and swore under his breath. "I have to go look for her."

"But where?" Pippa asked, watching his muscles bunched with tension even as he rolled his shoulders.

"I don't know, but I can't sit here waiting. I'll leave a note for Dad and Goldie. He'll be helping out here at the cottage for the time being."

Wanting to help, she impulsively offered, "I'll go with you." She suspected she surprised herself as much as she'd surprised him.

He gave the offer a flicker of consideration, then shook his head. "There's nothing you can do. I'll call or text you when I find out anything."

His easy dismissal of her irritated her. "I do know Chantaine better than you do."

"What's to know? The island isn't that big," he said.

"Did you know about Bebe's Crepes?" she asked.

"No, but—" He broke off and raked his hand through his dark hair. "Okay. But my first priority is finding my mother. If you're afraid someone may be able to identify you, you'll just have to duck behind the seat."

"Yes. Just let me put the flowers in water and grab my baseball cap," she said.

"I'll go ahead and call Goldie and ask him to come back now. I don't want my dad freaking out here by himself."

Pippa quickly placed the flowers in a pitcher she filled with water because she couldn't find a vase. Hearing Nic's low voice in the background gave her a sense of urgency. She raced to her car to grab the baseball cap. She'd put her hair in a topknot again, refusing to fight with it this morning. Pulling it down, she looked for an elastic band so she could put it in a ponytail and slip it through the back of the cap.

Hearing Nic's feet on the gravel of the driveway, she glanced up and pushed her fingers through her hair self-consciously.

"You should wear it down more often," he said.

"Oh, so I can look like I put my finger in an electrical socket?" No one had ever pretended to like her hair. She'd heard of a treatment that might tame it, but the idea of the hours it would take to accomplish it put her off.

"I like it," he said with a slow grin. "It's kinda wild. Makes me wonder if you have a wild streak underneath."

"I don't," she assured him and stuffed the unruly mass through the back of the ball cap as best as she could. "Shall we go?"

"I'm ready," he said and tucked her into the passenger side of his Mercedes.

"Has your mother mentioned any particular places in

Chantaine that she wanted to visit?" she asked as soon as Nic pulled out of the driveway.

"Since she moved into the cottage, she's just talked about how happy she is to be here, how beautiful it is."

"Hmm. Where are we headed first?" she asked.

"The beach," he said.

"That's a bit to cover. I don't supposed you've heard her talk about any specific beaches," she said.

"I've heard her talk about Chantaine a lot," he said, narrowing his eyes in deep thought. "She used to tell us bedtime stories about Chantaine before we went to sleep at night when my father was gone."

"Gone?" she asked.

"In prison," he said. "His conviction was overturned on a technicality. For a while there, she wouldn't let him come back."

Shocked by his revelation, she blinked. "I'm sorry. I didn't know. That must have been difficult."

"It was the gift that keeps on giving. My older brothers never forgave him. My younger brother just withdrew."

"But they've been in touch with your mother since she's been ill," she said.

"They won't talk to her if there's any chance they have to speak to my father," he said.

"Oh, my goodness, they're as bad as my family," she blurted. "If not worse."

He shot her a sideways glance, but kept his focus on the road. "Yeah."

"I'm sorry, but I'm just shocked. You never told me about all of this. Of course, I'd heard things about your father from my family, but you just said his conviction was overturned."

"Yeah, well, everyone's got a few skeletons in their closet. Even Stefan with his surprise daughter," he said.

Pippa bit her lip. It had been both scandalous and traumatic for the entire family and country for Stefan to learn he'd fathered a child fifteen months after the fact. "As soon as he'd learned about her, he'd done his fatherly duty. He's been a wonderful improvement over the example he had, let me tell you."

"Does that say more about your father or Stefan?" he challenged.

"My father wasn't involved with us. He procreated so that there would be children to carry on the work of the Devereauxs. The more he procreated, the more he could stay on his yacht and the less he would have to do." Her heart was slamming against her rib cage. She'd thought she'd settled all this as a child. Heaven knew, it was old news. "Stefan *reads* to his daughter most nights."

"Okay, okay," he said. "No need to yell."

"I wasn't yelling," she said, then reviewed her words and felt a slap of embarrassment. "Was I?"

"Just a little, but I probably deserved it," he said and pulled the car alongside the beach. "Let's check here." He opened the door for her and they scanned the beach from each direction.

"Did she mention this as one of her favorite beaches?" she asked, staring past rows of hot bodies.

"No. It's just the closest to the cottage. Why do you ask?"

"Well, Chantaine's beaches may share sand and

water, but they each have their own personalities," she said.

"Such as?"

"This is more of a singles scene, a pickup beach. As you can see from the demographics, a younger crowd frequents this beach. Farther north near the resorts, you'll find the celebrities and international visitors. Even farther north, there's a family beach where you'll see more children."

His hair whipping in the wind, he narrowed his eyes. "What's the name of the family beach?"

"St. Cristophe," she said.

"It was on the tip of my tongue," he said. "Let's go there. She went there often as a child before her parents died. She talked about eating fruit, cheese and crackers at the beach. I just hope she didn't decide to go into the water."

They both got into the car, traveling in silence up the coast. Pippa could sense Nic's tension. "If you could just persuade her to leave a message before she leaves…"

"Tell me something new. Maybe she'll listen to you if you say something to her," he said.

"Me? Why would she listen to me?" she asked, surprised at the suggestion. Amelie had only just met her.

"She's grateful to you for the use of the cottage and you're female. She thinks I'm just being overbearing and protective," he said.

"I'll give it a try," she said, full of doubt. "Maybe we could get a list of things she wants to do."

"Like a bucket list?"

She cringed. "That's morbid."

"But part of the program at this point," he said, clenching his jaw.

Pippa's heart twisted. She hated it for all of them, but Nic was only speaking the truth. "St. Cristophe Beach is just a few more kilometers north. We should be there soon."

As soon as the sign for the beach greeted them, Nic again pulled onto the side of the road and helped her from the car. Pippa scanned the beach. "Do you see her?"

He shook his head. "Let's split up. I'll go south. You go north. Call my cell if you find her and I'll do the same. Okay?"

She nodded in agreement and walked northward. The breeze was picking up and the clouds were rolling in, bringing the air temperature down. With Amelie's slight frame, Pippa feared the woman could become easily chilled even though it was summer.

Walking along the beach, she looked from one side to the other. Chantaine's beaches had their share of rocks and trees. Going barefoot could lead to serious discomfort. One more thing to worry about if Amelie had impulsively removed her shoes.

"Look! Isn't that Princess Phillipa?" a woman's voice called.

Pippa froze. Bloody hell, now what could she do.

A woman and several children raced toward her. Oh great, her security detail was going to kill her.

"Your Highness," the woman said, making an awkward curtsy. "Boys, take a bow. Girls, curtsy."

Pippa couldn't help smiling at the woman's delight and friendliness. "It's not necessary. I was here just taking a little walk. St. Cristophe is such a lovely beach. Are you enjoying your day?"

"Very much," the woman said.

The children echoed, "Yes, ma'am."

"Even more so seeing you here," the woman said. "Is there any chance you would give me an autograph? It would be a dream come true."

Seeing a small crowd forming, Pippa knew she'd better make the best of it. "Now, I didn't want to make a big production of this, so you're going to keep my little escape to the beach a secret. Won't you?" Fat chance with Facebook and Twitter alive and well.

She began to shake hands, sign autographs and make pleasant conversation. It really wasn't that difficult. The people were so lovely and kind. Her cell phone rang in the small purse she carried. "Excuse me for just a moment," she said and drew back slightly from the crowd.

"I found her," Nic said. "She was sitting beside a tree sleeping."

"I'm so relieved for you," she said. "But I've been discovered. Go ahead and take her home."

"How will you get back?" he asked.

"I'll figure out something. Or someone will alert security and it won't be necessary. I just wish my car wasn't in your driveway."

"I'll have Goldie take care of it. Where do you want it?"

"Close by, but he doesn't have the key."

"Goldie won't need it," he said. "I'll text you when he's close. He'll grab a cab ride back. *Ciao.*"

Pippa opened her mouth to protest, but she knew Nic had hung up, so she turned back to the crowd and continued to chat, sign autographs and even pose for a few photographs. Yes, there was going to be an inquisition in her very near future. Several moments later, her cell signaled a text. Certain it was from Nic, she didn't bother to look and began to say her goodbyes.

"It was lovely meeting all of you," she said. "But I really must go. *Ciao.*"

She climbed the sandy hill to the road and after walking south a short distance, she spotted her vehicle. Unfortunately she also spotted the vehicle belonging to her security man Giles. Dread tightening her stomach, she walked toward the man. She really didn't want to lose Giles as her personal security guard. He was, after all, the oldest security member on the force. With the exception of her secret meetings with Nic nearly a year ago, he regarded her as a sweet but boring student who posed very little security threat. Plus he was given to taking nice long naps in the afternoon.

"Your Highness," he said wearing an extremely displeased expression. "You didn't inform me of your plans to visit the beach today."

"I know," she said. "I'm terribly sorry. It was an impulse after lunch. I mentioned my plans to pop into a café for lunch, didn't I?"

Giles shook his head. "No, ma'am, you didn't."

"Oh, it must have slipped my mind. You know I usually pack a lunch, but I forgot this morning. My recent studies have been a bit depressing, detailing the causes of deaths of all our ancestors. I just felt a walk on a family beach would clear my head," she said, hoping she was boring the bloody stuffing out of him.

"But you usually prefer the more isolated Previn Beach," he said.

"I know. I guess I just wanted to see happy families playing on the beach. I do apologize. I would never want to trouble you."

"I know you wouldn't," he said. "But you must apprise someone of your whereabouts. If something happened to you, I would never forgive myself."

"You are absolutely correct and I'll never do it again," she lied and felt guilty, but she couldn't change the course she'd started and she wouldn't if she could.

"But you should have informed your Giles or someone," Frank, the head of security said to her. Because one interrogation wasn't enough.

"I know," Pippa said. "But I also know that Stefan has said that he wants us to make more impromptu public appearances."

"Impromptu to the public, not to security."

"So sorry," she said, and tried to conceal her insincerity. It seemed to be growing easier. She hoped she wasn't becoming a lying wench.

Frank sighed and began to pace across her public den. "Your Highness, except for your lapse with *Mr. Lafitte,* you have been an easy royal to protect. Since then, your studies and family have dominated your life. We don't wish to intrude, but if you continue to be unpredictable, then we will need to provide further security."

"I apologize again for not giving you more information today. I will do my best to be as predictable as possible in the future," she said.

Frank gave a sideways tilt of his head. "Perhaps I wasn't clear. We need you to be transparent."

Pippa gave a slow nod. The last thing she wanted to be was transparent. "Of course. And that's exactly what I shall be. Transparent. Predictable," she quickly added.

"Thank you very much, Your Highness," Frank said. "It is only our desire to protect you."

"I know," Pippa said. "And I'm very grateful," she added, exaggerating.

Frank smiled and nodded. "Thank you, Your Highness. I knew we could count on you."

Pippa lifted her lips in a smile as he left her suite. She'd just bought herself a couple more days of freedom. She hoped.

The following day, Pippa skipped visiting the Lafittes and even texting Nic. She felt as if she needed to stick to being predictable and transparent for at least one full day. That next night, however, she tossed and turned as she tried to sleep. She couldn't be what she needed to be for her family. She couldn't be what she wanted to be for the Lafittes.

She finally fell into a fitful sleep full of images of Nic and Amelie. Strong, strong Nic who would never admit pain or vulnerability, yet his dark eyes said something far different. Unable to sleep, she paced her bedroom and tried to work. She finally gave in and sent a text to Nic. I'm going to need a different disguise.

When a civilized time of day finally arrived, Pippa took a shower and got ready to go to the library. She sat down to work, and even though she had the concentration of a water newt, she forced herself to focus. Some time later, a package was placed beside her.

Glancing up, Pippa caught sight of a big bald man walking away from her. She lifted her hand. "Sir?"

The man didn't turn around. Pippa frowned, staring at the package. She glanced around her, then turned it over. The package bore the initials PD. Curious, she eyed the package with a sideways glance and slid it onto the chair beside her. Nic Lafitte was crazy. Who knew what scheme he had in his wicked mind?

She glanced back at her own laptop and with her heart racing, she tried to stare at the screen. Forget concentration. She would just like to be able to *read* the words on her screen. After seven tries, she gave up, grabbed the package and walked to the ladies' room. She went into a stall, ripped open the package and pulled out a gray-haired wig. Pippa couldn't help snickering. Her curiosity shooting upward, she pulled out the rest of the contents of the package. A hat, an ugly gray dress, tennis shoes and a key to a car.

She fished out a scrawled note at the bottom of the package. "The car is old, gray and rusty. In America, we call it a POS mobile. More later."

POS mobile? She couldn't wait to hear his explanation, she thought as she changed into the ugly gray dress. After she finished dressing, she carefully folded her other clothing and placed it into the package. Walking out of the restroom, she looked into the mirror and gaped. She looked at least thirty years older if not more. Pippa snickered again. *Well done, Nic.*

Following her instincts, she walked out the back door of the library and looked around for an old gray, rusty car. She immediately spotted it. The car was the most hideous vehicle she'd ever seen. Pippa walked to it, unlocked the door and got inside.

She turned the key and pressed the accelerator. The engine coughed to life. The summer heat combined with her wig and droopy dress made her feel as if she were suffocating. Pippa pushed the button for the air-conditioning, but only hot air blew from the vents.

"Bloody hell," she muttered and drove out of the parking lot.

Nic heard the sound of an engine backfiring outside his window. Glancing away from his tablet computer, he saw a gray-haired woman in a black dress exit the car and felt a ripple of pleasure. She'd come. He hadn't been sure she would. Pippa was an odd mix, and he'd already learned the hard way her first loyalty was to her family. She'd probably endured some pressure from her security guy and maybe even her family if they knew about it.

He was surprised she continued to visit. After all, her conscience should be clear. She'd made a dying woman's wish come true. Heading for the door of the guesthouse, he wondered why Pippa clearly felt the need to do more.

He stepped outside and caught sight of her walking toward the back door. "May I help you, miss?" he called, relishing the opportunity to tease her.

Whirling around with her hands on her hips, she stared at him, the gray curls of the wig so stiff they didn't move. "Very funny," she said. "As if you didn't handpick this lovely disguise."

"It worked, didn't it?" he asked as he strolled toward her.

She gave a reluctant nod. "Yes, but the car is another matter."

"I'll get Goldie to do something about the engine backfiring. We wouldn't want to call attention to you."

"The car may be a little over the top," she said. "It's distinctive and there's no air-conditioning."

"That must be hard on a woman your age," he said and bit back a grin. Lord, he felt like someone had turned on the light for the first time in two days. His mother had been alternately ill and sleeping. "I wasn't sure you'd come."

Her expression of contempt waned slightly. "You made it easy." She sighed. "How is she?"

He shook his head. "Not good. Sick or sleeping for close to thirty-six hours. It seems she gets a burst of energy and uses up all of it, then she can barely lift her head for days. I never know when one of these dips is the beginning of the—" He broke off. "Something bad."

"I'm sorry," she whispered. "I'm really sorry."

Feeling as if he'd revealed too much, he looked away from her and shrugged. "Part of the program. I'll deal with it. Good thing I've got Goldie. He's a licensed practical nurse, too."

Pippa blinked. "Goldie appears to be a man of many skills. Where on earth did you find him?"

"He and my father were in prison together. Goldie's record wasn't expunged, but he was a good guy. I hired him and he developed a hobby of educating himself. I paid for all the courses, but they've ended up benefiting me."

He felt her gaze on her for a long moment.

"I would like to meet him, please," Pippa said. "So far, I've only caught glimpses of his talents and abilities."

His gut tightened with something strange he almost couldn't identify. It took several seconds. Jealousy? He racked his brain to remember when he had felt this way before and couldn't. He led the way to the house. "Sure, I'll introduce you to Goldie. He's in the main house probably putting together a gourmet meal for dinner."

"He's a chef, too?" she asked.

"Oh, yeah, that was another one of his certificates. It's paid off in spades."

"The palace would *love* to have someone like him…."

"Don't even think about it. But if you do, he'll turn you down flat. He's the most loyal ex-con ever," Nic said.

"That remains to be seen," Pippa said. "The Devereauxs have seduced more than a few of the best of the best."

He stopped at the front door and turned around to meet her gaze. "I know that better than most."

Her cheeks heated and her eyes darkened. She cleared her throat. "Um…"

"Yeah, um," he echoed, saving her a response and opened the front door. "Let's go inside."

He guided her past the foyer into the kitchen. "Goldie," he said in a low voice.

The multitalented man appeared within two seconds, wearing an apron around his waist. "Yes, sir."

Goldie was sixty, but looked fifty because he worked

out. He was bald, muscular, with a gold hoop in his right ear. He usually wore a black T-shirt and black pants. He looked intimidating, but Nic knew he had a heart softer than that of a teddy bear. "Her Royal Highness, Princess Pippa Devereaux, this is Gordon Goldwyn."

Goldie gave a solemn bow. "Your Highness, my pleasure," he said.

Pippa smiled. "My pleasure," she said. "You're a man of many talents. Thank you for delivering my car to me at the beach and also leaving the envelope and car for me."

"I'm honored to serve," Goldie said respectfully.

"How is it that you are talented in so many areas?" she asked.

"I'm a lifelong student. Some things I learned got me into trouble. I'm fortunate that Mr. Lafitte encouraged me to explore my interests. Would you care for a drink or something to eat?"

"I'm fine. Thank you very much."

Goldie nodded, then turned to Nic. "Can I get something for you, sir?"

Nic waved his hand. "No, thanks. Any sign of my mother?"

"No, but your father is getting restless watching her," Goldie said.

"You're saying he could use some TV time. Sports Central," Nic said.

Goldie nodded. "A game would be even better."

"I got a million on DVD," he said.

"Then you've got what he needs," Goldie said.

At that moment, his mother walked into the room, looking gray and gaunt. "I'm thirsty," she said.

Nic rushed to her side. "What are you doing?"

She leaned against him. "I'm Lazarus rising from the dead. Hopefully, I'll do it a few more times," she said and stared at Pippa. "You look familiar. Are you someone who went to school with me?"

"Not quite," Pippa said with a smile. "But I would have loved that."

His mother frowned. "Were you in the orphanage with me?"

Pippa shook her head. "No, but you and I went to Bebe's Crepes together."

His mother stared at her for a moment, then smiled. "Princess Pippa," she crowed. "I love the look," she said, stretching out her hands. "You're my old best friend Rosie."

Pippa nodded and he saw that she was holding back her laughter. "Thank you so much. I'm sure Rosie is a most excellent person."

His mother nodded. "She is, but you are, too." Her eyebrows furrowed. "May we please have some refreshments?" she asked.

"What would you like, ma'am?" Goldie asked.

"Something fruity," she said. "Orange juice or lemonade."

"I'll bring both," he said. "Please take a seat in the den."

Nic assisted his mother to sit on the sofa. "There's no need to treat me like an invalid," she complained.

Nic gritted his teeth. Every other day, if not more often, his mother *was* almost an invalid. Yes, he was happy as hell that she didn't want to be treated like one. In his mind, that meant she might be around a little longer.

Pippa put her hand over his and met his gaze as if she knew everything he was feeling. Still dressed as a gray-haired lady wearing a baggy dress, she looked like an angel to him. An angel he wanted more than he'd ever wanted anyone else.

Chapter Five

Pippa concealed her alarm at how weak Amelie appeared. Just two days ago, she'd seemed an entirely different woman, going off by herself for a jaunt to the beach.

"I want to go on another adventure soon," Amelie announced as she sipped lemonade. "I'd like to go today, but I'm too bloody tired. Tomorrow will be a different story."

Pippa caught sight of Nic rubbing his forehead and face. She could see his shoulders bunch with tension. "Just let someone go with you so we don't have to call out a search team."

"A search team isn't necessary," Amelie said with a stubborn tilt of her chin. "I was fine."

"You were asleep on a public beach. You overestimate your energy level," he said.

She waved her hand in a dismissing gesture. "Plenty

of people doze on the beach. It's one of the pleasures of life. You wouldn't understand because you don't know how to relax."

"If you would agree to a GPS monitoring anklet…"

Amelie's eyes widened in indignation. "I'm not on house arrest. I refuse to be treated like a prisoner during my last days."

"It's just for tracking. Safety. It would give me some peace of mind," Nic added.

"Well, it wouldn't give me peace of mind walking around in public with an anklet designed for criminals."

Nic sighed. "I'm worried about you. What if you collapse and there's no one there to help you? Is that really the way you want to go?"

Pippa cringed at his bluntness, but she could tell he was feeling pressed. She honestly wouldn't like to be in his situation.

Amelie lifted her chin. "I don't get to choose the way I want to go. If it were up to me, I'd transform into a butterfly and float away, but the doctor says that's not possible."

A tense silence followed. Pippa felt it inside her and took a deep breath to ease it. "Well, I can see that the genes for independence and outspokenness are quite strong in both of you. I'm sure both of you enjoy those qualities in each other."

Nic glared at her, but Pippa forced herself to smile. "Mrs. Lafitte, perhaps you and I could go on an outing tomorrow or the next day, depending on how you're feeling. With my new disguise, I believe I'm safe to go anywhere."

Amelie smiled in delight. "Call me Amelie. And you

don't look a thing like yourself. That wig is so horrible, I think you may look even older than I am."

"Thank you," she said and shot Nic a wry look.

"I've been thinking I'd like to learn a new hobby. Years and years ago, I learned to knit, but I've forgotten everything. Do you know of any knitting shops on Chantaine?"

Ignoring Nic's astonished expression, she nodded. "I know of one downtown. If you feel like it, we could also have lunch."

Amelie seemed to brighten at the suggestion. "Lovely. This will be wonderful. I like having something to look forward to." She paused and glanced at Nic. "Have you heard anything from your brothers?"

"No," he said, and Pippa noticed the slight clench of his jaw. "You should let me call them again."

She shook her head. "You did that last year when I had my last treatments and they all visited then. It was a disaster with your father. I was just hoping things could be different now." She sighed. "There are some things we can't change. Best not to focus on them. I'll look forward to my outing with you tomorrow," she said to Pippa. "I think I'll sit outside by the pool with a book and this lovely lemonade."

"It's a beautiful day," Pippa said. "I think you'll enjoy it."

Goldie appeared in the doorway. "Can I get you something to eat?" he asked.

Amelie made a slight face. "If I tell you I'm not hungry, you'll tell me I need to eat something to keep up my strength. Crackers," she said.

Goldie's face fell. He'd clearly hoped her appetite had improved. "Yes, ma'am."

"Are you sure I can't join you outside?" Pippa asked.

"No, thank you, darling. I just want a little Chantaine sunshine," Amelie said and carefully rose from the sofa.

As soon as Amelie left, Pippa turned to Nic. "What is wrong with your brothers? Even my terribly dysfunctional family came together at the end of my parents' lives. Surely your brothers could do the same. It's the only humane, compassionate choice. You must make them come here at once."

Nic leaned toward her and gave a short laugh. "Here's a news flash, Princess. There's no royal decree available for the Lafittes. Besides, we don't respond well to attempted force or manipulation. My older brothers are holding on to a mile-wide grudge against my father. My youngest brother makes sure he's too busy to be contacted."

"But you must have some influence with them," she said, appalled at the situation.

"My oldest brothers would make the trip if they didn't have to face my father," Nic said. "My mother won't allow that. She refuses to turn her back on my dad even though she's earned the right more than once."

Frowning, Pippa rose and paced across the lush burgundy carpet placed on top of the ceramic tile floor. "There's got to be a way. Perhaps Goldie or I could take your father for a drive—"

Nic shook his head. "Not gonna happen. My mother wouldn't allow it."

"Well, we will just have to figure out another way," she said.

"We?" he echoed, rising to walk toward her.

Her stomach dipped as he moved closer. She kept trying to forget his effect on her, but every time she felt she was successful in staying focused on Amelie, Nic did something to upset her equilibrium. Unfortunately, it took very little. Seeing him stand and breathe was apparently problematic for her.

"I'm still not sure why you feel my mother's problems have anything to do with you," he said, looking down at her and resting his hands on his hips.

"Technically, I suppose they don't, but I would think any compassionate person would want to help," she said.

"Including Stefan?"

She bit her lip. "If Eve had anything to say about it, yes, he would help. I know you believe Stefan is a monster, but he's not. Just as he believes you are the very devil, and you're not."

"Good to know you don't think I'm the devil," he said.

She opened her mouth to retract her statement, then decided against it. "I will try to come up with a solution for your mother and your brothers. In the meantime, I can take Amelie shopping tomorrow, but I'll be busy the day after. I'm supposed to escort some soccer player around the island, then accompany him to a charity fundraiser that evening."

He lifted an eyebrow and his eyes glittered with something that gave her pause. "Is that so? Is the fundraiser at the St. Thomas Hall?"

"Yes, as a matter of fact, it is."

"This should be—" His lips twitched. "Fun. I'm invited to the same fundraiser."

"Oh," she said, her stomach taking a downward plunge. "You probably weren't planning to attend, were you?"

"I hadn't decided, but I could use some entertainment. May as well."

"But what about your mother?"

"It will just be for the evening," he said. "Goldie can call me. I'm not glued to Chantaine. I'll have to leave for business commitments within the next couple of weeks." He paused. "I'm at peace with my mother, and she's at peace with me. We have no unfinished business."

Pippa felt the oddest sense of calm and excitement from Nic. She'd never, ever felt that combination before. She took a deep breath and pushed past her feelings of panic about her feelings. That peace Nic had just mentioned, that was what was important. She felt it and knew it deep inside her. "I'm so glad that you have a good relationship with your mother. It will help you after—" She broke off, not wanting to say the words.

"After she's gone," he said.

Pippa nodded slowly.

"Because you didn't have the best relationship with your mother," he said.

"It wasn't horrible," she said quickly. "It was just distant. Our family was different. We weren't raised the way most other children are raised."

"It's different being royal," he said.

She nodded.

He reached out to take her hand in his. His fingers felt strong and sure wrapped around hers. "Most people don't have perfect childhoods. You take the good and screw the bad stuff."

His simple words gave her the biggest rush. They reverberated inside her. She wanted to be that person who could *take the good and screw the bad.* Every once in a while, though, she felt caught between herself as the chubby preteen who didn't feel worthy of her parents' attention and a grown woman who was on her way to earning her doctorate. The touch of his hand just made her want more… At that moment, Nic made her feel she was capable of anything she wanted to do and be.

A loud cough sounded. Mr. Lafitte stood on crutches at the entrance of the room. "Where's Amelie?" he asked, looking more than a little rough around the edges. His hair stuck up in a wild Mohawk and his jaw was heavily whiskered. "Is she okay?"

Pippa automatically pulled her hand from Nic's while Nic turned to his father. "She's fine. Outside by the pool."

Mr. Lafitte slumped forward slightly. "Good. As long as she's not swimming."

Nic winced. "Good point. Goldie," he called, "can you see my mother?"

"She's in a lawn chair, sir."

"Good." Nic took a quick breath. "Can I walk you to your car, Great-Auntie Matilde?"

Pippa felt a flash of realization. She'd forgotten she looked thirty years older. She smothered a laugh at herself. She'd been concerned that she was giving Nic mixed signals.

Well, she would have if she didn't look like his grandmother. Walking out of the cottage, she waved at

Amelie and strode the rest of the way to the horrid vehicle she would drive to the library, where she would change out of her outfit and return to her identity as Princess Pippa.

Nic opened the door for her.

"I hope it's cooler now. I burned up on the drive over here," she said.

"Goldie did a little magic. You should be more comfortable now."

"Thank you," she said.

"Thank you." He leaned toward her slowly and pressed his mouth just next to hers. It could have been a kiss on her cheek, but it just missed the mark. It could have been her mouth, but it wasn't. He almost made her forget that she was dressed like his grandmother.

Nic watched Pippa putter away in the POS mobile. She continued to make him admire her. He tried to name a woman who would be willing to disguise herself as a woman thirty years older and drive a wreck of an automobile just to check on a dying woman who was not related to her. Pippa was different. He'd known that from the beginning.

He returned to the front door.

"Nic, darling, come sit with me for a moment, please," his mother called. "Ask Goldie to bring you a Scotch. Or whatever it is that you drink."

"No need," he said. "It's early for that."

His mother glanced up from her wide-brimmed hat. "Haven't you heard? It's five o'clock somewhere." She rang the little bell Goldie had given her, insisting that she ring it anytime she wanted anything.

Goldie immediately appeared. "Yes, Miss Amelie."

"Please fix a drink for Nic. His usual," she said.

Nic sank into the chair beside her. "How's the book?"

"I fell asleep, so I don't know," she said. "But I'm loving the sunshine. You will have many stars in your crown for bringing me to Chantaine."

"That was Pippa's doing," he said.

"And you're quite taken with her," his mother said and sipped her lemonade.

"I wouldn't say that," he said, irritated at her suggestion.

"No, but I'm dying, so I can speak the truth," she said and shot him a knowing glance from the top of her sunglasses. "I would never ever suggest going after a royal especially because Paul and I made a bit of a mess with the Devereauxs back in the day. That said, I can tell the princess is also taken with you."

Goldie delivered his Scotch and Nic took a long drink. "Yes, that's why she dumped me like garbage several months ago."

His mother waved her hand dismissively. "Family's a tricky thing. You ought to know. I'm quite impressed that she's made such an effort to please a dying woman. Especially when her family wouldn't approve. I can't help believing some part of her is trying to help you."

"If so, then that part is buried very deep," Nic said dryly.

"You have to find your own way. I'll just tell you that some people are worth fighting for. Some people are your destiny," she said.

"You're speaking of Dad," he said, always stunned by the fervency of her devotion to his father.

"I am. He would steal for me. He would die for me. He would go to prison for me. He would do anything for me. I hope you'll know that kind of love," she said and leaned back against the chaise longue.

After a lovely lunch and bit of shopping spent with Nic's mother, Pippa prepared herself for her afternoon and evening scheduled with Robert Speight, the world-famous soccer player from England.

"Aren't you excited?" Bridget asked as she *helped* Pippa get ready for an afternoon outing. "He's so hot. Stefan protested. He wanted to put you with a count from Italy, but I insisted. You deserve a treat after all the academic work you've been doing along with being such a good auntie. Good Lord, don't you ever go shopping?" Bridget continued. "All I see are long skirts and blouses."

"I haven't had a lot of time for shopping," Pippa said, wishing she didn't feel such a strong sense of dread about the setup with the soccer player. She feared he was going to be quite disappointed and bored.

"Well, there's always catalogs and online shopping. For that matter, the palace stylist would be happy—" She broke off as she whisked through the hangers of clothing in Pippa's closet. "Don't you even own a cute little pair of shorts?"

"I'm sure there are some in there somewhere. I just prefer skirts. They're more comfortable," Pippa said and reached for a beige linen skirt that flowed to her calves.

"Absolutely not," Bridget said, scooping the skirt back from her. "If you insist on wearing a skirt," she muttered, pushing through a few more hangers. "Ah," she said, pulling out one of Bridget's few above-the-knee skirts. "Here, this one will work."

"I'm not sure it fits anymore," Pippa murmured, holding the pink skirt against her. "And I think I may have stained the blouse that goes with it."

Bridget pulled out a white scoop-neck cotton blouse. "There. It will be perfect with sandals. Why did you cancel the salon appointment I made for you yesterday? I told you about the new treatment. Smooth, shiny hair and because you're Miss Practical, you won't have to spend so much of your time styling it every day."

"I don't spend that much time, now," Pippa said. "I either pull it back or put it on top of my head."

"Hmm," Bridget said and studied Pippa for a long uncomfortable moment. Bridget took her hand and led her to the sitting area of Pippa's suite. "I'm not sensing a lot of enthusiasm about your outing with the soccer player." She sighed. "Please tell me you're not still pining for that terrible Nic Lafitte."

Pippa looked away. "Of course I'm not pining for him. But I'm not pining for a setup, either. Think about it. Did you like it when Stefan set you up with men hoping for a romance or marriage?"

"I hated it," Bridget said. "Fought it with every bit of my strength, but most of those men were at least ten years older than me. Robert is your age. And he's regarded as one of the most eligible bachelors in the world. I'm not trying to arrange a marriage. I just want you to have a little fun. You're due."

Pippa gave a slow nod. "I appreciate the sentiment. You're sweet to want me to have some fun."

Bridget met her gaze and groaned. "But you're not

at all interested. Well, at least give the poor man a try. Trust me when I say I didn't have to do any coaxing to make this happen. He was more than happy to spend the day and evening with you. And who knows? You may have a fabulous time. Promise me you'll *try* to have fun."

"I'll do my best and I'll also try to make sure that Mr. Speight is entertained," Pippa said.

Pippa treated the date as if it were a project. She planned to take the soccer player on a tour of the island, stopping at a few of the famous beaches. If time permitted, she'd arranged for a brief turn on the royal yacht.

Robert Speight was an impressive specimen. He stood over six feet tall with a well-muscled body. His hair was red and skin extremely fair. The exact opposite of Nic, she thought, and immediately wished she hadn't made the comparison. Their date started out well enough with Pippa giving a running commentary on the history of Chantaine as she showed him points of interest. It was only when she saw his head rolling back against the headrest, his eyes closed and his mouth open that she got her first clue that she'd begun to bore the poor man.

Thank goodness she'd arranged for a picnic lunch at a private beach. She and Robert sat on a large blanket and ate food from a gourmet basket prepared by the palace chef. Robert asked for photos, but kept fighting the yawns.

"Sorry," he said sheepishly. "Late night last night partying," he said waggling his bushy red eyebrows suggestively. "If you know what I mean."

She didn't, so she just made a vague little sound. "I

thought it was very generous of you to lend your name to the charity fundraiser this evening. So many people are looking forward to meeting you."

He shrugged. "I have to do a few of these every now and then for the sake of my image. It helps me get other endorsements. This one included exotic beaches and a date with a princess. What's not to like?" He leaned toward her and placed his hand over hers. "I've heard Chantaine has some nude beaches. You want to take me there?"

Pippa blinked at the proposal and tried not to laugh. She'd spent a lifetime trying not to be photographed in a bathing suit. A nude beach was totally out of the question. "I'm not really permitted on the nude beach," she whispered. "Photographs live forever. If you have time tomorrow, I can arrange for a driver to take you."

"But it would be much more enjoyable with you," he said.

"I'm so sorry," she said and took back her hand. She was going to have a chat with Bridget tomorrow, she promised herself.

Later that afternoon, Pippa received a visit from the palace stylist, Peter, to make sure she was properly dressed and coiffed. Dressed in a designer gown that reminded her of a pink cocktail napkin, she bit her teeth. Peter applied more makeup than she wore in a year. He sighed and swore over her hair. "A keratin treatment would change your life."

"It takes too long," she said.

"It's not as if you would have to sit in a salon like the rest of the world. We would bring the cosmetologist to the palace. Your hair would be straight for three to four months after one treatment."

Pippa stared into the mirror at herself and made a face. "I don't know if I want it straight."

Peter lifted one eyebrow. "As you wish, Your Highness."

"Your way of saying I'm crazy," she said.

Both of Peter's eyebrows flew upward, which was quite an accomplishment given the Botox he regularly had injected into his forehead. "Pardon me, Your Highness if I offended you."

"It's true. You think I should get the treatment and have straight hair. Straight hair is more fashionable than crazy, wavy hair."

Peter seemed to work on his restrained. "It's my job to keep the royal family informed of current fashion. Your hair…" He began and moved his hands, but couldn't seem to find the words.

"I hate my hair and love my hair because it's different," she told him. "You have to admit, it's not like anyone else's hair in the family."

Peter tilted his head to one side. "You make an excellent point, Your Highness. We shall begin to capitalize on your hair," he said. "We shall make your hair a new trend. We can name it the Princess Pippa hairstyle. Perfect."

Alarm shot through her. "No need to go that far," she said.

He lifted his hands. "I can see it now. Magazine shoots, commercials. It will be fantastic publicity for the royal family."

"Not in my lifetime," she said quietly.

He sighed. "Begging your pardon, ma'am, you give this impression of being a people pleaser, yet you somehow stop me in my tracks when I try to expand you."

"And you like me for that, don't you, Peter?" she said more than asked, unable to hold back a grin.

Peter shook his head but smiled. "I do. Let me spray you one more time," he said lifting a can of hair spray.

She lifted both her hands to block him. "I'll die if you do."

"An exaggeration," he said.

"You would know because you're the master of exaggeration," she retorted, her hands still braced to shield herself from the hair spray.

Peter groaned. "You make this difficult for me, ma'am. What if this man is your future husband?"

"No worries," she said, adapting a phrase she'd learned from Bridget. "He pushed hard for me to take him to a nude beach."

Peter frowned. "A cad. In that case, perhaps I should give you sea salt spray. It will take your curls to a new level."

Pippa laughed. "No need. Thanks for your help tonight."

"Someday, a man will sweep you off your feet."

Pippa laughed again, and her mind automatically turned to thoughts of Nic. She clamped down her thoughts and feelings. "I prefer my feet on the ground."

Thirty minutes later, she joined Robert Speight in a limo headed for the charity event. "Nice dress," Robert said, staring at her cleavage. "Are you sure I can't talk you into a trip to one of your nude beaches tomorrow?"

Pippa refused to honor the subject, let alone the question. "Did you know that I'm working on a doctorate in genealogical studies? I had some extra time this afternoon while I was waiting on alterations for my gown. Did you know that you may be distantly related to Attila the Hun?" The truth was just about anyone could be distantly related to Attila.

Robert shot her a blank look. "Attila the Hun?" he echoed.

"Yes, he's quite famous."

"I'm drawing a blank," Robert said. "Can you refresh my memory?"

"He was a ferocious warrior. The Romans were terrified of him. He was excellent with a bow and an amazing horseman. Quite the sportsman," she said.

Robert stuck out his chest with pride and smiled. "Like me."

"Exactly. He was known as a conqueror." *And barbarian.*

"I've got to make a little speech tonight. Maybe I could mention him," he said. "Maybe spice things up for people interested in history."

She opened her mouth to correct him, but couldn't quite make herself do it. "Just as long as you understand that I said that you *may* be related to Attila. I would need to do an in-depth study to verify the possibility."

"Hey, it's a good story. That's all that counts to me," he said, leaning toward her as if he were going to kiss her. "You're cute. Let's make some private plans after the event."

"Oh, I—" The limousine pulled to a stop. She glanced out the window, thankful for the interruption. "We're here."

"Yeah," Robert said as the driver opened the door. "First time with a princess. In more ways than one," he added against her ear as he folded his hand around her waist.

Pippa's stomach rolled.

She stepped out of the car and felt a thousand camera flashes as she strode toward the entrance of the building. Robert grabbed her hand and she struggled to free it. She pointed at a camera and she took advantage when he loosened his grip. Clasping her hands firmly together, she walked inside and smiled at the crowd that applauded.

"Pippa, Pippa!"

She was surprised to hear so many call her name. She'd always thought of herself as the anonymous Devereaux.

Robert put his arm around her and whispered in her ear, "Give me a kiss. They'll love it."

She bit her lip and turned her head. "I see some of your fans," she said.

"Where?" he asked.

Moments later, they entered the ballroom and Pippa waved to the crowd. There, several people screamed out loud. "Rob, Rob!"

"There you go," she said, but she needn't have. Robert was fixated on the crowd, waving and throwing kisses.

They were led to the head table and Pippa took her seat. The rest of the guests took their seats. Instinctively, she glanced around and her gaze landed on a man with broad shoulders, dark eyes and dark hair. Tonight he wore that Stetson as if to proclaim to all of Chantaine and her family that he didn't give a damn.

She liked him even more for that.

"This is fun," Robert said. "Just tell me it's not another rubber chicken dinner," he said.

"Lobster," she said and barely managed not to roll her eyes.

She felt Nic's gaze on her. He was silently laughing.

"So that guy's name is Atowla?"

"Attila," she said. "Attila the Hun." She was caught between a barbarian and a pirate. She wasn't sure which was worse.

Chapter Six

A server discreetly handed Pippa a piece of paper with her sorbet. Putting it in her lap, she opened it and glanced at it. *Meet me on the second floor in 5. N.* Pippa took a quick sip of water and briefly met Nic's gaze. She shook her head.

Her so-called date whispered in her ear. "It's time for more pictures," he said. "Stand up and I'll give you a passionate kiss. The press will love it."

Pippa nearly choked. "I was just going to tell you that I need to, uh, powder my nose. I'll be back shortly."

Robert's face fell. "Well, damn."

"I won't be long," she said and stood. She gave her security man a wave of dismissal and quickly walked to the hall outside the ballroom. Restroom was to the right, she remembered. Pippa had attended several events at this venue. The second floor offered a lovely view of the beach. Her stomach took a dip. Nic clearly remembered that fact, too.

She headed toward the restroom.

"Pippa."

She automatically paused, her heart leaping at the sound of Nic's voice. Pippa sucked in a quick, sharp breath and forced herself not to turn around. She didn't need to because Nic was at her side in seconds. "This is not a good idea. Go away," she whispered.

"Your Highness," a woman called. "Princess Phillipa."

Pippa frowned and turned at the distress in the woman's voice. She stared into the lovely heart-shaped face of a very young-looking woman. She was dressed in a miniskirt and tank top.

"You can't have him. I'm having his baby."

Pippa dropped her jaw. "Pardon me?"

"You can't have Robert. He belongs to me. He's all excited about being with a princess, but it will pass. He'll come back to me. He has to," she said and began to sob.

Pippa instinctively gathered the girl into her arms and glanced searchingly at Nic. "You're getting too upset," she said.

"He belongs to me. I'm having his baby," the young woman continued to sob. "He belongs to me."

"Darling, I wouldn't dream of taking Robert from you. This was just a charity appearance for both of us."

The girl pulled back, her baby blues filled with tears. "But he was so excited about being with a princess. He told me he couldn't make a commitment. Big things were coming in his future," she said, her voice fading to another sob. The woman buried her face in Pippa's shoulder again.

She met Nic's gaze again. "Please ask a server to give Robert a note. Robert's friend and I will be upstairs. He should join us immediately."

Nic lifted a dark eyebrow and dipped his head. "As you wish, Your Highness."

As soon as he turned away, she felt a rush of relief. "Let's go upstairs," she said. "I didn't hear your name."

"Chloe," she said and sniffed and swiped at her cheeks as Pippa led the way upstairs. "You're much nicer than I thought you would be. I was sure you would steal Robert from me."

"Oh, Chloe, I wouldn't dream of that," she said with complete and total honesty. She wouldn't take Robert if he was handed to her on a silver platter. She guided Chloe into a room and propped open the door.

Just a couple moments later, she heard voices coming from the hall. Nic's and Robert's. The door swung open and Nic and Robert stepped inside.

Robert's eyes widened. "Chloe, what are you doing here?"

Chloe bit her lip. "How could you leave me, Robert?"

Looking incredibly awkward, Robert shrugged his wide shoulders. "It was just temporary." He shot a quick glance at Pippa. "The princess required my presence for the charity event."

"I did not," Pippa said, unable to contain herself. She wanted to punch the scoundrel. She clenched her fists.

"Okay, well, I had to show for the charity event. The princess was just a bonus," he amended.

Nic cleared his throat. "I think Chloe has some important news to share."

Chloe gulped and appeared to force a smile. "I'm having your baby," she said.

Pippa looked at Robert and saw the tall, strong athlete turn as pale as ghost. "Baby?" he echoed.

"Yes, I'm having your baby," Chloe said and walked toward him.

Robert fainted backward. Nic caught him just before he would have hit the floor.

Pippa sighed, crossing her arms over her chest. "Are we going to have to call the medics, too?"

"Let's try something a little more basic," Nic said. "Can you get a glass of water?"

She glanced around the room and saw a stack of paper cups and pointed at them. "There's a water fountain in the hall."

"I'll take care of it," Chloe said.

"Get two cups," Nic said and gently lowered Robert's head to the carpeted floor.

Chloe ran out of the room. Seconds later, she returned.

"I think you should have the honors," he said to Chloe.

"What do you mean?" she asked, clearly confused.

"Throw the water in his face," he said.

Chloe's eyes widened in alarm. "In his face."

"It's the best thing for him," he said.

"Are you sure?"

"Couldn't be more sure," he said. "If you don't do it, then I will."

Chloe took a deep breath and threw a cup in Robert's face.

The athlete blinked and shook his head.

"It worked," Chloe said with a delighted smile. "You were right."

Nic nodded and extended his hand. "Can you give me the second cup?"

"Of course," she said and gave it to him.

"You coming around, Speight?" Nic said as the man lifted his head.

"Yeah," he said, rubbing his hand over his face. "Why am I wet?"

"So many reasons," Nic said. "You okay? Are you conscious?"

Robert lifted himself up on his elbows. "Yeah, I'm good."

Nic nodded and dumped the second cup of water on Robert's head.

Robert scowled and swore. "Why the hell did you do that?"

"In Texas we would say you need a good scrubbin'," he said in his Texas drawl. "I just thought I'd get you started. Pops."

After Robert pulled himself back together and dried himself with some paper towels, he returned to the ballroom and Nic arranged for a car to take Chloe back to her hotel.

Pippa felt the pressure of passing time. She knew her absence would be noted if she didn't return soon, but she wanted to thank Nic for his help. After stepping just outside the door, he returned and strode toward her.

"You okay?" he asked, his dark gaze intent on her.

She laughed. "Of course I'm fine, thank you. I wasn't the least bit enamored of Robert from the beginning."

Nic walked closer. "Are you sure about that?"

Pippa frowned. "Of course I'm sure. Do you really think I could be so easily won over by a man just because he's a world-famous soccer player?"

"You fell for me pretty quickly in the beginning," he said, lowering his mouth to half a breath away from hers.

Her heart skipped. "I was young and foolish."

He laughed, and the deep, hearty sound echoed inside her, making her feel alive. "It was six months ago."

"Eight months," she corrected.

He lifted a brow. "I didn't know you were counting."

She opened her mouth, but at the moment, she couldn't deny... Anything.

His mouth brushed hers, and the sensation made her felt as if she were melting and blooming at the same time. His mouth searched, plundered and empowered hers. She felt sensual, womanly, and it sounded crazy, but she felt as if she could fly. It was such an amazing, euphoric sensation that she didn't want it to ever end. During a moment that felt like centuries or seconds, she slid her arms around Nic and reveled in the strength of his body. It seemed to flow into hers.

She craved more of the feeling. There was more, she thought. More...

Nic pulled back slightly. "Let me take you away," he whispered. "For just a while."

Every fiber of her wanted to say yes, but her duty and obligation screamed no. "I want—" She took a breath and tried to clear her head. "They're expecting me for the end of the dinner. After twelve minutes, people start to notice when a royal is gone." She swallowed over the craziness rolling through her, but she fought the drowning sensation she felt when she stared into his eyes. "They actually notice before that, but if there's a distraction such as a famous soccer player, we get a bit more time."

"After the dinner, then," he said.

Her stomach dipped as if her amusement park ride had abruptly plunged and risen and plunged again. "Oh," she said. "Uh, I—" She broke off and shook her head. "This is crazy. We tried it before. It didn't work out."

"Why?" he asked, his gaze wrapping around hers and holding it.

She opened her mouth to answer, but the words stopped in her throat.

"What's the problem, Princess Pippa? Cat got your tongue?" he asked and kissed her again.

Pippa melted again, feeling as if she were having an out-of-body experience. His arms felt better than chocolate, his mouth, the same. She felt as powerful as the ocean. She clung to him, but duty tugged at her. It was so ingrained that she couldn't quite forget it.

Pippa pulled back. "I have to go."

"Chicken," he said.

Something inside her wanted to prove him wrong. "Blast you," she whispered, and wiped her mouth as she ran from the room.

Although she was bloody distracted, Pippa finished the interminable evening. With photos, but no passionate kisses. She took a separate limo to return to the palace, all the while consumed with thoughts of Nic. What if she could have met him? Where? She felt a terrible aching need to be with him, but she knew she couldn't. For a thousand reasons. She arrived to find Bridget waiting in her quarters, bouncing with excitement.

"Tell me all about it," Bridget said. "How hot was he?"

"Too hot for me, given the fact that a, he pushed to go to a nude beach."

Bridget's jaw dropped.

"B, he wanted to French kiss me in public for the sake of getting photographs with a princess."

"Oh, my—"

"And c, congratulations are in order. The very young mother of his baby showed up at the charity event."

"He has a child?" Bridget asked, her eyes wide with horror and shock.

"He is a father-to-be. I believe the popular term is baby daddy."

Bridget gave an expression of pure disgust. "Oh, how horrible. I don't know what to say."

"Just say you won't set me up again," Pippa said. "Please."

Bridget winced. "I'm so sorry." She lifted her hands. "I just wanted you to have a little fun."

"I know your intentions were good," Pippa said. "They always are. You have a good heart and you love me. I know you love me. I just need to find my own way in this area." She decided to make a bigger push. It was her moment. "As you know, my birthday is right around the corner. Everyone is pushing for the palace to make budget cuts. I've decided I want a little more control over where I go. I'm going to request more limited security."

Bridget shook her head, fear filling her eyes. "Oh, no, you can't do that. Not after what almost happened to me. Not after what happened to Eve."

"If you recall, you actually had security when you were leaving that charity event when you were almost stampeded by that gang. I think it makes sense to follow what other royal families are doing. I'm *way* down the list to take the throne and heaven knows I have no interest. Current practices suggest I be given security for official events with a panic button for my use at all times. Do you know how much the head of security grilled me because I took a walk on a family beach last week?"

"It's the social media," Bridget said. "People with camera phones are everywhere, tweeting, taking photos. You can't possibly expect anonymity or privacy, Phillipa."

"It doesn't help to have security nipping at my heels every minute," Pippa said.

"I thought you had a soft spot for your security man. You seemed to have an easy enough relationship with Giles before, well—" Bridget broke off. "Before the Lafitte incident."

Pippa felt her irritation grow. In the past, she would have just sighed and fallen silent. "All of you made entirely too much of a fuss. Can you honestly say you never dated someone Stefan would have considered inappropriate?"

"Stefan considers any man he doesn't choose to be inappropriate," Bridget scoffed and began to pace.

"He almost didn't approve of Ryder until he figured out Ryder could be the new health minister. But Lafitte was different. His family—" Bridget shook her head. "There's just too much bad history between his family and ours. Plus his father had to have been a terrible influence on him."

"Some people might say the same about the influence our father had on us," Pippa muttered.

Bridget shot her a sharp look. "What are you saying?"

"I'm saying I want my personal business to be my business. I'm saying I want to make my own decisions about security and dating."

"We just all adore you and we don't want you to be hurt," Bridget said.

"I realize that, but I'm not four years old. I'm a grown woman. I may be the youngest daughter, but I don't need all of you looking after everything in my life. I want you, Tina and Stefan to stop it. Now." She barely kept herself from stomping her foot for emphasis.

Bridget blinked, then sighed. "You may be able to persuade Tina and me, but good luck with Stefan."

It was a good thing she didn't care what the tabloids said about her, because she would have become extremely depressed the following day. *Princess Phillipa Dumped by Soccer Player* the headline read with photos from the charity event and her impromptu visit last week on the beach. Not cover-girl shots. Pippa had always shrunk from any potential emphasis of her image. She was no fashion leader, that was certain. Her sisters Fredericka and Bridget had seemed to do enough of that for everyone, thank goodness. It had taken the focus off her. Her other sister, Valentina, had been a bit less fashionable, more normal in her figure and ultimately more concerned with relationships than her image.

That was probably the reason the weight of royal appearances had worn heavy on Tina's shoulders and she'd become the wife of a Texas businessman rancher. Tina made occasional appearances for the family and attended to a few royal duties, but her focus was happily fixed on her marriage and young daughter. Over the years, Pippa had filled in the gaps on the schedule or substituted when one of her siblings couldn't make an event.

She hadn't spent a lot of time thinking about what she truly wanted for herself because she'd been so busy finding ways to avoid causing trouble or being in the spotlight. Ever since she'd gotten involved with Nic all those months ago, she found herself fighting a restlessness that seemed to grow worse every day. She wished it would go away. She'd thought once she'd broken off with Nic that she could go back to normal, but normal didn't fit anymore. Sipping a cup of tea and sitting inside the small suite where she'd lived since she was a teen, she stared outside her window to one of the palace courtyards and felt like a caged bird. She didn't like the feeling at all.

Taking a deep breath, she prepared herself for her meeting with her brother Stefan. He'd requested the meeting first thing this morning. She suspected he had something on his mind and she intended to do what she'd heard Eve say on more than one occasion. Pippa was going to give her brother, the crown prince of Chantaine, a piece of *her* mind.

She walked down the long hallway to the opposite wing of the palace, then up the stairs to the office where her brother worked. On rare occasions, her father had also worked here.

Her brother was a working prince and he'd spent most of his adult life living down their father's yachting playboy prince image. All the Devereaux children had been raised to understand that duty was first and foremost. Some had accepted the duty more easily than others.

Pippa lifted her hand to knock on the door.

Stefan's assistant immediately responded with a slight bow. "Good morning, Your Highness. His Highness is ready for you."

"Thank you," she said and walked through the outer office into Stefan's office.

Stefan stood and smiled. "Thank you for coming on such short notice," he said and moved from behind his desk to embrace her.

Pippa hugged him in return, noting he wore a suit, signaling he had other official meetings today. "As if you would let me refuse you," Pippa gently teased him, taking in the office. The decor combined the history of the Devereauxs with Stefan's interests in horses, his studies in leadership and economics and a few of Eve's homey touches from Texas.

She also noticed a wooden toy on the corner of his desk and pointed at it. "For Stephenia?" she asked, smiling as she thought of his toddler daughter.

"Eve and the nanny bring her to visit. I like to have

at least a couple things in the room that she's allowed to touch. I don't want her to remember my office as the no-no room," he said.

"I like that," Pippa said. "It's a lot different than the way we were raised."

Stefan nodded. "That's the plan. Please have a seat."

Pippa sat on the edge of one of the leather chairs. She would have preferred to remain standing. Standing somehow made her feel stronger. "How is Eve?" she asked.

His eyes lit at the mention of his wife's name. "A bit of nausea and I think she's more tired than usual, but she's trying not to let me see it. I've asked her assistant to limit the number of invitations she accepts. We'll see how long that works. She can be as stubborn as—" He broke off. "As I am."

Pippa laughed. "One of the many things we love about her."

Stefan nodded, then turned serious and she could tell he was going to start discussing the reason he'd invited her to his office. "I'd like to go first, please," she said breathlessly.

His eyes flickered in surprise and he paused a half beat, then gave a slow nod. "All right. Go ahead."

Pippa took a teeny, tiny breath and clenched her hands together. "My birthday is next week," she said.

Stefan smiled. "I know. That was part of the reason I asked you here."

"Really," she said. "Well, I've been thinking about this a lot and I believe I'm ready to drop my security back to official events only."

Stefan stared, again in surprise.

"It's really the current trend among royals and I know you're trying to keep us up-to-date. All of our expenses are being scrutinized by the government and the press, and I think it would be an excellent way to show that we can be economical."

Pippa sat back and waited for Stefan to respond.

"I'll take it under advisement. However, my first response is no. With the brawl Bridget and Eve faced last year, we've learned that we can't count on all our citizens behaving in a welcoming or even civil manner."

"If you'll recall, that was an official event and security was present."

His eyes narrowed with irritation and dark memories. Pippa understood the dark memories. Stefan had been falling in love with Eve when she'd been injured. "I said I would take it under advisement, but you must understand that I regard your protection as a very serious responsibility."

"I appreciate that very much," she said. "But I'm insisting."

He tilted his head to one side in shock. "Pardon me?"

Pippa's stomach clenched. She knew that expression. He'd used it far more often with Bridget because her older sister had felt perfectly free to argue with Stefan. Pippa, on the other hand, avoided arguments like the plague. Except this time.

"I said I'm insisting. I don't do a lot of insisting, but I am this time. And I think you should also know I'm considering moving out of the palace."

Another shocked silence stretched between her and her brother.

"And how do you plan to pay for this apartment?" he challenged.

"I earn a small stipend with the research I do, and I have a savings account. It's true most of my clothes have been provided by the palace, but I don't need a different dress every day. It's not as if everyone is watching every move I make."

"You underestimate how interested our people are in you," he said. "As evidenced by the crowd you drew during your impulsive walk on the beach last week."

Pippa winced. She wondered who had ratted on her. It wasn't as if Stefan spent a lot of time on internet social sites. "Yes, and everyone was perfectly polite."

"You'll be entirely too vulnerable if you were to move away from the palace," he said.

"Entirely too vulnerable to what? I would still have a panic button and I could have alarms set up in an apartment. Admit it. Jacques will be of age soon enough and you would allow him to live away from the palace."

"That's different," Stefan said. "He'll be a young man and would feel trapped here."

"The same way I feel trapped," Pippa said.

Stefan looked as if he'd been slapped and she felt a stab of regret. "I thought you liked having access to the family, the twins and Stephenia, the family dinners."

"I do," she said. "I love my nieces and nephews. I love my family. There's no reason I still can't babysit and attend family dinners. I just need some space."

Stefan sighed, then straightened his shoulders. "Perhaps you just need a break. When I tell you what I have planned for you, I know you'll be pleased."

Pippa felt her stomach twist with dread. There was

always a catch involved when Stefan had a *plan*. "No, really," she began.

He held up his hand. "You've had your turn. Now it's mine. I've arranged for you to take a holiday to the coast of Italy for your birthday."

Pippa immediately thought of Amelie and shook her head. "That's a lovely thought, but this isn't a good time for me to take a holiday. Due to my studies," she added.

"It's only for a few days and the break will be good for you. You'll have only two appearances to make during your trip. One celebrating the anniversary of a museum and the other will be a christening ceremony for a new cruise ship that will be making stops in Chantaine. I've arranged for an escort for you. Count Salvatore Bianchi. He's a bit older than you, but his family is considering opening several wineshops here, so we'd like to further that relationship. And who knows? Perhaps the two of you will hit it off," Stefan said, wearing his most charming smile.

Pippa felt a twist of suspicion. "Just how much older is Count Bianchi?"

Stefan shrugged. "I'm not sure. He's a widow with children. I believe one of them goes to school with Jacques." Jacques, her nineteen-year-old brother.

"So what you're saying is he could be my father," Pippa said.

"Age is just a number, Pippa. I assure you that you'll have more in common with the count than the soccer player Bridget arranged as your escort. My assistant will give you your itinerary later today and the palace stylist will help you with your attire for the trip."

"And if I don't want to go?" Pippa said.

"The arrangements have been made. People will be expecting you. Besides, I can tell by our discussion today that you need this holiday. You *will* enjoy it," he said and stood.

"Because His Royal Highness decreed it," she muttered and also rose.

A flicker of irritation passed over Stefan's face. "I've always counted on you for your sweetness."

She felt a quick surge of pain at the prospect of disappointing Stefan. "I'm sorry. I'll go on the trip, but Stefan you need to understand that it won't change my intentions regarding my security and moving out."

"We'll see," he said.

Chapter Seven

Two days later, Pippa managed to make her way to the Lafittes' temporary cottage. She drove the rickety car from the library wearing the terrible disguise over her clothes and pulled off the wig as soon as she pulled into the cottage driveway. Unbuttoning the too-large matronly blouse, she stepped out of the car and pushed down the hideous skirt.

She heard a wolf whistle and glanced up to see Nic smiling at her as he leaned against the guest quarters door wearing jeans and a black T-shirt that outlined his broad shoulders and muscular arms. "Don't stop now," he said, referring to her awkward striptease.

She bundled up the disguise in her arms and rolled her eyes as she walked toward him. "I despise this outfit."

"But it gets the job done," he said.

Unable to argue his point, she pushed open the gate. "How is your mother?" she asked.

"Restless. She may need an outing," he said. "A short one. Any ideas?"

"I'll think of something. Have you made any headway with your brothers?"

"Heard from one and I'm hounding the others. I may have to resort to unconventional methods of getting their attention."

She shot a sharp glance at him and he shook his head. "You don't want to know."

"Actually, I do," she said. "I may need to use subversive tactics with my own family at some point."

She felt his glance at her, but didn't meet his gaze. "Okay. I'll send a fake officer to stop them on their way to work. This officer will deliver a message."

She met his gaze. "That's drastic."

Nic shrugged. "Drastic times…"

She couldn't help smiling at his creativity. "Well done."

He shot her a half grin. "It's only the first step. I have others planned if this doesn't work."

She nodded. "What are we doing with Amelie this afternoon?"

"I don't know. Depends on her mood."

"How is her appetite?"

"Temperamental at best," he said.

"Maybe she'll take a few bites of gelato."

"You'll have to put on your disguise again," he reminded her.

"I know. I want to cool off until then."

Nic opened the door for her and she stepped inside

the cool foyer. Pippa walked toward the den and saw Amelie and Paul cuddling on the sofa and watching television. She hesitated to interrupt, but Paul glanced up at her.

"Hey, y'all come on in," he said.

Amelie glanced up at her. "It's Pippa!"

The delight in Amelie's voice grabbed at her heart. "Yes, I'm here for just a while."

"We should have another adventure," Amelie said.

Nic gave a low groan from behind her.

Pippa smothered a smile. "We should plan something."

"I want to do something now," Amelie said. "Paul is feeling better tonight."

Pippa remembered her earlier suggestion. "Would you like some gelato?"

Amelie's face lit up. "Perfect." She turned to Paul. "Do you think you can manage a ride in the car?"

"I can do anything for you," Paul said. "And gelato sounds good, too," he said with a rough chuckle.

Pippa's heart twisted at the obvious love that flowed between the two of them. Reluctantly, she put on her costume again. The four of them got into Goldie's SUV and drove to Chantaine's best gelato shop. They ordered ten flavors. Amelie took a teeny bite of each of them. When they returned, both Amelie and Paul were worn out.

Pippa stripped off her disguise again. "I hate this disguise," she muttered to Nic as they sat by the pool. "I think I hated it from the beginning," she said. "Do you think your mother enjoyed the outing?"

He nodded. "My father did, too. They won't admit it, but it helps if the trip is a short one."

"How do you think your father is dealing with your mother's illness?" she asked.

"Depends on the day. Sometimes he's in denial. Other days he's trying to grab the moment. He's definitely not fit for making business decisions."

"So you're doing that for him?" she asked.

He nodded, his head still resting against the chair, his eyes closed.

"He's lucky to have you stepping in for him," she said.

"Someone has to," Nic said.

She stared at Nic as he sat in the chair, in his jeans and T-shirt, his head tilted back. "But why you?" she asked.

He cracked open an eyelid. "Because no one else would."

"Does that mean you would have preferred to let one of your brothers take on this challenge?"

"I would have preferred to have just about anyone take on the challenge, but I knew no one would. My father is an ex-con. Trust in his business is precarious at best. I have to both check behind him and authenticate his company to his customers."

"If his business is so precarious, how are your mother and he surviving so well?"

Silence settled between them, making Pippa wonder about the mysteries of Nic's family. Suddenly, it dawned on her. "You're taking care of them, aren't you?"

Nic sighed. "His business has huge potential, but with the economy and his reputation, it's a struggle."

Pippa thought about all Nic was trying to do for his parents and felt an overwhelming sense of admiration and something deeper, something she couldn't quite name, for Nic. "You're quite the amazing son."

"You would do the same in my circumstance," he said.

Pippa shook her head. "I wouldn't know how to do everything you're doing," she protested. "Plus my relationship with my parents wasn't half what yours is."

Nic pulled his head from the back of the chair and met her gaze. "But you were there at the end."

Pippa took a deep breath, remembering both of her parents' deaths, and nodded. "Most of us were. Stefan and Valentina pulled us together. It wasn't easy. I think they suffered because of it."

Nic nodded. "It's a tough time. If there are more people, there's a bigger cushion."

"But you have none," she said.

He shrugged and cracked a grin. "I'm from tough stock. We've had to scrabble for everything. No royalty in my blood."

"Hmm," she said. "Bet there is. Just about everyone has a bit of royalty in their background."

He chuckled. "You would know. Your Highness genealogist. Bet you can get me that information by next week."

Pippa's feeling of lightness sank. "Not next week now that Stefan is sending me on a trip," she said glumly.

"Where?"

"The place isn't the bad part. It's my escort."

Stefan's eyes widened. "Another escort?"

"Yes, that's what I said. I also told him I want to

ditch my security and move into an apartment away from the palace."

"Bet that went over well," Nic said in a dry tone.

She laughed. "Not at all. He ignored me."

Nic nodded. "You may have to go ahead and make your move before he has approved. And be prepared to be have your title taken away. Stefan is known for his priority on loyalty."

Her heart twisted at his words. He'd described Stefan perfectly. "I hate the idea of disappointing him. He's always counted on me not to cause any trouble."

"Sometimes you have to cause trouble if you're going to be who you're meant to be," Nic said.

His words vibrated through her. "When did you learn that?"

"When I was about eight years old," he said.

She smiled. "Wise words."

"Children are wiser more often than not. Where are you headed and when?"

"Capri, Italy, in three days. This is supposed to be a birthday gift, but I have to make two appearances and I have an escort who has a child as old as my youngest brother."

"Stefan's idea?" he said more than asked.

"Yes, they're trying to make a match. Bridget was trying to give me a hot, young sports guy. Stefan is always about the man who can bring added value to Chantaine. Ultimately, he was thrilled that Bridget fell for a doctor who became our medical director."

"But you have to live with the choices," Nic said.

She nodded. "I do."

"My mother will be crushed if we don't get a chance to celebrate your birthday," he said.

Pippa racked her brain for a time she could break away. "Friday afternoon."

"Night," he said.

She blinked at him. "Night?" she echoed. "How am I supposed to do that?" she asked.

"Creativity, ingenuity," he said. "You're a Devereaux," he said in a slightly mocking voice. "You can do it."

Pippa sighed. "I'll try to figure it out," she said. "I need to put on my disguise so I can return to the library."

"Unless you want to stay here," he said, his tone seductive.

Pippa wanted to stay far more than she should admit to anyone, including herself.

Nic told his mother about Pippa's birthday and she immediately asked Goldie to make a cake and instructed him to get ice cream and noise-making toys. At seven o'clock on Friday, Pippa arrived in a rush, wearing her horrid costume, and he'd never seen a more welcome sight. Greeting her at the gate, he helped her disassemble her disguise.

"You have no idea what I had to do to make this happen," she said, ripping off her wig and raking her fingers through her hair. She pulled a band from her wrist and pulled her hair up into a ponytail.

"We'll make it worth it," he said and led her toward the front door of the cottage. He knocked first.

She frowned at him. "Why are you knocking?" she asked.

"Don't discourage me. I'm being polite."

"Oh," she said, realization crossing over her face.

"Come in," a female voice called.

"Amelie is awake," she said.

Nic opened the door and Pippa walked inside.

"Surprise!" the small group cried. Streamers filled the air.

Pippa gaped. "Oh, my goodness." She clasped one of the streamers in her hand. She clearly couldn't help grinning. "How cool is this. You shouldn't have done it. I didn't expect it."

"We wanted to celebrate," Amelie said. "You deserved a party. Bring the cake, Goldie."

Seconds later, Goldie carried in a birthday cake with lit candles.

"Is that a fire hazard?" Nic joked.

Pippa frowned at him, then returned her gaze to the cake. "Oh, wow," she whispered.

Nic felt a ripple of pleasure at her obvious delight. "Ready to blow out those candles, Princess? Make a wish," he coached next to her ear.

"Just one?" she asked.

He chuckled. "As many wishes as you can fit in while you're putting out the candles."

"Okay," she said and bit her lip. She inhaled deeply and blew out the candles. Milliseconds after they were snuffed out, she looked at him and smiled. "I did it."

"So you did," he said.

"Time to cut the cake, eat the gelato, open gifts," Amelie said.

"Gifts," Pippa echoed. "There weren't supposed to be any gifts."

"Why not?" Amelie asked. "If there are birthday parties, there should be gifts."

Goldie served the cake and gelato, along with champagne. Mr. Lafitte then presented Pippa with a wrapped box.

"It's from me," Paul said.

"Really?" Pippa said and unwrapped the gift which held a box of chocolates and a bottle of champagne, along with a gift certificate to one of her favorite local shops.

"You did too much," she said, clearly surprised and delighted. "I didn't expect this."

"We Lafittes like the element of surprise. Don't forget that," he said with a broad wink.

"Thank you, Mr. Lafitte," she said and brushed a kiss over his cheek.

"Call me Paul, sweetheart," he said.

"Thank you, Paul," she said and another gift was given to her. She opened it to find a long knitted scarf.

Her eyes filled with tears, Pippa looked at Amelie. "Oh, no, you didn't."

"I fear I did," Amelie said with a laugh in her voice. "I realize it's not the best handiwork, but hopefully my effort will warm your heart."

"I will treasure it," Pippa said through a tight throat. She tried to remember when she'd had a birthday that had made her feel more special. She couldn't. For various reasons, her birthday had often been overlooked. There had been conflicting schedules. Her brothers and

sisters had been busy. There were always more pressing obligations.

Tonight, however, she was the most important part
of the Lafittes' evening. "I don't know what to say. You
are—" Her voice broke and she swallowed hard over
the lump of emotion lodging in her throat. "You have
no idea how special this is for me."

"Bet you had gourmet cakes and birthday balls,"
Paul said.

"I had birthday cakes and birthday balls, but only
a couple of times. My parents were rarely around for
my birthdays. It was also sporadic for my brothers and
sisters. Everyone was so busy," she said and shrugged,
fearing she'd revealed too much. She bit her lip and
smiled. "But this is fabulous. You've made me feel so
special."

"That's because you *are* special," Amelie said and
reached to embrace her.

Pippa hugged the woman and Amelie's gaunt frame
frightened her. She was so thin. She felt so fragile. At
the same time, Pippa had learned that Amelie was a
strong, strong woman.

Goldie poured her another glass of champagne, but
Pippa asked for water. She had to drive back to the
palace.

"This has been delightful," Amelie said. "But I'm
pooped. Tomorrow I'll be stronger, though, I promise,"
she said, wagging her finger.

"Of course you will," Pippa said. "I would expect
nothing less. I have to go away for a few days, though,
so I'll check in when I return."

Amelie frowned. "Away? We'll miss you."

"I'll miss you, too," Pippa said, hating the prospect of leaving the Lafittes behind. With Amelie in such fragile health, Pippa wondered if something would happen to her when she was gone on the Italian holiday.

"Good night, darling. Happy birthday," Amelie said. Paul followed, giving her a kiss on her cheek.

After they left, Pippa turned to Nic. "I should probably go."

"You didn't finish your cake," he said.

How could she? she wondered. She could barely breathe, let alone swallow Goldie's cake.

"You're gonna hurt Goldie's feelings," Nic added.

She winced. "I can't eat that entire cake," she whispered.

"Let's take part of it to the guest quarters. That should help," he said. "Bring your champagne."

She shook her head. "I have to drive back to the palace," she said.

"I'll handle that," he said.

"How?" she asked.

He shrugged. "Trust me."

Pippa decided, for once, to trust him. Heaven knew, she'd seen an entirely different side of him with the way he was dealing with his mother's illness. "Lead me on," she said, lifting her glass of champagne.

She followed him out the door and he led her into the guest bungalow. A breeze flowed through the window, more delicious than any central air-conditioning could ever be. "This feels nice in here. Have you had a hard time adjusting to the small quarters?"

"There are interruptions from my parents when I'm

working sometimes, but for the most part, I've liked it. I don't need that much space," he said.

She laughed. "I'm thinking of your yacht. It's huge."

"That's different," he said.

"And your ranch in Texas?" she asked. "Your big, big ranch? Is that different, too?"

"And your big, big palace?" he returned.

"I live in a small suite in the big, big palace," she said. "And I'm prepared to live in a small apartment."

"Why are you making the big move now?"

She shrugged and moved around the small den of the bungalow. "It's overdue. It just took me a while to see that."

"Have a seat," Nic said from behind her.

Too aware of his presence, she felt a dozen butterflies dancing in her stomach. She sank down onto the sofa and took a sip of her second glass of champagne. Nic sat beside her holding the plate with her piece of cake and soft gelato.

"It was better a few minutes ago," he said, scooping up a bite with a spoon and lifting it to her mouth.

She opened her mouth and swallowed the sweet treat. "It really is delicious. Goldie could be a bakery chef."

"Goldie is a lot of things," Nic said. "Bodyguard, medic, mechanic, cook. Hell, he would make a great nanny."

She smiled. "He's so big and brawny. That's a funny image." She took another bite of cake.

"All packed for your holiday?"

The cake stuck in her throat and she coughed. Nic handed her the glass of champagne. She took a quick sip, then shook her head. "No, I've procrastinated. The palace stylist chose some things for me, so I'll take them. I hate to admit it, but I'm dreading it, which is ridiculous. Who wouldn't be happy with a trip to Capri?" She made a face. "But with those appearances and the fact that I'm supposed to spend time with the count, it doesn't feel like a holiday. It feels like an assignment."

"Do you have any free time?"

"The last day," she said.

"I could meet you," he said.

Her heart stopped, then started at his suggestion. "Oh, that would be—" *Fantastic,* she thought before she stifled herself. "We shouldn't. I'm sure my bodyguard will be there."

He shrugged. "We could get around him," he said. "But if you'd rather not—"

"Are you sure you can leave Amelie?" she asked.

He nodded. "She's been fairly stable. It would be just a day or two. To be honest, I have business with a colleague in Rome. I've been putting it off. I could take care of business, then meet you in Capri."

Although she knew it was insanity to even consider a secret rendezvous, Pippa could not make herself say no. She opened her mouth to try to form the word and her lips refused. Her whole body and being wanted to be with Nic and she was bloody tired of denying herself. "Yes," she finally said and closed her eyes. "But this could be messy. You know that, don't you?"

Nic laughed. "I've been dealing with messes since I was six years old."

She wondered what it was about Nic that made her feel stronger. When she was with him, she felt as if she could do almost anything.

He met her gaze and he must have read her feelings in her eyes. Pulling her slowly toward him, he gave her a dozen chances to turn away, but she didn't. She couldn't. But she couldn't help wondering why he continued to pursue her. He was experienced. He could have any woman he wanted.

"Do you want me just because you can't have me?" she whispered, the fear squeezing out of her throat.

"No," he said. "Besides, we both know I can and will have you. The question is when," he said and lowered his mouth to hers.

Pippa melted into him. She was afraid to trust him, afraid to trust her feelings because she never really had before, but her fear of missing him was bigger than her fear of trusting him.

She kissed him back with all the passion in her heart and felt his surprise and pleasure ripple through her. He paused just a half beat before he kissed her more thoroughly.

She slid her fingers through his hair, craving the sensation of being as close to him as possible. He leaned back on the sofa and pulled her on top of him. She felt his arousal, swollen against her, and the knowledge made her even more crazy. She squeezed his shoulders and biceps and shuddered against him as he took her mouth in yet another kiss that took her upside down.

Pippa couldn't remember feeling this way. Even though she and Nic had been involved before, they'd never gone all the way. Now she wondered how she could possibly fight how much she wanted him.

She felt his hand tenderly rub her back. "Hey, you

know where this is headed, don't you?" he asked against her mouth.

Pippa moved her mouth from his and buried her head in his shoulder, taking desperate breaths.

"Pippa, are you sure you're ready?" he asked.

He wasn't going to make it easy for her. He was going to make her choose. And maybe that was part of the reason she wanted him so much. It was time.

She lifted her head to meet his gaze. "Yes, I am."

He sucked in a quick, sharp breath and chuckled. "I'm ready, too, but I want you to think about it a little longer."

Pippa blinked. "Pardon me, are you refusing to be with me?"

He rose to a sitting position with his arms still around her. "I don't want you to do something impulsive and regret it."

Anger flickered through her and she narrowed her eyes. "You sound like my family. You sound like you don't trust me to make my own decisions."

"It's not that. I'm protecting you," he said.

"That's what they say, too," she said. "No one trusts me to make my own decisions. No one," she said and pushed away from him.

"I'm going home," she said.

"I have to drive you," he said. "You've had too much champagne."

Pippa stood, wrapping her arms around her waist, feeling humiliated. "Goldie can take me."

"I will take you," Nic said, rising.

Pippa bit her lip, feeling rejected and vulnerable. She wanted to hide.

"Pippa, you know I want you," he said and cupped her chin with his hand. "How much of a demonstration do you need?"

She swallowed over the desire pulsing through her. "It seems so easy for you to turn it off," she whispered.

He took her hand and placed it over his chest where his heart thundered against her palm. "Does that feel easy? I can show you more," he said as he moved her hand to his hard abdomen.

"S'okay," she said breathlessly.

"What do you want?" he asked.

"You've confused me," she said, clinging to him.

"Well, damn," he said. "Why would I do that?"

She looked up, studying his face. "I thought you would be the ruthless type when it comes to sex."

He held her against him for a long moment. "I am, but for some reason just not with you," he said.

Confusion and a half dozen other feelings swarmed through her like bees. The part of her that knew she was no beauty queen stabbed her with self-doubt. Pippa had made it a practice not to think about image, but all the criticism she'd received from the press over the years suddenly bombarded her. Maybe she wasn't sexy enough. Even though he'd been aroused, he'd been able to stop without a great deal of effort. At the same time, she'd lost all sense of time and place and could have gone much further without a second thought.

Self-conscious, she pulled away. "I really should get back to the palace," she said.

"Pippa—"

"I don't want to talk right now, if that's okay. I have

so much I need to do in a short amount of time to get ready for this trip."

With Goldie following in another vehicle, Nic drove her to the palace, and the silence between them was so uncomfortable that Pippa could barely stand it. Yes, she knew she'd told him she didn't want to talk, but now she would be leaving for her holiday, and she would just be full of doubts. Maybe it was for the best. Maybe this had been a close call and she could get her head back on straight with this trip.

He stopped a block away from the palace. "Can you make it the rest of the way?"

"Of course," she said. Overwhelmed by all the feelings tugging her in different directions, Pippa bit her lip. "Thank you for the birthday celebration and the ride to the palace. Listen, there's no need for you to make a special trip to Capri. I'll be there only a day and—"

"Are you saying you don't want me to come?" he asked, his gaze dark and penetrating.

She took a deep breath. "I'm saying you know my situation. I may not be able to spend time with you. The decision is completely up to you. *Ciao,*" she said and got out of the passenger side of the car.

Chapter Eight

Pippa arrived in Italy the next day. Count Bianchi greeted her at the airport. He was nearly bald with a paunch, but she tried very hard not to compare him to Nic. It was difficult because she had begun to compare every man to Nic.

"A pleasure to meet you, Your Highness," he said.

"And you, Count Bianchi," she said.

"Please call me Sal," he said. "You're such a lovely young woman. I'm pleased to have you by my side."

"Thank you very much, Sal," she said. "Tell me about your children."

During the ride, to Sal's chateau, she learned that Sal's oldest child was, in fact, older than her by five years. Sal also had several grandchildren. He showed her several photos and mentioned his wish to marry again.

Pippa rode the fence by praising his children but not

encouraging any discussion of her interest in him. After a quick respite in her room, she shared dinner with him in his formal dining room. Finally, they made the trip to the museum where Pippa made a brief speech encouraging historical and genealogical research.

Pippa begged off when Sal invited her to join him for a nightcap.

The following day, she geared up for a ride on a yacht, complete with photos. Afterward, she helped christen a new cruise ship with the count by her side. Every second, she damned Stefan for arranging this. Someone had clearly given the count entirely too much hope and she had to find a way to let him down easy. A chauffeur drove them back to his estate after the event.

"Have you enjoyed yourself?" the count asked, leaning toward her.

Pippa discreetly scooted away. "It's certainly been a long day. I'm more than ready for a good night of sleep."

"I understand you'll be in my country tomorrow night," the count said. "I would love to show you Capri. I know several restaurants and beaches that might please you."

"I couldn't trouble you," she said. "You've already done too much for me."

The count sighed.

"Sal, may I ask you? How long has it been since your wife passed away?" she asked.

He looked at her in surprise. "Ten months and three days."

She smiled and took his hand. "You're still counting days," she said gently. "I don't want to be presumptuous, but I don't think you're ready for a new wife. I know you're lonely, but I encourage you to take your time. You're a good man. You deserve a good woman."

He inhaled and smiled at her. "I'm an old fool to think I could attract a young princess like you."

She shook her head. "It's not that," she rushed to assure him. "I can tell that you're still not over your wife. I'm sorry for your pain, but at the same time, I know you're fortunate to have experienced that kind of love."

"Yes, I am," he said and began to talk about his former wife. Nearly an hour later, they arrived at his home. He appeared startled by the passage of time.

"I'm sorry if I've bored you," he said, clearly chagrined.

"No apologies necessary. I treasure a good love story, and that is what you and your wife had," she said.

"You're such a warm, lovely person. I wish I were at a different place in my mourning," he said.

"The right time will come," she said and pressed a kiss against his cheek. "The right woman will come."

He gave a soft chuckle. "Funny how the young can teach us so much," he said and helped her out of the limousine. "If I can ever do anything for you, it would be my pleasure," he said and kissed her hand.

"Thank you, Count Sal. My biggest wish for you is someone who will provide comfort to your heart. In the meantime, enjoy those grandchildren."

Sal gave a light laugh. "I'll take your advice."

The following morning, Pippa left the count's estate. After her last meeting with Nic, she wasn't sure he would meet her. She'd been so temperamental. He'd been so calm. His calmness infuriated her. She felt as if she couldn't control her passion. She didn't want to feel alone in her feelings and wanted to know that he felt the same way.

As she walked into her room with a lovely view of the ocean, Pippa stood in front of the open windows and inhaled the sea air. Her resort was located just outside the busy section of the beach, so she was able to enjoy the view without the crowds thronging to the pebbled beaches. Although Chantaine had its share of rocky beaches, Pippa had to confess Capri offered breathtaking vistas of steep cliffs, narrow gorges and limestone formations.

The sight was so beautiful she thought it might just clear her mind, and that was exactly what she needed. She refused to wonder if Nic would show or not. She had one day to truly relax and enjoy herself and that was what she intended to do. Pulling on the bathing suit the palace stylist had purchased for her, she glanced in the mirror and shrugged. Not too bad, she thought, then slathered herself with sunscreen from head to toe and grabbed her cover-up.

Situated on a hill, the hotel offered several decks with lounge chairs for sunning and enjoying the gorgeous views. Pippa accepted the assistance of staff to position an umbrella over her as she reclined in a chaise longue. She stared at the rocky coastline, willing it to clear her head. It occurred to her that Amelie would have loved this. The thought made her unbearably restless. Perhaps a magazine or book, she thought, rummaging through her bag. She pulled out the book on French history she'd been reading just before bedtime during the past month.

A shadow fell over her. Another waiter, she thought. Pippa had never been one to overindulge, especially when it wasn't even lunch yet. But perhaps a mimosa… She glanced up to see Nic standing over her.

Her heart lurched and the rush of pleasure she felt was so powerful that she couldn't squeak out a sound, let alone a word of greeting. He was dressed in jeans, a shirt and a ball cap, and his expression was gently mocking.

"Still pissed?" he asked.

She could argue that he was the basis for her *irritation* and confusion, but she was so bloody glad to see him that she knew it would be a waste. "Not too much."

"That's good. You want to chill here on the deck or are you in the mood for a little adventure?"

"Adventure," she said without waiting half a beat. "I'll tell my security I'm taking a tour."

Within a half hour, she was riding on the back of a motorcycle, clinging to Nic for her very life as he zigged and zagged around the curvy streets. If Stefan or Giles knew, they would have her head. Nic took another curve and she burst out laughing at the thrill.

"What's so funny?" he yelled at her.

"I'm terrified. I've either got to scream or laugh," she yelled back.

He nodded in approval. "We're just getting started."

After a lovely but terrifying ride, Nic pulled into the driveway of a chateau with stairs descending to a dock where several boats were moored. "What now?" she asked.

"We're going for another ride, this one on the ocean. You don't get seasick, do you?" he said, taking her hand.

She shook her head. "I'm a Devereaux. It's not allowed. My father never would have permitted it," she said as she walked down the steps with him.

"What trait would he have chosen over seasickness in his children?"

"Oh, I don't know. Two heads," she joked.

He stopped and looked at her and laughed. "You ought to get out more. I think it's good for you."

"And you?" she asked.

"Haven't had a lot of time for that lately," he said, his smile fading for a second. "But we've got today and a boat at our disposal."

"How did you arrange it?" she asked.

"My friend owns this chateau. He's out of town and he said I could use the house, the boat and the pool. I have access to a ski lodge in Switzerland he has used, so it all evens out." They walked across the dock and he helped her into a boat.

"Where are we going?" she asked.

He shot her a mysterious smile. "Places you can reach only by boat."

Joining him on the motorboat, Pippa reveled in the wind in her face. Nic didn't coddle her with a slow speed or by taking it easy on the curves. The wake made the ride bumpy enough that she had to sit down a few times.

"You're a fast pilot," she shouted to him. "Have you ever raced?"

He nodded. "But now we need to get to a special place."

"What special place?" she asked.

"You'll see soon enough," he said. He glanced over

his shoulder toward her. "Come here," he said extending his hand. "Wanna drive?"

Surprised by the offer, accepted his hand and he pulled her onto the seat next to him. "We have to slow down just a bit," she said.

He lowered the speed and she took the wheel. It was her first time because heaven knew her brother wouldn't have ever permitted it, let alone security. She gripped the steering wheel with her hands and turned it away from a huge yacht headed for the port side of their craft. The wake of the yacht created ripples, making the boat bounce against the waves.

Pippa laughed at the bumpiness but held tight.

"Doing good," Nic said, placing his hand at her back. It was a steadying sensation. Supportive, but not controlling. "Head this way," he said, pointing left.

She drove several more moments, then turned the wheel over to him. "Thank you. That was glorious," she said, unable to wipe her smile from her face.

"Glad you enjoyed it," he said, then revved up the speed again. "Hold on, Your Highness."

After several minutes, Nic slowed as they drew close to a series of rocks jutting from the ocean. "Where are we going?"

"Guess," he said, slowing the speed even more.

In the distance, she saw a rowing boat. Realization hit her. "The Blue Grotto," she said, so excited she could hardly stand it. "I know it's supposed to be a huge tourist spot, but I've always wanted to see it."

"I was hoping," he said.

"But it's supposed to be incredibly crowded." She glanced at Nic. "Why is it deserted? Is there a problem?"

"I bought an hour for us. No other boats during that time," he said.

She blinked. "That would be obscenely expensive," she said. "Stefan would throw a fit if he knew."

"He doesn't have to know," Nic said with a smile. He pulled closer to the rowboat and dropped anchor. The guide from the rowboat pulled right up next to their motorboat. Nic and the guide assisted her onto the rowboat.

"Buongiorno," the man said. "I'm Roberto. I will be your guide."

"Buongiorno and *grazie,* Roberto. I'm very excited to see the Blue Grotto," she said.

Nic hopped aboard. "Just tell me you've got a great singing voice," he said and shook Roberto's hand.

Roberto's mouth lifted in a wide grin. "The best. When I tell you, you must lie down in the boat." He turned to Nic. "Hold on to your sweetheart."

Pippa sank to a sitting position. Nic sat behind her and wrapped his arms around her. "Just following orders," he said.

She laughed, feeling the same terror and exultation she'd felt on the motorcycle and the speedboat. As they drew closer to the famous cave, she and Nic reclined in the boat.

"Prepare to enter the Blue Grotto, a spectacle providing thrills since the Roman times. Statues of pagan gods rest on the floor of the grotto. Once inside, you will see a surreal view that will make you feel as if you are floating through a clear sky. The reflection of the sunlight produces a unique transparency. There is no bluer blue," Roberto said. "Stay low, then you may sit up for a few minutes."

Sitting cradled in Nic's arms, Pippa stared in wonder at the blue universe on which they floated. They could have been riding on the sky if not for the lapping sound of the ocean against the cave walls.

"Put your hands in the water," Roberto said.

Both Nic and Pippa dipped their fingers into the cool water.

"It's so beautiful," she said.

"As are you, *signorina*," he said, and began to sing *"Bella Notte."* The acoustics were amazing. She almost didn't want to breathe because she didn't want to miss a nuance of the experience. Surrounded by Nic's strength and the wonder of the Blue Grotto, Pippa wanted to absorb everything. This was the kind of magic she wanted to store up inside her for sad, bad days.

When Roberto sang the last note, she glanced up at Nic. "This was amazing," she said.

"Quite a show," he said and took her mouth in a kiss.

After they boarded the motorboat, Nic took them back to the chateau. "Are you starving?" he asked. "My friend offered me anything in his pantry and refrigerator, but I thought we'd order takeout. The view is great and I thought you'd just as soon skip a public restaurant."

"That sounds perfect," she said and joined him as they climbed the steps to the chateau. Chugging her water, she sank onto a chair on the patio which overlooked the sea and sighed in contentment as she heard Nic call in an order to a restaurant.

Nic sat down across from her, lifting a bottle of beer to his lips. "You like Capri?"

"How could I not?" she said and shook her head. "I've never had a day like this."

"It was pretty good, wasn't it?"

"That's an understatement, and you know it," she said.

He chuckled at her response.

"Perhaps you do these kinds of things on a far more regular basis," she said.

"I've had some thrills, but the person you share it with can make a big difference," he said. "You need to make any calls to your security guy?"

She made a face at the reminder. "He said for me to call him when I returned to my room." She drummed her fingers on the table. "I suppose I could tell him I've returned and I'm safe and sound."

"Your choice," he said and took another drink from his beer.

Her stomach dancing with a combination of anticipation and apprehension, she placed the call. Her security man seemed satisfied. "I'd like to freshen up," she said and Nic pointed her to the toilet.

When she looked in the mirror, she nearly didn't recognize herself. Her cheeks and lips were flushed a deep pink. Her eyes looked so blue against the contrast of her skin and her hair was wilder than she'd ever seen it. Pippa chuckled and shook her head. It was hopeless. There was no use trying to tame it.

Dinner arrived and she and Nic enjoyed a meal of pasta, seafood and wine. Pippa knew Nic joked to diffuse tensions and cover his feelings, but she knew underneath it all, he had his share of stress. She'd never seen him this relaxed since she'd met him.

"You enjoy the sea. It's therapeutic for you," she said, touching his arm.

"It can be. It's not always." He shrugged. "What about you? Do you enjoy boating?"

She shrugged. "I haven't always. When I was a child, my father was known for spending as much time on his yacht as possible. He missed birthdays, appointments so he could escape on his yacht. In retrospect, he must not have been a very happy man."

"Tough being crown prince," Nic said with a wry grin.

"Perhaps. Some are better suited for the job than others. Stefan takes it very seriously, sometimes too seriously in my opinion. He's very controlling. I remember once when I was a teenager, we were on a family outing on the yacht and I asked if I could take the wheel just for a moment."

"Let me guess," Nic said. "He refused. There are plenty of men who can't give up the wheel."

"Why did you let me?" she asked. "For all you knew, I could have wrecked the boat."

"You're excessively responsible, Pippa. If you'd been concerned, you would have asked for my help. Plus, you underrate your abilities," he said in a matter-of-fact voice as he took another sip of red wine.

"You can't know that. I could be a total klutz," she said. "For all you know, we could be in a hospital from my flipping that boat."

He shot her a sideways glance full of humor. "I have excellent instincts."

She sighed and took a sip of her own wine. "Well, I can't argue with that."

"Anything else you want to argue about?" he asked, swirling his wine in his glass.

She couldn't help chuckling. She had been a bit contrary. "No."

"Good," he said. "Want to go for a swim in the pool? We can turn out the lights."

Pippa was still wearing her swimsuit under her clothes. The invitation for an evening swim was irresistible. She stood. "I'm ready."

He chuckled at her immediate reaction. "I should have asked earlier. I'll grab some towels. Let's go."

Cutting the lights, Nic grabbed some towels and led her down to the pool with a flashlight. Pippa tripped on a step, but he caught her against him. "Okay?" he asked.

"Yes. It's so dark," she said, laughing nervously.

"That's the idea," Nic said and led her the rest of the way to the pool. Clouds cast a filmy cover over the moon, but there was some light reflected against the water of the pool.

"It's beautiful," she said.

Nic jumped into the pool, the splash spraying over her legs. "It is," he said, with a wicked smile on his gorgeous wet face. "Come on in."

She paused half a second and jumped in. Two seconds later, she felt Nic's arms around her. "It's a little chilly."

"You'll warm up in a minute. Trust me," he said, pulling her against him.

She looked up into his face, feeling a crazy joy at the sight of the droplets on his face. "You're not warm," she said. "You're hot."

"I'm that way every time I get around you," he said and dipped his mouth to hers for a quick kiss.

The brief touch of his mouth on hers made her sizzle and burn deep inside.

She instinctively wrapped her legs around his waist.

"I like that," he said, pressing his hand at the back of her waist.

Everything that had been brewing between them for months tightened so much that she could hardly breathe. "Whew," she breathed.

"Take it easy," he said. "You okay?"

"Yeah," she breathed.

"You look like you need another kiss," he said with a half grin and lowered his mouth.

She sank into his mouth, feeling him, inhaling him. She couldn't get enough. His tongue slid past her lips and she savored the taste of him, the feel of him wrapped around her. The buoyancy of the water only added to the sensuality of the experience.

Nic slid his hands over her thighs and cupped her hips as he gave her a French kiss that made her feel as if she were turning upside down. She felt the same excitement race through her that she'd experienced earlier today when she'd driven the boat.

He squeezed her against himself. "I love your laugh," he muttered against her mouth.

"Good thing," she said. "I can't remember laughing more than I do with you."

"Hold your breath." He kissed her again, twirled her around again and sank, inch by inch underwater. It was a crazy, sexy, amazing experience kissing Nic that way. Seconds later, he rose, bringing her to the surface. She sucked in a quick breath of air, staring into his face. His strong, sexy face was covered with droplets of water. His eyes bored into hers.

The electricity between them sizzled and burned. She lifted her hands to cradle his face. "You're quite an amazing man."

He stopped dead. "That's quite the compliment," he said.

"I'm just telling the truth," she said.

"Good to know," he said and untied the top of her bathing suit. His hands slid over her breasts.

She inhaled quickly.

"You want me to stop?" he asked.

She hesitated a half beat. "No," she whispered.

He leaned his forehead against hers. "Pippa, I'm not gonna wanna stop," he said.

Her heart slamming against her ribs, she bit her lip. "Neither am I."

They played and frolicked in the pool. He kissed and caressed her, coaxing her out of the bottom of her bathing suit so that she swam nude with him. They got each other so worked up that he almost took her in the pool. Instead, he dragged her from the pool, wrapped a towel around her, another around him and half carried her up the stairs to the house.

Carrying her to the master bed and following her down, he seemed to devour her. And Pippa wanted him to consume her.

"Are you sure you're okay with this?" he asked, clearly reining himself under control.

"Yes," she said and stretched her arms out to him.

Nic slid his hand between her thighs, testing her

readiness. He rubbed and caressed her, making her wet with wanting. Sliding his finger inside her, he drove her even further. He made her want deep inside her.

"Nic," she said, squeezing his arms.

"You want me?" he asked, his voice raspy with his own desire.

"Yes," she said, close to pleading.

He slid his lips down to her breast, taking one of her nipples in his mouth. The sensation electrified her. She felt the instant connection between her breast and lower, deeper inside her.

"I want you inside me," she said. "In me."

In some corner of her mind, she knew he was putting on protection. Seconds later, he pushed her thighs apart. He thrust inside her and she felt a rush of shock and burning pain at the invasion. "Oh," she said.

Nic stopped, staring at her in surprise. He swore under his breath. "You should have told me."

"I wasn't thinking about it," she said. "My mind was on—" She wiggled as she grew more accustomed to him. "Being with you," she said and wiggled again.

His gaze darkened and he fastened his hands around her hips. "You're gonna make this tough on me," he said in a rough voice.

"Hopefully, it won't be all bad."

Nic groaned and began to move in a slow, delicious rhythm. Pippa felt the beginning of exquisite sensations sliding throughout her.

"You okay?" he asked in a low, uneven voice.

"Yessss," she said. "This is sooo—" The twist of tension growing inside her took her breath.

The pulsing rhythm continued, and she clung to him,

staring into his dark gaze, taking and feeling taken. His jaw tightened with restraint, he reached down between her legs and sought her sweet spot, sending electrical impulses through her. The combination of his possession and his caresses were too much.

She jerked and rippled in response. Suddenly, her body clenched in indescribable pleasure and she arched toward him. "Nic," she called, feeling as if her voice were separated from her body.

He held her tight and she felt and heard his own climax ripple through her.

It was the most profound experience of her life and she knew she would never, ever be the same.

Their harsh breaths mingled in the air. The sound was as primitive as what she'd just experienced. At this moment, she felt Nic inside her body, her mind, her blood. She wondered if she would ever breathe without being aware of him again.

Chapter Nine

Nic lay on his side and pulled Pippa against him. She was half asleep. He tried to take in the impact of what they'd done. Nic had known it was inevitable. He had known they would make love. He had known she would be his.

He just hadn't known how much it would affect him. Months ago, when he'd first met Pippa, he'd wanted her, reluctantly felt a need for her. Something primal had driven him toward her. He'd hoped it had all been about sex, but now he knew he'd been wrong.

Something in his psyche was tangled with this woman, and he wasn't sure how in hell he could untangle himself from her. Aside from the fact that she felt so soft and right nestled against him, he felt himself wanting more. Wanting something he hadn't known was possible.

It didn't make sense. Other women had made themselves available to him. Sometimes he'd accepted their overtures. Sometimes he'd refused. Now, he felt himself falling deeper than he'd ever expected.

He frowned as he luxuriated in her naked body against his. He'd thought that once he took her, he would be okay. He would be rid of the itch that plagued him day and night for her. But it hadn't worked. Now that he'd taken her, it was almost as if he was more committed. He wanted her more.

That was strange as hell.

He slid his hand over her crazy, curly hair. She sighed and the sound did something crazy to his gut. He felt incredibly protective of her. More so now. He knew she was mostly asleep, but her hand closed over his, as if she were protecting him. The notion was amusing, but the gesture stole his heart.

The rude ping of his cell phone awakened Nic. It took a few pings, but he finally recognized the sound. Grabbing his cell phone from the bedside table, he pulled it up to his ear. "Yes," he said.

"Nic," his father said. "Your mother's in trouble. She needs help. The regular doctor can't be reached."

Nic sat up straight in bed. "What's wrong?"

"Her belly's distended. She's in pain," his father said.

"I'll take care of it," Nic said. "I'll be there soon."

Pippa opened her gloriously blue, groggy eyes. "What's wrong?"

"Amelie is having problems. Her belly's distended."

Pippa frowned, rising in the bed. "Oh, no. Your doctor isn't available?"

Nic scowled. "He should have been. She may need

to have some sort of draining from fluid buildup. I may have to find another doctor."

Pippa blinked, then frowned again. "If it takes too long, maybe I can find another doctor."

"Who?" he asked.

"My brother-in-law, Ryder McCall," she said.

"Won't that cause problems for you?" he asked.

"What's more important?" she asked. "My problems, or your mother's?"

Two hours later, they were on a plane, in different rows, to Chantaine. Even though she wasn't sitting next to him, Pippa could feel Nic's tension reverberating throughout the jet. She wished she could help him, but ultimately, she knew she couldn't. Ultimately, she knew Amelie would die. And she would die soon. The question was how could they make Amelie's passing easy. The jet landed in Chantaine and she exited the plane ahead of Nic.

Needing to get away from the watchful eye of Giles, her security man, she made a quick trip to the ladies' room.

Nic called her on her cell. "I can take her to a clinic, but that won't guarantee her privacy. The news could get out that she's here."

"Wait," she said. "Let me see what I can do."

She took several deep breaths, then dialed the number for her brother-in-law, Ryder. He immediately answered.

"Ryder McCall," he said.

"This is Pippa," she said. "Don't reveal who you're speaking to. It's an emergency."

He paused a half beat. "How can I help you?"

"There's a cancer patient who needs some kind of draining. I'm hoping you can help."

He paused again. "Where can I meet you?"

Pippa gave him the address. An hour later, she arrived at the cottage and met with Nic. "Ryder is coming."

"Can he help?" he asked as they stood in the den. Amelie was in the bedroom, bloated and suffering.

Paul banged his crutch on the floor. "She's in pain. What's taking so damn long?" he demanded.

"Ryder will be here any moment," Pippa tried to reassure him.

"Ryder?" Paul echoed. "Who the hell is Ryder? What kind of doctor is named Ryder?"

Seconds later, Pippa's brother-in-law strode into the house. He met Pippa's gaze. "How sick is she?" he asked.

"She's terminal," she said in a low voice. "We want to keep her as comfortable as possible," she said.

Ryder met her gaze. "You should share this with your family," he said.

"My family wouldn't understand," she said. "You know how much they hate the Lafittes."

"I don't understand the grudge," Ryder muttered.

"I need your help and your confidence," she said.

"The first is easy. The second is not. Soon, you must tell your family about this," he said.

Pippa felt her stomach twist. "There's enough trouble today," she said. "Please help Amelie."

Moments later, Goldie drove Amelie to a local clinic

where Ryder performed the procedure that would bring her relief.

Just a few hours passed and Amelie was brought home.

"Thank you," Nic said, clearly weary from the whole experience. "How much trouble will this cause you?"

Pippa shrugged. "Ryder will give me some time. It's more important that Amelie is okay."

Nic's gaze grew shuttered. "You know it's only a matter of time for her," he said.

"I know that," she said. "But I want her to be as comfortable as possible."

He took her hand and clasped it for a long moment. "How did I get so damn lucky to know you?"

She smiled. "That's an excellent question. I feel the same way about you."

In the middle of the night, Pippa returned to the palace. Happily enough, she didn't have to endure a screening from her security detail. Unfortunately that didn't extend to Bridget. Her sister could out-snoop any P.I., and Pippa was doomed to face her questions.

"How was the count? Was he a prick? Was he determined to get into your pants?" she asked as Pippa gulped down her first coffee of the day.

"He was lovely. Just older. We both realized that he was still in love with his wife and he should take his time before getting involved with anyone else even though he was lonely."

Bridget blinked. "Really?"

Pippa nodded. "Really."

"So what did you do for the rest of your trip in Capri?"

"I took a tour," Pippa said.

"A tour?" Bridget echoed, chagrined. "The least the count could have done was to give you a proper tour of Capri."

"I didn't want him to do it," Pippa said. "He was a sweet man, but I used up all my patience during the two days I spent with him. I just needed to take a break after that."

"I suppose I can understand that. I feel bad that you've experienced such bad matchups from Stefan and me," Bridget said.

"There are worse things," Pippa said.

"True," Bridget said. "Ryder went out last night to help a terminal cancer patient."

Pippa's stomach clenched. "How terrible."

Bridget shook her head. "He has a difficult job."

Pippa nodded. "Yes, he does," she murmured.

Bridget shrugged. "Well, did you enjoy Capri? I hate to think the whole trip was a waste."

Pippa nodded again. "Yes, I got to see the Blue Grotto. It was amazing."

"Did you really take a tour?" Bridget asked.

"Yes," Pippa said. "The sight of it was amazing. Worth the crowd."

Bridget shook her head. "Better you than me. I would love to see it, but I couldn't stand the crowds."

"It wasn't that crowded when I was there," Pippa said. "I guess I got lucky."

"Did the guides sing for you?" Bridget asked.

"'*Bella Notte*,'" she said with a smile.

"How romantic," Bridget said. "A shame you didn't have a handsome man accompanying you."

"It was beautiful," Pippa said.

Bridget sighed. "You're a saint. You know how to make the best of everything."

"I would never call myself a saint," Pippa said.

"That's because you don't know what demons the rest of us are," Bridget said with a dirty giggle.

"You overstate your evil," Pippa said. "Most of us just do the best we can."

"That attitude is what makes you a saint," Bridget told her.

Guilt stabbing at her. She was lying to her family. "Please don't call me a saint. I'm not worthy of that," Pippa said.

Bridget tilted her head, studying Pippa's face. "If you insist," she said. "But if anyone ever deserved sainthood—"

"It wouldn't be me," Pippa said in a flat voice.

Stefan wouldn't meet with her the following day. His assistant said he was too busy. After soldiering through her brother's romantic aspirations for her with the count, Pippa was more than peeved, so she took a rare move. She sent him an email and text. In general, the family was instructed not to bother Stefan with personal texts. She usually respected the instruction. After all, she knew he had a terribly demanding schedule and she didn't want to add to his burden. Today, her patience wore thin.

Happy birthday to me. I'm moving out and ditching my security. Cheers, Pippa.

Seconds later, she received a text from Stefan. I order you not to make any changes before you and I have an opportunity to talk.

She sent a return text. Apologies. You used up your orders when you tried to match me up with a man nearly the age of our father. *Ciao.*

Then she turned off her phone. Pippa felt a rush of adrenaline race through her. Her heart hammered against her rib cage. She was so rarely defiant. She exulted in the feeling. For a moment. Then she realized she needed to find a place to live. Immediately.

She spent the morning making calls to apartments, eliminating those without a security gate. By afternoon, she had a list of properties and made visits. At five-thirty, she signed a lease for a one-bedroom apartment. It cost a little more than she'd hoped, but the situation was perfect for her. Now if she could just ditch her security detail.

Pippa finally turned on her phone again, dreading the incoming voice mails and messages. She was immediately deluged by messages from Stefan, some of which had been written in all capital letters. She deleted them without reading and sent one last message regarding her security and the fact that she was ready to make a press release regarding her status change in security.

A half beat later, her phone rang, and her stomach immediately tightened. Pippa saw that it was Stefan and considered pushing the ignore button. *Coward.* Scowling at the truth in the accusation, she picked up the call. "Good evening, Your Royal Highness," she said.

"What in bloody hell has gotten into you?" Stefan demanded. "I realize getting you together with the count was a stretch, but your overreaction is totally unnecessary."

"It's not an overreaction. I just turned twenty-five," she said.

"But you've never complained before," Stefan said. "I can't allow you to move out and dismiss your security. Are you sure you're not having some sort of women's issue?"

If his pompous attitude weren't so offensive, she would have laughed. "Pretend I'm male and this will all seem overdue," she said.

"But you're not. You're my youngest sister and it's my duty to protect you."

Her heart softened. "That's so sweet, Stefan, and I do appreciate it, but I will die of suffocation if I stay at the palace. It's time for me to go."

"I don't understand this. You've always been so reasonable," he said.

"Acquiescent," she corrected. "I feel like Rapunzel, but with bad hair."

Stefan sighed. "At least continue your security."

"No. My security is a leash. It's unnecessary except when I make appearances assigned by the palace. Trust me, the citizens of Chantaine will cheer when they see another expense deducted by the palace."

"They won't know about it until after the fact," Stefan said and swore. "Promise you'll still attend family dinners," he added.

"I will," she said, her heart softening again. "You're so busy you won't notice that I'm gone."

"I already notice," he said.

Pippa felt her eyes burn with tears. Her emotions

caught her off guard, but she refused to give in to them. "I promise to babysit your new child," she said. "None of the new generation of Devereauxs will escape my terrible singing voice."

Stefan laughed. "I love you, Pippa."

Pippa's heart caught. For her hardnosed brother to admit such feelings aloud was monumental. It was all she could do to choke the words through her throat. "And I love you."

They hung up, and Pippa began to weep.

The following day, she enlisted the help of security to help her move into her apartment. She was able to make her move under the radar of Bridget because her sister was busy with the construction of the new so-called ranch. Pippa didn't want her security man to get a hernia, so she insisted he get help.

By noon, she was moved into her apartment. Surprisingly enough, she had more room in her new quarters than her previous suite at the palace. She felt a strange combination of relief and anxiety.

Sinking down onto the antique sofa that seemed so out of place in her new surroundings, she took a deep breath. She was free. That was what she'd wanted. Right?

A knock on the door startled her. She rose, looked through the peephole and saw Nic standing outside her door. She whipped the door open. "How did you find me? And how did you get through security?"

"Goldie," he said with a shrug. "You gonna invite me in?"

Fighting a sudden, strange awkwardness, she nodded. "Of course."

He stepped inside and glanced around. "Downsizing?" he asked.

"Actually the apartment is larger than my quarters at the palace," she said, folding her arms over her chest.

"Really," he said more than asked as he glanced around the apartment. "Did they put you in the palace dungeon or something?"

She laughed. "No, but I had no children, so I didn't need a larger suite. How did Goldie find out about my move?"

Nic shrugged. "Goldie has his ways. I don't question him. He just gets the job done. Why didn't you tell me about your plans for the big move?"

"Besides the fact that I didn't know if it would all work out, I don't owe anyone an explanation about my plans," she said.

He gave a low whistle and dipped his head. "As you say, Your Highness."

She wrinkled her nose at his response. "Truthfully, would you feel the need to make explanations about your own living arrangements?"

He met her gaze and gave another shrug. "Touché. I'm just curious what inspired all this."

"It's been a long time coming," she said, walking toward the balcony window. "Stefan fought it every inch of the way. I know he means well, but it will take him a long time to understand what I said about feeling like Rapunzel with very bad hair."

"I like your hair," Nic said.

She laughed, her heart warming at his comment. "That's not the point. I must confess I'm a bit worried that it was so easy for Goldie to find me. If he can get through the security, others could, too."

"Not likely," Nic said. "Many foreign nations could learn a lot from Goldie."

"But how did you get through?" she asked.

"I'm interested in buying the entire complex," he said.

Pippa blinked. "Pardon me?"

"It's just a story, but you never know," he said. "Have you ordered pizza?"

"What do you mean?"

"It's a tradition. Whenever you move, you order pizza for dinner because you're too tired for anything else," he said.

"I hadn't thought of it, but—"

"It's on me," he said with a sexy smile. "Because I didn't get here fast enough to help you move in."

Her heart softened. "That's very nice," she said.

"I have ulterior motives," he confessed. "I want you to share it with me."

"I can do that," she said.

Forty-five minutes later they sat with their feet propped on the boxes, munching on a loaded pizza. "I would have chosen vegetarian," Pippa said, but took a bite of her second slice anyway.

Nic shook his head. "No. Moving day turns everyone into a carnivore."

"If you say so," she said, smiling at him. "What made you put Goldie on me?"

"When I didn't hear from you, I got worried. I didn't know how hard your family would be on you once they learned about your relationship with the Lafittes."

"They still don't know," she said, taking a long draw from her glass of water.

He shot her a look of disbelief. "You sure?"

"Reasonably sure. I can't believe neither Stefan nor Bridget would be able to hold back their opinions if they knew. They're both extremely outspoken," she said.

"Bet Stefan hated that you moved out. I don't think he thought you would go through with it," he said.

"Hate is a mild term for it," she said, smiling at him. "And you're right. He didn't believe I would go through with it even though I'd warned him."

He grinned at her in return. "I'm surprised the palace didn't disintegrate from his temper tantrum."

"The palace has endured temper tantrums over the course of several centuries," she said. "I must confess I wonder if Stefan has cracked a few walls."

"Well, he's turning the tide. He's no playboy prince," Nic said. "That kind of will is going to shake some foundations."

Pippa nodded. "That's a good way of saying it. Stefan has fought to overcome my father's reputation."

"I'd say he's doing a pretty damn good job."

"He is. I've tried to support him, but I had to move away from the palace. I couldn't stand the restraints anymore."

"The timing's interesting. Did the Lafittes have anything to do with your decision?"

"Perhaps," she said. "You're all such independent sorts, even Amelie. You made me aware of how trapped I feel."

"And how do you feel now?" he asked.

"Great," she said, reluctant to reveal even her tiniest regret.

"And a little scared," he said.

"I didn't say that," she said.

"Your mouth didn't, but your eyes did," he said and cupped her chin. "You're gonna be okay, Pippa. You're stronger than anyone thinks."

"What makes you so sure?" she asked.

He gave a dry chuckle. "You've already proven yourself ten times over."

The strength in his gaze both empowered and aroused her. The combination of feelings was strange but undeniable. She leaned toward him and he took her mouth. The room began to spin.

The kiss turned into another and another. Soon enough, he'd removed her blouse and skirt. She pushed away his shirt and jeans, and he was inside her. This time, slowly.

"Okay?" he asked, his restraint vibrating from his body.

"Yes," she said, drawing him into her.

The rhythm began. She took him and he filled her. More than ever, they had more in common. She was a rebel just like him, and their joining was more powerful with the knowledge of it.

The next morning, Nic awakened before dawn on the mattress on which they'd collapsed on the floor. Pippa breathed in a deep, even sleep. She'd been exhausted and he could still feel her tiredness against him. But Nic had tasks calling him, even at this time of day. His businesses, his father's business, his mother's illness.

He tried to make himself slow down and relax for just a few moments.

"You're awake," Pippa whispered and turned her face into his throat.

His heart stuttered. "How did you know?"

"Your whole body is tense. I can almost feel your mind clicking a million kilometers an hour," she said.

He felt the slightest easing inside him. "I thought you were asleep."

She gave a soft chuckle that tickled his throat. "Not."

He tugged her fabulous, curly hair with one hand and slid his hand low between her legs. "As long as you're awake."

She gave a soft intake of breath. "Oh, my."

"Oh, yeah," he said and began to make love to her.

An hour later, they took a shower together and had to hunt for towels. They dried off with blankets instead which provided even more of a distraction.

Nic dressed in the clothes he'd worn the day before. Pippa stood before him with a damp blanket wrapped around her.

"Will you be okay?" he asked.

"Of course," she said. "I have a dozen boxes to unpack. My biggest fear of the day is a visit from Bridget or a call from Tina."

He rubbed her shoulders. "You can handle them."

"Yes, it just won't be fun," she said and made a face.

"Call me if you need me to break any legs," he said.

She laughed. "Now that would go over well."

"I'll check in on you later, but seriously, call me if you need me," he said.

"I will," she said. "And I may take a break from unpacking to visit your mother."

"She would like that," he said. "She did okay physically after the procedure to drain extra fluid, but I can tell it bothered her to need it."

She sighed. "I wish I could change this for her."

"You already have," he said.

"Have you been able to reach your brothers?" she asked.

"Two down, one to go," he said. "They said no the first three times I talked to them. I've got them up to a maybe."

"You're amazing and they're stupid," she said.

"It's complicated with my dad," he said. "If I hadn't been successful on my own so young, I may have shared their attitude. The weird thing about that success is that it freed me to forgive him."

Pippa loved him even more for his ability to express how he'd grown. Not every man could do that. She reached for his hand. "You're a good man."

His hand enclosed hers. "Careful. Never forget that I come from pirates."

Chapter Ten

Nic chewed through another two antacids as he stared at his electronic tablet and tried to figure out when he could break away for a two-day business trip. His mother had seemed more tired than usual lately, sleeping more during the day. He didn't know what in hell to do. If he left and she passed, he would never forgive himself.

He had thought that spending the day and night with Pippa in Capri would rid him of the increasing edginess he'd felt 24/7. Being with Pippa calmed a part of him, and he'd thought just a little time away with her would give him the break he'd never admit to needing.

He'd known going into this that it would be no picnic, but he would never have predicted the effect the situation would have on his body. He had begun to feel like a caged animal, rarely sleeping longer than three hours at night. The knowledge of his mother's impending death seemed to squeeze his throat tighter and tighter every day. He was always running out of antacids. He'd been determined to keep his emotions under strict control, but his frustration at his inability to change his mother's pain and the ugly progress of her disease wore him down.

He heard the sound of his mother singing outside his window and immediately glanced outside. He stared in disbelief at the sight of her as she approached the pool. It was 1:00 a.m.

Alarmed, Nic raced out the door. "Mother, what in hell are you doing?"

Amelie glanced over her shoulder. "Oh, hello, darling. What are you doing up so late?"

Nic felt a sliver of relief. At least she was lucid. He let out a half breath. "Finishing up some work," he said, moving toward her. Although she was still eating, she looked thinner.

Amelie tilted her head, sympathy creasing her brows. "You're not sleeping well, are you?" she said more than asked. "Come here and sit with me for a few minutes. I was going to go for a swim, but it can wait," she said as she sank into a chair.

Nic shook his head, but joined her. "You can't go swimming. Dr. McCall said you have to wait for five days after the procedure to swim or take a tub bath."

She frowned. "I could have sworn it's already been five days." She waved her hand. "My memory's not the best lately. The pain meds help the pain, but they make me sleepy. Makes for a difficult choice." She sighed. "But enough about me. I'm sick of it all being about me. How are you and Pippa?"

"What do you mean me and Pippa?" he asked, rubbing his jaw.

"Well, there's obviously something between you. It's a wonder the sparks don't burn down the cottage. What are you going to do about it?"

"It's complicated," he said.

She laughed. "You think I don't understand complications?"

"She's very devoted to her family. They hate me. It's an impossible situation for her. I can't ask her to give up her family," he said.

"Pippa is a very strong woman. You're a strong man. The two of you together, you may be able to achieve something that seems impossible," she said.

Nic couldn't see it. He couldn't see asking such a thing of Pippa after all she'd already done for him and his mother.

"You have no faith," she said. "You'll have to find your way. But remember what I said."

"I will," he said.

"And I wish you wouldn't suffer so much about the fact that I'm dying. I'm going to be fine. I'm a bit worried about your father, but I think if you get him a dog, it will help."

Nic blinked. "A dog?"

His mother nodded. "He'll need the blind adoration and companionship. Trust me on this."

His stomach knotted at the direction of their conversation. "We don't have to talk about this."

"Yes, we do," she said and put her hand over his. "I'm worried about you."

He clenched his jaw. "You don't need to worry about me. You raised me to be strong."

"Yes, but you don't have superpowers. Deep inside, you think you should be able to save me, and the fact that you can't is ripping you apart. If I'd known it would be this hard for you, I would have stayed in the States and worked with hospice. This has been too much of a burden on you."

"I wouldn't have it any other way," he said. "Except for you not to die," he said, his eyes stinging with emotion.

"Oh, darling, you will always have me with you," she said. "I promise. And I believe you'll feel it. It will hurt terribly in the beginning, but I'll always be with you. You're doomed. You have my genetic material and that won't go away."

He laughed at her words, struggling with a dozen emotions, most of them sad and wrenching. "Is there anything else I can do for you?"

"You've already done it. You've given me this wonderful gift of time in Chantaine. Now live your life," she said. "If you need to take care of business, do it. But don't forget your heart. Never ever forget to have fun and to have heart. Promise?" she asked.

He took a deep breath. "I promise."

She looked wistfully at the pool. "Are you sure you won't let me cheat and take a quick dip?"

"One more day, and you can be a dolphin. But not until."

"You're such a tyrant," Amelie said. "But I'm tired again anyway. Good night, darling. Try to get some rest. You know how cranky you get when you don't get your beauty sleep."

He rolled his eyes. "I'll try," he said and helped her to her feet and walked her to the front door. At that moment, he knew what he had to do. She hadn't asked for it, but there was one more thing his mother wanted and he was damn well going to do it for her.

The next day, Pippa came to visit. She began pulling off her disguise the second she climbed out of the car. "Hate this," she muttered. "Completely and totally hate this."

Even her griping made Nic feel a little lighter. He stepped outside his door and grabbed her from behind. She gave a squeal.

"It's me," he assured. "The gray wig brings out my primal urges," he said.

She laughed breathlessly and turned toward him. "You're insane."

"I do my best," he said. "It's damn good to see you." He took her mouth in a long kiss that made him want far more than a kiss.

"I've been unpacking," she said. "I didn't think I had that much, but I clearly underestimated. Plus, I had nothing in my refrigerator and couldn't ring the chef for breakfast or dinner."

"Oooh, tough break, Your Highness. Sure you don't want to move back into the palace?" he asked. "I know Stefan would take you back."

She shook her head. "There will be adjustments. That's expected. Nothing a toaster and microwave won't cure. Plus I'm told my security detail is retiring at the end of this week. The true beginning of my new life will start then."

"Yeah, just be careful," he said. As much as Pippa's security had been a pain in his backside, the fact that she'd had it had given him a measure of relief.

"Oh dear, you're sounding just a bit like Stefan," she said.

"Cut me some slack. I can be protective, too," he said.

She nodded. "I know. It's not totally bad when not taken to extremes," she said. "How are your mother and father?"

"Dad is getting stronger. Mom is getting weaker. It's going to be tricky keeping my dad occupied," he said.

She frowned. "Do I need to take him on an outing?"

Nic chuckled at the image of Pippa taking his dad to the knitting store or brunch. "Nah, I'll just get Goldie to wear him out with some extra workouts."

She nodded. "And what about you?" she asked and he felt as if she were turning a searchlight on his insides.

"I'm good," he said with a shrug.

"You lie, but I understand," she said and squeezed his arm. "I'm sorry this is so hard for you, but you wouldn't be the man I—" She broke off. "You wouldn't be the man I admire you if it weren't hard for you."

"Yeah, well," he said and picked her up off her feet.

Her eyes widened. "What are you doing?"

"Just checking your weight. Making sure you're not wasting away without a chef."

She laughed. "I'm not suffering that much," she said.

He pulled her against him and slid her down the

front of him. "I'm headed out of town tomorrow. Can you come over tonight?"

She nodded.

He felt a rush of relief. "I'll send Goldie to pick you up. Wear this and you'll be fine."

Pippa groaned. "As soon as my security guy retires, I'm burning the wig."

"Don't rush it. You never know when you'll need it."

"Where are you headed?"

"Back to the States for business and one personal mission. Let's go see my mom. She'll fuss if she knows I kept you from going inside," he said.

Pippa saw the weariness stamped on Amelie's face. Nic's mother tried to hide it, but it was unmistakable. Still, Amelie seemed happy to see her and Pippa promised to visit with her the following day. Not wanting to tire her further, Pippa gave the woman a hug and left. Nic walked her to the dreadful machine that was her covert car.

"I'll see you later," he said, pulling her against him. His strength tugged at her. She didn't know how he kept everything together. She just longed to help him as much as she could.

"Later," she promised and kissed him, then drove away.

Hours later, she ate a frozen dinner and tried to play catch-up with her academic work. First, she waited for her security detail to leave for the evening, then she waited for Goldie's call. Her stomach danced with nerves on her way to see Nic.

The more time she spent with Nic, the more she felt

as if she were making a commitment toward him. With the way her family felt about the Lafittes, she just didn't see how anything between her and Nic could end well. Pippa closed her eyes against the thoughts. She couldn't think past tonight. There was too much to work out and she knew she couldn't do it all at once.

But she could be with Nic tonight, hold him and treasure the way she felt when she was with him, the way she felt in his arms.

When Goldie pulled into the driveway, he immediately got out and opened the door for her. "Your Highness," he said with a dip of his head.

"Thank you, Goldie," she said. "But I already told you to call me Pippa."

"Yes, you're welcome, Your—" The big man broke off and smiled. "Your Pippa," he said.

She smiled. He was such a gentle giant.

"I'll take you home whenever you like," he said. "Enjoy your evening."

Pippa walked the few steps to the guest suite and lifted her hand to knock on the door, but it opened before she had a chance.

Nic caught her hand and pulled her inside. "What took you so long?"

"I waited for my security detail to go home," she said.

"Good for you," he said. "Have you had dinner?"

She nodded. "As a matter of fact, I have."

"Are you going to tell me what you ate?"

She shook her head. "No."

He chuckled. "That tells me enough. Goldie put together some appetizers and he baked a pie."

"A pie?" she echoed. "Is there anything he can't do?"

"Not much," he said. "Have a seat. I'll get you a glass of wine."

They shared easy conversation while they ate the appetizers. Pippa was almost too full for pie.

"The proper way to eat this apricot pie is with ice cream," Nic said.

"À la mode," she said. "But I can't imagine eating a full slice."

"Then we can share," he said and scooped up a bite for her. The gesture was both generous and sensual.

"Delicious again," she said. "What time do you leave tomorrow?"

"We're not going to talk about tomorrow, but I'm leaving around 5:00 a.m."

Pippa gasped. "You should go to bed and I should leave. You need to get your rest."

"I can sleep on the flight, but I like your idea of going to bed," he said, his dark gaze wrapping around hers and holding tight.

She took a last sip of her wine and met his challenge. "Then what are you waiting for?"

He immediately took her hand and led her to the bed. He skimmed his hand over her crazy, curly hair. "I didn't expect to want you this much after the first time we were together," he said, kissing her. "How can I want you more?"

Her heart hammered in her chest. "I hope I'm not the only one who feels this way," she whispered. "It's almost too much."

"I know," he said. "I've never felt this way before."

"That's a relief," she said and tugged at his shirt.

"Maybe for you. It's hell for me," he said, and began to undress her.

They kissed and caressed each other into a frenzy. He made her breathless and she did the same to him. Finally he filled her and they stared into each other's eyes.

Pippa wasn't sure if it took seconds or moments later. She only knew she felt taken all the way to her soul.

"I want you," he muttered. "I need you. I—"

He didn't finish, but she craved the words, the emotion, everything that he was. Her heart and stomach clenched, and she arched toward him as he thrust deeply inside her.

Her climax sent her soaring.

"It's never enough," he said. "I can't get enough of you."

Thank goodness, she thought and wrapped herself around him from head to toe. She clung to him with every fiber of her being, wanting him to draw her strength into him.

"I want you with me," he said next to her ear. "All the time."

Love me, she thought. *Love me just for me, that's all I want.* She wished he would say, *I'll take care of you forever.* The thought took her by surprise. Pippa didn't want to be the one taken care of. She wanted to be the woman strong enough to stand up and take care of her man and give him anything he needed from her.

"I want to be with you anytime," Pippa whispered. "Every time."

They made love again and afterward, Pippa realized that Nic needed rest. He might deny it, but the truth was he needed rest. She knew he needed far more rest than he could possibly get tonight.

Relaxed against him, Pippa fought sleep. "I need to go back to my apartment."

Nic swore. "I wanted to talk you into staying here all night."

"It will be easier for you to rest tonight, then wake up to leave tomorrow without me here," she said.

"Says who?" he said.

"Says me," she said and lifted her hand to stroke his forehead. "You have a tough trip ahead of you. Business and something else you're not telling me."

He leaned his head back and narrowed his eyes. "How do you know?" he challenged.

"I just do," she said. "Besides, you said you had a personal mission, too."

He scowled at her, then chuckled. "I'm going to bring my brothers back. Even if I have to kidnap them."

Pippa gasped, then bit her lip. "Well, bloody hell, if anyone can do it, you can."

He laughed louder this time and put his hands on either side of her hand as if she were the most precious thing in the universe.

"If you get arrested," she began.

"Would you pay my bail?" he asked.

"Oh, yes," she said without a second thought. She squeezed his hands. "Call me anytime," she told Nic.

"I will, unless a police officer does…asking you to make bail," he said and gave a dry chuckle.

"You're a bad, bad boy with an amazing heart," she said.

"That's why you fell for me from the beginning," he said.

She bit her lip. "Yeah, maybe. Just promise me you'll take care of you," she said.

"I will. Spend some time with my mother," he said. "She's on the edge and I have a feeling you could bring her away from it."

Surprised at his belief in her ability, she shook her head. "I'll visit her tomorrow, but you know I can't control her future."

"Yeah," he said. "I think being with you makes things better for her."

"I'll do my best," she promised. "My very best."

Pippa reluctantly dragged herself from Nic's bed and washed her face and pulled on her clothes. Stepping out of the bathroom, she felt Nic step behind her and wrap his arms around her. "What are you doing?"

"Drawing your life force into me," he said.

She giggled. "That sounds ominous if it were possible."

"How do you know it's not?" he asked.

"I'm taking a wild guess," she said, turning in his arms.

"Well, damn," he said.

"Well, damn," she echoed, and they kissed. She caressed his mouth and squeezed his body tight. "Kick your brothers' asses down the street like a can and bring them here to Chantaine."

He drew back to meet her gaze. "That's pretty strong language for a princess," he said.

"Just sayin'," she said.

"How cool are you?" he said. "I'll get the job done.

Thanks for sticking with me," he said with a gaze that held all kinds of crazy emotions she was determined to ignore but couldn't. "I'll see you soon," he said.

She kissed him and headed toward the door. "*Ciao, darling*," she said. "Be safe."

Goldie drove her home even though it was 2:00 a.m. He didn't even blink at the time. Pippa took a deep breath and leaned her head back against the seat. "You're kind to drive me back to the apartment at such a crazy hour."

He shrugged. "Crazy is relative," he said.

"You're quite amazing," she said. "With all your skills. Nic and I ate your appetizers and a few bites of your amazing pie last night."

"Cooking relaxes me. I'm glad you enjoyed the food I prepared," he said.

"It was delicious. Is there anything that helps you relax? You spend so much of your time working," she said.

Goldie took a deep breath. "I'm addicted to yoga."

"Really?" Pippa asked. "Does it make that much of a difference?"

"Yes," Goldie said. "Relieves pain, allows me to relax and sleep."

"Do you go to a special studio?" she asked.

"Sometimes," he said. "Otherwise, I use a DVD or cable on TV."

"What station?" she asked.

He smiled. "Eight. You can DVR it. Meditation and acupuncture can help, too."

Pippa thought about the prospect of having needles

stuck inside her and shook her head. "If you say so," she said.

"Take it slow. You will learn your truth," he said.

"Goldie, what do you think of this whole crazy situation with me, Nic, Amelie and Paul?" she said.

"You're more powerful than you know," he said.

She thought about that for a moment. "I hope so, but speaking of power—you are quite powerful and talented. Why do you stay with the Lafittes?" she asked.

"They are my home," he said. "I would do anything for them."

His resolute statements sent chills through her. "I wish I had your talent and your fortitude," she said.

"You have both," he said. "Don't fear them."

Goldie pulled into her apartment complex, flashing a pass, then driving toward her apartment. "I'll escort you upstairs," he said.

"It's not necessary," she said.

"It is for me," he said, pulling to a stop. Stepping outside the car, he opened her door and walked with her to her second-floor apartment. "I'll wait outside. Knock on the door to let me know you're okay."

Pippa ventured inside her apartment. For just a half beat, she felt lonely and insecure. Then she gave a quick walk-through to her bedroom. She realized she was okay and opened the door. "No one here but me," she said to Goldie. "Perhaps I should get a cat."

Goldie chuckled. "Good night, Your Highness," he said.

Pippa spent most of the next day with Amelie. Nic's mother knitted, chatted and dozed on and off throughout the day. Pippa noticed that Amelie's energy came and went in short spurts. Paul lumbered restlessly on crutches. Nic had been correct about his father's need to release pent-up energy. Goldie stepped in and helped occupy Paul.

Pippa remembered Amelie when she'd had so much more energy. She'd been so lively, engaging. Irresistible. She still possessed her charm even when sleeping. Her stubby eyelashes rimmed her eyes. Her face growing more gaunt every day, full of wrinkles, crinkles, hollows and bones, defined her character. Her stubborn chin told the world she would push it to the max, till the very end. Amelie was nothing if not a fighter.

Pippa felt her throat suddenly close shut at the realization that Amelie was going to die, and it would be soon. She'd known all along that Amelie's time was short, but Pippa realized she'd been in denial. Amelie's time was all too close. Pippa left a little later than she'd planned. Goldie gave her a sandwich and followed her home.

Pippa took a shower and fell into a dreamless sleep. She awakened to the sound of her cell phone beeping. Glancing at the caller ID, she saw that Bridget was on the line.

Reluctantly, she accepted the call. "Good morning, Bridget. How are you?"

"When did you move? Why didn't you tell me? I went to your suite and you weren't there. Stefan won't discuss it, but he's clearly furious. How could you do this to us?"

"I moved a few days ago. It took place quickly because I had to do it before I lost my courage. I couldn't continue to live in the palace. I felt so trapped," Pippa said.

"We all feel trapped," Bridget scoffed. "The key is stealing your freedom whenever you can."

"You're a better fighter than I am," Pippa said. "I needed to finish the big fight so there could be peace for me, for everyone."

Silence stretched between them. Bridget gave an audible sigh. "I want to argue with you, but I can't. I obviously haven't had enough coffee." She gave a growl of frustration. "Maybe I'm just jealous that you got out before I did."

Pippa smiled. "You're right on my heels with your ranch in sight. You have Ryder and your boys. I have… genealogy."

"I still may find a man for you," Bridget said.

"Oh, please. If you love me, Bridget, stop," she said and laughed.

"Everyone deserves a second chance," Bridget said.

"Maybe in five years," Pippa said.

"That was cruel," her sister said. "Don't forget, there's a family dinner tonight."

"Lovely," Pippa said. "I'll have the whole table glowering at me."

"Don't be late," Bridget said. "*Ciao,* darling."

Chapter Eleven

"I want to go to the ocean," Amelie said at three-thirty.

Pippa blinked. "The ocean?" Today had been a duplicate of yesterday with Amelie knitting, chatting and sleeping except for this latest request.

"Yes, I want to swim," Amelie said, standing. "I'll put on my suit."

Pippa followed the woman to her feet. "I'm not sure that's wise. I don't think you're supposed to be swimming."

"Why not?" Amelie asked.

"Well, because of your condition," Pippa said.

"Oh, you mean the draining procedure. I'm permitted to swim after five days. I don't suppose you have a suit. I'm not sure mine would fit. Perhaps I should go by myself."

No. "I'll come up with something. Goldie can help me," Pippa said. "Go change into your suit." She wondered if Amelie would tire before they were able to leave. As soon as Amelie walked down the hallway, Pippa called for Goldie. Somehow she ended up with shorts and a tank top.

With surprising energy, Amelie returned wearing a caftan, the strap of her swimsuit peeking through the shoulder sliding over her too-slim frame. "Ready to be a little fish?" she asked with a singsong tone in her voice.

"Ready," Pippa said. "Goldie said he'll drive us."

Amelie frowned. "But what about Paul?"

"He's already given Paul a good workout. Paul is napping in the extra room," Pippa said.

"Excellent," Amelie said. "Let's go. Another adventure."

Heaven help them all, Pippa thought. Moments later, they trudged through the sandy beach toward the ocean. Partway there, Amelie pulled her caftan over her head and dropped her towel on the sand. She lifted her head to the sun and smiled like a child.

Pippa's heart caught. She picked up her cell phone and clicked a photo and another. She was no photographer, but she hoped the photos somehow captured Amelie's love of life.

"Let's go," Amelie called. "Before the water gets too cold."

Pippa tossed her cell phone into her bag and ran toward the ocean with Nic's mother. The water was already cold. Pippa muffled a shriek. "It's a bit nippy."

"Could be worse," Amelie said. "We're lucky it's not winter. The waves are so calm."

Amelie reached for Pippa's hand. "Isn't it lovely?"

Pippa took a deep breath and looked at the beautiful

blue ocean with the slightest caps of white. Both she and Amelie wore water shoes to cushion them from the rocky ground.

Amelie smiled but her teeth chattered. "I always wanted to be a fish or a dolphin," she said. "Or a butterfly."

"You're all of those in one," she said.

Amelie laughed. Her lips were turning blue. "You're such a lovely person. The perfect princess." Her smile fell. "The one thing I'll miss is meeting my grandchildren. You could have my first grandchild."

Pippa stared at Amelie in shock. "Grandchild?" she echoed. She felt her insides clench. Could Amelie sense something? In fact, she was late with her period, but because she wasn't regular, pregnancy wasn't a concern. Nic had worn protection.

"Don't worry, it will all work out. You'll have a beautiful baby," Amelie said.

Pippa wondered for a moment if Nic's mother was suffering from some kind of delusion. "You've grown cold. We should go back."

"Just a moment longer," she said. "I want to feel the water and the waves a moment longer."

Pippa laced her fingers more tightly through Amelie's and began to count. She was torn between protecting Amelie's pleasure and her fragile health. Amelie stumbled, then dipped her shoulders underneath the water.

"Amelie," Pippa said.

Seconds later, Amelie ducked her head beneath, frightening the bloody hell out of Pippa. She tugged on Amelie's hand, pulling her above the surface. "What are you doing?" she asked Nic's mother.

"It was so nice under the water," Amelie said, beaming. "I feel like I'm nine years old again."

Pippa put her arms around Amelie and squeezed her tight. "Let's get our towels. I want you cozy and warm."

Amelie's teeth chattered as Pippa led her to their towels. Goldie rushed out to help them into the car. "Turn on the heat, please," Pippa said.

"But it's—" Goldie broke off and met Pippa's gaze. Understanding flowed between them. For Amelie, it may as well have been winter. Her body was so thin and she'd become chilled in the water.

"I hope she won't get sick from this," Pippa said, scrubbing Amelie's arms.

"She won't," Goldie said. "You did the right thing, Your Highness. She was determined to go to the sea. We're lucky you went with her."

They returned to the cottage and Pippa helped Amelie into cozy pajamas, then into bed. Only after Goldie's promise to frequently check on Amelie did Pippa agree to leave. As she climbed into cab, she noticed the time. Bloody hell. She was going to be late for the family dinner.

Rushing, rushing, rushing, she took a shower, dressed herself and pulled her errant hair into a bun. Forget cosmetics, she told herself. She drove to the palace and raced up to the private dining room and burst inside. Everyone was there, her brother, his child and his pregnant wife, Eve, her sister Bridget, her husband, Ryder, and the twins. For one stunning moment, they were silent. Damn them.

"Hi," she said, forcing a big smile. "I'm so sorry I'm late. Time got away from me." She sank into the empty seat. "How are you feeling, Eve?"

Eve shot her a look of sympathy. "Better, thank you. How are your studies?"

"I'm getting there," Pippa said and glanced at Bridget. "How's the ranch?"

"Well, if we could get the plumbing and the kitchen straight, we'd be most of the way there," Bridget said. "Why is your hair wet?"

"I just took a shower," Pippa said and reached for her glass of water. She eyed the wine, but remembering what Amelie said, she wasn't sure she should do much drinking. She didn't think she was pregnant, but she supposed it was remotely possible.

Her hand shook as she held the glass of water. *Pregnant? No.*

"What's for dinner?" she asked brightly.

"Beef, rare," Eve said, wincing slightly. "Stefan's favorite."

"Mashed potatoes for Eve and anyone else who wants them. It's the only thing she can eat. That, and bread."

With the help of her screaming niece and nephews, Pippa made it through the meal. She gave a sigh of relief as dessert was served. Bananas flambé served with a flourish. She took a few bites, then discreetly motioned for one of the servers to take her plate.

"This had been wonderful, but I should leave. Back to work early tomorrow," she said and pushed back her chair.

"I'd like a word with you," Stefan said. "In my office."

"Our suite," Eve said. "Stephenia would love a bed-time hug and kiss from her aunt Pippa."

A flicker of irritation crossed his face, but he appeared to mask it with a quick nod. "Our suite will be fine." He said good-night to Bridget and her family, then the four of them made their way to Stefan and Eve's suite. Pippa had noticed Stefan had appeared more remote than usual this evening, but she'd just thought he was either still peeved about her move or his mind was on something else altogether.

Once inside the suite, Pippa kneeled down and extended her arms to Stephenia. "Come give me a big hug."

The little girl rushed toward her, her curls bobbing. Laughing, she threw her little body against Pippa. Her uninhibited expression of joy and complete trust tugged at Pippa's heart. "Now that's a hug," Pippa said and kissed the toddler's soft cheek. "You are such a sweet and smart girl. I bet you've been busy today."

Eve nodded with a wry expression on her face. "There'll be an early bedtime for Mamaeve tonight, too. Come along, Stephenia. You need to pick out your book. And Stefan—" she said but stopped.

Pippa saw the silent communication between the two of them and wondered what was going on. Surely he couldn't still be so upset about her move from the palace.

Stefan brushed a kiss over his daughter's cheek. "Sweet dreams," he said, echoing Eve's frequent night-time wish.

As soon as Eve and Stephenia walked toward the

bedrooms at the other end of the suite, Stefan turned toward Pippa. "How are you?"

"Well, thank you. And you?"

"Also well. Your studies?"

Pippa resisted the urge to squirm. She'd been forced to put her academic work aside during the last week. "Demanding as always."

"You've been quite busy since you returned from Italy," he said. He pulled out a computer tablet and turned it on.

The uneasiness inside her grew. "Moving makes for a busy time." She hesitated to ask but went ahead anyway. "What is your point?"

"Some photographs of you were posted on a social network just before dinner. I'll be surprised if they don't make the rag sheets by morning." He showed her a series of photos of her holding hands with Amelie in the ocean. "The woman looks familiar," he said in a cool voice.

Her stomach knotted, yet at the same time an overwhelming relief swept through her. "Good eye, Your Royal Highness. That's Amelie Lafitte."

Stefan clenched his jaw. "What in hell have you gotten yourself into?"

Pippa sighed. "I got myself involved with a family experiencing a tragedy."

"What tragedy? I'd heard Amelie had been ill for some time, but if she's swimming, she must have recovered."

Pippa shook her head. "Amelie is terminally ill. She's—she's dying."

Surprise crossed his face. "I'm sorry to hear that."

He cleared his throat. "That said, any association with the Lafittes is understandably forbidden. You must stop your involvement at once."

Pippa shook her head. "Oh, I'm sorry. That's not possible."

Stefan tilted his head to one side in disbelief and disapproval. "Pardon me, of course it's possible. You merely send a message to the Lafittes with your good wishes, but tell them you're unable to continue the association."

"I can't and won't do that. At this time of all times, I would hate myself for pulling away from them."

Stefan's jaw tightened again. "Pippa, after I received these photos, I asked my security detail to investigate the situation with the Lafittes. It has been brought to my attention that you've used family connections to secure a cottage for them. Not only that, Paul Lafitte, whose presence in this country is illegal, is living in this cottage. How do you think your cousin Georgina will feel when she learns you've used her cottage to house a criminal?"

"He's not a criminal," she said, unable to fight a stab of impatience. "He's a man with a broken foot and he's about to lose the love of his life."

"Pippa, this is not up for discussion. What you've done is illegal and dishonest."

"I'm not proud of being dishonest with all of you. I've hated every one of the lies I've had to tell, but your attitude made it impossible."

"I don't think you understand what a black mark this will make on our name. I insist you sever your relationship with the Lafittes," he said. "Please don't force my hand on this."

Pippa fought a sliver of fear, but her anger at his manipulation was stronger. "Are you threatening me? With what? Let's not keep it a mystery."

He paused, then narrowed his eyes. "If you don't stop your association with the Lafittes, I'll be forced to consider revoking your title."

Pippa absorbed the potential loss and made her decision in less than two breaths. "Then do what you have to do. I'll do what I must do. Helping the Lafittes through this painful time is the most important thing I've ever done in my life. If I lose my title over it, then c'est la vie. Good night, Stefan," she said and walked out of his suite.

Her heels clicked against the familiar marble palace floor. It crossed her mind that if Stefan carried through with his threat, this might be the last time she walked these halls. Worse yet, she realized, she might lose her relationship with her family. Her chest tightened with grief. Her hands began to shake and she balled them into fists. As much as her dysfunctional family drove each other crazy at times, Pippa loved them with all her heart. She would never get over losing them.

Deep in her heart, though, she knew that she would hate herself if she turned her back on the Lafittes. Stefan had forced her to make an impossible choice. She prayed she would have the strength to live with the consequences.

The connecting flight from Madrid began its descent into Chantaine just after 8:00 a.m. Nic rubbed his eyes, which felt like sandpaper. He looked at the passengers beside him and behind him. By some miracle, all three of his brothers were on the flight. Alex, his youngest brother, sat beside him gently snoring. Paul Jr., who went by James, and Michael sat across the aisle in the row behind them.

The plane had a bumpy landing. Nic hoped it wasn't a sign of what was to come for the rest of his brothers' visit.

Alex awakened, rubbing his face. He narrowed his eyes at Nic. "Looks like we made it. Are you sure our father isn't in a Chantaine dungeon somewhere?"

"You never know with Paul Lafitte, but he wasn't when I left," Nic said. "Besides, you're not here to see your father. You're here to see your mother," Nic said. "If you're man enough."

Alex scowled, but Nic knew that very same challenge had gotten Alex and Nic's other brothers onto the plane. He'd made a strong, no-holds-barred demand, and thank goodness, his brothers had responded.

"There's a car waiting," Nic said. "When we get to the cottage, you'll have a good meal."

An hour later, the driver drove the limo toward the cottage. The ride was mostly silent, but Nic figured he would be paying the price for the intimidation and manipulation he'd used to bring his brothers to his mother. Despite their anger, their brothers drank in the sight of their mother's island.

"Not bad," James said. "Never visited Chantaine before. Mom always said it was beautiful. She was right."

Alex gave a dry chuckle. "Who says they would have let us on the island?"

"You got on this time," Nic said.

"Because you've donated a ton of money and enhanced Chantaine's economy," Alex said.

"There are worse ways to spend money," Nic said.

The limo pulled into the driveway.

"Quaint," Paul Jr. said.

"A friend helped out," Nic said. He wondered how Pippa was doing. He knew that moving from the palace was a huge change for her. He and his brothers got out of the limo and walked to the front door.

Paul opened the door. On crutches, he looked at his four sons in shock. "Well, I'll be damned."

"We've already done that several times over," Paul Jr. said. "Where's Mom?"

Paul's expression hardened. "She's asleep, and if you can't show her respect and kindness, you can go the hell back where you came from," he said and slammed the door in their faces.

Silence followed.

"Same ol' dad," Michael said.

"Yep, sonofabitch, but he was always protective of her," Alex said.

"When he wasn't in prison," Paul Jr. said.

"This is stupid," Nic said. "Let's just go inside. Dad will have to deal with it. I'm sure Goldie has a great meal for us."

"Who's Goldie?" Paul Jr. asked.

"You'll know soon enough," Nic said and inserted his key into the door and pushed it open.

Paul had apparently hobbled to the back of the house. Nic turned on a baseball game and Goldie immediately showed up with platters of appetizers and sandwiches, along with beer. Beer before lunch may have seemed inappropriate, but in this case, it was for the best. His brothers commented on the food and the game while downing a few beers.

Finally, his mother appeared in the back of the den. "She's here," Nic said, turning off the TV. His mother was gaunt and tired, but clearly delighted to see her sons.

"Am I dreaming?" she asked, lifting her lips in a huge smile.

"Go," Nic said in his brother Michael's ear.

"Me?" Michael asked.

Nic nodded, and half a breath later, Michael sprang to his feet and enveloped his mother in hug. "I'm sorry I haven't—"

"No sorries, no apologies," Amelie said, hugging him in return. "I'm so happy to see you."

A moment later, James rose and pulled her into his arms. "Mom, I've missed you."

Alex finally stood and made his way to his mother. "I'm the worst of your sons," he confessed.

"No," she insisted with a smile. "You are all the best sons any woman could want because you came to see me before—" She broke off, her smile fading. "Before I turn into a butterfly."

Nic's heart wrenched at the sight before him. It had taken an enormous effort to make this happen. He just wished it hadn't been necessary.

His mother pretended to eat and sipped some lemonade while she enjoyed the visit with her sons. Amelie asked each of them about what they were doing. None were married and none had children, much to her disappointment. She encouraged all of them to enjoy Chantaine as much as possible during their visit, but Nic knew his brothers were leaving at 5:00 a.m. the next day.

After a while, Nic could tell she was growing tired. "We should let you rest," he said.

"In a bit. I have something to say first," she said. "You're not going to like this, but I raised you to be extraordinary men, so now's the time for you to man up."

The room turned silent. His brothers grew restless.

"Take a deep breath. Listen. It won't be that long. You can handle it," she said. "The truth is your father broke the rules because he was determined to take care of me. He was determined to keep me in the same way a princess should live because, after all, I could have been a princess. How do you compete with that? How do you produce a lifestyle fit for a princess, even though I didn't ask for it?"

His mother's words sank into him. He'd never realized what a burden his father had taken on when he'd stolen his mother from Prince Edward. It made him think of his current relationship with Pippa.

"Can't deny that was tough," James said. "But he made our life a living hell by destroying the family reputation."

"True," his mother said. "But that was a long time ago. It's time to get over it."

Silence followed.

"Excuse me?" Michael said. "Get over it? His disreputable dealings are the gifts that keep giving. We had to move out of the state to reestablish ourselves."

"Well," his mother said. "It's time for you to get over it. You've reestablished yourselves. Paul is nursing a broken foot. I have two things to ask of you," she said. "Be true brothers. Stand together. Be family. And forgive your father," she added.

Nic felt his brothers close up like locks at Fort Knox. "Love you, Mom," he said and moved toward her to give her a hug.

She embraced him in return. "Thank you," she said. "You made a miracle."

"No, it was you," he said. "I just added a little muscle."

"I'm getting tired. I should go to sleep. Can we get a photo of me with my boys?" she asked.

Goldie took a few photos and his mother went to bed. His brothers sacked out in the guest room and guest quarters. Nic considered calling Pippa, but he was drained. He resolved to call tomorrow afternoon, after his brothers left and he caught up with some rest.

Nic arranged for the limo that took his brothers to the airport in the early predawn morning, then went back to sleep. Hours later, a knock on the door awakened him. Goldie, wearing a tortured expression, dipped his head. "I'm so sorry, sir. Your mother has passed on."

Chapter Twelve

Numb from the news, Nic dialed Pippa's number as he paced his room an hour later.

"Hi. Welcome back," she said.

Her voice was like oxygen to his system. "Thanks," he said. "I have some bad news." He paused a beat because he'd already had to say the same thing several times. "She's gone."

"Oh, Nic, I'm so sorry. I'll be right over," she said.

"Good," he said, feeling a shot of relief that bothered him. Now, more than ever, he needed to keep himself in check. There was just too much to do and his father was a mess.

He made several more calls, unsure what to do about a memorial service. Thank goodness, his mother had made her burial wishes clear in her will. She wanted her ashes spread in Chantaine. Nic suspected his father would fight it.

He heard a vehicle pull into the driveway and immediately went to the door. Pippa stepped from the car and rushed into his arms. "I'm so sorry. How are you?" she asked.

Feeling her in his arms was a balm to his soul. "I'm okay. We knew this was coming."

"But you're never really ready," she said, pulling back to search his face.

"True, but we were more prepared than most," he said and led her into the den.

"How is your father?" she asked.

"Not good," Nic said. "He was having some pain with his foot, so he spent the whole night on the patio. My brothers were sleeping in the guestroom. I think my father must have taken an extra dose of pain reliever because he didn't even wake up when my brothers left early this morning. Goldie went in to take her a croissant and some juice. He was the one who found her. My father was horrified that she died alone." His throat closed up.

Pippa took his hand in hers. "But your brothers, did she see them?"

Nic nodded.

"It's almost as if she was waiting to see them again and that gave her permission. You did a wonderful thing by bringing them here," she said.

"Trust me, I had to be damn ugly to them to make it happen," he said.

"And now there are other things to be done. Arrangements," she said. "How can I help you?"

Nic took a deep breath. "I need one more favor. My mother wanted her ashes spread here in Chantaine."

"And a memorial service, too," she said, her eyebrows furrowing together in concern.

"Yeah," he said.

"I'll do my best. Not sure Stefan is speaking to me at the moment," she added in half jest.

"Why? Is he still upset that you moved out of the palace?" Nic demanded.

Pippa waved her hand in a dismissive gesture. "Stefan's always bothered about something. It's his nature. What about your brothers? You said they'd already left."

"They're on their way back," he said. "I'd like to do this quickly and get my father back to the States. There are too many sad memories for him here and he's going to have to find a new normal for himself."

Pippa nodded. "Okay, I'll go out by the pool area and make a few calls," she said and left him to his list.

Fifteen minutes later, she returned, relief on her face. "I was able to get permission for your mother's service. Because the weather has been good, I wondered if you would like it to take place outdoors. There's a lovely green park on the other side of the island that people use for all kinds of occasions including memorial services. Chairs can be set up for your family."

"That sounds good. Thank you," he said, mentally checking the decision off his list. Nic felt as if he had a million-mile journey in front of him. Pippa made everything feel easier, but soon enough, he would be back in the States and he would be handling everything by himself. Again.

Two days later, Pippa took a seat at the end of a second row of chairs arranged for Amelie Lafitte's memo-

rial service. She didn't want to call attention to herself.
By a stroke of luck, or fate, she'd located a minister
who had lived in the same orphanage as Amelie. She
was pleased that someone who had known Nic's mother
would lead the service.

It was a beautiful morning. Amelie would have loved
it.

"Excuse me, is that seat taken?" a familiar voice
asked her.

Pippa looked up and surprise raced through at the
sight of her sister-in-law, Eve, and her sister Bridget.
She stood, feeling as if her heart would burst with gratitude. "I don't know what to say," she said. "I can't believe you're here."

"Of course we're here. You're family. This is where
we're supposed to be. Stefan didn't come because he
didn't want to turn things into a madhouse," Eve said.
"But he sends his condolences to you and the Lafittes."

Pippa hugged Eve. "You must have given him a
Texas-size lecture because the last I heard, I no longer
had a title," she said.

Bridget rolled her eyes. "He's got to make that threat
to each of us at some point. He just can't stand not having control sometimes, most times," she added and held
out her arms. "Come here. Shame on you for suffering
by yourself. Why can't you be more like me and make
everyone suffer with you?"

Bridget's remark made her laugh despite how emotional she felt. "I knew none of you would approve,"
Pippa said. "But I couldn't turn my back on them."

"That's one of the many reasons we love you," Eve
said as she took her seat. Bridget also took hers.

Within the next moments, many people arrived, taking seats and crowding around the area. "I didn't know this many people remembered Amelie," Bridget said, surprised at the number of people gathering in the park.

"You would understand if you'd met her. I wish you'd had the opportunity," Pippa said, her eyes suddenly filling with tears. "She was a magical person."

Bridget covered her hand in comfort and the Lafitte men arrived, filing into the front row of chairs reserved for Amelie's family. Seconds later, the minister stood at the front of the group and began to speak.

He delivered a heartfelt message with touches of humor as he described Amelie as a child and how she seemed to have held on to her sense of wonder despite life's trials. Nic then read a message his mother had written for the occasion. The sight of him so strong delivering his mother's last words wrenched at her. She knew he had to be suffering but wouldn't reveal it. Pippa wished with all her heart that she could help him.

As the service drew to a close, Pippa noticed Bebe, the proprietor of Amelie's favorite creperie, move toward the front of the crowd. "Please forgive the interruption, but Amelie was such a joy. We were so thrilled to receive a visit from her a short time ago and she was just as beautiful as ever. Several of us who knew her have asked and received permission to plant some buddleia in her honor. We've planted one already. It's over there," Bebe said, pointing to the flowering bush to the left of the crowd.

Eve gave a loud sniff. "Now that could make even me cry. A butterfly bush."

"And look," Bridget said. "There are butterflies."

Pippa saw the beautiful butterflies fluttering and met Nic's knowing gaze. Amelie had often said she wanted to be a butterfly. In that moment, she felt the bond between Nic and her solidify. They would always remember, together.

Nic asked her to come to the cottage after the service. She had arranged for a catering service to bring food. With all the turmoil of the past few days, Nic, his brothers and his father might have forgotten to eat, but their hunger would remind them soon enough. When she arrived, they were silently eating. Nic introduced her to his brothers and they all responded politely. Moments later, they all scattered except Nic.

"It was a beautiful service. I believe Amelie would have approved," she said.

"Yeah, especially with those butterflies. That caught me by surprise," he said, shoving one of his hands into his pocket. He'd pulled off his necktie and opened his shirt. Dark circles rimmed his eyes. Pippa knew he hadn't gotten much sleep.

"What else can I do for you?" she asked.

He pulled her into his arms. "Oh, hell, Pippa, you've already done more than I could imagine. The rest is up to me. I'll pack up my dad and we'll head out tomorrow."

Surprise rushed through her. She'd known he planned to leave soon, but not this soon. "Tomorrow?"

"Yeah, I need to get him away from Chantaine. I'll send in a team to clean up the cottage," he said.

"I can make those arrangements," she said.

"No, you've already done enough. Too much," he

said and sighed. "When I said fate would bring you and me together, I had no idea it would be for this. Or that it would turn out this way."

Pippa felt a twist of nerves at his words. "What do you mean 'turn out this way'?"

"Well, I've got to leave now. I've got to get my dad straight. There's no one else to do it," he said.

Alarm shot through her. "Are you saying goodbye?"

"No. I'm just saying I'm not free to be here with you right now. When I get my Dad settled, we'll see if you're still interested," he said.

Pippa stared at him in disbelief. "Of course I'll still be interested. Why wouldn't I be?"

"Your family still hates the Lafittes," he said. "In their eyes, I'll never be good enough for you."

"My family is rethinking their stance on the Lafittes. Besides, what's important is how I feel about you, not how they feel about you."

"We'll see, darlin'. You've taken a lot of heat for me. You deserve a break to decide if I'm worth the trouble," he said.

"But, Nic," she began and he covered her mouth with his index finger.

"Trust me. This is for the best," he said and lowered his mouth to kiss her.

Two weeks later when Pippa hadn't heard from Nic, she wasn't at all sure this *break,* or whatever Nic called it, was for the best. Plus, there was the matter of her increasingly regular nausea. When she counted the number of days since her last menstrual period, she broke into a sweat and got sick to her stomach again.

Even though she'd known she was late a couple weeks ago, she figured it was due to stress. After all, Nic had always used protection. So nothing could happen, right? The combination of her symptoms and that strange conversation she'd had with Amelie just before Nic's mother had died gnawed at her.

It took several more days for Pippa to work up the nerve to take a pregnancy test. She even dragged out the old disguise of the hated gray wig and ugly clothes and paid cash at the pharmacy so that no one would recognize her. She nearly fainted at the result. Positive. Perhaps she should get another test. She did, three of them, actually, from different pharmacies. The results were all positive.

She knew she needed to tell Nic, but this wasn't the kind of news she could give over the phone. It wasn't as if she could send a cheery little text saying Guess who's going to be a daddy? She knew he must be terribly busy making up for lost time with his businesses and helping his father create a new life, but the lack of contact from him only fueled questions and doubts inside her.

She and Nic had never discussed marriage, and she really didn't like the idea of him proposing just because she was pregnant. She wanted Nic to propose marriage because he didn't want to live without her.

Pippa rolled her eyes at herself. As if Nic Lafitte would ever allow himself to want a woman that much.

Suffering more and more each passing day, she avoided her family. Her older sister Valentina may have gotten pregnant without the benefit of marriage, but she'd had the good sense not to tell Stefan until she was on another continent. Pippa didn't want to even think about how to break the news to her brother.

She plunged herself into her studies and made progress that impressed even her. At the rate she was going, she could wrap up the last of her dissertation within a couple months. She wondered if she would be showing then. Another week passed and she hadn't heard from Nic. What did this mean? Had he forgotten her? The possibility made her ill. What if this had just been a fling for him? What if he hadn't fallen as deeply for her as she had for him? What if she was truly alone? And now with a baby on the way... Even with all the hours she'd been putting in for her dissertation, she was sleeping for only a few hours each night. She avoided looking in the mirror because she knew she was looking more tired and miserable with each passing day.

Pippa had successfully begged off two family dinners, but when Stefan called for an official meeting of all adult Devereauxs, she could no longer hide. The meeting was held in Stefan's office, which indicated potentially serious business. As Pippa entered the office, she noted the additional chairs. Bridget, her older sister Ericka, who lived in Paris, and her younger brother, Jacques, who'd responded to Stefan's missive by leaving his soccer team mid-tour. Ericka and Jacques were both talking on their cell phones.

"Pippa, there you are," Bridget said, then frowned at her. "Oh, my goodness, you look dreadful. What have you been doing to yourself? You need to let me set up a day at the spa for you."

"I've just been trying to make up time on my dissertation. Burning the midnight oil," she said.

"Well, don't burn any more. How are the Lafittes?" Bridget asked. "I apologize for not calling sooner. I've been so busy with the building of our ranch and both the twins got sick."

"I know you're busy. Nic and his father have gone back to the States. They both had a lot to do after Amelie's death," she said.

"Hmm," Bridget said, her mind clearly whirling. "He's been in touch, though, hasn't he? He hasn't just abandoned you after you helped his family."

"He hasn't abandoned me," Pippa said, even though she felt that way. "He's just terribly busy right now. Do you know why Stefan has called the meeting?"

"No," Bridget said.

"It must be big if he insisted that both Jacques and I come immediately," Ericka said and gave Pippa a hug. "I hope no one is ill."

Jacques turned off his phone and approached his sisters. "We're all here except Valentina. I'm stumped about this one. Stefan can go over the top easier than most, but I don't know—"

He broke off as Stefan and Eve entered the room. His assistant closed the door behind him. "Please be seated," Stefan said, his face, devoid of humor.

Pippa's stomach clenched at his expression.

Stefan gave a heavy sigh and sat on the edge of his desk. "As you all know, our father wasn't perfect. We can be thankful to him for our lives, our positions. Nothing will change that. However, he had a mistress for several years. She was a small-time actress. Her name was Ava London."

Pippa felt a stab of surprise, not that her father had

stepped out on her mother, but that Stefan knew the identity of this woman. She slid a sideways glance at Bridget, whose mouth gaped open.

Stefan gave another heavy sigh. "During their affair, Ava gave birth to two children."

Pippa and her siblings gasped in unison. Her mind whirled at the implications.

Stefan nodded. "According to the advisers, this development shouldn't affect succession. The son, Maxwell Carter, is thirty years old and is living in Australia. The daughter, Coco Jordan, is a—" He cleared his throat. "She's a nanny in Texas."

Pippa felt her stomach roll with the news. She couldn't help thinking about her own unborn child. "What else do we know about them? Did Ava raise them? What—"

Stefan shook his head. "Ava made an agreement with my father. He would support her until her death if she gave her children up for adoption and didn't reveal their existence. Ava passed away two weeks ago and her attorney is determined to follow her wishes, which are to ensure that her children know that they have Devereaux blood."

"Great," Bridget muttered. "This sounds like a public relations nightmare."

"It is," Stefan said. "The two children may also have some rights to an inheritance."

Bridget scoffed. "But they haven't had to perform any duties," she protested. "We've spent our life serving."

"True, but our attorneys have not been able to determine the legalities concerning their inheritance," he said.

Pippa skipped over the money issues. She had tried to be aware of economics ever since Stefan had begun to complain about frivolous costs. Her biggest expense had been the cost of her degree and she'd been fortunate to receive scholarships. "What are they like?"

She felt Bridget stare at her. "What do you mean what are they like? They're illegitimate Devereauxs."

"But they're people, human beings," Pippa said. "She's our half sister. He's our half brother."

Eve met her gaze and smiled, giving her a thumbs-up.

"Leave it to Pippa to bring in the human element," Stefan said and gave a half smile. "Both of Coco Jordan's parents have died. She's finishing her education after taking care of her mother during a terminal illness. Her parents left her no inheritance, so we're not sure how she'll respond to the news that she could gain financially from being a Devereaux. The advisers and public relations staff want to control the release of this information, so we will be inviting her to Chantaine as soon as possible."

"Mon Dieu," Ericka said. "You're going to bring her here? Why will you not pay her off and bury this information?"

"Because in a contemporary media environment, we have learned it's impossible to bury this kind of information. Our goal is to take this distressing news and to somehow make it work for us."

"We call that taking lemons and making lemonade," Eve said in her Texas drawl.

"So what's our new *brother* like?" Jacques asked sarcastically. "Knowing our luck, he's a drug dealer or something."

"Not that bad," Stefan conceded. "His adoptive parents live in Ohio. He graduated with a degree in engineering and has been working in Australia for the past few years." He paused a half beat. "He hasn't responded yet to our communications."

"Has the daughter?" Bridget asked.

"Yes," Stefan said. "But she hasn't yet accepted our invitation to come to Chantaine."

"Do you think this is a strategy to make us give her money?" Jacques asked.

"Jacques," Pippa said, "must you be so suspicious? Maybe this has taken her off guard, too. If she stuck with her mother during an illness, she can't be all bad."

The room turned silent because they all knew that Pippa had just helped the Lafittes during their difficult time. Pippa's stomach continued to churn. The realization that her father had denied his own children hit too close to the bone with her. She hadn't been able to talk to Nic yet. How would he respond to the news about her pregnancy?

Suddenly, her feeling of nausea overwhelmed. "Excuse me, I need to leave," she said and ran for the toilet connected to Nic's office. After she was sick, she splashed her face and mouth with water. Glancing into the mirror, she braced herself for what she would face on the other side of her door.

Taking several deep breaths, Pippa opened the door. All of her siblings were standing, waiting. Bridget crossed her arms over her chest, tapping her foot. "Do you have something you want to tell us?" she asked.

Pippa bit her lip. "Not really," she said.

Eve chuckled and the sound eased something inside her.

Stefan narrowed his eyes. "Pippa," he said.

She sighed. "Eve's not the only one who is pregnant," she said.

Stefan's face turned to granite. "Lafitte," he said in disgust. "I'll make him pay."

Her stomach turned again. "No," she said and raced for the toilet again.

Bless her Texan heart, Eve saved Pippa from a grueling discussion with Stefan. Pippa decided she needed to thank the heavens for Eve on a more regular basis. Eve had come through for her in several critical situations.

Pippa returned home and breathed a sigh of relief. She wished, however, that she would hear something, anything, from Nic. She finally gave in, called his cell and left a message. "Hope you and your father are okay," she said. "I need to talk to you when you get a chance."

Less that twenty-four hours later, she got a return call. When she saw the caller ID, her heart hammered so fast she could hardly breathe, let alone speak. "Hi," she said.

"Hey," he said. "It's been nuts here. My father took too many sleeping pills and he's been in the hospital. He's in rehab right now and I'm working on interim housing for him. How are you?"

How could she top his troubles? "I'm fine. I just thought we should touch base," she said, pacing the small den of her apartment.

A short silence followed. "You sound different. Are you sure you're okay?"

"Yes," she said. "I'm fine."

"I would have called you, but I've been slammed with my dad's issues."

"I understand," she said, adding as much backbone to her voice as she could muster. "I'm sorry he's struggling."

"Yeah. I could have predicted it. The good news is my youngest brother has started checking in on him," Nic said.

"That's wonderful. I know your brothers' relationship with your father has been, well, precarious," she said.

"That's a nice way of saying their relationship with him was in the toilet. Flushed repeatedly," Nic said. "My two other brothers don't appear to give a rip, but Alex is working at it. There's hope anyway."

"That's good," she said. "I'm glad."

Another awkward silence stretched between them. "You sure you're okay?"

"I'm fine," she insisted.

"How are the Devereauxs?" he asked.

"In perfect health," she said.

"Good to hear. Stefan breathing down your throat?" he asked.

"No more than usual," she said.

"I need to go," he said. "I'll call you in a couple of days. I'm glad you called. It's so good to hear your voice."

The call was disconnected and it took several seconds before she began to breathe again. His last words vibrated through her. *It's so good to hear your voice.*

He called and left a message the following day. She missed it, damn it, because she was in a meeting with her professor. Three days after that, there was a knock at her door. She looked out the peephole. It was Nic. Her heart hammered against her rib cage. She felt a jolt of nausea rise from her belly.

"Just a moment," Pippa called. She willed her stomach to calm down. Turning away from the door, she took several breaths and told herself she would get through this. She walked to the door and opened it. "Hi," she said.

"Hi," he said, studying her. "Are you okay? You don't look well," he said.

"It's good to see you, too," she said and headed for the toilet. Moments later, she returned to her small den where Nic stood with a brooding expression on his face.

"You're not sick, are you?" he asked.

"Not really," she said. "I've just had some nausea lately."

He frowned. "That was one of my mother's symptoms," he said.

Her heart softened. "Oh, it's not that. I'm not sick that way, Nic."

"How can you be sure?" he asked.

"I just am. Trust me," she said.

He searched her face for a long moment. "Then what is it?"

She took a deep breath. "Why don't we sit down? Would you like water or ginger ale?"

"Ginger ale," he echoed, clearly disgusted.

"Water," she said and laughed. "Have a seat." She filled two glasses with ice and water and brought them into her small den. Giving one of the glasses to him, she sat across from him. "I didn't expect you."

He took several swallows of water. "I didn't like the way you sounded."

She winced. "How is your father?"

"Okay at the moment. Alex is checking in on him." He set his glass down on a coaster on a lamp table. "What the hell is going on? Something's wrong. If you want to dump me, just say it."

Pippa dropped her jaw in astonishment. "That thought hasn't occurred to me."

"Then why are you acting so weird?" he demanded.

"I wasn't aware that I was acting weird," she said.

"Well, you are," he said.

"We haven't seen each other in nearly a month and we didn't talk for almost three weeks," she pointed out.

"I told you what was happening with my father," he said.

"Yes, but that doesn't change the fact that we didn't communicate for three weeks."

He frowned at her. "You're still not telling me what's going on," he said. "Spit it out."

She took a sip of her ice water, hoping the cool hydration would help calm her nerves. "What made you come to Chantaine?"

"You," he said.

She gave a nod, but didn't say anything.

"And I missed you," he admitted.

"That's good to know," she said in a dry voice.

"What the hell—" He broke off. "What's going on?"

"I'd rather not discuss it at the moment," she said. "I'd rather hear your true feelings for me."

He met her gaze for a long moment, then raked his hand through his hair. "You're more important to me than I had planned," he said.

"What had you planned?" she asked.

He shrugged. "I knew we would be together."

"So you planned for a fling, a temporary affair," she said.

"Yes."

His honest answer, which she'd asked for, stabbed at her.

"What had you planned?" he asked.

His question caught her off guard. "I don't know that I made any real plans," she said. "I just knew I couldn't turn away from you. The situation with your mother made it even more intense. I wanted to be with you. I wanted to be there for you." She closed her eyes and allowed the words to tumble from her heart. "I fell in love with you, and now I'm afraid I'm in this all by myself."

"You're not," he said. "But I don't want to be a wedge between you and your family. You would grow to hate me for that."

"It's not right for you to make that decision for me. Don't you see that in another way you're treating me like Stefan does? You're treating me like I don't know my own mind and heart." She clasped her hands together tightly and voiced her worst fear. "Are you sure this isn't some kind of smokescreen to hide the fact that you don't really love me and you don't want to be with me?"

His eyes lit with anger. "That's the most ridiculous thing I've ever heard you say."

"It isn't at all ridiculous to me, and it occurs to me that if I have to extract a commitment from you, then maybe I don't want it after all," she said, feeling a terrible wrenching sensation inside her.

He pulled her against him. "What do you want from me?"

"Not much," she said. "Just undying love, devotion and adoration."

"You've had that for months," he said.

She was afraid to believe him. "Why didn't you tell me?" she asked, her eyes burning with tears.

"I had to wait for you to catch up," he said and cupped her face.

Pippa finally saw everything she'd been afraid to wish for right there in his eyes.

"I love you, Pippa. I just don't want to make your life a living hell. I want to give you an opportunity to—" he shrugged "—come to your senses."

"Too late for that," she said, laughing breathlessly. "Besides, if being without you means I'm coming to my senses, then I don't want to do that." She bit her lip. "But there's something else I have to tell you."

"What?"

"I'm pregnant."

Epilogue

Nic felt as if Pippa had hit him upside the head with a two-by-four. In a way, she had. It took three seconds before his mind moved into high gear. His immediate response was primitive and protective.

"You have to marry me," he said. "Your brother may want to kill me, but our child deserves a father."

Pippa winced. "That was romantic," she said in a wry voice.

Nic sweated bullets. He couldn't lose her. He had to protect her. He had to protect their child. He had to make her see everything he'd tried to hide. "I love you. I want to be with you all the time. Forever. I just didn't know how we could work it out with your family. Cut me some slack. I didn't plan on falling for a princess."

"That's much better," she said and pressed her face against his chest. "I wanted you to want me for me, not just because I'm having your child."

"That was never an issue," he said, stroking her crazy curls with his hand. He couldn't believe his luck. Pippa was pure gold without her title and somehow he'd managed to win her heart. "So am I gonna need to do the pirate thing and steal you away?"

She laughed and the husky sound vibrated against his chest. "No. I think everything will be okay once you talk with Stefan."

Nic anticipated a rough discussion, but was determined to do whatever was necessary for her and their baby. "I'm up for it."

"My family can be difficult," she said.

"You're worth it," he said and sealed his promise to her with a kiss.

Later that day, Nic met with Stefan. Nic didn't blame Stefan for being protective of Pippa. She was worth protecting. If the situation were reversed and Stefan had gotten his sister pregnant, Nic would have knocked him into next week. Nic admired Stefan's physical restraint and did everything he could to reassure the prince that he was devoted to Pippa. Nic suspected it would take a while to win over Pippa's clan, but he would keep chipping away at it.

Despite their differences, Nic and Stefan had a lot in common. One thing they both agreed on was that Nic and Pippa should get married right away. Three weeks later, he pledged everything including his troth, allegiance, love and devotion to Pippa. He was in it for good and he was relieved that she was, too. Nic hadn't known he could love a woman this much, but he'd never met anyone who brought him so much peace and happiness at the same time. He knew it wasn't possible to be any happier than he was with Pippa.

Until Pippa took him to a level he'd never imagined months later, when she gave birth to a beautiful baby girl. Pippa insisted that they name the baby Amelie and Nic had a feeling that the baby was gonna wrap him around her finger the same way her mother had. He was damn sure he didn't deserve all this joy, but he wasn't giving up the treasure he'd been given for anything. Her Highness was stuck with him, and thank God, she seemed to be just as happy about it as he was.

* * * * *

THE PRINCE'S
SECRET BRIDE

RAYE MORGAN

To my friend Patty Jackson,
who is going to London to see the Queen!

Raye Morgan has been a nursery school teacher, a travel agent, a clerk and a business editor, but her best job ever has been writing romances – and fostering romance in her own family at the same time. Current score: two boys married, two more to go. Raye has written more than seventy romance novels and claims to have many more waiting in the wings. She lives in Southern California, with her husband and whichever son happens to be staying at home at the moment.

CHAPTER ONE

PRINCE Nico of the royal House of Montenevada pulled down his cap and turned his collar up, partly against the misting drizzle, but also in order to avoid being recognized. His family had been back in power less than six months and he was already sick of the toll it was taking on his private life. He hadn't spent five years leading a rebellion in the mountains so that he could be treated like a rock star. He'd thought they were fighting for bigger things. Now he wasn't so sure.

The dark streets were pretty much deserted and only dimly lit by flickering street lamps. A lone car went by. Then a cluster of giggling teenagers, late for their curfews. As he started over the Gonglia Bridge, he passed a young woman whose eyes were strangely vacant; she seemed to gaze right through him. Her mass of blond crimped curls was wild around her pretty face, but that seemed to be a style that was popular these days and he didn't think twice about it. That otherworldly look in her eyes stayed with him, though, and when he reached the high point of the bridge's arc, he turned and looked back to see what she was doing.

"Hey!"

What he saw had him running back. The crazy woman was about to jump! In the half a minute since he'd passed her, she'd climbed out on the scaffolding and was leaning over the inky waters that rolled beneath, racing down out of the mountains toward the sea.

"Hold it!" he yelled as he flung himself at her.

She looked up, startled, and tried to avoid him, twisting away so that she was even more dangerously close to crashing down into the river. He grabbed her roughly. There was no time for niceties. Gripping her upper arm, he sank his other hand into her thick hair and yanked her back onto solid surface. She fell against him and he had just time to take in the soft, round feel of her breast as his palm un-intentionally slid over it, before she turned on him like a scalded cat.

"Get away!" she cried, glaring at him and backing away. "Leave me alone!"

He grimaced, annoyed with her, annoyed with anyone who would make such an obvious play for attention as jumping from a bridge. And then her soft blue jacket fell open enough for him to see her body and he realized that she was pregnant. That put a different light on things. He winced, knowing from experience that a pregnancy could change everything—for everyone involved. He looked deeply into her wide dark eyes and saw something that tugged at his sympathies after all.

"I'd be happy to leave you alone," he said, trying to shave any harshness from his comments, "if you think you could refrain from flinging yourself into rivers."

She shook her head impatiently. "I wasn't trying to jump."

"Really? You were doing a pretty good imitation of a bridge jumper."

"No, I was just looking for my things." She looked away distractedly. "He…he threw them over the side of the bridge and…" Her voice trailed off and she met his gaze again, her own eyes hooded. "Never mind," she said, hunching deeper into her jacket and turning away.

He'd only heard half her muffled words but he was willing to join in. "What were you looking for? Maybe I can help you."

"No." She seemed to be trying to put distance between them. Glancing at him sideways, she began to move away. "You can't help me."

It was dark. He was large. And male. He knew he probably looked threatening to her. He didn't mean to. But what the hell? He had better things to do with his time than to follow a crazy woman around. So he shrugged.

"Fine. Have it your way."

She glanced back over her shoulder. "I will, thank you."

He slowed, then came to a stop and watched as she hurried away. He supposed it was best to leave her alone, just as she'd demanded. Still, he hated to do it. She bothered him. There was something in the way she moved, to quote an old song.

Besides, this town was only a few months into recovering from a war and the place was crawling with unsavory characters who had nothing better to do than to make trouble for someone else. It was a problem he and his brothers were going to have to deal with very quickly. One of many. And right now it could be a problem for this troubled lady.

You can't save them all.

Those words echoed painfully in his head and he shook them away. Gordon Greiva, his best friend and comrade-in-arms, had said that often in the old days when they'd been fighting for their country's liberation. *Nico, let it go. You can't save them all.* The irony was, Gordon himself had died in that final battle.

No, he couldn't save them all. Truth to tell, he didn't have the greatest track record in saving much of any of them. And what could he do to help this one? Not much. She'd certainly made it clear she didn't want his help.

With a careless shrug, he turned away and started back toward the other side of the bridge. He needed a drink.

He heard the pub before he saw it, music and laughter an appealing invitation to step into the crowd. But he hesitated in the doorway, peering inside. He would love to go in, order Scotch, neat, and sit back and let that liquid fire burn its way into his soul, restoring him to something resembling real feeling again. It was tempting. He could see himself sitting there in the darkened room, letting the smoke and conversation wash around him while he contemplated life and all its twists and turns.

But he knew that picture was a fantasy. As soon as he sat down, the waitress would look at him sharply, then whisper to one of the other customers. The buzz would begin as people craned their necks, staring, until finally someone would get brave enough to come over and start talking. And once the ice had been broken, the flood would come, people wanting to rehash the war, people wanting to know why everything wasn't instantly wonderful now that the good guys had taken over again. And who knew if it was a bar full of patriots or a refuge for disgruntled losers. You paid your money and you took your chances. But tonight, he didn't feel up to testing those waters.

Turning away from the pub, he looked back at the river. He couldn't seem to shake the image of his distressed jumper, her wild curls floating around her face, her dark eyes filled with mystery. He wondered if she'd found what she'd been looking for, and if she was going to have any trouble making her way home. The bridge looked ominous from this angle, like a path into dangerous territory. The wet streets were empty. It was getting late and time for him to make a decision as to where he was going to spend the next few hours.

He started down the walkway that fronted the river feeling vaguely uneasy, his hands shoved deep into his pockets, his gaze running restlessly over the scene. And then it sharpened. Something was moving down by the riverbank, where various debris was piled up around a short pier. He stopped and looked harder, then swore softly and vaulted over the river wall to get to the water's edge. It was her.

A few quick strides brought him to where she was bending over a large black plastic bag.

"What the hell are you doing?" he demanded.

She looked up, startled once again. Straightening, she pushed at her damp hair, leaving wet strands plastered to her forehead. "It's none of your business."

She'd been crying. Once he saw the tears on her cheeks, he knew he was a goner. It *was* none of his business, but there was no way he could stay out of it now. She was far too vulnerable. Only a cad would leave a woman like this to fend for herself in the night.

Still, his impulse was to growl and start ordering her about. He restrained it. He knew enough about women to know that wasn't going to work out well. Taking a deep breath, he said carefully, "Why don't you tell me what you're doing. What's wrong?"

She stared at him for a moment, then shook her head. "Please, just go. I'm really busy here. I've got to find…" Her voice trailed off and she went back to trying to move the huge plastic bag.

Instead of leaving, he moved closer. "You've got to find what?"

She shook her head and threw a hand out as though covering the waterfront. "My bag. My things."

He frowned. She could hardly be talking about this big plastic bag she seemed to be so intent on moving out of the way. He reached around her and moved it for her, revealing only more, smaller plastic bags, all filled with suspicious substances. It was obviously trash someone had stacked there, along with things that had washed up on the shore.

"What sort of bag?" he asked her. "What did it look like?"

She straightened and looked around, her bottom lip caught by her teeth, her eyes worried. "I…I'm not sure…"

He resisted the impulse to throw up his hands. "Then how are you going to find it?"

Tears welled in her dark eyes and she

turned her head away, her damp curls flopping limply against her neck in a way that somehow touched him. He could see her finely cut profile against the lights from across the river. Her features were delicate, yet strong in a determined sort of way. Her body was slender despite the pregnancy. Her legs were long and exotic, like a dancer's, and her short skirt showed them off in a way that would turn any man's head. She moved like a dancer, smooth, fluid motion, like a song brought to life. But that thought made him want to laugh at himself for thinking it. He wasn't usually quite so sentimental.

Then she turned and his gaze dropped to her full breasts and the way they strained against the soft sweater she wore under her jacket, and he felt a reaction so quick and so hard, it threw him off guard for a moment.

"I don't need help," she said, but her voice quavered and the tears were still in her eyes.

Something caught in his chest and he grimaced. No, he wasn't going to let her get to him. At the same time, she obviously couldn't be abandoned here. He'd already noticed someone skulking farther down along the river. No, he was going to make sure she got to safety—wherever that might be.

But he wasn't going to care. Never again. That part of him was gone—and good riddance.

"Just go away," she said, wiping her eyes with her sleeve. "Just go."

"I'm afraid to leave you here," he shot back. "You might try another shot at river-rafting."

She glared at him. "I was *not* trying to jump into the river."

"Really? Then what were you doing? Practicing high-bar techniques for Olympic trials in gymnastics?"

She didn't answer, turning away instead.

"I'll admit it seems unlikely for someone in your condition…."

"Condition?" she asked. Then she looked down and gasped softly, her hands going protectively to her rounded belly. "Oh. I forgot."

"Forgot?"

He stared at her. Females didn't "forget" pregnancy. There was something very odd about this woman. But something distracted him from the subject. For the first time he noticed there was something dark and shiny in her hair. He touched it and drew back his fingers. Blood.

"Hey. What's this?"

She reached up but didn't quite touch it

herself. "I don't know." She frowned. "Maybe I hit my head when I fell. Or…or…" She looked up at him questioningly. "Maybe it's where he hit me."

Her words sent a blinding flash of outrage slashing through him. The thought of someone deliberately hurting her made him crazy for an unguarded moment.

"Who?" he demanded. "Where? What did he do to you?"

A look of regret for having mentioned it flashed across her face and she turned away. "I don't know," she said, shaking her head. "I don't know."

"Wait." He grabbed her arm to stop her from starting off. "This is serious. I'm taking you to the police."

She jerked from his grip and began to back away, her eyes wide. "No, I can't do that. No." She glared at him, shaking her head, looking fierce. "I can't go to the police."

"Why not?"

She hesitated, looking past him.

He frowned. He could think of only two reasons why someone wouldn't want to go to the police, neither of them good.

"Look, I'll be with you. I'll handle things. There's nothing to be afraid of."

She flashed him a scathing look. "It must be nice to be so sure and cavalier about other peoples' lives," she said. "Who do you think you are, anyway? King of Carnethia?"

He looked at her sharply, but no, she really didn't seem to know she was talking to someone pretty close to that mark.

"Just someone trying to help you," he said softly.

"Really?" She tossed her damp hair and sent him a penetrating look. "And what do you expect to get out of it?"

He gave her a half shrug and a well-practiced look of pure boredom. "I was hoping for a simple thank you, but even that seems to be out of the question."

For just a moment, her gaze faltered. "Why should I trust you?" she asked, pushing hair back out of her eyes.

"You don't seem to have a lot of choice, do you?" he grumbled, moving restlessly. "Look, if you don't want to go to the police, there must be somebody I can call to come get you or something." He pulled out his cell phone and held it poised. "Give me a number."

She shook her head and looked away.

"Come on. We've got to get you out of this drizzle, at least." He looked back at the storefronts along the riverside. It was late and most of the shops were closed. "How about that little café there? It'll be warm and dry."

She looked up. He could see she was tempted.

"A nice hot cup of coffee? Come on. I'm buying."

She glanced at the café and a look of longing came into her face. "I'm so hungry," she admitted softly.

He snapped the cell phone shut and put it back in his pocket. "That does it. Come on. Let's go."

Turning, she looked searchingly into his face. He wondered what she saw there—a helpful new friend or the hard-bitten man he knew he'd become? It seemed she hadn't recognized who he was. That was a relief. So she wasn't particularly political. Good.

"Let's go," he said again, putting his hand lightly at her back to urge her along.

He entered the café warily, scanning the scene like a soldier on point. Simple booths lined one side of the room. Wrought-iron tables and chairs filled the center. Posters and advertisements covered the walls and pop music was playing on the speaker. The place was almost empty. A pair of young lovers had a booth at the back but they were lost in each other's eyes and paying no attention. An elderly couple was finishing up a meal toward the front. Involved in some sort of argument, neither looked up. That left the waitress and she just looked bored and very sleepy. No one reacted.

Who knew—maybe he was becoming unrecognizable. That would certainly be an improvement.

He led her to a booth in a protected corner and sat across the table from her.

"An omelet and a tall glass of milk," he ordered for her, giving the bored waitress a quick, cool smile. "And I'll take a cup of espresso."

"Eggs," the mystery woman said thoughtfully, as though she were considering whether she really liked them or not. "Okay." She sneaked a look back at the counter. "But that pie looked awfully good," she mentioned.

He stifled the grin that threatened to soften his mouth. "Okay. A large piece of the apple pie, à la mode, too. We'll share it."

As the waitress left with their order, the woman gazed at him wide-eyed with that searching look again.

"Do I know you?" she asked softly.

He looked at her sharply, afraid she'd realized who he was, but all he saw was bewilderment in her beautiful eyes, and he relaxed. If she felt he looked familiar, but couldn't quite place who he was, that might at least make her trust him a bit more.

"Not that I know of," he replied lightly. "We met on the bridge just tonight."

"Ah. Of course."

"And I don't know your name," he noted.

She nodded as though she thoroughly agreed, and he prodded further.

"My name's Nick," he said, fudging a bit. "What's yours?"

"Uh…" She looked trapped for a moment and avoided his gaze, looking about the café as though she was going to find the answer to his question in the atmosphere. "Marisa," she said quickly as her eyes focused behind his head. "It's Marisa. Marisa Fleur."

"Marisa," he repeated. "Pretty name." He stuck out his hand. "Nice to meet you, Marisa."

She put her small, fine-boned hand in his and for the first time, she actually smiled. "Nice to meet you, too, Nick."

The beat of his heart stuttered. There was no way to deny it. For just a second, he was afraid his heart had stopped. The feel of her small, smooth hand in his, the beauty of her sweet smile, the warmth that came momentarily from her dark gaze, all combined to shock him as though someone had hit him with a stun dart. He blinked, drew in a sharp breath, and quickly pulled his hand away from hers. *What the hell...?*

"And thank you," she was saying. "It might not seem like it but I really appreciate you taking the time to...well, to help me."

He nodded, avoiding her gaze, still shaken by the involuntary reaction he'd had to her smile and touch. "No problem," he said gruffly.

He risked looking at her and it was okay. Whatever spell had swept over him seemed to be gone for now. Still, forewarned was forearmed. He was going to be on his guard from now on.

He waited for her to take a few bites of her omelet before trying to question her. Her color was better by then, and she'd lost most of that trapped look.

"So," he said, nursing his espresso in both hands. "Are you ready to tell me what happened?"

She looked up at him, eyes wide. "You mean on the bridge?" she asked.

He nodded.

She looked down. "I…well, I think a man came up from behind and knocked me down."

His hand tightened on the slender cup. "Did you know him?"

"I don't think so. No," she amended quickly. "No, I'm sure he was just a mugger or something. He grabbed my purse and then he threw my bag over the side of the bridge." She gazed at him earnestly. "That's why I was climbing up on the railing. I was trying to see where my bag had gone."

"And that was what you were looking for along the side of the river?"

She nodded. "I know there's not much hope in finding my purse, but if I could find my bag…"

"It's a suitcase?"

She hesitated, looking uncertain. Then she nodded again.

He frowned. There was something odd and off-kilter about all this. "When did it happen?"

She hesitated, shrugged, then her eyes lit up as she remembered. "Just before I saw you the first time. I think maybe you scared him away."

The waitress brought them a huge slice of pie on a ceramic plate. A rounded mound of vanilla ice cream was melting on top. Marisa smiled again and he frowned to keep from letting it get to him.

"So you're here from out of town?" he noted as he handed her a fork. "Where are you from?"

She looked down again. "I really can't talk about that," she said evasively.

He shrugged. "Do you know anyone in town?" he asked.

She didn't answer but the look on her face said it all. What was he going to do with her? The realization came to him with a sick feeling in the pit of his stomach. He was going to take her home. At this time of night, what else could he do?

They rose to leave and he turned to let her go first, and as he did so, his gaze fell on an advertising poster on the wall behind where he'd been sitting. Marisa's Flowers it said, along with an address and telephone number.

Marisa's Flowers. He turned slowly and watched as she walked ahead of him out of the café, and that feeling in the pit of his stomach got sicker.

CHAPTER TWO

MARISA.

It wasn't her name but it felt like a near fit. Close enough—for now. Her real name was there, right on the tip of her tongue, but every time she thought she had it, it slipped away again. But it would come. She had no doubt about that. She'd hit her head pretty hard and it had knocked her silly for a moment. Give her a little time and a bit of rest and it would all come back. If only she could find her suitcase….

She glanced at the man walking beside her. He was near thirty, large and hard and there was something just a little bit dangerous about him. There was something appealing, too, despite his icy demeanor. But she needed to be careful. She'd been wrong about men before. Hadn't she? She couldn't think exactly how, but she knew it was true. She wasn't thinking too clearly right now but she did know one thing: men were nothing but trouble. She'd best get away from this one as soon as possible.

"Thanks for the late-night snack," she said, keeping her tone light. "I'm sure you've got places to go and people to meet, so I'll just say goodbye here."

She stuck out her hand. He took it but not for the handshake she'd expected.

"Where are you going?" he said, looking down at her, his hand warm on hers.

She tugged, but he wasn't letting go. Looking up, she winced—partly at how tall he was, but mostly for the look of resolve in his silver-blue eyes. The man wasn't going to go gently into the dark and foggy night, was he?

She hesitated. What she really wanted to do was get back to looking for her suitcase. She needed that bag with an urgency she wasn't really clear on—but she needed it badly. She wanted to comb both sides of the river until it turned up. But something told her he wasn't going to go for that.

"I know where I'm going," she said quickly. "You don't have to worry about me. I've got…uh…someplace to stay."

He cocked one dark eyebrow, and it was

the sexiest thing she'd ever seen a man do. She gaped at him, astonished at her own reaction. He was masculine magic—a gangster right out of a thirties film, a movie star dining at the Copa in the forties, a military commander from the fifties, a rock star from the sixties, Italian royalty from any decade at all. He had the presence common to all those icons, a sort of magnificent sense of command that took her breath away.

And he didn't believe a word she'd said, making her shiver with the sort of expectant chill she only got from a really good thriller.

"Fine," he was saying as she was pulling herself back down to earth. "I'll go with you to make sure you get to your destination without any more bridge diversions."

She felt that under ordinary circumstances, she would have talked back and insisted on going her own way, but she was still getting over the shock his insolent eyebrow had given her, so she nodded and began to make her way along the riverfront sidewalk, her companion beside her, and not an idea in her head as to where she would go.

She had to make up her mind soon. They couldn't just wander around the city. She bit her lip and tried to think of some way to get into a doorway that would pass muster as her final objective.

Meanwhile, they walked.

It was late and the streets were deserted, but there was a man in the block ahead, leaning against the wall of a building, playing his guitar. As they got closer, she could see that he was standing near the entrance to a sort of nightclub. Music and laughter floated out, but the man was playing to his own muse, standing under a light. He wore dark glasses and there was a cup on the ground near his feet. Maybe he was blind.

Maybe. But she shivered. Something about him…

Maybe it was just the night. As her mother used to say, *nothing good happens out there after midnight.*

Her mother? She tried to grab hold of that concept, tried to see a face, but it slipped away before she could focus. A feeling of loss filled her, but she tamped it down. Never mind, she would think of it soon enough.

Turning to her companion as they reached the crosswalk, she put her hand on his arm. "Let's go this way," she said, nodding down a direction that would avoid the guitar player. "I think this is quicker."

He came along without comment and in a moment or two, she was breathing evenly again. Funny. She didn't know why, but the man playing his guitar on the previous block had reminded her of something…something she didn't want to remember.

Which shouldn't be a surprise, she supposed wryly. After all, she wasn't remembering much. Was this going to be a long-term problem? Possibly. But right now it was mostly annoying. And her mind was full of so many things, she didn't have time to worry about it.

The first order of business was to get rid of this man so she could go back and find her suitcase. Something told her that was the key to getting herself back to normal. As they came to another corner, she stopped and smiled at him quickly.

"There it is," she said, gesturing down the block. "I can handle the rest of this on my own," she added breezily. "Thanks again."

She turned to hurry off, but his hand stopped that, his long fingers curling around her upper arm.

"Marisa," he said, a smile teasing the corners of his wide mouth as he looked down into her wide eyes, "this is Embassy Row."

She turned and looked. Sure enough, the

street was lined with stately mansions, and even in the dark, she could see the placards identifying the countries.

"So?" she said, trying to remain nonchalant. "I…I'm staying with the Hungarians for now." She looked up to see if he was buying it.

He laughed shortly. "Liar," he said calmly. "The Hungarian embassy has been closed down for years and they haven't sent a new delegation yet." He shrugged. "Want to try again?"

She glared at him. He was becoming insufferable.

"Look, I don't want to argue about this. I appreciate your concern, but you have no hold over me." Very deliberately, she peeled away his fingers, making a graphic statement to back up her words. "And I'd like to be on my own."

"You can't be."

She wrinkled her nose, frowning up at him. "What are you talking about?"

That wonderful eyebrow rose again. "You're carrying a baby with you, no matter what you do," he said flatly. "And that means you need to take a little extra care, don't you think?"

Looking down, she bit her lip. He was right. She could see the slight bulge of her tummy.

She was pregnant! It startled her every time she remembered. How had this happened?

Well, she supposed it was in the usual way. Still, you'd think she would remember something like that. At least, she should remember the man involved.

She wished her mind would clear. She was so confused. She knew it would be crazy to go with this man she didn't even know. Of course, in some ways it was even crazier to go roaming the streets when she didn't know where to go or what to ask for. What was she going to do, sleep under a bridge or in a doorway like a homeless person?

But that seemed to be what she was right now. Until she figured out who she was and where she was going, she was homeless.

"I'll be honest with you, Marisa," he went on. "You're a grown woman. If you want to wander the streets of this city at all hours, ordinarily you could be my guest. But right now, things are different. You've got to think about that baby you're carrying."

She blinked at him, not sure where he was going with this.

He considered her levelly. "I think you'd better come home with me."

That shocked her. She gasped softly, wondering if he really meant it—and how he meant it. What kind of a home was he talking about? What sort of situation?

She looked up with a wry smile. "What will your wife think?" she tried, fishing for information.

A cold shadow passed through his gaze. "I'm not married."

She shivered, then tried to make light of the circumstances with a quip. "That's what they all say. Right after they claim to read *Playboy* for the articles."

His mouth twisted. Despite himself, he almost grinned. "Okay," he admitted, "I'll plead guilty to being male."

She wondered if that meant he was acknowledging a certain attraction. She thought maybe it did, and that made her want to smile, too. Better to make a smart-aleck crack instead, she decided hurriedly.

"Wise move," she retorted with a nod. "Next you might as well throw yourself on the mercy of the court. That'll get you a lighter sentence."

"If you're the court, I'd think twice," he shot back. "But either way, here's the truth. I'm not married."

He wasn't married. Was she? No, she

didn't think so. Despite the fact that she was pregnant, she couldn't picture herself married. It just didn't feel like it.

She studied him with her head to the side, considering. "Do you have any children?" She only asked because he seemed so concerned about the baby she was carrying.

"No. But I care a lot about children. And I think it's only fair to give a baby the best first nine months you possibly can."

She nodded. Of course she agreed. Who wouldn't? But what did that mean, exactly? If she couldn't even remember why she was pregnant....

"Come on," he said, starting off across the street. "You're dead on your feet. We've got to have a doctor look at you before you pass out."

"Doctor?" She found herself going along with him again. What had happened to her determined effort to peel off? It seemed to have melted into the mist. "Where are you going to find a doctor at this time of night?"

"I've got one where I live."

That made her do a double take. "Really?"

"Yes." He glanced at her sideways, a half grin just for her. "I've also got a sister who will take care of you. So you don't have to worry about my intentions."

She wanted to protest, to say she hadn't been a bit worried, but the words stuck in her throat.

"Once we get there, I probably won't even see you again. Carla will handle everything."

"Will she?" He was walking quickly now and she was hurrying just to keep up.

"Yes. She's capable of handling just about anything. The entire country, even."

"Well, if she can handle you, I'm sold."

They stopped at the crosswalk on a major road. Two cars sped past. Looking back, she thought she saw someone duck between two buildings. That gave her a start, then she relaxed. She was imagining things. This night was taking a toll on her sanity, wasn't it? She felt an overwhelming need to bring things to rights as much as she could.

Nico took her arm. "We're almost there," he told her.

Instead of starting off across the street, she hung back, putting her own hand on his.

"Okay, listen," she said seriously. "Before we get there, I've got a confession to make."

His eyes darkened as he looked down into hers. "Really."

"Yes." Taking a deep breath, she closed her own eyes for a moment, then opened them and blurted out, "I don't know where I'm going or what I'm doing."

He almost smiled. "That's been obvious from the first moment I saw you."

She pressed her hand on his and gazed earnestly up into his eyes. "No, I'm serious. I really don't know who I am."

He blinked and the smile faded. "That's why you made up that name, Marisa Fleur?"

She gasped. "How did you know?"

He shrugged. "I saw the sign in the café and figured it out pretty quickly."

She sighed, shoulders slumping. "I wish I was a better liar," she muttered.

"What was the point of lying?" he said sensibly. "You got hit on the head and you're a little confused. That's why you need to see a doctor."

She looked at him in surprise, then realized what he saw when he looked at her. He saw a woman under suspicion of wanting to commit suicide. Maybe he thought she'd wanted to jump because she was pregnant and had no husband. And why wouldn't he think that? She had no wedding ring on her finger. That made her bite her lip. She probably wasn't married, but she really didn't know. And why was her impulse to lie about it all? Was she trying to hide something?

But all that was crazy. She wasn't suicidal. She was confused, but not ready to end it all. Was she?

No, of course not. Why couldn't she keep things straight? She'd climbed up on the bridge to try to see where the man had tossed her suitcase. She had hoped to see where it had landed, or where the river might have taken it, so that she could get it back and find her things and clear everything up. That was all. Nothing earthshaking. She hoped.

"Come on," he said. "I live right across the street."

She looked at where he was pointing and gasped.

"Wait a minute. Isn't this Altamere? The royal palace?"

"Yes. Come along." He started across the street and she came along willingly, gaping at the huge Gothic building they were headed for.

"Oh my," she said softly.

He glanced down at her. "Have you been here before?"

"What? No. I don't think so. But…" She looked at him questioningly as he used a remote to open the huge iron gates. "Do you work here or something?"

"No, Marisa," he said, closing the gates behind them and nodding to a security guard. "I live here."

"Wait." Grabbing his arm, she stopped and stared up at him, her eyes huge with wonder. "Ohmigod. You're one of the princes, aren't you?"

He smiled, his blue eyes shining with amusement. "Guilty as charged."

That did it. The world started to swirl and if Nico hadn't caught her, she would have hit the ground for the second time that night.

CHAPTER THREE

"ALL I can say is, it's about time you brought a woman home."

Nico turned to throw a stern glance at his lively, dark-haired sister as she entered the parlor where he'd taken Marisa just after she'd fainted in his arms. But his next words were directed at the silent-as-a-ghost butler standing near the door.

"Chauncy, has Dr. Zavier been contacted?"

"Yes, Your Highness," the man responded with a slight bow. "He is on his way here now."

"Good."

He turned back to Marisa, looking down at her, where she lay on the velveteen couch, with a frown of concern. She hadn't stirred since he'd carried her in. Did that have any connection to the bump on the head she'd taken earlier on the bridge? He took her hand in his again and felt her pulse. She was lying very still with her eyes closed, but he couldn't see any other evidence of injury. Her breathing was normal.

What the hell—maybe she was asleep.

"She's very pretty," Carla noted, leaning on his shoulder to look at the exceptionally pretty blond woman. "Though I thought brunettes were more your type."

He had to bite back the sharp retort that rose in his throat. Maybe Carla had forgotten about Andrea.

Andrea. Just thinking her name slashed another jagged tear into his heart. A vision of wild, lustrous auburn curls filled his mind's eye. Memories of her dancing green eyes, her soft skin, her rolling laughter swept over him in a wave that threatened to choke him. He pulled away from his sister and began to pace the Persian carpet, fighting back the crippling anger that always came when he thought of his loss.

Marisa was a very different type. Slender and light, her blond hair curling into an impenetrable mass that didn't quite reach her shoulders, she was nothing like the woman he had loved. But just seeing Marisa lying there on the couch brought back his most painful memories.

Andrea had been on the cold, hard ground that awful night, over a year ago now. They'd been pinned down by a sniper and his rounds were still biting in around them as he'd worked frantically on her wounds. Ripping apart his shirt to use to bind her torn flesh, he tried desperately to stop the bleeding. He cried out encouragement, prayed aloud, promised things and begged. But the blood kept coming, slowly draining her life away. And finally, there was nothing to do but to cradle her lifeless body in his arms and curse and sob out his anguish and promise revenge.

But that was then. This was now. And the woman on the couch wasn't in danger of dying. Still, she was alone and vulnerable and she carried a child, just like Andrea. He couldn't ignore the parallels.

"This is hardly a date, Carla," he rebuked her curtly, just because he had to funnel his anguish into anger in order to keep it under control.

"Well, brother dear, it's as close as you've come lately," she said cheerfully, pushing back her thick black hair and bending over Marisa.

He glanced over, regretting that he'd snapped at her, though not quite enough actually to apologize. He knew it hadn't been easy for Carla, growing up during a war with three older brothers always taking precedence. He should cut her some slack.

Carla had lived a strange, schizoid existence, sometimes thrust into the midst of bloody battles as the family fled attack, at other times treated as though she were the proverbial pampered princess to be kept away from ordinary life as long as possible. Their mother had died two years ago and their father, the king, very recently. When she'd been alive their mother had always acted as though Carla's primary role in life was to wait for the right eligible swain to present his credentials and get permission to sweep her off her feet. So Carla had waited. But the war and other things had cluttered the time up and now, in her early twenties, he knew she was beginning to fear she had waited too long.

Seeing the look in his eyes, Carla knew he was thinking about her situation. She appreciated his compassion, but a little action on her behalf would be more useful. Princesses were usually betrothed by now. And no one seemed to be doing anything about it.

When she'd taken her fears to their aunt Kitty, the older woman had reassured her.

"Don't worry, dear," she'd said, patting her

hand lovingly. "I'm sure your brothers will always need looking after. If you don't get married, there will always be a place for you at the palace."

It had been a shock to realize her aunt didn't think much of her chances either. If only she'd been born beautiful, the way her brothers were handsome, things would have been so much easier. She wasn't bitter, but it did seem unfair.

"You seem beautiful to me," her father had always said, but that, obviously, didn't help at all.

She'd decided, if it came down to it, she would run away to another country, change her identity and join a dressage team training for the Olympics. Why not? She was good at working with horses. Better that than feeling like a piece of furniture half of the time.

The woman Nico had settled onto the couch was beautiful. Carla smiled as she looked her over. She was as happy to admire beauty as the next person. But as she looked, she noticed the woman's rounded stomach.

"Uh-oh. It looks like she's got a little traveler along for the ride." She shook her head, frowning. "Darn. Does that mean she's already married?"

The prince moved away restlessly. "I'm not really sure about that."

"Oh?" She straightened and gazed at him questioningly.

He shoved his hands down into the pockets of his slacks. "She's…well, it's a bit complicated, but she got mugged tonight and now it seems she's not sure who she is."

"Amnesia?" Carla's silver-blue eyes, so like Nico's, glittered with interest.

"Maybe."

Carla turned back to look at her. "No traditional rings." She tilted her head, considering the silent woman. "I'd say she's unattached."

"Carla…" he said warningly.

"But then, I'm an optimist." She allowed herself a quick look of concern before she went back to needling her brother. "Of course, you've as good a chance as anyone at turning her head."

He groaned.

"But that doesn't explain why she fainted." Turning, she gave him an arch look. "You've obviously terrified the poor dear. What on earth did you do to her?"

"Nothing at all," he said defensively. "She just…well, when she realized who I was…"

Carla laughed and threw up her hands. "Of course. That would be enough to scare any girl into a stupor."

He turned away with a snort. "Where's that damn doctor?"

"He was probably sound asleep when Chauncy called him," Carla said, getting a confirming nod from the butler. The doctor's house, where he lived with his wife and the two nieces they'd taken in when they had been orphaned, was at the far edge of the compound. "It is after midnight. Don't worry, he'll get here." She smiled as she watched her brother go back to pacing the floor.

Marisa was lying very still, her eyes closed, her mind drifting. If she stayed very quiet, maybe she could pretend she was asleep and dreaming and she could put off the reality of her situation. The murmured voices of the others in the room were muted, washing around her. Still, try as she might, she couldn't help but hear what they were saying.

It was all a little too much right now. Somehow she had walked out of her own everyday reality and stepped into a fantasy— she'd just been carried into a palace in the arms of a prince, for heaven's sake! And she couldn't even remember how or why she got here.

Carefully, she tried to reconstruct her day, but she couldn't remember anything that had happened before she found herself on the cold bridge walkway with a lump on her head. She'd tried to shake off the dizziness and she was aware of a man throwing her suitcase and purse over the side of the bridge. What had happened to him? By the time she'd regained her feet, she'd noticed Nico coming toward her and the man who'd attacked her was nowhere to be seen.

The rest was a muddle of clearing her head and walking along with the man she now knew was Prince Nico. There was a stop for something to eat in a café, but what had happened there was blurry. And then the prince had brought her here.

He and his sister were talking as though they didn't think she could hear a thing they were saying. She knew she ought to open her eyes and sit up and join in, but she still needed a moment or two to regroup. Just a moment or two.

"Be serious for a minute," the prince was saying, reacting in exasperation to something his sister had said. "And tell me what we're going to do with her."

"Don't think twice, Nico. I've already got the

second-floor maids up, running a bath, preparing the peach room, laying out nightclothes."

His tone turned reluctantly admiring. "I have to admit, you're nothing if not efficient."

"I do my best. Just trying to make sure that your little treasure has a place to lay her head."

"Excuse me, Your Highness."

Marisa frowned slightly at the new voice that was practically a whisper, then realized it was the butler.

"Yes, Chauncy?"

"I hesitate to intrude, but I thought it might be wise to point out another factor that might have upset the young lady."

"And what is that?" Nico sounded just a bit impatient and she could see why. The man sounded conniving to her, too.

"We live in perilous times, Your Highness. I don't think you can afford to rule out the possibility that she might be… affiliated with the opposition in some way and was shocked to find herself ensconced with the enemy, so to speak."

"Nonsense. Chauncy, you see enemies behind every bush."

"Of course, Your Highness. I beg your pardon for speaking so candidly."

Marisa lay very still and wondered if she

was part of the opposition. She didn't know
the answer to that question, but she did know
she had to get out of here. Carla had called
her a treasure. What on earth had she meant
by that? Unbidden, an old Carnethian folk
song trailed its way into her mind. The refrain
repeated, "Oh what a lucky girl, to be the
prince's plaything." The phrase was said with
bitter irony and added a bad feeling to this
crazy mix. Royalty played exotic games in a
rarified atmosphere she wasn't used to. She
didn't belong here.

And something was tugging at her—some
responsibility she hadn't met, or some errand
she hadn't completed. She had to go, even if
she didn't know where.

Reluctantly, she opened her eyes, just as
the doctor arrived, but it was the prince's gaze
she met first. The connection that sparked
between them made her gasp softly. She
hadn't realized before just how blue those
eyes were, or how provocative. She saw
something there that set off alarms inside her
and sent her heart into a thumping frenzy.
But maybe she was imagining things,
because a moment later his look was cool
and impassive and he was speaking to the
doctor as though she were a homeless person

he'd found in the street. Which she was, wasn't she?

The only time he revealed a flash of emotion was when the doctor turned to him almost accusingly.

"This woman is pregnant," he said, looking sternly at the prince.

Nico's face hardened and he stared at the man. "I just met her tonight," he said icily.

It was obvious the two men didn't care much for each other, but Marisa didn't have time to dwell on that fact. Dr. Zavier examined her quickly and dispassionately, then declared her well enough for now. He found nothing physically wrong, other than a bump on the head, and prescribed lots of rest and plenty of fluids and promised to look in on her in the morning.

Marisa agreed with that diagnosis. She was fine, really. Just tired and a bit confused. She sat up as the doctor left, then looked hesitantly into the prince's eyes, wary of seeing whatever that was she'd seen a few moments before, but his gaze was bland, revealing nothing more than vaguely impatient interest, and she relaxed. She was probably being a ninny and she hated that. Squaring her shoulders, she resolved to be stronger from now on. Just as soon as that was possible.

Nico introduced her to Carla, his sister, who immediately took over and ushered her down the hall and up the stairs and into a warm bath, chattering in a friendly manner all the while. Two chambermaids helped and Marisa didn't have to do a thing. Before she knew it, she was clean and smelling delicious with her dirt-stained clothes exchanged for a silky night-dress that felt like heaven. And finally, Carla led her to a luxuriously plush canopied bed in a beautiful room decorated in peach and gold. By the time Marisa had caught her breath, she knew it was all too much.

"I should go," she protested weakly, knowing she was in danger of letting herself be seduced by all this cosseting.

"Nonsense," Carla told her cheerfully, turning back the bed and providing a step-stool. "It's late. You need to sleep. You can go in the morning."

"But, my clothes…"

"They're being cleaned for you. In the meantime, look here." Carla threw open a tall wardrobe set against the inner wall. "You see all these?" she said, sweeping her hand along the length of the display inside. Bright cloth hung from every hanger. "They belong to my cousin Nadia. She's just about your age and size. Minus the pregnancy, of course, but you're barely showing. Feel free to use anything here that you like."

Marisa shivered. This was beginning to remind her of a fairy tale. Fairy tales didn't always have happy endings. She could think of a few where the young innocent visitor was lulled into a false sense of security by all the riches laid before her, only to come to a bad end when she finally realized what the evil captors actually wanted from her.

"Uh, where *is* Nadia?" she asked.

Carla shrugged and pretty much evaded a straight answer. "Good question. That's something we'd all like to know."

She drew the heavy drapes closed over the lacy liners at the window and Marisa turned slowly, following her movements. She was hesitant to seem to be looking a gift horse in the mouth, but still….

"I… I don't really know why you're being so nice to me," she said carefully. "I mean, you don't know anything about me or where I came from or…"

Carla's good-natured laugh rang out. "Well, neither do you, from what I hear. We're all playing this by ear, aren't we?"

Marisa couldn't help but return her smile. "I guess you're right," she said reluctantly.

"You get into that bed and get some sleep," Carla said, turning to go. "There's a bell rope if you need anything."

"Carla," Marisa said quickly, "thank you."

Carla stopped at the doorway and looked back. She hesitated, then sighed. "I'll be honest, Marisa. It's lovely having you here, but the bottom line is that Nico is in charge when our oldest brother, Crown Prince Dane, is out of town. I'm sure you know—but then, maybe you've forgotten—that our father, King Nevander, died last month after a long illness. So now we're preparing for a coronation. The Crown Prince is in Paris making international alliances. Nico is the de facto ruler here at home for the time being. And Nico gets what he wants. If he thinks you're welcome here, you're welcome here. So relax and enjoy it."

With a wave she was gone. Marisa stared after her. Somehow her last words had not been comforting. The more she heard the prince wanted her here, the more she began to think she didn't want to be here. Instead of heading for the bed, she turned and hurried toward the wardrobe, reaching in to grab something to wear for a quick escape. She'd barely taken down a beautiful pink sweater when a soft rapping on her door told her this wasn't going to be quite so easy.

"Come in," she said, tensed in uneasy anticipation.

Prince Nico entered the room, just as she'd been afraid he would. Funny, but he looked more handsome, taller, harder and just a bit scarier than he had when she hadn't known he was royal. Biting her lip hard, she tried to hold back any evidence of being swept away. She absolutely refused to seem awestruck. She'd been impressed with him before, but once she realized he was royalty—like it or not, that had its effect. The royals were stars. How could it be any other way?

"How are you feeling?" he asked, gazing curiously at the pink sweater.

"I'm fine. Absolutely fine." She pressed the sweater to her chest. "I…listen, I'm sorry to be such a bother to everyone." She gazed up at him earnestly. "Really. I think I should go. You know…"

His handsome face was impassive but his blue eyes shimmered silver in the lamplight. "You can't go."

"Oh." That startled her for a moment. Why couldn't she go? It didn't make any sense. Was he just throwing his royal weight around? Or did he have some ulterior motive? She wasn't sure why she was so suspicious of everyone. But then again, maybe she did have a hint or two as to why that might be. After all, she'd been assaulted tonight. Time to guard herself a bit more carefully, perhaps.

"Well, I'm sure you have better things to do than to look after me. I mean…here you are, a prince and all." She shook her head and tried to convince him. "If I'd realized that from the beginning, I would never have gotten…" The word *involved* was the one she was going for, but the connotations scared her off. "…tangled up with you," she said instead, then frowned, wondering if maybe that was worse.

The faintest of smiles quirked the corners of his mouth. "Too late. I'm entangled." Reaching out, he took the hanger with the pink sweater from her hands and walked it back to the wardrobe.

She gazed at him, nonplussed. "But why?"

He hung up the sweater, then closed the door and turned back. "That doesn't matter."

Her warning system was setting off tiny

alarms again. "Sure it does. I don't understand why you think you have any responsibility for me and my child."

He gazed at her for a long moment before answering that one—long enough that she began to feel self-conscious. She *was* standing there in a filmy nightdress, after all. Hardly the way one would want to appear in an audience with a prince. Unless, of course, one had seduction in mind. That sent blood rushing to her cheeks and she crossed her arms over her chest, wishing she had the sweater back to hide behind.

"We care about all our subjects, Marisa," he said at last.

Right. She almost laughed aloud at that one. Especially when she considered the hint of mockery she heard in his tone.

"Maybe so, but you don't invite them all to come and stay in the palace, do you?"

His blue eyes seemed to smile. "No. You've got me there. I'll have to admit it. You're special."

That gave her the shivers. "Why?" she demanded, though she wasn't sure she really wanted to hear the answer.

He glanced down. She knew her pregnancy was pretty well hidden by the folds of the gown, but it almost felt as though he had X-ray eyes. He was very obviously referring to her child as the reason he was taking extra care to protect her. Her hands went involuntarily to her belly once again and she bit her lip, wondering if she could trust him—or if this was just a way to lower her defenses.

"Are you married?" he asked bluntly.

"What?"

"You're pregnant. The usual order of things would require a husband somewhere in the mix."

She looked down. Funny, she couldn't remember who the father was right now—but despite the fact that there had been a moment there, when she'd still been groggy from the mugging and this amnesia or whatever it might be was still new to her, that she'd been startled to find she was with child, she was now well aware that she was carrying a baby close to her heart. She would never lose sight of that for a moment.

"I'm not married," she said firmly.

He cocked his head to the side. "Can you remember…?"

"No." She lifted her gaze to meet his. She knew instinctively that she had never voluntarily submitted to the authority of a husband.

And she was beginning to feel very similarly about the authority of a prince. "But I know I'm not married. I can feel it."

He frowned. "Perhaps your husband was killed in the war."

She shook her head, chin high. "No."

His eyes darkened. "You seem very sure."

"I am. Look." She held up both hands. The simple rings she wore left no room for the traditional Carnethian doubles all married women wore in this country. "I would remember. I just can't believe I would forget a thing like that. Or if there were anyone in my life that I was in love with."

He nodded slowly. "Maybe the answer will be in your luggage. I'll send out men to search for your suitcase first thing in the morning."

Her suitcase! That sense of urgency came over her again. She looked toward the door. "I really should go," she began.

"You're not going anywhere," he cut in, sounding like a man whose patience was still holding, but not for much longer. "The doctor said you needed rest."

"Yes. But that doesn't mean I have to get it here. Look, I can take care of myself."

"I have no doubt of that. But what about your baby?"

"What about my baby?" she said defensively. "It really has nothing to do with you."

For just a moment, she thought she saw him wince, as though her feisty words had hurt him somehow. Despite everything, she regretted it. And that was a real problem. Her impulse was to do anything she could to make him happy. And that made her want to scream.

"Your Highness," she said, purposefully using his rank as a way to distance herself from him. "I may not remember my name at the moment. And I may not be too clear on where I came from."

She paused for a moment as a picture swam into her mind, a hazy, misty picture that wouldn't quite come into focus. She blinked, thinking the clouds would clear in a second or two and she would see it perfectly.

"Are you remembering something?" he asked, stepping closer.

She drew in a quick breath as the picture evaporated before her eyes. Looking at him, she twisted her mouth slightly. "Not anymore," she said coolly.

He nodded. "Let me know if you do," he said, searching her face as though he thought the answers might appear there.

She sighed. Here was the problem. He saw

her as a victim, someone who needed to be taken care of. She'd been through a lot today and taken some hard knocks, but she knew one thing for sure—she was no victim. She could take care of herself. She was going to have to pull herself together enough to show him that inner toughness before it was too late.

"Get some sleep," he told her, starting to turn away. "We'll discuss your situation tomorrow. I'll see you in the morning."

"Not if I see you first," she muttered to herself as she listened to the sharp sound of his boots on the tiled floor of the hallway.

CHAPTER FOUR

MARISA stared at what she could see of the flowered canopy above her. Not much moonlight slipped in around the heavy drapes. She'd slept for an hour or so, but something was gnawing at her and she was completely awake now. If she was going to try to find a way out of this place, now was the time. She had to go. She didn't feel right being here in the first place. This memory thing was driving her crazy. She was so sure she would remember everything if only she could find her missing bag. There was a compulsion driving her. She had to hurry back to the river and find her bag before anyone else did. And the most chilling thought of all. If she never found it, would she ever remember who she was?

Sitting up, she leaned against the headboard and tried to make a plan. She was in the palace. There were guards. There were probably alarms on the windows and doors. So how was she going to get out of here?

Well…how about a bold walk right out the front door? Why would a guard even want to stop her? She was a guest in this house and she wanted to leave. What could be simpler?

Slipping out of bed, she went to the wardrobe, bypassing the pink sweater for a light training suit in more earthy tones. The pants were stretchy and fitted just fine around her belly. The top was a little snug around her bust. She was ready to go.

In moments she was making her way carefully down the wide staircase and into the dimly lit marble foyer. Catching sight of the front-door guards through the glass, she stopped and chewed on her lip. Now that she was down here, coming face to face with a couple of men likely to have overly aggressive authoritarian complexes didn't seem like such a good idea. Maybe she ought to try a side door or window first, something in one of the rooms that opened off the foyer. Turning she dismissed first one doorway, then another. A semi-dark room appeared to her left. It seemed to be a library of some sort, with floor-to-ceiling windows. Light from the moon cast a silver aspect across the floor that was almost inviting. She slipped inside, heading for the windows. Surely she would be able to open at least one of them, and if she could get through into the garden without triggering the alarm…

Prince Nico sat in semi-darkness, sunk in the depths of a huge leather chair in the palace library, a glass of amber liquid in his hand. The night was stretching out long and lonely ahead of him. He wished there was a switch that could turn his mind off. It was running like a rat in a wheel. At this rate, he was never going to be able to sleep.

The cause was plain enough. Marisa. Marisa with her amnesia and her adorable bewilderment and her strangely vulnerable eyes and her determined bravery. And most of all, with the mystery child she carried. For some reason she had appeared out of the mist and walked into his life, conjuring up all his old ghosts and setting them free to torture him once again. He had a feeling he wasn't going to be able to sleep for a long time.

And why was that? What had she done to him? There was no real reason for it. Marisa looked nothing like Andrea. Her personality was very different as well. So why had she captured his imagination like no other woman had done for a long, long time?

Throwing back his head, he groaned softly. He knew exactly what it was—he just had to face it.

First, she was pregnant and at just about the same stage Andrea had been when she'd been killed. That just naturally reached out and twisted his heart in ways not much else could. He wanted to protect her, to keep the world and all its ugliness away from her, to make sure nothing happened before she delivered her baby. His own baby had died with Andrea. A double tragedy. A double outrage. The pain had been unbearable. If he had the power, he would make sure that never happened to anyone again.

Okay, was that enough? Did that answer the questions roiling inside him? He lifted his glass and looked at the way a shaft of moonlight turned the drink inside to liquid gold and knew he hadn't begun to give a full answer.

Ah hell. He took another long sip and put the glass down on the table at his elbow. Maybe he'd had enough to drink now to be honest with himself.

"She turns me on."

There. He'd said it. And now he hated himself.

It was true. She'd stirred something in him he hadn't felt since he'd lost Andrea. Despite everything, she'd resurrected a sensual response he'd thought had been destroyed that horrible day on the mountain. He hadn't felt the slightest interest in another woman for over a year. He'd wondered, fleetingly, if maybe that part of his life had died with the woman he loved.

No more worries along that score. Every time he saw Marisa he couldn't stop looking at her mouth and wanting to taste her, wanting to cup those full, rounded breasts that strained at the material of her skimpy top in the palms of his hands. Even her rounded belly appealed to him. When he'd seen her in that filmy nightdress, her dark nipples just barely showing through the lace, he'd thought his arousal was going to be so obvious, she wouldn't be able to miss it. He wanted her in a deep, primal way that almost shocked him—the dominant male urge to stake his claim.

What the hell was wrong with him?

Closing his eyes, he let himself think about Andrea. He very rarely did that. It hurt too much. But right now he felt he needed to remind himself of what really mattered in his life. For just a moment, he saw her again, felt her again. He remembered the day she'd told him she was pregnant. He'd covered her face with kisses and they'd clung together, laughing their joy into the air, planning how it was going to be to bring a new baby into the world at the same time they were helping to usher in a new life for their country. He felt the joy again, just for a few seconds, and then her image began to slip away, like a wisp of mist, into the night. A lump rose in his throat and his eyes stung.

"Don't go," he whispered softly to himself.

He heard something. Opening his eyes, his heart lurched. There she was right in front of him! The light from the hallway made a halo effect around her body, while the moonlight lit her hair with silver.

"Andrea?" he whispered in wonder, rising from the chair.

But in that same instant, he realized who it really was. Marisa. Disappointment and then anger flashed through him, as though she'd been deliberately impersonating his lost love. He stood, barring her way, glaring at her and all she represented to him in his useless agony.

"Oh!" Marisa gasped, jumping back. He'd startled her. If she'd seen him there, she never would have come this way.

He stood in her path, immovable, looking dark and dangerous "Where exactly do you think you're going?" he demanded.

She took in a deep breath and stiffened her spine. A part of her had known he would probably find a way to try to stop her. Now that she'd spotted him, she could see a glass of liquor on the small table beside where he'd been sitting. He'd been drinking. Would that mellow him or make him more menacing?

"I want to go home," she said quickly. "I didn't want to bother you again, so…"

The words died in her throat as her eyes grew accustomed to the gloom and began to see him more clearly. He was barefoot and his shirt was unbuttoned, hanging open as though he'd begun getting ready for bed and then decided to come down here for a drink. His eyes were darkly haunted, his mouth a hard, relentless line that told her he could be cruel. But what really took her breath away was the gorgeous landscape of his hard, muscular chest. She hadn't seen muscles like that since…well, she couldn't remember ever seeing a man like this—not face to face, anyway. It suddenly felt as though there was an elephant sitting on her chest.

"How can you go home if you don't know where home is?" he asked evenly.

He had a point there and she managed to drag her gaze away from his beautiful torso to look into his eyes and try to deal with it.

"You don't understand," she said. "I don't belong here. I'm not comfortable. I need to leave."

"You need to stay." He grimaced and tried to soften his tone a bit. "You can't get out, anyway. The moment you open a door or a window, alarms will go off and sirens will sound and the dogs will be released. You wouldn't get two steps out of the house before the guards and dogs would bring you down." He looked at her narrowly. "And they play rough. This is serious business, Marisa."

She didn't waver. "You could call them off."

He sighed. "So you could go wander the streets of the city? Be serious. We've just overthrown a vicious regime and there are still plenty of their supporters around. There are murders in the streets every night. No one on either side is willing to give anyone the benefit of the doubt." He shrugged his wide shoulders. "It's a cold, cruel world. You're better off here."

"That's your opinion."

He stared down at her without speaking for a long moment.

His silence was making her jumpy. "You really have no right to stop me, you know," she added stoutly.

"You think not?" he said softly, moving closer. "You haven't been paying attention, Marisa. I have every right."

She blinked up at him. He was so close she caught a hint of the liquor he'd been drinking. Against all reason, it smelled sweet and enticing. She had to fight back the urge to lean toward him. Funny how his physical presence drew her in even while his inflexible words put her back up.

"Because you're a prince? Are you giving me some sort of...of royal order?"

His mouth twisted and his eyes glittered. "Exactly."

"Oh really!" She tried to glare. "I didn't realize restoration of the royal family was going to change all our lives in quite such a personal way."

"Get used to it," he said, speaking very softly again. "It's for your own good."

His tone was making her very nervous and the way his gaze kept dropping to her mouth was causing butterflies in her stomach. There was a pulse between them, a rhythmic sensuality that was getting as obvious as jungle drums. He was going to kiss her, wasn't he? All the signs were there. And that was no good at all. She had to get away from him before that happened.

She licked her lips, trying to think of a killer phrase or bit of logic, something that would permanently win this argument and let her turn on her heel and stomp off. But it was too late. As she stood there, transfixed, he moved even closer and his hand went to her hair, fingers spiking in until he'd cupped the back of her head in his palm and her will had turned to Jell-O.

He looked down into her face as though he was struggling as hard to stay away as she was. This close, she could read the turmoil in his eyes, despite the darkness. Could he hear how hard her heart was beating?

She shook her head slightly, trying to pull away, but his hand tightened. She felt the warm sizzle of his breath on her face and then his mouth came down on hers and something magic happened. Her mind was screaming at her to get away, but her body wasn't listening to that anymore. She didn't resist at all.

Instead, she sighed softly and curled herself into his embrace as though she'd been starved for male affection for a long, long time and needed this in order to survive.

He pulled her up against the length of his solid body. She put a hand up to stop him, but it landed on his exquisite chest and she flattened it against a rounded mound of the hardest muscles she'd ever touched. She couldn't think anymore. She could only feel. And what she felt was hypnotic and wonderful.

His mouth was hot and hard and sensual in a way she'd never known before. He tasted so good—but then, temptation always tasted good, didn't it?

When he pulled back, she found herself yearning toward him, as though she couldn't stand to lose his heat. Slowly, he disentangled their limbs until she was standing all alone again.

"I shouldn't have done that," he said gruffly, holding her off.

Looking up at him, she couldn't speak. She'd never been kissed quite like that before, and she wasn't sure how to react. Her gaze went to his mouth and she tried to say something, but no words came.

He made a sound of pure disgust, startling her until she realized he was responding to his own actions, not hers.

"Marisa," he said, looking away and raking his fingers through his own hair, "if you must go, of course, you must go. But not now. Not in the middle of the night. The city isn't safe."

Huh? Oh. That again. She'd almost forgotten.

They'd been arguing about her desire to leave. Somehow it had slipped her mind. Good thing he'd reminded her. Taking a deep breath, she wished she could go back to the fray, but her thought processes didn't seem to be working very well. Did kissing a prince tend to turn your brain to cotton candy? Maybe so. At any rate, she was feeling warm and fuzzy and all the fight she'd been so full of had oozed away.

"Go back to your room," he said shortly, looking back at her as though it was a painful thing to do. "You can go in the morning. I won't stop you."

Picking up his glass, he turned and left the room. And Marisa found herself moving like a zombie, but doing exactly what he'd told her to do.

* * *

Marisa stretched and yawned and looked about the room. Someone had pulled back the heavy drapes and sunlight was streaming in, catching on the rich embroidery of the bed covers and the elaborate flocking on the wallpaper. The room was enchanting. She knew she'd never had such a beautiful place of her own before and she smiled, enjoying it for a moment. She'd slept well and she felt good. She was going to let her mind slowly drift into full awareness, and surely she would remember all those things that had been hiding from her since last night. Her name was Marisa and she'd come to the city from a town called…

She waited expectantly. Nothing happened.

Okay, just relax. It was going to come to her. *Just drift and try to picture it.*

Still nothing.

Oh come on! This was so darn frustrating! Why couldn't she remember? It was right there, just out of reach.

Maybe…maybe something else was getting in the way. Maybe if she just let herself think about it for a moment, let the memory of the prince and his touch and his taste…

No! A spasm of pure reaction made her stretch out and then curl up again. She couldn't go there. Thoughts like that made her stomach fall, like riding on a roller coaster. It was too dangerous.

She'd been kissed by a prince. That was not a good thing. The chorus from that nursery-rhyme tune wafted into her brain again. *Oh what a lucky girl, to be the prince's plaything.*

"Not in this lifetime," she promised her reflection in the big mirror on the other side of the room. No, she wasn't going to let the prince's kiss corrupt her thinking. She had enough common sense in her soul to fight it. At least, she hoped she did.

"I'm getting out of here," she told herself out loud and with determination. "I'm going to leave the palace and hunt down my suitcase and once I have that, I'll be able to figure out what is going on. I don't need a royal intervention."

"Nobody expects a royal intervention," said a teasing voice that just barely preceded Princess Carla appearing through the doorway. She smiled at Marisa, blue eyes dancing.

"Good morning, my dear. I hope you won't begrudge me a morning visit, no intervention implied."

Marisa laughed. "You caught me talking to myself. I feel foolish."

"Don't." Carla plopped down on the side

of the bed. "We all need to give ourselves a good talking to now and then. So, tell me, have you remembered anything?"

Marisa shook her head. "Not really. It's so odd. I feel fine and nothing is really wrong. I remember myself as a person, but not the specifics of how I got here. Does that make any sense?"

"No." Carla laughed. "But I think I know what you mean." She took Marisa's hand and looked earnestly into her face. "And you don't remember who the father of the baby is?"

"No. Not at all." Marisa hesitated. She had the urge to go on, to unburden herself to this friendly princess—she seemed so open and welcoming. But she knew it would be wise to be a little discreet. Some deep instinct was warning her that spilling her guts just might get her into big trouble.

"For some reason," she went on carefully, "the father of the baby doesn't loom large in my desire to know the truth. It seems almost irrelevant. It makes me think he hasn't been a factor in my life for quite some time."

Carla nodded. "You don't have the traditional rings," she reminded her. "So it doesn't seem you would be married."

Marisa nodded.

"Well, I think we should call in a specialist. Dr. Zavier is all very well, but what does he know about these things? Tell you the truth, he's always been our family doctor but I've never cared for him much. We really need to get some expert advice on what to do with you."

Marisa smiled at her intensity. "I appreciate all you and your brother are doing, but this really isn't your problem, you know."

"Sure it is." Carla grinned. "We like you." She waved a careless hand in the air in a mock show of royal hubris. "And anyway, what else do I have to do today?"

That made Marisa curious. She'd never wondered much about what being a princess might be all about, but she would never have a better opportunity to find out.

"Carla, what do you do with your time?" she asked her.

"Me? Oh, I'm quite busy. I do good works."

Marisa wrinkled her nose. "What sort of good works?"

Carla made a face. "Oh, I don't know. I have a list of them somewhere. I'll find it and get back to you." They laughed at each other again. "To tell you the truth, I haven't really begun yet. From what I understand, representatives of different charity groups and other organizations come to me and I go speak to them at their luncheons. Help them with fundraising. Cut the ribbon at openings. Hit ships with bottles. Things like that." She shrugged. "At least, that's what I'm told. Isn't that what princesses do?"

Marisa frowned. "I thought they partied with the jet-set crowd."

Carla leaned forward conspiratorially. "You know, I thought that too. But so far…" She looked back over her shoulder to make sure they weren't being overheard. "My brothers are pretty protective. We grew up in exile, you know. It was very different for us. Over the last few years, with the war and my mother passing away and now my father too, we haven't really had much partying in our lives. But I'm looking forward to giving it a try."

Marisa smiled at the younger woman, thinking she was glad to have her for a friend—for the moment at least. Reaching out, she gave her a hug. "Be careful out there, Carla. No wild affairs with rock stars. That doesn't do anyone any good."

"Oh no, of course not!" She blushed prettily. Sliding off the high bed, she started toward the door. "Come on downstairs, sleepyhead," she said. "The morning room is laid out with plenty of things for break-fast. I'm going to go ahead and eat now, because I have a gown fitting in half an hour. But you can eat any time you choose. See you later."

Marisa hesitated. It was on the tip of her tongue to say again, "But I have to leave." She knew she was getting to be a one-note samba on that score, so she held her tongue. But before Carla got completely away, she took a deep breath and asked the question that had been bothering her since her midnight encounter with the prince.

"Carla, who is Andrea?"

Carla spun around and stared at her. "Where did you hear that name?"

"Your brother. I startled him and he called me Andrea."

Carla's gaze was troubled. "I don't know why he would have done that," she said shortly. "She's dead."

Turning back toward the door, she walked away with a determined step. Marisa's breath caught in her throat. No wonder he'd seemed so haunted last night. If he'd actually thought she was someone he'd loved and lost, even for a moment, that must have cut like a knife. She sighed. She really did have to leave this place. Everything was way too complicated for her.

"I suppose I just wasn't meant for the royal life," she muttered to herself as she slid out of bed and padded to the bathroom.

CHAPTER FIVE

PRINCE NICO was on the terrace that flared out over the estate from his bedroom suite. From where he sat, he could see the gardens and the small forest beyond them. To the right were the ancient Gothic buildings that housed certain agencies of the government. To the left was the entry yard, the guard building, the gate to the rest of his country and all its citizens. He could feel them out there, just waiting for things to get better. He only hoped they would be patient a little longer. He felt like a man sitting on a powder keg. If he and his brothers didn't get off the dime soon, the whole thing would blow up in their faces.

But he wasn't really thinking much about that today. Today, sitting at a wrought-iron table, he was having coffee and reading the morning paper.

At any rate, he was trying to read it. He

stared at the headlines, but all he could think about was Marisa. What was he going to do with her? The new government was not yet able to use DNA or fingerprints or any other sort of identity confirmation. All records had been destroyed in the war. Unless she regained her memory, or someone turned up who knew who she was, there wasn't much hope of identifying her and he was going to have to find a way to care for her without getting involved himself.

Of course, she had every right to walk out of the palace and never look back. He knew that. But he wanted to avoid that at all costs. She and her baby needed protection.

At the same time, he knew he couldn't keep her here. It was perfectly obvious he wouldn't be able to keep his hands off her if she was around all the time. Quickly, he mused over various options as they presented themselves to him and soon he thought he had a pretty good idea.

Chauncy appeared with a glass of orange juice and the morning mail. He looked up at the man who had served his family for so many years.

"Ah, Chauncy. I'm glad you're here. I need you to make some arrangements for me."

"Of course, Your Highness."

He outlined a plan to have teams sent out to try to find Marisa's suitcase as the first order of business, then got down to the matter at hand.

"What I have in mind is some sort of an old-fashioned boarding house, a nice place, well-decorated, with private rooms off a central living room and dining facilities."

Chauncy went very still and his brow showed the tiniest of frowns. "Might I ask what such a place would be for?"

"You may indeed. I'd like it to be a home for nice women, especially women who may have babies on the way and need a place to stay. There should be a sort of den-mother person hired to make sure everything runs smoothly." He frowned, thinking. "A cook, I suppose, a housekeeper, a gardener and that sort of thing. You can handle the details, I'm sure."

Chauncy coughed discreetly.

Nico looked up at him questioningly. "Yes?"

"Your Highness, I'm sure you have some specific young ladies in mind. Perhaps if you filled me in on just what your plans are…"

Nico's brow lowered appreciably. He would have preferred to keep things on a theoretical basis, but he realized that was unrealistic. Surely Chauncy already guessed the truth, so what was he waiting for?

"It's for her, of course," he said shortly. "Marisa. She needs a place to stay. She also needs consistent medical care, actually, but she will resist that." He nodded as he thought that over. "This way we can keep an eye on her and provide for things like a decent diet and doctors' visits and such without worrying that she's in any sort of jeopardy."

Chauncy looked stricken and tried to hide it. "Might I suggest that, pure as your motives obviously are—if the tabloids got hold of this they wouldn't see it that way."

"Hmm?" Nico looked up at the older man. A look of surprise flashed over his face.

"Oh my God. You're right." He laughed humorlessly. "What was I thinking? They would assume I was setting up a comfortable bordello for myself, wouldn't they?"

"I'm afraid so, Your Highness."

The prince sighed and threw down his pen. "Okay, back to the drawing board," he muttered. "I'll have to think of something else."

"I have a suggestion, Your Highness."

"Yes?"

"I know of a residence hotel for young women who come to the city looking for work. It's clean and well-run. I happen to know there is an opening right now."

Nico frowned, considering. "Do you vouch for the place?"

"I do, sir. My sister runs it."

Nico's eyes widened. "Your sister? When did you get a sister?"

"I've always had one, sir."

Nico stared at him. He'd known this man all his life. More than a servant, Chauncy had often seemed to be his father's best friend. He winced now, missing his father and the wise counsel he so often gave. Having Chauncy as backup was invaluable. He loved the man. Why hadn't he known he had a sister? But that was neither here nor there at the moment.

"Well, that might be the answer to the problem. How soon do you think she could move in?"

"I'll be happy to take her over this morning, Your Highness."

"Oh. That soon?" Nico swore at himself the moment the words were out of his mouth. The sooner the better. Wasn't that the whole point? It would be best if he knew she was well taken care of but he never had to see her again. And he could get on with his life.

"Very well. That might just fit the bill.

And in the meantime, don't forget to start the great suitcase search immediately. Thank you, Chauncy."

Chauncy bowed his way off the terrace but Nico hardly noticed. Now that he'd taken care of that little problem, he should be able to rest easy. Instead there was a restless anger smoldering inside him. Rising to go inside, he cracked his knee on the wrought-iron table and cursed harshly, barely resisting the urge to throw the damn thing over the railing.

Oh yes, he could tell this was going to be a great day. Still muttering curses, he limped off to change into other clothes. He was headed for the palace gym. If there was one thing he needed, it was a good, exhausting workout.

Marisa searched through the garments in the wardrobe and picked out a cute yellow sundress. She never wore things like this—at least, she didn't think she did. Still, somehow she was attracted to it today. But it had been raining the night before. Was a dress like this going to be appropriate? She went to the window to look out and judge the weather.

The rain had cleaned the city and the sun was giving it a special shine. Everything looked warm and inviting. There was a lovely view from her vantage point. The window faced the front of the palace and she could see out past the iron fence, past the barricades left from the war, into the surrounding neighborhood with its wealthy homes.

And as she was looking over the handsome estates across the street from the palace, she also saw, just out of the corner of her field of vision, someone slip behind a stone wall and duck down, out of sight. Funny. She stared at the place where she'd seen it happen for a long moment, but there was no movement. Still, she was sure she'd seen someone go into hiding. She couldn't think why anyone would be keeping watch on the palace and trying to hide that fact, but there was something ominous about it. She made a mental note to tell the prince what she'd seen, shrugged and turned back to dressing.

Everything had looked warm and sunny outside, so she put on the dress without a qualm. Looking in the mirror, she liked what she saw. Her belly protruded a bit, but the bloused waist hid most of that. She looked pretty good, if she did say so herself. Looking around the room, she wanted to hug herself. This was all so nice.

Whoa there, she told herself quickly. There

was no point in growing to like this lifestyle too much. By noon, she should be out of here, but for now, she made her way downstairs and for the first time, took a really good look around.

What she saw staggered her. The place was a palace, for heaven's sake! The floors were marvelously inlaid with marble and other luminous stone, highlighted here and there by large sumptuous Persian rugs. The walls were richly textured with velvet-like coverings and huge ancestral paintings hung on every wall. The furniture was large, mostly heavy and reeking of age and quality, with fancy carvings and gilded decoration. It was enough to make her feel very small and ordinary. She tried to imagine what it must have been like for a young girl to come here straight from the countryside to work as a maid. Terrifying!

She wandered for a few minutes, awestruck, then found herself staring at the morning room where, rumor had it, breakfast was to be found. An older man and a middle-aged woman were just leaving. They looked startled to see her, but both nodded, glanced at each other, and left the scene as she nodded back.

"Probably wondering if I'm actually one of those new employees who's lost her way," she muttered. But never mind. Here she was, alone with piles of wonderful food.

There was a table set for breakfast, but she didn't want to stay and risk ending up eating with the prince. Very quickly, she filled her plate with bakery items and chunks of fruit, then grabbed a steaming cup of coffee before trying the French doors to the garden outside. One opened at her touch and she was outside, heading for the small forest of fluttering trees she could see on the other side of the garden pond. Balancing her cup and her plate, she walked fast, hoping to get into the shelter of the trees before she was seen.

A few more steps and she was home free, following a well-worn path that soon led her to a bubbling brook snaking its way through the woods. Putting her cup and plate of food down on a large, flat rock, she wandered down to the stream's edge, enjoying the cool, clear water.

What a place this was! It was like being in the middle of an ancient forest in the center of a bustling city. Looking up at the sky beyond the treetops, you wouldn't even know a busy population was rushing about only a couple of blocks away. The music of the brook masked any traffic noise from just beyond the fence, but she could hear the sound of the breeze rustling the leaves and the cheerful chirping of birds in the trees…and the sound of someone on a cell phone, coming her way down the forest path.

"Oh bother," she cried softly, knowing right away it was going to be the prince. Yes, she could hear that it was his voice. She couldn't run into him alone again, like last night. Looking around quickly, she searched for some place to hide. There was a little brush-covered island accessed by strategically placed logs. Without giving it a second thought, she bounded across the stream, stepping on one log then another and vaulting her way into the brushy area.

Unfortunately, the bush turned out to be a lot more threadbare than it had looked from the banks. She crouched down anyway, knowing that she wasn't well hidden at all and praying he would be too involved in his conversation to notice her there.

He came into view and it looked as though she might be in luck. He was arguing with someone, speaking sharply, and he passed through the little glen without a glance her way.

Obviously dressed for a workout, he looked very different from when she'd seen him before. Shiny black compression shorts hugged his muscular upper thighs like a second skin and his loose-fitting tank top revealed a pair of very strong shoulders and the gorgeous bulge of some extremely fine biceps. She gulped. Every time she saw the man, he just looked better.

Just as he was about to pass by completely, he stopped short, looked back, and did a double take at her breakfast, neatly set out on the flat rock. He cocked that majestic eyebrow, then broke off his conversation and closed his phone, tucking it into a pocket as he turned back in her direction.

"Marisa, come on out, I can see you," he said, looking mystified. "And anyway, you left your plate of goodies behind." He shook his head as she rose from the bush, her cheeks hot. "What the hell are you hiding for?"

Despite the fact that her embarrassment was only too obvious and visible, she held her chin high and pretended to have a scrap or two of dignity still left.

"One would think, being royal and all, that you would have better manners," she said, clinging to the theory that a good offense was the best defense.

"Manners?" He stared at her, completely out to sea.

"Yes." She cast a careless gesture into the air with her hand. "Seeing a lady in distress at being found in the forest, a real gentleman would walk on by, pretending he hadn't seen a thing."

He shook his head as though he really didn't know what to make of her and had given up trying.

"A real lady wouldn't be hiding in the bushes in the first place," he noted sensibly. "Anyway, what if you were stuck there? Caught by a bramble or with a sprained ankle or something. Being a real gentleman, it would be my duty to come to your rescue."

She gaped at his presumption. "I can rescue myself very well, thank you."

"Can you?" He was relaxing into amusement and he gave her a half grin that sent her pulse spinning, but it didn't last more than a few seconds.

"Come on," he said, growing somewhat impatient. "Take my hand." He offered it to help her back across the logs.

"I can do it myself," she said dismissively. "I got here on my own. I can get back." But she stared at the first log thinking, *How the heck did I get here, anyway?* It suddenly looked like a long leap. One misstep and she would be in the water. She hesitated, trying to decide where to plant her foot.

"Give me your hand," he ordered, leaning out as far as he could without landing in the water himself. "Give me your hand or I'm going to come over there and pick you up and carry you across."

She looked up into his eyes. He meant it. Her heart began to thump against her chest at the thought. She put her hand out and he took it in his and guided her back across the logs with no problem at all.

And once he had her safely on the bank, he released her hand and stepped away from her. Obviously he was as anxious to avoid a repeat of what had happened the night before as she was. That should have been a relief, but somehow it was an annoyance at the same time.

Their gazes met and held for a second or two, but it was so obvious they were both thinking about the midnight kiss, they quickly disengaged.

"How are you feeling?" he asked her. "Did you sleep well last night?"

"Yes, actually. I slept very well."

She glanced at him sideways. His stance

was wide and balanced like an athlete. She had to admit he had better legs than most men. From all evidence, he had better almost everything than most men. In fact, he was a prince a girl could dream about. As long as she remembered it was all fantasy anyway.

"Any change in your memory problem?" he asked.

She shook her head. "No."

He didn't say anything more. She knew he was looking at her in her yellow dress. She wished she had the nerve to look into his eyes and try to judge what he was thinking. Did he like what he saw?

Marisa! Don't go there!

Swallowing hard, she looked up at him and he looked into her eyes and then both gazes skittered quickly away again.

"Have you talked to Chauncy?" he asked, kicking at a stone with his foot.

"No." It seemed an odd question. She turned his way but pinned her gaze to a woodpecker in the tree behind him. "Why?"

He cleared his throat, then said quickly, "He and I have devised a plan for you."

That set off warning bells all through her system. How dare he? Now she could look him fully in the face.

"Oh really?" she said, trying to remain calm. "I don't suppose it might have occurred to you to consult me? Or even that I might have plans for myself?"

He frowned. "You don't understand…."

"Oh, I think I do."

She took a deep breath and counted to three. There was no point in getting hysterical. She'd already made a spectacle of herself by attempting to hide in a bush.

Nice and easy, that was the ticket. Another deep breath. *Okay*.

Looking into his blue eyes, she tried to look as earnest as she felt. "Seriously, I appreciate all you've done for me, but I need to be on my own. As soon as I finish my breakfast…"

"Breakfast!" He turned to look at her plate of delicious-looking pastries. "Is that what you call it? What is that stuff you're eating?"

She blinked, not sure what he was complaining about.

"Carla told me to go ahead and take anything I wanted from the spread in the morning room. I'm sorry if…"

"No, you're welcome to the food, it's just your selections I have issues with." He scowled at her. "Are you still having a hard time remembering that you're pregnant?"

She flushed. So that was the crux of the problem. She should have known. "No, not at all. I'm aware of it every minute. This baby means everything to me."

"Really? Then where's your glass of milk? Why aren't you eating eggs? Or maybe a little oatmeal."

"I've got fruit. Look." She pointed out a nice red strawberry sitting proudly on the plate next to a piece of sugar-encrusted pastry, dabbed with whipped cream.

"Have you had any nutritional counseling at all?" he demanded.

She rolled her eyes at him. "Well, if I knew that, I'd be remembering things, wouldn't I?" Her gaze sharpened. "What do you know about nutritional counseling for pregnant women?"

The flash of some emotion she couldn't identify told her she'd said something it would have been better not to say. She took a step backwards, a quiver of unease shivering down her spine. But before he got a response out, his cell phone rang. Swearing softly, he pulled it out, looked at the caller ID and gave her a quick nod.

"I've got to take this call," he said shortly. "I'm sure you can find your way back to the palace by yourself."

"Of course." She gave him a look of manufactured disgust. "I can see it from here."

He hesitated. "If I don't see you again before you go, I just want to say…"

It was evident he couldn't say what he really wanted to. She blinked at him, waiting.

"It's been very nice having you stay with us," he said stiffly at last, making it sound like a rote pleasantry that meant nothing. "Good luck to you in the future."

He turned away quickly, not waiting for an answer. She bit her lip as she watched him walk on into the depths of the tiny forest, cell phone to his ear. The worst part was, she knew very well she was overwhelmed with disappointment to see him leave.

"And that only proves that I'm late for the leaving myself," she muttered as she collected her pastries and headed back toward the palace.

She had no idea what he'd been talking about but his attitude seemed to show that he also realized she had to go. In fact, he was pretty much saying goodbye, wasn't he?

Perfect. She was as good as gone.

A half hour later, Prince Nico had showered and was dressing for a meeting with the prime minister. He had a lot of complaints about things the PM was doing and he needed to marshal his arguments. He should have been thinking up strategies. Instead, he was mooning over a woman. And he couldn't seem to stop.

At first he'd told himself it was because she was pregnant, but since he'd kissed her, he knew better. Against all logic, he wanted her badly—so badly his insides were churning with a deep, hungry restlessness that was making him feel like a caged beast.

"But don't worry," he muttered darkly to his reflection as he finished using his electric shaver for a little touch up. "I'm not going to do anything about it."

At any rate, soon this all would be moot. Chauncy should be getting her packed up at this very moment. By the time he got back from meeting with the PM, she would be gone, and he would never see her again.

Ouch. He didn't know why that made him feel sick to his stomach. He should be happy. He should be celebrating.

"Whoopie," he muttered, looking through his ties for a good one. Celebrating was the last thing he felt like doing. He wished he could go back to the gym and put his body through another torture routine. Anything to get his mind off Marisa.

Instead, he went out restlessly onto the terrace and leaned on the railing. And there she was, walking on a path through the rose garden, still in the yellow sundress. He knew he should go back in and ignore her, but he couldn't. This might be the last time he ever saw her. She seemed to dance along the walkway, making an enchanting picture with her light-blond mass of curls catching the sunlight and floating around her face like a halo, her long, lovely legs, her rounded breasts, her pretty face, her slender arms with the hands fluttering like elegant birds. For the rest of his life he would have that picture and all he would have to do was close his eyes and dredge up the memory of her in that yellow sundress and he'd be happy.

Happy? He slapped himself in the forehead. Was he nuts? She didn't make him happy now, so why would memories do it?

He watched as she headed into the house through the French doors. There was no getting around it, she could surely brighten a life. Not his, of course. But somebody's.

He turned back into his room and felt like

kicking something. But he had no time for that. The prime minister was waiting.

He was almost finished creating the perfect knot in his tie when Carla came barging into his room, waving a set of papers.

"Bad news," she cried, her cheeks bright red and her eyes sparkling with anger. "Look at these," she added, thrusting the papers at him. "The wash maid found them concealed in Marisa's clothes."

He looked at them curiously as she spread them out on his dresser where he could get a better view. The papers had the patina of ancient parchment. Each was covered with ink forming odd symbols, the like of which he'd never seen before. Stained and tattered, they looked like something that might have turned up in a treasure chest dug up in some excavation site. He reached out and touched one of them gingerly, afraid it might crumble. The symbols meant nothing to him.

"What do you mean they were concealed in her clothes?" he asked, fingering the paper and frowning.

"In the linings. Part of the stitching had come loose and the maid pulled these out. Can you believe this? The whole amnesia thing is obviously a hoax."

His head came up and he stared at her levelly. "What are you talking about?"

She nodded wisely. "It looks like your little bird is a lousy opposition spy after all."

CHAPTER SIX

PRINCE Nico stared at his sister Carla.

"You think Marisa is a spy?" he asked skeptically. "What evidence do you have of that?"

"Just look at these!" she cried, waving a hand at the papers. "We've caught her red-handed."

"I don't get it," he said, shaking his head. "How does this prove she's a spy?"

She looked as though she thought he was being willfully obstinate. "What are you talking about? She came here pretending to be a lost soul with amnesia, and yet now we find secret papers hidden in her clothes, papers written in code. It's pretty obvious she's up to no good, isn't it? Chauncy thinks so."

"Has he seen these?"

"Yes. Chauncy was with me. He has no doubt she's a spy. We swore the maid to secrecy, but it's bound to get out." She gave her brother a challenging look. "What'll we do with her?"

Nico stared at the papers. This did look bad, but he couldn't quite join the posse yet. "You tell me, Carla. What do you think we should do?"

"Have her arrested, of course."

He gave her a pained look. "On what grounds?"

Carla shrugged dramatically. "She's carrying secret documents about."

"When did that become a crime?"

She blinked and looked rebellious. "You can declare it a crime, can't you? You're the caretaker prince while Dane is away."

He groaned. "Carla, we're trying to establish the rule of law in this country. Once any group starts making their own laws, you can throw out that brand-new constitution."

"There must be something you can do. It's just obvious she's trying to undermine our family. Can't you see that?" She looked thoughtful. "Maybe we should put her under questioning. You know methods, don't you? From your time in the war?"

His face darkened. "Carla, if you understood what you're talking about, you wouldn't say such things."

"It's a new time, Nico. You're always telling me that. We have enemies everywhere. We have to take extreme measures to protect ourselves."

"Within the law." He turned from her, beginning to realize how serious this could be. He would stick to the law, of course, but what if more came out and the law said he had to hand Marisa over to the authorities? Everything in him rebelled at the thought. He just couldn't believe she could be spying here.

And yet, what had she been doing skulking about in the woods, hiding from him? Had she hoped to overhear his phone conversations? He tried to remember who he'd been talking to. The Greek ambassador. Nothing particularly classified there. But maybe she was waiting to hear whomever he might be calling next. Who knew? And if she was spying, whom was she spying for?

Shaking that thought away, he picked up the phone to call the butler. "Chauncy, cancel my meeting with Grieg. Tell him I'll call him later. And get Trendyce over here. I need to talk to our Intelligence Coordinator."

"Immediately, Your Highness," the butler

responded. "And as to that other matter, the transfer of the young lady to my sister's residence hotel?"

Looking into his wide mirror, Nico noted the haggard look in his own face. "We'll have to put that on hold for now. But keep it in abeyance. We may be making use of your sister's hotel soon enough. We'll have to see how this pans out."

"As you wish, Your Highness."

Carla flopped down on his bed and watched as he talked and then closed his phone. "What are you going to do?"

He glanced back at where she sat, looking young and naive, as usual. "I'm going to have Trendyce take these papers and find out what the hell is going on."

"Good. And the police?"

He turned to look at her. "Carla…"

"She needs to cool her heels in a jail cell for awhile," his young sister said stoutly. "I've just been reading a history of England. Opposition spies were always being arrested in the old days."

Nico shook his head decisively. "No, no jail cell. The woman is pregnant, Carla."

"Are you kidding? What if that's phony, too? What if this whole thing is a ruse to play on your sympathies and wheedle her way into your good graces?"

"Dr. Zavier confirmed the pregnancy." Nico frowned. "And anyway how does that track with her desire to leave?"

Carla made a sound of deprecation. "That's just another ploy to get your sympathy."

"You think so?"

"Of course it is." Carla dangled her legs over the side of the bed. "I say she goes to the tower."

He swung around to stare at her. "Carla, we don't have a tower."

"Yes we do. The prison at Elmgore."

He shook his head, looking at her incredulously, wondering if the family hadn't protected her from real life for much too long. "You can't call that a tower. And this isn't medieval England."

She stuck her nose into the air. "It ought to be."

He stared at her again. A part of him wanted to laugh, but this situation was far from amusing. A very painful knot was developing deep inside him and he knew it was only going to get worse.

Marisa knew something was wrong. The sweet, friendly and funny Carla of midnight and morning had transformed into a tight-lipped young woman with a cool gaze now that it was almost noon. What had happened?

Was it because she was balking at the plan Nico and Chauncy had cooked up to put her out of the way and into a residence hotel on the other side of town? She didn't blame them, really. If she'd been in their shoes, she might have thought it was a good idea. After all, it got her out of their hair but under supervision, so no one could claim they'd abandoned her to the winds of fate. Good for them.

But bad for her. She had no intention of being managed. She wanted to get out in the mix and start looking for her suitcase—and her place in the world. Surely it would come back to her as she walked around the city. Wouldn't it?

So when Chauncy had told her what the plan was, she'd very politely told him she thought it stunk. And she wanted to talk to the prince about just how badly.

Chauncy had tried to dissuade her, telling her Nico was busy and was off to see the prime minister and other things to put her off. But she was having none of it. She was leaving all right, but not before she told Nico just what she thought of his plan.

It had been shortly after that awkward confrontation that everyone had begun treating her as though she'd developed a communicable disease. But really, Carla's attitude was the one that puzzled her the most. Carla had been such a darling and now she acted as though they were enemies. It was disappointing, and truth to tell, it rather hurt her feelings.

Never mind. She was leaving. But she had to see the prince before she went. So she was wandering through the house, trying to figure out where his room was, and suddenly she came face to face with him on the stairs.

"Marisa," he said, stopping on a step above her.

"Prince Nico," she replied, searching his face to see if he had turned on her, too.

"I was just coming to look for you."

"That doesn't surprise me," she said, meeting his gaze and holding it. "I want to know what's happened. What's wrong?"

His eyes darkened with what looked to her like suspicion. That stung. He was dressed for business and obviously ready to go out. Now he looked like her picture of a prince again, cool, detached, superior. There was no way a man like this would have kissed her.

"What are you talking about?" he asked softly.

"All of a sudden people are looking at me as though I'm the...the enemy." All her bravado evaporated. "Please tell me. I know there's something. What happened?"

He nodded slowly, his gaze distant. "Very perceptive of you, Marisa," he said coolly. "Come with me. I'll show you what happened."

He continued down the stairs and she followed, heart beating harder and harder as her anxiety grew. Now she was really getting scared. After all, she didn't know a thing about herself. What if they had found out something very bad? What if she'd committed a crime? Or really was allied with their enemies? How could she defend herself or protect herself when she just didn't know?

He led her into the library where he swept the miscellaneous books and papers off the table onto the floor and put down a folder instead. Opening the folder, he took out three pieces of faded paper and spread them out on the table.

"These are what happened," he said, standing back so she could see them.

She leaned over them. They seemed to be ancient documents covered with odd symbols. For just a moment, something about them struck a bell. She looked harder. Could she be remembering something? But no, nothing else flickered in her memory banks. She turned back and looked at Nico.

"What are these?"

He studied her for a moment before answering. "You don't recognize them?"

"No. Should I?"

He searched her eyes for a bit longer, then shrugged. "They were sewn into the lining of your skirt."

"They were…" She looked puzzled as she figured this out, then gasped. "What right do you have to snoop into my clothes?"

"Your clothes were in my house being laundered by my laundry maid," he said, his voice rough as gravel. "I reserve the right to check for evidence of spying."

"Spying!" Her heart fell.

"That's what we're talking about."

Spying. Oh my.

"Funny," she said nervously, trying to joke. "And here I thought you were going to accuse me of stealing the silverware."

"Marisa, this could be disastrous. Be serious."

She was. She'd just been vamping, hoping for a sudden burst of insight to help her along.

She had no idea what these pages of odd symbols represented, but there was no denying, it looked bad. She stared at them for another moment or two, trying to force memory. But nothing came. Disappointment almost choked her. This couldn't go on this way. Eventually, something had to give. Didn't it?

She shook her head, looking at him with all the veracity she could muster. Would he believe her? Why should he? He didn't really know anything about her. And right now, she didn't know much about herself. But she was pretty darn sure she wasn't a spy.

"I'm telling you quite honestly, I don't know what these are."

"Never seen them before?"

She shook her head, her eyes filled with sadness. "Not that I remember."

His eyes narrowed as he watched her closely. "Ah yes, there is always that pesky memory thing at work here. Pretty convenient, isn't it?"

She was tempted to let anger rise in her voice, but she held it back. She was in big trouble and she knew it. "Believe me, if I could get rid of this...memory block or whatever it is, I would."

He stared down into her eyes for what

seemed like forever, then turned away. "I've called in the intelligence services to decipher these symbols," he told her as he walked toward the window, hands shoved down into his pockets. "I'll talk to you again once they've made their report."

She assumed she was being dismissed. This was not going to be a good time to bring up her own questions, but she needed a few answers of her own. She made a quick exploration into his hard gaze and decided to chance it.

"About Chauncy and this plan you two cooked up," she began.

He swung around to face her straight-on. "Forget that," he said shortly. "Things have changed. You're staying here for the rest of the day. We'll decide what to do with you once we get this straightened out."

She knew better than to bring up her need to leave again. "What are the options that are on the table?" she asked instead.

"That depends on the report," he responded.

She wanted to ask more. If she was a spy, was she considered a traitor? What kind of penalty did spies get these days? Should she be looking for ways to escape this place? That was pretty obvious. Too bad it didn't seem very possible.

She needed a champion in her corner,

someone to lean on, someone on her side. The trouble was, the man who fit the bill was the very man accusing her.

By late afternoon Marisa was a nervous wreck. She'd spent hours in her room, waiting to be called down to hear the verdict. She couldn't read, she couldn't eat, she couldn't even think very straight. Was she a spy or wasn't she? And if she was, was she at all good at it? It hardly seemed likely.

The one positive sign was that she couldn't believe it. Sleuthing didn't seem to be a talent that came naturally to her. She just didn't seem to be the espionage type. As she tried to analyze it, she couldn't imagine that someone as bumbling and careless as herself—and as incompetent at hiding in bushes—could be a spy. Of course, maybe she was the sort of spy who sneaked around photocopying documents when no one was home instead of hiding out and overhearing conversations.

She sighed. No. Probably not.

A maid had brought her a nice lunch she hadn't touched, but other than that, she'd seen no one. There were books and magazines to read, and a television in the corner, but she couldn't keep her mind on anything but this

accusation. It was so strange to be in agony
and not know for sure what she was agonizing about. It was like shadow-boxing with a
rival you couldn't really see. How could you
possibly get anywhere? Or even know if you
were making any progress?

Finally a rap came on her door.

"Marisa? I'm coming in."

Her heart leaped. It was Nico. She jumped
up off the bed and looked around wildly, as
though she needed to sweep something under
the rug or hide evidence of wrongdoing. But
there was nothing and no one. She'd changed
into the stretchy running suit again, so she
didn't even need to cover her knees. Feeling
almost sullen, she sat back down on the bed
and waited as he entered.

"Well?" she said, looking at him expectantly. "Am I a criminal or not?"

He stood looking at her for a long moment,
hands loosely at his hips. His tie and suit coat
were both gone and his crisp white shirt was
open at the neck. Inanely, she wondered
where he'd come by such a nice tan, then remembered that he seemed to make a habit of
walking around the grounds in shorts and a
tank top. That would do it.

"Our decoding crew has been working on

it all afternoon and can't make heads nor tails of the symbols," he told her. "You wouldn't want to give them a clue, would you?"

She flashed a dark-eyed glare his way. "I told you, I don't know a thing about them."

"Yes, but they were sequestered in the lining of your skirt. I'm afraid that means we're going to assign you custody of the entire issue until we get evidence otherwise."

She stared at him for a moment, then closed her eyes. "Of course," she said, sadness seeping into her voice. "In the meantime, I'm under house arrest for the duration. Isn't that the story?"

"Basically, yes."

She looked at him, feeling drained. She was tired of this, tired of being suspected, tired of not knowing enough about just what was involved to be able to fight it.

"Don't you see what a corner that puts me in? How can I make any progress in finding out who I am if I'm stuck here?" She sighed, fighting back tears. "I'm sure this isn't legal. The law must be on my side." She shook her head, searching for an idea. "Maybe I should talk to the police."

He grimaced. "Marisa, don't you understand? There are very few laws that are operative right now. Everything is in flux. Parliament is in turmoil trying to establish a new set of rules that will deal fairly and completely with all our people. But nothing has been established yet. In fact, right now, you have no recourse."

"I have no recourse at all?" Her eyes were huge with tragedy. "You can do whatever you want with me?"

If only it were that easy.

He almost grinned. It was hardly fair but he had to admit, the more upset she got, the more attractive he was finding her. Here he was staring down a woman who might be here as a viper in the bosom of his family, and all he could think about was how much he would like to kiss those cherry-pink lips again.

"As of right now, yes. There may be repercussions later, but I can risk that."

"Oh!" She closed her eyes and hugged herself, holding in the agony.

He felt a flash of sympathy for her and frowned hard to hide it before moving a step closer. "Marisa, do you understand why we're doing this?"

She turned her face away. "I understand that you're keeping me here against my will," she said stubbornly.

He sighed. She looked small and vulnerable sitting on her bed with her legs crossed in front of her. "I know you're unhappy. I know you feel you're being mistreated."

Moving closer, he dropped down to sit on the bed beside her. This was touchy. He was working hard at holding back his natural inclination—when in doubt, shout and force issues. That wouldn't work. Actually, it seldom did. But it was frustrating to know that, locked inside somewhere, she had the answers if only she knew how to find them. He was going to have to work hard to keep from doing anything that would just close her off. After all, he needed those answers.

And then it came to him—more than that, he didn't want her hurt. Something touched him as he looked at her. He thought it was probably because of Andrea that he felt so protective of Marisa.

Probably. Maybe.

"I've been wracking my brain trying to think of a way to explain this to you, Marisa. If you'll listen for a few minutes, I'll do my best to clarify it."

She met his gaze for only a second or two, nodded her compliance, and turned her gaze away again. Looking at her, he wasn't sure this was going to do any good, but he knew he had to try.

"Marisa," he began. "I don't know where you were during the war, or what side you were on. That's irrelevant now. But I want to go over a little history with you, just to clear things up."

He paused and she nodded again without looking at him.

"Since your memory of basic things that don't explicitly apply to you seems to be intact, you might remember that the rule of the House of Montenevada goes back over six hundred years. The only interruption has been over the last fifty years when the Acredonnas with their National Party had control. We spent the last five years fighting to get our patrimony back. Not because we felt some God-given right to rule, but because the Nationals were ruining the country and we have a responsibility to our people to protect them and take care of our heartland and its resources. And so the struggle began.

"Now that we've prevailed, we must fight hard to make this a decent country again. There are many forces arrayed against us. There's no guarantee that this is going to succeed. The Nationals are gathering strength in their enclaves. They are going to try to wrest power back away from us. We know that fight is coming. It's in this context that we have to be totally over the top in our security methods. *Have* to be. There is no alternative. If we let one thing go, that one little thing is bound to be the chink in our armor, the fatal flaw that can bring down the whole structure of our regime. We have to be more than careful. In fact, we sometimes have to be ridiculous."

She hadn't said anything for a long time and that seemed unusual. She was sitting with her head down, her mass of curly, lovely hair completely hiding her face. Reaching out, he broke the rule he'd set for himself that he wasn't going to touch her, and he pushed her hair back so he could see her eyes. They were brimming with tears.

"Marisa…"

She looked up at him as the tears began to make trails down her beautiful cheeks and her lower lip trembled with misery. "Oh Nico…"

His heart lurched.

"I just don't know," she admitted to him, sniffing helplessly, her heartbreak clear in her voice. "I can't even swear that I'm not one of them, because I just don't know."

He believed her. Everything in him believed her. If she was lying, if she was trying to pull one over on him, she was doing a wonderful job, because he was ready to do anything he could to help her right now. It was beyond his control. Before he knew what he was doing, he had her in his arms. And then there was no way to avoid kissing away her tears, murmuring sweet comfort and holding her close. She responded as though she was just as much a victim of this wave of emotion as he was.

He'd meant to calm her, to stop the tears and make her understand that he was on her side, that he wasn't going to jump to any conclusions, that he would do everything he could to make sure she got every benefit of the doubt.

But what started as simple comfort quickly became much more. He kissed her lips and when they opened, he just naturally entered her mouth and then his hands slid down her body and pulled her closer. She was softer than she looked, but with an underlying strength that warned him not to take her lightly. She was alive, vibrant, a force to be reckoned with. Her body felt so good, her skin so smooth, her kiss so hot. He felt an excitement he hadn't known for a long, long time.

She arched into his embrace, turning to take him against her and hold him tight. She was hungry for what he offered and she couldn't pretend otherwise. His own body tightened like a spring, coiled and ready, aching to plunge. She was soft and warm and smooth and he wanted every part of her to be his. He heard a deep sound and realized it was his own groan of a need to take her as his own.

Every part of him longed for her, agonizing to join her body with his. It felt like something that had to be, and yet he knew it was so wrong. Breathing raggedly, he pulled away from her, angry at himself, angry at fate, throbbing with the need to have her and wishing he could change that. He forced himself to breathe evenly, catching his breath, then looked at her, expecting frowns and recriminations.

Instead, she was smiling. "Oh!" she cried, as though something was startling her. Her hands went to her belly and she began to laugh.

"I feel it!" she said, eyes shining. "Oh Nico, I feel the baby."

Just like that, she'd forgotten what they'd just been doing. But he didn't blame her. He looked at where her hands were planted and suddenly he was smiling, too.

"Is this the first time?" he asked her.

"Yes. At least, this is the first time I'm sure it's the baby. Oh, I feel as though I've been invaded by butterflies!" She laughed up at him, impulsively inviting him to share her joy. "Oh here, you try. Can you feel it?"

He couldn't feel a thing, but it didn't matter. As his palm cupped her belly, he felt as intimate as he'd ever felt with a woman. He and Andrea hadn't gotten to this stage. It was sad that Andrea had never felt their baby move. And yet, he was rather glad Marisa was traveling on to a level beyond what he'd experienced with the woman he loved. That seemed to make it more possible to appreciate her happiness without feeling a corresponding sense of pain for Andrea.

At least there was no doubt she was pregnant. And there was no doubt he was going to be involved with this woman in ways that were impossible to maintain. If he wanted to avoid that, he was going to have to do something quickly to stem this rapidly growing connection between them. He had to put a stop to it.

And he would. Very soon.

In the meantime, he had work to do. It was a bit awkward pretending he hadn't just been kissing the hell out of her, but he managed to do it, telling her how things were going to be and preparing her for what was coming next.

"Marisa, I've had men scouring the city for your suitcase all day. So far, no luck. They did find this, however." Going to the door, he reached outside and he pulled in a large suede purse he'd left there and put it down in front of where she sat on the bed. "Do you recognize this?"

She frowned, looking inside, checking the pockets, unzipping the zippers, hoping to find something, anything, that would strike a chord. It was completely empty. Picking it up, she tried carrying it the way she assumed she usually carried her purse. She just wasn't sure.

"You know, it feels right." She looked up at him like a child, eager to please. "I like it. It might be mine." Then the clouds of anguish came back into her eyes. "Why can't I remember?"

Watching her, he didn't have a doubt in the world that she was telling the truth, as far as she was able to.

"I've got a memory expert flying in from Berlin tomorrow," he told her.

She looked stunned. "Just to see me?"

He smiled at her surprise. "Of course. Who else has amnesia around here?"

"Gee, I didn't realize I was so special."

She said it with a trace of bitterness, but there was a smile on her pretty face. He wanted to kiss her again, wanted to touch her, to make love to her for hours. But most of all he wanted to stay with her, and that meant he had to go.

He'd kissed her twice now. That was twice too many times and it couldn't happen again. He was going to have to find a way to keep his distance. That was the only way any of this could work.

CHAPTER SEVEN

"WE'RE going to keep her right here." Meeting with Carla in the library after talking to Marisa, Prince Nico was firm.

Carla reacted in surprise. "What? Here in the palace?"

"In the palace." He gazed levelly at his sister. "I will not have her in a prison."

"No prison?" Carla frowned. "But wait, Chauncy said his sister could…"

The prince held up his hand to stop her. "I'm telling you right now, Carla, that I don't think she's guilty. I've got Doctor Stein coming in from Berlin to examine her. Meanwhile, Intelligence says it may take weeks to break the code on those papers. I want her here for the duration. And that's the end of it."

Carla drew in a sharp breath. "Oh Nico. You haven't fallen for her, have you?"

His head reared back before he could stop himself. "No, of course not." Why was it that he didn't sound convincing, even to his own ears?

Obviously, Carla wasn't sold. "Are you crazy? What if she's married?"

He winced. Everything in him wanted to reject that possibility. If she was married and he was kissing her the way he'd been kissing her… No, that went against all his principles. It couldn't be. "I thought you agreed she wasn't married."

She shrugged and looked worried. "I thought the signs were good. But I don't know. She is pregnant, after all, so we know someone has been in her life. If it turns out she's married and you've let yourself fall in love with her…"

"I'm not in love with her," he said, exasperated. And he wasn't. Fascinated, yes. A bit smitten even. But not in love. He knew love. This wasn't it.

Carla was skeptical, but she held it back and pretended to believe him. "Good. Because, like they say, that crazy little thing called love can make you crazy. Or at the very least, break your heart."

He knew that. No one had to tell him about

heartbreak, especially not his naive little sister. But he held his tongue. He didn't want to give her any more ammunition anyway.

Carla was shaking her head and staring at him as though she couldn't understand what had come over him. "Okay, so she won't go to prison, at least not yet. But I don't understand why she has to stay here. You don't really know anything about her. She's basically nothing but a stranger. Why do we have to keep her here?"

He turned from her. That was a question that was very hard to answer. He was tempted to say, "Because I want to," and leave it at that. But sometimes the truth just wasn't good enough, especially when Carla was prattling on and on about love. This wasn't really that. But for some reason, he couldn't stand to think of her away from his protection. He could protest that it was just the baby she was carrying until he was blue in the face, but he knew very well there was more to it than that. Still, it was no one's business. He was acting monarch while Dane was out of country. And he could do what he wanted to, damn it all!

"Tell me one thing." Carla frowned at him like an interrogator. "Is she really pregnant?"

"Carla, we've been over this before. Dr. Zavier is the final word on that."

She nodded, looking thoughtful. "I know, but if she's a spy, you have to question everything, don't you?"

He didn't answer and she went on.

"Well, how is this going to work?" Her eyes glittered with the possibilities. "Are you going to keep her locked in her room? Maybe put a guard on her?"

He half smiled at his sister's constant search for drama. "No, Carla. I'm going to put her in your custody."

"What?"

"Yes." He had to grin at her reaction. Shock was written across her face. But he was warming to the idea as he thought more about it. "She'll stay with us like a guest, only you'll be in charge of her safekeeping. And she will be your companion."

Carla's mouth was open but no words came out. It seemed she was half appalled, half intrigued with the idea. "But…"

"Pretend you're both in the tower and you have the key."

"Oh." That captured her imagination right away. She thought for a moment, then beamed. "That might work."

Yes. It would work. For everyone but him. Because he was going to keep his distance, no matter how much he was tempted to get closer to Marisa. He was going to stay away. Maybe he would even find a reason to take a few business trips.

This was all nonsense anyway. He had more important things to think about. They had a country to build here. Love was for those who didn't have anything better to do. He was busy.

Marisa was trying to talk herself into going downstairs. She had no idea how she would be received, but it was time for the evening meal. She was just shoring up her determination to brave the possible enmity of the others when Carla appeared in her doorway.

"Hi," she said, her eyes big and soulful. "May I come in?"

"Of course." Marisa's smile was not as friendly as it might have been that morning, but if Carla was ready to make amends, she was ready to let bygones be bygones herself. She tensed, waiting to see how it was going to be.

Carla came all the way in, looked at Marisa and emitted a huge sigh that sent her shoulders drooping. "Nico sent me up here to ask you to join us for dinner."

Marisa's heart skipped a beat. He didn't have to send Carla. He could have sent a maid or Chauncy. Sending his sister was a good sign, wasn't it?

"Thank you," she said, and meant it.

Carla licked her lips and squared her shoulders. "And I want to apologize for being mean to you," she said, looking very contrite. "And I want to suggest we declare a truce until we learn what the truth is. Okay?" She looked hopeful.

"That would be great," Marisa said, amused at Carla's poses.

"Okay, good." Suddenly the younger girl looked happy again. "But I have to warn you," she added. "If it turns out you're really a spy, I'm going to hate you."

Marisa grinned. "If it turns out I'm really a spy, I'm going to hate myself," she told her.

Carla laughed and stepped forward impulsively to hug Marisa. By the time they were on the stairs, they were friends again and chattering like friends. Entering the huge, high-ceilinged dining room, Marisa looked around at the wonderful paintings that covered the walls—mostly seventeenth-century semi-nudes in the style of Rubens— and that might actually be the real thing for all she knew. The table was huge and set with sterling silver and crystal goblets that sparkled in the light from the heavy chandelier, but only one end was populated with about a dozen diners. She looked about quickly for the prince, but didn't see him.

A few older relatives were there, and the couple she'd seen that morning at breakfast. She was introduced to a pair of young cousins from Belgrade who were staying at the palace while they attended classes at the newly reformed university. But as they took their seats, an elegantly attired middle-aged woman who was introduced to her as Lady Julia announced that Nico had been called away on business and wouldn't be joining them after all.

The sense of disappointment almost choked her. That set her back on her heels a bit, and made her color warmly. If she really cared this much, it was obviously time to back off. Sure he'd kissed her, but he was a prince and princes played around. It even said so in nursery rhymes. He was a prince and she was, for all she knew, a spy. There was no point in dreaming for things that were just downright impossible.

Gritting her teeth, she plastered on a smile

and made small talk with the others at table. There was no way she was going to let anyone know that she wished the prince was there. No way at all.

Dr. Stein arrived the next morning. He spent an hour with her. Dr. Zavier had covered her physical vitals, so Dr. Stein concentrated on her emotional health, asking her questions that seemed far removed from the situation at hand. In the end, he told her to rest and to try to avoid stress. He thought she would recover her memory slowly over the next few weeks and promised to keep in touch to monitor her recovery. Other than that, he wasn't especially helpful, and she felt as if she had just wasted the time she'd spent with him.

She saw Nico a bit later in the morning, but only from a distance, and then he was gone again, heading for meetings with various members of the government. That was just as well, though it was funny how often she thought of things she wanted to talk to him about. For a man she hadn't even known two days before, he was certainly looming large in her consciousness. But that was probably because she didn't have much memory of anything that had happened before they met.

Her mind had a big empty playground to fool around in and only Prince Nico as a toy.

She helped Carla cut flowers from the gardens for the huge bouquets that decorated all the public rooms of the house. She spent time in the little forest. She discovered a wonderful selection of historical volumes in the library, along with an exquisite collection of rare ancient cookbooks, which really drew her eye. By that afternoon she'd gotten to know most of the other residents of the palace a little better, including the people who had been at dinner the night before and other various relatives and old friends of the family.

There was Lady Julia of course, who acted as hostess for the royal family when they had banquets or balls, and as companion to Carla when she needed one. There was an uncle named Sergei, the Duke of Norgate, who seemed to be Nico and Carla's mother's brother. He was always wandering the halls, trying to get someone to come play chess with him. There were nieces and nephews and there was much talk about the fascinating Cousin Nadia whose clothes Marisa was wearing.

"Nadia lives close to the edge," Carla told her as they were sitting down for lunch. "Nico says she's always just one step away from a full-color spread in the tabloids." She smiled, her eyes glowing. "She's wonderful."

Nico entered the dining room in time to overhear what she'd said. His gaze met Marisa's and he nodded quickly, but responded to his sister's comment as he took his seat at the table.

"Our 'wonderful' cousin Nadia is a disaster waiting to happen. Like a snowball rolling downhill, she's gathering steam and scandal, which will eventually explode over all of us."

There was much nodding and a murmuring of agreement from the others at the table.

"She'll most likely ruin our reputation with the people," Uncle Sergei intoned dolefully. "It's bound to happen."

Marisa frowned. "Do you really think that whatever a madcap cousin of the family does is going to rebound on all of you?" she asked curiously.

"Oh yes," Lady Julia replied. "We've seen it happen before. The tabloids can take a one-day story and turn it into a month-long campaign against royalty in general."

It still seemed far-fetched to Marisa. "But I thought that was what royalty was for," she joked. "To get into scrapes that provide endless entertainment to the populace."

Talk about a lead balloon. The ones who didn't glare at her resentfully stared down at their plates and avoided her gaze. The silence was deafening. Her joke didn't seem to be funny to the royalty involved and she quickly wished she'd kept her sense of humor to herself. She glanced at Nico, biting her lip, and found that his blue eyes were sparkling with amusement at her faux pas.

"Well, there you go," he said at last, giving her a sly sideways smile. "In Rome they had circuses. In Carnethia we have the adventures of Nadia to keep us from being bored with it all. And incidentally, to keep us buying papers."

She flushed, appreciating him for making the effort to try to cover for her. The talk went on to other things, but she didn't join in again. She sat staring down at her plate and pushing her food around with her fork, but all the time, she was conscious of the prince sitting two places up from where she sat and of not much else. Her gaze met his one more time as he excused himself and left for an afternoon at the parliament.

That marvelous eyebrow rose. He made a quick gesture. Was it her imagination, or was there a special message in his eyes as he gave her one long, last look? A message that said, Marisa, I'd love to take you out into our little forest and ravish you beside the stream but I've sworn to stay away from you. You make it difficult when you sit there looking so beautiful. But I've got to be strong. Either that, or take another cold shower.

But as he made his way toward the exit, Carla leaned over to whisper to her. "I think Nico was trying to tell you you've got spinach in your teeth," she murmured confidentially.

Marisa laughed out loud. Everyone turned to look at her and her face flushed again as she gave herself a quick lecture on keeping a level head about her. She stared at the wall until he'd left the area and she could risk looking around the room again. Oh brother. She was going to have to find something to do with her time so she could hold back these crazy fantasies. If he'd had any idea what she was thinking!

She spent the evening on the computer, researching amnesia and coming up empty as far as solutions went. She heard the prince return in late afternoon and she stayed where she was, waiting until he'd gone to his suite before she ventured out and made her way to her own room. That was going to be her pattern from now on. She was going to avoid seeing him alone. That seemed to be her only answer to the problem.

But at least she was admitting to herself that a real problem existed. She had a crush on the prince.

She couldn't help it! She'd tried to keep from letting this happen. And she was sure it was only temporary. Once she had her memory back, she would forget all about the prince and his incredibly addictive kisses. Absolutely. No doubt about it. After all, she was armed with her little song about being the prince's plaything and she was never, ever going to let that happen to her.

Of course, it would all be a lot easier if she didn't keep thinking about those kisses and how wonderful it had felt to be in his arms. She'd been swept away both times, but she'd also noticed, both times, that he'd pulled away from her as soon as he could and his regret that he'd let himself embrace her that way was unmistakable. In other words, he was attracted to her completely against his will.

Well, she was going to make sure he didn't do anything else with her to regret. She had her own life to lead—just as soon as she found it again. And she knew she wasn't sticking around. So there was no point to getting involved with the prince. No point at all.

The next few days went by in a very similar manner. By the end of almost a week of imprisonment in the palace, she had to admit it was rather a pleasant incarceration, as that sort of thing went. Still, she was a captive, unable to do what she wanted to do when she wanted to do it or to move on with her life.

Move on to where? That was the question. There had to be a way to break this darn deadlock in her head. Where, oh where was her memory? So close and yet so far. It was very frustrating.

And yet, in some ways it was becoming irrelevant. The pattern of her days was taking on a pleasant rhythm, lulling her into a sense of normalcy she didn't deserve to feel.

And then there was the prince. There was no denying that there was a spark of something dangerous between the two of them. But so far, they'd gotten pretty good at ignoring it and letting it simmer under the surface. Still, every time her gaze met his and she felt that jolt of excitement, she got a yearning inside that was hard to ignore.

Everyone at the palace was preparing for

the coronation. Nico's older brother Dane would become the new King of Carnethia. That was one reason Nico was working such long hours, and another reason security was being emphasized more and more. There were factions who would just as soon make sure that the coronation never happened.

She'd told the prince about the man she'd seen skulking behind the wall across the street from the palace. He'd sent out guards to scour the neighborhood but they hadn't found anything. Now they were going through the houses that faced the palace one by one, just in case. She felt a little guilty that she'd stirred up such a commotion, but Nico had convinced her that it had to be done. The royal family was in a defensive position, whether it wanted to be or not.

"And we still don't know what the papers sewn into my skirt are all about," she noted that afternoon after he'd told her the latest about the search. "And we still haven't found my suitcase."

He'd found her in the library, poring over the antique book section. They seemed to run into each other there more and more often lately. She was fascinated by the old cookbooks she'd found there and he was doing research into previous government actions, attempting to get a handle on what his own government was trying to accomplish today and how to avoid some of the harmful consequences of the past. They seemed to be able to meet more naturally in this room with its wonderful deep-cherry paneling and tall beveled windows, than anywhere else in the house.

"The analysts are at a dead end in identifying the symbols. They think the script is probably from an old language that hasn't been well documented yet." He turned and smiled at her as he slid a huge volume back into its place on the shelf. "Chauncy has a theory that you're an archeology student carrying documents to a museum in London. Maybe something special your professor uncovered in an ancient tomb."

She brightened. "Well, that's better than his last theory, that I was a spy." She smiled, thinking of it. How much fun it would be to be an archeology student, digging around in abandoned civilizations and making wonderful discoveries. Could she…? She gave it a moment, but nothing touched a chord or brought up a compatible memory.

So she was a bit deflated when she

finally asked, "But how does that explain the amnesia?"

His eyes darkened as he looked down at her. "How do *you* explain it?"

She was tempted to say she didn't. But she really owed him some sort of attempt, so she made one.

"I think when I got knocked down on the bridge, the bump I took on my head knocked me silly." She touched where it had wounded her and was glad to feel that it had pretty much healed. "I'm assuming that it did something to jolt my memory center or something, and it just hasn't cleared up yet. But it will." At this point, she wasn't sure if she was still sounding confident or if she was beginning to show a little desperation.

"You don't think there might be a psychological component? Perhaps some reason, something you were running from, that made your mind happy to blot out reality for a time?"

She hesitated. She'd suspected something along those lines herself, but it was a scary thing to contemplate. That was why her mind shied away from it. How did you protect yourself if you didn't know what was coming at you?

Instead of responding, she looked up at

him, her helplessness in her eyes, and he moved toward her. His body language was echoing the message his eyes were conveying. He wanted to take her into his arms and hold her close and kiss her until the vulnerability evaporated and she didn't have that troubled look anymore. She lifted her face in his direction, stripped of all defense against him. She ached for him and she let it show.

He almost kissed her. He was so close, she could feel his breath on her cheek, smell his masculine scent, feel the heat of his body. His lips were inches from hers. But at the very last second, he pulled away. Looking back at her, he swore softly, turned and walked from the room.

She closed her eyes and swayed and wished she didn't care.

Though Marisa did love working in the library, the funny thing was, she seemed to have an even stronger preference for working in the kitchen and had a real affinity for cooking. Whenever she had nothing else to occupy her time, she found herself gravitating in that direction. She definitely knew how to cook, and though she hardly ever seemed to need instructions, she was having a great time incorporating recipes from the antique cookbooks she'd found in the library. She cooked up some great meals. Everyone treated her like the wonder of the year, oohing and aahing over her culinary creations, especially when it came to fancy desserts.

"You should see her in the kitchen," Carla told Nico at dinner the night she concocted a chocolate truffle marquise to die for. "She's got the whole staff whipped into shape."

"Well, they are kind of an amateur lot," Nico said, almost apologetically. "We were going to hire a French chef but we haven't gotten around to it yet."

"I think we should hire Marisa," Carla said, waving a chocolate-stained spoon in the air. "She's better than any chef we've ever had."

By this time Nico had taken a forkful of the marquise cake and his eyes glazed over. "Wow," he said. He looked at Marisa as though he were seeing her for the first time. "Wow," he said again, and took another bite.

"See? I told you." Carla gurgled happily. "She's a chocolate genius."

"A chocolate genius." Something in that phrase seemed to zap inside Marisa's head, like a rubber band being snapped. For just a moment, she felt a bit faint.

"What is it?" The prince was up and out of his chair immediately, coming to her aid. "What is it, Marisa? What's wrong?"

She shook her head and tried to smile. "N-n-nothing. Really, I'm okay. I just felt a little light-headed for a moment. I'm fine, really."

He left her side and went back to his chair, but she could feel him watching her for the rest of the meal. His concern touched her, but at the same time, terrified her a little. How could it be that the two of them seemed to be entangled in some sort of emotional vortex when neither of them wanted to be at all?

That night she had trouble sleeping. No matter which way she tossed and turned, she couldn't get comfortable.

"This is all your fault, I'll bet," she whispered to her baby. "But you're definitely going to be worth it."

Dr. Zavier had done an ultrasound and told her it looked as if her baby was most likely a little girl. Lying there in the dark, she started going over names for her child. It was better than counting sheep.

But not good enough. She just couldn't sleep. Maybe it was because she was so hungry. Finally, in desperation, she rolled out of bed, put on a fluffy robe, and headed downstairs to the kitchen. She had only been rifling through cabinets for a few minutes when Prince Nico appeared in the doorway.

"What are you doing?" he asked.

"Oh!" She jumped. "I'm sorry. I didn't mean to disturb you." She frowned. "But what are you doing still up?"

He rubbed his neck and looked tired. "I'm still working on some things I brought home from Parliament," he said. "I didn't realize it was so late."

"You should go to bed," she said sternly, pulling her robe up tightly against her neck and glad it was thick and fluffy.

He blinked at her vehemence and for just a moment, she thought he might actually relax into a smile. "How about you?" he responded, glancing at her belly area.

"I couldn't sleep. I just need…" She bit her lip and looked at the huge stainless-steel refrigerator.

"You're hungry?" he said, incredulous. "You ate like a truck driver at dinner."

She was instantly indignant. "I did not! And besides, remember, I'm eating for two."

This time there was no doubt about it, his blue eyes had an authentic twinkle to them.

"Of course." He tilted his head as though allowing her this point. "My mistake."

Nodding, she went back to going through the cupboards. "I just don't understand why there isn't any marzipan in this house," she complained.

"Marzipan?" He came closer and looked over her shoulder into the cabinet.

"Yes. How can you run a kitchen without marzipan? I've been searching all the shelves."

"Can you use a tube of almond paste instead?" he asked, reaching around her to point it out.

"Oh." She moved a little to the side. He was awfully close. "Well, it's not perfect, but I guess it will do." She took down the tube and put it on the counter. "Thanks," she said, giving him a fleeting sideways smile that quickly turned serious again. "Now, where do you suppose I could find a tin of smoked salmon?"

He choked. "Wait a minute," he said. "Marzipan and smoked salmon?"

She wrinkled her nose. "It doesn't sound right, does it? But I don't know, it just feels like something I've got to have."

"Hold everything," Nico said wisely. "You know what this is, don't you?"

She looked at him blankly. "No. What?"

He aimed a significant look at her belly. "It's the baby talking."

She grimaced. "My baby wants marzipan and salmon?"

He shrugged. "Could be. Have you ever wanted that combination before?"

Slowly, she shook her head, her gaze now caught by his in a way that sent tingles down her spine.

"I wouldn't think so," he said wryly, moving closer. "In fact, I'll bet it's pretty much a first for this kitchen."

"You think so?" she echoed, unable to pull her gaze from his.

"I do."

He was standing so close and his eyes held her mesmerized. She swallowed hard, knowing she should break the connection, but not quite able to do it.

"Let's see," he said softly, and before she knew what he was doing, he'd reached in under her robe and placed his hand on her stomach.

"Oh!" she said, but she didn't pull away. "What are you doing?"

"Shh," he said sternly. "I'm listening."

He was joking. Wasn't he? Had to be. But she stood very still, breathless, while he got a faraway look in his eyes and pretended to be channeling her baby's thoughts.

"Hmmm," he said, mouth quirking at the corners. "Smoked salmon and marzipan are just the appetizers. She wants cotton candy, bagel dogs and a pint of peppermint ice cream. Oh, and peanut butter."

Marisa's eyes grew round. "Peanut butter! Oh, yes!"

An actual grin softened his face. His hand left her belly but only to move to her chin, where he tilted her face up toward his. She looked up dreamily, held in his spell and happy to be there. Her heart was pounding and her head was light. He was going to kiss her, wasn't he? She could almost taste it and she yearned toward him as his head began to lower.

"Once this baby is born," he was murmuring, "we'll have to put in a special kitchen if these crazy food cravings continue."

It took a half second for his meaning to register. His lips had almost touched hers. But when she realized what he was saying, she drew in a sharp breath and jerked back away from him. Her hands rose to hold him off and she stared into eyes that no longer held her in their spell.

"What makes you assume I'll still be here when I give birth to my baby?" she demanded.

He drew back as well and all humor faded. His eyes were dark and unreadable. "I'm not assuming anything," he said stiffly.

"Yes, you are. You're acting as if you're sure I'm still going to be here." She moved sideways against the counter to get away from his compelling presence. "Is anything actually being done to find out who I am?"

"Marisa…"

"Nothing's happening, is it?"

"Of course things are happening. These investigations take time."

Right. She glared at him. Suddenly she was thunderstruck by the idiocy of her recent compliance with it all. She was pretending to be a guest here. How had she let herself float into this situation? She was no guest. It was high time she paid more attention to what was going on.

"Don't you have to come up with some sort of charges to keep a person against their will? Tell me, Your Highness. Am I a prisoner here?"

His mouth twisted. "Marisa, I thought we had gone over this the other day. Didn't you understand the seriousness of the problem?"

She shook her head. It was overwhelming to

be surrounded by so many pitfalls and not know which way to turn. The biggest black hole that gaped in front of her was the danger of falling in love with this man. It would be so easy—and it would mean complete disaster. How to ruin your life in one simple step.

Suddenly, she felt like crying. She wanted to go home. If only she knew how.

"I don't know why I'm letting you do this," she whispered, shaking her head and holding back tears.

His frown was merciless. "You're letting me do this because you don't have any choice. Believe me, this is the best of all your options."

She knew he was right. He could have let her go to jail as a suspected spy. Instead, he'd ensconced her in this velvet prison. But that was the catch. Going through normal channels, she would have known what she had to do to get out again. Here, she wasn't so sure. How was she ever going to win her own release?

Blinded by tears, she threw him one last angry look and turned to go back to her room, forgetting all about the food her baby had ordered up. It was just as well. She wasn't hungry any more.

CHAPTER EIGHT

PRINCE Nico hit the wall and executed a perfect flip turn against the tile, then stroked strongly back across the pool, swimming as hard as he could. He'd already spent an hour in the gym, then another half hour running on the track. Now he was hoping a good hard swim would finally rid him of this aching restlessness that was driving him crazy.

He had a country to run. How the hell had he let himself get sidetracked by a pretty blonde who couldn't even remember her own name? If he were more like his brother Dane, who steamrolled through the female population like a force of nature, he would bed her and move on. If he were more like his younger brother Mychale, he would enjoy a game of sweet seduction and everyone would know it was not to be taken seriously. But he was Nico, the careful one. He'd only had one love in his life. He didn't expect ever to have another. And yet, there was something about the woman that wouldn't let him go.

It was impossible. Even if he were ready to fall in love again, she was completely wrong for the role. She was lovely and talented and a delight to be around. But who was she? Where was she from? Who were her people? And most important, perhaps—what had she done during the war?

He could hear Dane laughing at these concerns, laughing at him and his earnest ways.

"Hell, Nico. You don't have to marry the woman. Just take her to bed. That'll either whet your appetite or kill this obsession. Either way, you'll be free of this useless agony."

"Easy for you to say," he muttered, as though Dane were really there with him.

Groaning, he vaulted out of the pool and stood, dripping water in every direction. Shaking his head to get rid of some of it, feeling like a wet and shaggy dog, he opened his eyes to find himself face to face with the woman he'd been agonizing over.

"Marisa," he said, surprised.

"Oh." She was beet-red. Obviously she was seeing more of him than she'd ever expected to. She had that deer-in-the-head-lights look that meant she was about to bolt for the door. "I...I was just..."

"Wait." Reaching out quickly, he grabbed her hand. "Don't go. We need to talk."

"Talk?" She sounded strangled and there was a reason for that. Standing here, staring at his beautiful wet body, she felt as though the pounding of her heart had taken over completely. She was nothing but one big, quivering hunk of womanly sensuality. Talking was not what came readily to mind in this situation. She often took this shortcut through the pool area to get to the potting shed, but she'd never encountered anyone using it before.

"Wait." Not letting go of her hand, he reached for a towel and threw it around his shoulders. "Is that better?"

"Better than what?" she murmured, still in a sensual daze. She looked up into his face. Drops of water shimmered on his eyelashes like diamonds. "Oh, Nico, I think I'd better go."

"No, I have something I need to say to you."

"Make it fast. Please?"

He pulled her hand in and pressed it against his heart. "I just want you to understand that we are doing the best we can at finding out your background. So many records were destroyed in the war. But as soon as we can clear you, we will."

That was nice. At least he seemed to take it for granted that the odds were she would be cleared. She nodded. "I know," she said softly, her gaze flickering toward where her hand rested against his gorgeous chest. She took a deep, shuddering breath. "Can I go now?"

"No." He shook his head, then steeled himself to go on. "Marisa, I guess you know I'm very strongly attracted to you. And I'm sure you understand how stupid and self-destructive that attraction is."

Her eyes widened as she looked up at him. "Well, thanks a lot."

"No, I don't mean…" He grimaced. "Oh, hell. Marisa, you know what I'm saying here. I'm only human. But I've got important things to do and I can't get caught up in an affair."

Her eyes flashed. "Well, who asked you to?"

"Marisa…"

He was in agony. His words just weren't coming out right. She could read it all in his face and she understood perfectly well. Despite everything, she smiled.

"Let me go. And stop talking. As they say,

when you find yourself in a hole, the best thing to do is to stop digging."

"But Marisa…"

"Hush."

Reaching up, she threw both arms around his neck and kissed his mouth, hard. His arms came around her and he kissed her back, even harder. His body was deliciously strong and provocative and she melted against him. Staying close, he seemed to breathe in the sense of her for just a moment, then drew back, a cloud shadowing his eyes as he took in her pretty face. He touched her cheek and smiled sadly.

"Don't worry," she said, her eyes shining. "I know there's no future for us. I don't expect it."

Slipping out of his arms, she left him, savoring the tingle his kiss had left on her lips. It was a shame, really, that he was a prince, because just on a man-woman level, she had to admit, she liked what he had to offer.

The fascinating Cousin Nadia finally came to visit the palace the next night after dinner. Marisa and Carla were listening to a new CD Carla had bought during the day when Nadia breezed in with the family's younger brother Mychale in tow. They drove up in a Lamborghini and sauntered in like film stars, sending the entire household into delighted hysterics.

"We can only stay a minute," the beautiful young woman told them regretfully. Tall and thin as a runway model, she had her jet-black hair pulled back in a tight, contemporary style that accentuated her modish pose. "We're headed for the regatta at Lake Lucinder."

Mychale didn't say anything at all. He merely seemed to be escorting Nadia and standing back with an amused look of sophisticated cynicism. From what she'd heard, he seemed to spend more of his time enjoying life with the society crowd.

"Marisa, this, at last, is Nadia." Carla dragged her forward to meet the woman she'd spoken of so often.

"A pleasure to meet you, I'm sure," Nadia said with a rather bored smile and a limp handshake.

Impressed with the elegance the woman managed to display, as well as her obvious ties to royalty, Marisa was a little nervous. The royals she knew well by now seemed like regular people compared to this. Nadia knew how to project an image.

"Oh, I'm sorry," Marisa said, mortified at the thought of imposing. "I'm afraid I'm staying in your room and using your clothes."

Nadia's smile grew warmer, as though finding a connection with the person she was meeting helped humanize the situation. "Think nothing of it. That's not my room at all—just where I park last year's frocks." She waved a casual hand, her gaze skimming over the loose summer dress Marisa wore with a sign of recognition. "Take them all. I'll never use them again."

"Oh." Marisa was fumbling for words when Nico came into the room.

"Hello, Nadia."

Everything stood still as he regarded his cousin with a jaundiced eye. For the first time, Nadia herself showed a hint of anxiety.

"Oh, Nico. I thought you'd be off at a business meeting tonight. You usually work later than this." Her smile looked a bit strained. "Shouldn't you be out revitalizing the economy of our country or something?"

"I do my best," he said, still gazing at her with a cool, level regard.

"So I hear."

"And I hear you are doing your best to re-vitalize the discotheque scene in Paris."

Nadia smiled nervously. "You heard about that, did you?"

"Your escapade at the Club Giroux? Doing a striptease on a table top? Yes, I heard about it."

"It was a mock striptease," she protested. "I didn't take off my bra and panties."

Nico's gaze darkened coldly. "You're to be commended for your high moral standards."

Nadia licked her lips and tried to smile in her usual carefree fashion, but it was obvious she was not enjoying this. "I suppose Dane called and told you about it."

"Actually, no. I saw it in the paper." The beautiful woman winced. "Nadia, do you understand how important it is to stay out of the papers? We're trying to rebuild a good country here and we need the firm support and respect of the people to do it. That can all be ruined if we become an object of scorn and ridicule and lose the support of the powers that be in the media."

Nadia pretended to be interested in looking over her latest nail job. "I've already heard this entire lecture from Dane."

"So he did talk to you?"

"Oh yes." She looked up at him, trying to maintain a bit of defiance in her attitude. "By the end of our conversation he was on the phone to the Bastille, trying to find out if they had an old leftover torture rack he could borrow." She rolled her eyes. "We did not part on friendly terms."

Nico stared at her for a moment, then seemed to relax a bit. "I take it the rack wasn't available."

"No, and I guess that's what made him so irritable."

Nico bit back a smile that threatened to soften his face. "Well, he's right, Nadia. We have to stay out of the tabloids."

"I understand." She looked at him and smiled tremulously, all defiance gone. "And from now on I'll work very hard at it. I'll be as anonymous as a church mouse at the regatta."

Everybody grinned at the thought of Nadia fading into the background. Wasn't going to happen.

"You'll be with her?" Nico asked his younger brother, Mychale.

Mychale's smile was laced with cynical amusement. "I'll keep her in line," he promised.

"I hope you do." His lip curled just a bit. "Sometimes I wonder if you're not as bad as she is. Some of the things I've heard about your exploits…"

"Gross exaggerations, every one," Mychale responded lazily, but Marisa detected a flash of anger in his eyes all the same. Evidence suggested the brothers had issues. "The papers love a good story, especially if they've made it up themselves."

Nico nodded, looking as though he had more to say but had decided to hold his tongue. He excused himself to get back to working on something in the library and the two visitors didn't stay much longer. Truth to tell, everything seemed a little deflated once they'd gone.

"They just seem larger than life, those two," Lady Julia murmured.

Marisa agreed with her, but her mind was on Nico. He'd looked tired during dinner and she had a feeling the visit from Nadia and Mychale had disturbed him somehow. Still, he seemed fine when he came out to get some papers from his suite and stopped by where she was helping Carla fold some antique linens for packing in storage boxes.

Carla had been explaining some of the reasons behind her family's dread of the tabloids.

"You know very well they are constantly in search of scandal among the royals. They love to stir things up. Look what they've done in other countries."

"Can't you just ignore them?" Marisa asked.

"I wish. But you really can't. People believe the ugly things they put out. It can destabilize an entire regime."

"Really?" Marisa was skeptical.

"Oh yes. Just look at what they are doing to my brother Dane right now. They've got this bee in their bonnet about the succession. He hasn't even been crowned yet and they are already worried about whether he can have children or not."

"What?"

"Yes. You see, there is a rumor that he's had war wounds which…well, make it impossible for him to have children. So they are obsessed with trying to figure out if he's already had a child with someone. It's all so crazy."

It was at this juncture that Nico stopped by and all talk of the tabloid trash evaporated quickly. He touched the linens they were folding, asked a couple of questions about the methods of storage, then turned to Marisa.

"What did you think of Nadia?" he asked her. "Was she all you'd hoped?"

Marisa laughed. "Every bit. And very

generous, too, to offer me the use of the clothes in the wardrobe."

His hard face softened. "She's a sweetheart, really," he said. "She just thinks she has to create excitement wherever she goes. We're hoping she grows up soon, before something spectacular happens." He frowned. "And now with Mychale egging her on, that might be delayed a while."

"Oh, Nico, they'll be fine," Carla said, taking a stack of linens that had been deemed suitable for current use and carrying them off to the linen closet.

Nico watched her go, then turned back to Marisa.

"One thing I appreciate about you is that you're a good counterweight to Nadia. It's good for Carla to see that there is another style that's more down-to-earth and still attractive."

She flushed. "What a wonderful thing to say. But I'm not royal."

"You have a natural nobility that's a lot more important."

She was speechless. He went on, talking about plans for Carla during the coronation, but Marisa was hardly listening. She couldn't get over what he'd just said. Did that mean he'd decided she probably wasn't a spy after all?

He was back on the subject of Nadia, talking about how she'd come to live with the family most of the time, since her parents had died, and that brought up the topic of Mychale.

"Your little brother is quite something," Marisa noted, stashing the last of the linens in a box. "What a cosmopolitan-looking young man. And so handsome."

Nico flashed her a look. "More handsome than I am?"

"Why, you're vain!" Marisa smiled with delight. "Who knew?"

"I am not. I was just joking." He smiled, then cocked his famous eyebrow. "But you still haven't answered my question."

That eyebrow still gave her chills. "Whether you or your brother is more handsome?" Studying him, she pretended to think it over. "You're more muscular, I think," she teased. "Harder. Stronger."

He flexed his biceps and she found herself laughing as she reached out to touch the closest bulge. The feeling of hard muscle beneath his cotton shirt was provocative in a way she hadn't expected. Suddenly her breath was a little harder to draw in. She looked up into his eyes, then quickly pulled her hand away. Swallowing, she tried to go on with the mock critique.

"But Mychale has that young, slender charm, like a greyhound," she said quickly, her tone a little forced. "And a profile a Roman would envy."

"Now you don't like my profile?" he asked her, his eyes knowing and as cynical as his younger brother's.

"Oh no," she said breathlessly. "I like your profile very much."

He took her hand in his and brought it to his lips. "And I like yours," he said huskily, holding her with his gaze. "And I like your mouth," he added softly, moving closer. "And your kinky hair. And the pulse that beats at the base of your throat. And…"

They both heard Carla coming back and drew apart. He dropped her hand, gave her a wistful smile and turned to go. "I like it all," he said as he left, mystifying Carla. "Don't change a thing."

There was a buzzing in her ears. Carla chatted as usual, but Marisa couldn't manage more than an occasional smile. It was a good half an hour before she had her pulse back down to normal. This was nuts. She was letting him get to her and she'd sworn she wouldn't do that.

She made herself busy for the next hour, but all the time she knew he was in the library, and finally she found herself heading there.

"I'm just going to look in and see if he needs anything," she told herself, knowing she was lying but unable to help it.

She hesitated in the doorway, then took a deep breath and stepped in. He was there, working over a pile of books. Aloof and morose, he seemed like a different person from the one who had teased her. He barely looked up, and when he did, he hardly seemed to see her. In the end, she just smiled and retreated again. But her sympathy was with him. He worked so hard and had so much on his shoulders—the welfare of an entire country. She began to wrack her brain, trying to think of something that might cheer him up. Finally she had to admit, she could only think of one thing.

Chocolate.

"You're being an idiot," she told herself helplessly as she marched to the kitchen. "He doesn't want chocolate!"

"You don't know that," her chocolate-fanatic side retorted. "Besides, do you have a better idea?"

She spun on her heel and found Nico standing in the doorway. Her heart leaped up. "Oh, Nico!" she cried, hurling herself into his arms. "You found me!"

He smiled down at her, holding on as though he knew just how precious she was. "Were you lost?" he teased softly.

"Oh, yes!"

"Well, you left enough bread crumbs. I could hardly have missed the trail."

She turned her tearstained face up and he dropped a kiss on her lips, then put her to the side so that he could walk over and nudge Umberto's body with his foot.

"Looks like he's still out. Too bad. I would have paid good money to see you swing that mallet at him again." He shook his head in raw admiration, then pulled out a cell phone.

"What are you doing?" Marisa asked him.

"Calling the police. We need to get him locked up before he comes to. I have a feeling he's going to be in a very bad mood."

Marisa shook her head. Everything was happening pretty fast, and she was trying to keep up. "He has two henchmen who are…"

"Yes, I know. I've got a couple of men with me. We ran into them outside. They've been taken care of as well."

"Oh."

She watched him talk into the phone and her love for him almost choked her. This was all so surreal. One minute she'd been fighting for her life and the next, here was the prince to take care of everything. But that meant they were back to the basic question—just what was he doing here?

"I still don't understand how you found me," she said and he closed his phone.

"Your suitcase showed up. The man who mugged you threw it over the side of the bridge, but it seems it never actually fell. It got caught up in the scaffolding under the bridge in such a way that it wasn't visible from the bridge or the ground. It wasn't until a painter was climbing under the rafters that he saw it."

"So you opened it?"

"I had to. Once I'd read your letter, I knew I had to find you. It was my only lead."

She nodded. "So you saw the key to the code."

"Yes. From there it just took time to figure out which chocolate company was yours."

She shook her head. "I'm so glad you're such a good detective," she noted. "I left the palace around midnight and Tom Verner, one of Umberto's men, grabbed me right away. In fact, he was the one who mugged me the other night. And I'm sure he was the one I saw watching the palace that time."

Prince Nico was frowning. "Why would he mug you?"

"To get the recipes. He wore a bandana over his face, but I knew it was him." She made a face. "Until I didn't know it anymore. For over a week."

"But your mind is clear now."

"Oh yes. Totally." Quickly, she explained Umberto's background, how he'd hoped to steal her company secrets and ended up taking control of DuBonnet Chocolatier to such a degree she had to go for help. "He worked with me for months, learning all our methods. But once I began to realize he didn't deserve to know our secrets, he'd already made me sign papers that gave him part ownership. So I sewed the coded recipes in my skirt and destroyed the other copies. I gave him false copies instead. When he realized it, he tried to force me to give him the real ones and that's when I ran. I was hoping to find my uncle and get his protection and help, getting control of my company again that way. But Tom followed me. He thought he would find the recipes in my suitcase or my purse, so he knocked me down and threw them over the side of the bridge, hoping to pick them up later downstream. Only the suitcase didn't show up. So he kept following me until I disappeared into the palace. He couldn't follow me in, so he waited for his chance."

"Thank God I found you when I did."

"Yes." She smiled at him, loving everything about him.

"But explain these recipes to me. What makes them so special?"

"The oldest ones aren't even chocolate. They're various methods of mixing ingredients with sugar to form the base of our candies. These methods were developed in that little monastery in the mountains where that strange code language was used. One of my ancestors was given sanctuary in that monastery in the thirteenth century. He came away with the recipes and started making sweets. Later, when chocolate came from the New World, the DuBonnets incorporated those recipes in a special way informed by the old ones. And that is why we have such unique taste and texture."

"And now you've ended up saving your recipes after all."

"Yes. Thanks to you." She sighed. "You gave me the refuge I needed to get the distance to understand that I had options. I didn't have to be a victim." She sneaked a glance his way. "So I'm not a spy. And I'm not an archeology student. But I am a cook of sorts."

More than an ordinary cook, still, less than royal—or anywhere near that. She knew the gulf between them was still huge, and it included his suspicions about her having leaked family information to the press. But he'd come to the rescue at just the right time and she'd needed him—more for emotional support than anything else, still, she had never been so glad to see anyone in her life.

The police had arrived and she and Nico moved outside so that they could watch the removal from a distance. The air was full of the scent of fruit trees blooming. It was spring. Time for renewal. They stood back and looked at her company and he put his arm around her shoulders, pulling her close.

"So this is your chocolate factory," he said, looking over the Tudor-style cottage that was its main office. "Looks like something out of a storybook. I expect to see the Seven Dwarves coming out of the doors and windows singing 'Hi Ho' at any moment."

She smiled, pleased with his tone. "Do you like it? It's really a wonderful place."

"I can see that."

She frowned. "Of course, Umberto is part owner."

"Don't worry, we've got lawyers to untangle that sort of problem."

She looked up, searching his face. "Nico, why did you come after me?"

He looked down into hers. "I wanted to make sure you were okay."

She tried to smile but suddenly there was a lump in her throat. "Was that all?" she asked, disappointed and trying to hold it back.

His brow furled thoughtfully. "No, there was one other thing."

"Yes?"

He looked down as though he could drown in her eyes. "I just wanted to know if you…"

The siren on the police car went off, making them both jump.

"Oh!" she cried.

He held her closer as the vehicles drove off.

"What was it you were wondering about me?" she asked, prompting him to get back on track.

"Oh, nothing much," he said casually, pushing her hair back so he could look into her pretty face. "I just was wondering if you'd like to get married. That's all."

"Get married?" She frowned. What on earth was he talking about?

"Yes."

She shook her head, completely perplexed. "Get married to whom?"

He looked around as though expecting someone else. "How about me?" he suggested. "I'm the one who loves you."

She blinked at him, waiting for the catch. But there was a smile growing in his eyes. "Are you kidding?" she asked at last. "You don't mean…"

"Marisa, are you going to make me go down on one knee?" he asked lightly.

"Nico, don't tease me!"

"I'm not. I love you. Maybe you hadn't noticed. Here, I'll show you."

He kissed her with passion and intensity and she gasped for breath when he was finished.

"You still haven't said yes," he demanded.

"But…"

"You hesitate. Do you realize what you're doing to my ego? Listen, there are plenty of benefits to marrying a prince."

Her smile was tremulous and tears filled her eyes. "I don't know," she said, trying to join in the spirit of the jest. "All those boring state dinners."

"We can find ways to make them interesting. We could invite chocolate makers from all over the world. You could be queen of chocolate."

She laughed. Was everything really going to be all right? It was hard to get her mind around that. There had to be a catch.

"But does Dane still suspect me of leaking family information?"

"No, not at all." He waved her worries away as though she shouldn't have given that a second thought.

"But *you* did. At least at first."

"Never. Not for a moment. And I told Dane that right after you left the room."

He was so candid, she believed him totally. She was so relieved.

"And anyway, the mystery is solved. Carla got home before I left this morning and she confessed everything."

"What? Carla?" This news was as shocking to her as everything else that had happened that day.

"Yes. You remember that Jans Hunsinger who hovered around her at the derby?"

"Of course."

"He charmed her and somehow he contacted her and got her to call him secretly. Chatted her up and got all sorts of info out of her. Turns out he's actually a writer for one of those rags."

"Oh no." Marisa gasped. "Poor Carla."

"Don't worry. She'll be okay. She's young and bound to make mistakes." He dropped another kiss on her lips. "She has to learn how to act like a princess. You already seem to be a natural." His mouth twisted in appreciation of the concept. "You're natural royalty. Chocolate royalty."

She laughed. Everything was making her laugh. She'd never been so happy. "You could say that, I suppose."

"I can see the headlines now: 'The chocolate queen deigns to marry a lowly prince of the realm.' I think the tabloids would love it."

"But Dane wouldn't." Her face changed. "Oh! Quick. Give me your hand." She placed his palm right over where the little foot was kicking. "Do you feel that?"

"Hey!" He pulled his hand back, startled. "This baby does more than talk, doesn't she?" he said, but he put his palm on her belly again and this time he smiled. "Marisa," he said. "That's amazing."

"Isn't it?"

Emotion choked him suddenly, and he thought of Andrea and the baby that should have reached this stage but never had. Marisa was so different from his first love. And yet, there were some very important similarities—strength, beauty, wonderful humor and just plain goodness. She was perfect. Even Andrea would approve.

"Nico, tell me honestly," Marisa was saying, searching his eyes. "What do you think about children?"

He shrugged. "She'll be the first. More to come."

Marisa's worry showed in her face. "Promise me that you won't love her any less than the others who come later."

He held her in the circle of his arms. "How could I? She's a part of you." He dropped a kiss on her neck, then another. "In fact, she'll always be first in my heart. After all, if she hadn't existed, we might never have met."

She sighed, running on pure happiness. "And all because of chocolate," she noted happily. "Want to go in and try some?"

He smiled. "I thought you'd never ask."

But he kissed her first, just because he could.

EPILOGUE

"Shhh." Carla put a finger to her lips and cautioned Marisa. "I can't tell you yet," she whispered. "It's a secret."

A secret. Marisa stared at her soon-to-be-sister-in-law in frustration. Here she was, standing in a cold, damp basement room in her wedding gown, and Carla was telling her she couldn't know where she was going or what would happen once she got there. What sort of wedding was this?

She knew Dane was opposed to her marrying his brother. He'd made that very clear. And Nico had made it just as clear that he would give up his right of succession before he would give up the woman he loved.

"Give it some time," Dane had urged just days before. "Later this year when this nonsense in the tabloids has died down we can look at a public announcement…if you still feel the way you do now. But we're barely getting our footing with the public. To have you marry a pregnant commoner of no standing will send the chattering classes into a frenzy. We can't afford that in this precarious atmosphere."

"If we wait," Nico had responded firmly, "Marisa's baby will be born out of wedlock. And everyone will assume the baby isn't mine."

Dane had given him a puzzled look. "But…the baby isn't yours."

Nico had smiled. "That's where you're wrong, brother. That baby became mine as soon as I realized how much I loved Marisa. I take full responsibility. Nothing will change that. And our marriage will confirm it."

Dane's anger began to show itself. "You're crazy," he'd said with a fierce frown. "Life doesn't work that way. And as for this insane marriage, I forbid it!"

Nico had set his jaw and turned away. With a sinking heart, Marisa had assumed that was going to be the final word. Later that evening, he'd told her he was taking a short trip to Paris and would be gone for a few days. Three days later, Carla had appeared in her room with news and very sparkling eyes.

"Come quickly! Nico is back. He's brought you a wedding gown. It's in my room. You're to put it on and then I'm to take you to the dungeon."

"What?"

"Don't worry. It's just the basement and wine cellar. We always call it the dungeon because…" She shrugged with a disarming smile. "Well, just because. Come on. There's no time to lose."

They'd rushed through the preparations. Marisa's heart was beating like a drum. She tried to find out what Carla thought of it all, whether she thought it was wise to go against Dane this way, but Carla refused to discuss it.

"We don't have time to talk," she'd said, slipping into a lovely blue silk number that was a perfect complement to the satin and lace Marisa was sinking into. "Hurry! Here's your veil."

"Oh," Marisa sighed. Beautifully studded with tiny freshwater pearls, it was a lacy fantasy. Once it was installed, looking through it felt like looking into a magical future. Was she really going to marry the man of her dreams? It seemed hard to believe.

"And your flowers."

White orchids with violet centers in a

stunning waterfall spray. Looking into the full-length mirror, she gasped. She looked incredible, if she did say so herself.

"Let's go."

And now here they were, waiting in the basement. Marisa looked around at the gloomy walls and shivered, wondering if the place had actually been used as a dungeon after all. Maybe that creepy sense of presence she was feeling was really the ghosts of past unwilling visitors and…

She stopped cold. The ground was shaking. Earthquake? Heart in her throat, she turned to look at Carla who was shaking her head.

"Look," she said, pointing toward the back wall. Marisa turned. The back wall had split and was rumbling open. A long, wide passage was revealed, flickering torches lining the way. And just inside stood what looked like a golden sleigh set on an electric track.

"Let's go," Carla said, picking up the bride's long white train and nodding toward the sleigh.

"What is this?" Marisa asked as they settled into the plush seats. The doors rumbled shut behind them and the sleigh took off down the track.

"This was the royal family's escape route

during the overthrow fifty years ago," Carla explained. "During medieval times it was the secret way out of the palace. During the Reformation, it was the secret passage to the royal family's private chapel. And now..." She smiled at her soon-to-be-sister. "Now it's the secret pathway to your wedding."

Marisa smiled back, but before she had time to ask more questions, the sleigh was slowing. They had arrived at the secret royal chapel, and there was Prince Mychale, looking elegant and debonair in tails, to escort her into the sanctuary.

"Hello, Your Highness," she said as she took his arm and stepped down onto the stone floor.

"Welcome, Marisa," he said, smiling down at her. "I can tell you'll be a wonderful addition to our clan. We're very pleased to have you."

"Thank you," she told him, her tone heart-felt. "I can't tell you how honored I am to be j-j-joining you." She still felt shy and tentative about how unworthy she was and about Crown Prince Dane's disapproval, and that made it difficult for her to talk about it casually.

Mychale had her pause with him at the doorway. An organ inside began to play "The Wedding March." Marisa gulped. This was it. Suddenly the doors were thrown open. For just a moment she was blinded by the light coming from the beautiful, high, stained-glass ceiling, but once her gaze cleared, she saw Prince Nico standing at the end of the aisle, waiting for her.

With a cry of delight she dropped Mychale's arm and ran to her love. He laughed, catching her up in his arms and twirling her for a moment. Then he stopped, setting her down where she belonged, and she noticed the priest who was waiting to perform the service. Her heart was beating so hard, she was sure she was about to faint. Carla came up and took her place beside her. She looked to see if Mychale was standing up with Nico, but he was off to the side, and she frowned, wondering why.

And then she saw why. An imposing figure entered the chapel and came directly toward where they were standing. Her breath stopped in her throat. It was Dane. What was he doing here? Her head snapped around as she looked at Nico, wondering if they should run for it. But Nico was smiling, and as she watched, mouth open in wonder, Dane took the position for the best man.

"Nico?" she whispered loudly.

He gave her a wink and nodded. "Dane's come around," he whispered back.

"Oh!" She smiled at the future king, joy rushing in her veins. "Oh, thank you, Your Majesty," she whispered so loudly, it seemed to ring from wall to wall.

Dane grinned at her. "I'm not a 'majesty' yet," he reminded her. "So I decided to put off trying to run everyone's life around here until I'm legally obligated to do so."

The priest cleared his throat and they all came to attention like naughty schoolchildren. It was time to begin.

Most of the short service left Marisa in a daze. She knew she'd said "I do" and she knew she'd given Nico a ring and received one of her own. And then she distinctly heard, "You may now kiss the bride," and she felt Nico's arms slide around her and his lips press to hers and she sighed, a sound of pure happiness. It was done after all.

He held her tightly, as if he was never going to let her go.

"Marisa," he said softly, close to her ear, "I promise you, as soon as we decide things are stable, we'll have a very huge and very public celebration of our marriage."

She shook her head, looking up at him with tears in her eyes. "Nico, I don't need the public. I just need you. I'll be your secret bride forever if need be. Just as long as we're together."

And somewhere close by, there was a loud, joyful tolling of a bell.

MILLS & BOON®

Why shop at millsandboon.co.uk?

Each year, thousands of romance readers
find their perfect read at millsandboon.co.uk.
That's because we're passionate about
bringing you the very best romantic fiction.
Here are some of the advantages of
shopping at www.millsandboon.co.uk:

* **Get new books first**—you'll be able to buy
  your favourite books one month before they
  hit the shops

* **Get exclusive discounts**—you'll also be
  able to buy our specially created monthly
  collections, with up to 50% off the RRP

* **Find your favourite authors**—latest news,
  interviews and new releases for all your
  favourite authors and series on our website,
  plus ideas for what to try next

* **Join in**—once you've bought your favourite
  books, don't forget to register with us to rate,
  review and join in the discussions

Visit **www.millsandboon.co.uk**
for all this and more today!

She didn't. But she did have a good ganache going on the stove—and some freshly picked strawberries from the garden. Working quickly, she cut off the tops, then cored the berries and stuffed them with the truffle ganache. After melting discs of white dipping chocolate, she drenched the berries, then with melted bittersweet dark chocolate, she painted little jackets with bow ties and buttons over the white "shirts." She stuck the green tops back on with white chocolate for "hair" and ended up with what looked like fat little men wearing tuxedos.

Looking at the final results, she smiled. They were cute as heck. Before she had time to think better of it, she slid two of them onto a small silver dish and headed for the library.

She looked in. Nico was leaning over the pile of opened books, his eyes tired and bloodshot, his shirt open at the neck, his hair rumpled as though he'd spent a lot of time thrusting his fingers through it. He was frowning down at his papers. Her heart began to pound. Was he going to order her out? Or ask her what on earth made her think he would want this kind of interruption? Or, even worse, give her a faint smile and pretend to appreciate what she'd made him, then politely dismiss her? For a fleeting moment, she wished she hadn't done this. But it was too late to back out now.

"Here," she said, putting the silver dish down in front of him. "I brought you something."

He looked up, his eyes moody and unreceptive. Looking at what she'd put in the dish, he straightened. A reluctant smile just barely broke the line of his mouth.

"That's very nice," he said. "Very clever." He looked at her. "Why didn't you bring them out for dessert so everybody could see them?"

"I didn't make them for everybody," she said, looking down into his eyes. "Just for you."

Leaning back in his chair, he looked at her warily, as though he was afraid to let her see what he felt. "Marisa," he said softly. "Oh, Marisa." His hand caught hers and he pulled her down into his lap. He looked at her face for a long time before he softly kissed her lips. "You're a special woman, Marisa," he said. "I wish…"

His eyes clouded and he didn't finish that thought. Putting a hand to the side of his face, she leaned close and kissed him.

"You're a pretty special man," she said, her voice husky with unshed tears. Rising from his lap, she looked back at him longingly, and left the room.

His unstated wish stayed with her into the night. She probably wished pretty much the same thing he did. But neither one of them could say it out loud.

The next morning at breakfast, the talk was all about the surprise visitors the night before. The young cousins from Belgrade hadn't been there to see them and had to be told all about it.

"Maybe *we* could go to the regatta," one said hopefully.

They both looked toward Nico as the rule-keeper and plan-maker.

"Sorry," he said, dashing their hopes. "You'd have to stay overnight and you've both got classes tomorrow."

They pouted, but there was no question that Nico's word was final. Looking across the table, Marisa felt a little sorry for them. But their request gave her an idea and she followed Nico out into the garden a few minutes later as he prepared to go for his morning run.

"I've been thinking," she said, trying not to notice once again how good he looked in shorts and a tank top. "We don't seem to be getting anywhere on my memory problem. The analysts aren't coming up with anything on the papers from my skirt. We're at a standstill and I'm really getting antsy about this. I think I should go out and mix with the populace a bit. Wander the streets. See if I recognize anything or if anyone recognizes me."

He gazed at her skeptically. "The better to run away from us?" he suggested softly as he began stretching for his run.

A flash of anger raced through her. After all this time, did he still think she was a liar and a cheat?

"No, Nico," she said firmly. "And if you think so poorly of me, I guess there's not much use in…"

"Hold on," he said, reaching out and taking her by the shoulders and gazing deeply into her eyes. "I don't think poorly of you at all. Not a bit. Surely you know that."

His hands slid down her arms, fingers caressing her flesh, and then he jerked away as though he'd pulled himself from the brink of doing something he knew he shouldn't. Turning away from her, he reached for his towel.

"But I wouldn't blame you if you were getting impatient to get out of the palace and try something new," he said quickly. "And that's why I thought you might like to go with us to the Carnethian National Derby Cup this weekend."

She blinked. "You mean the run of the horses at Brolney that we hear about in legend and song?"

"Yes."

Her heart jumped. That sounded like fun. "I don't think I've ever been."

His half grin was infectious. "It would be surprising if you had. It hasn't been held for the last fifty years."

"Oh." She laughed.

"Dane is still in Paris so I'll have to go to represent the family. It's important to bring back these old traditions in order to help the people feel that they really have their country back." He gave her a look. "I think you would enjoy it."

"You think so?" It was funny how such a simple thing could raise such expectations. She was feeling like a new person.

"Carla's coming. So why don't you come along too? You could use a diversion."

She wanted to hug him, she was so happy. "I-I'd love to."

He was still looking at her with that half-bemused, half-affectionate expression, as though he'd decided he couldn't pretend he didn't like her after all. "I know it's been rough on you all this week," he added.

She wanted to laugh and dance and kiss him. "No, actually, it's been very pleasant. Carla is a darling and the food is good and…" She couldn't really add that the host was sexy and romantic and made her blood sing, could she?

"We'll have to keep your pregnancy covered up as much as possible at the races," he was saying with a thoughtful frown. "We don't want to start any rumors."

That stopped her in her tracks. "What sort of rumors?"

He looked at her sideways and put the towel around his neck. "A pregnant woman is always the hub of rumor central, especially when she's staying at the palace. Surely you can see that."

She frowned, her lovely mood dimming. "I suppose so."

"You'll be there as Carla's friend," he said, making it up as he went along. "Who could take exception to Carla bringing a friend along?"

He stopped and looked at her, glancing down at her rounded belly.

"How are you feeling?" he asked, obviously referring to her pregnancy.

"Very well. No complaints." She smiled,

hand on her tummy. Dr. Zavier had stopped in the day before and given her a checkup. He seemed to think everything was proceeding normally. "Lots of moving. No real firm kicks yet, but once that happens, I'll make you try to feel it. Okay?"

She held her breath. The question was more important than she'd realized as she was asking it, and now the answer was the most important thing in the world. Did he want to feel her baby kick? Or did he want to distance himself from the whole thing?

He was impassive for a long moment, and then he smiled.

"Okay."

His smile was so natural and genuine, it made her heart skip a beat. And then he was off, jogging past the garden as he headed for the perimeter of the property. She watched him go, enjoying the beauty of his muscles at work and the way his dark hair caught the sunlight, savoring him as though she knew she was going to have nothing left of him but memories very soon.

Carla was excited about the plans for the weekend. So were the Belgrade cousins, Jan and Jols.

"This is even better than the regatta!" one of them crowed.

"The only thing more exciting will be the St. Tupin's Day Ball next month," said the other.

"There's a ball next month?" Marisa asked Carla as they walked out to the day parlor.

"Oh yes. It's basically for me. I've got to come out. And Dane thinks we should do it before the coronation."

"You're not out? I thought you high-society girls did that at about eighteen."

"We do," Carla said, batting Marisa with a tea towel for using the term. "All things being equal, I would have come out a long time ago, except the war got in the way the last few years. So now, we're having a great big ball. It's so exciting! Lady Julia is going to present me." She sighed. "I feel a little foolish, of course, being so old and all. But you notice I'm not married, or even engaged, so it's assumed I'd better put myself out there."

"Carla! They'll be standing in line."

"Hmm. Maybe. We'll see, I suppose." She looked at Marisa speculatively. "But I have a favor to ask you. If everything turns out okay and you're not a spy and all, would you be my official companion at the ball?"

Marisa blanched. "Oh Carla, I'm bound to be aggressively showing by then."

"I don't care." Carla smiled at her with candid affection. "Spy or not, preggers or not, you're the best friend I've ever had. And I want you there." Her big eyes turned to puppy-dog pleading. "Please say yes."

Marisa took her hands and held them. She was very fond of the girl and wanted to do anything she could to make her happy. It broke her heart to think that she had no friends to speak of. She only wondered if Carla realized how tentative her stay here really was. She wasn't supposed to be a friend. She was actually a prisoner. Why was everyone skipping that part?

"Of course I'll be there if it is at all possible. I promise."

And she bit her lip, wondering if she'd just become a liar.

They spent the afternoon planning for the trip and deciding on their wardrobes. Marisa had a great selection as Nadia spent a lot of time going to special events and had the clothes to wear to them. She finally picked out a day outfit of a navy blue shift with a white jacket, and red-and-blue scarf at the neck—very chic in a preppy way. Carla was going through one outfit after another and still couldn't decide.

"I'm supposed to be thinking about being attractive to a possible marriage prospect," she fretted. "Dane thinks I should dress like a nun. Mychale says be trendy. Aunt Julia counsels a little cleavage." She rolled her eyes.

Marisa laughed. "What does Nico say?"

"He's the only one who says, 'Be yourself.'" She looked doleful. "But he doesn't really mean it. I'm supposed to zero in on someone upright and smart and educated—but royal—and make him fall in love with me. That's not so easy, you know."

"No, I wouldn't think so." She felt a pang of sympathy for the girl. "Does he really have to be royal?"

"Yes. Dane is very keen on us all marrying royalty, just to help shore up our credibility as a country."

Marisa had another pang of sympathy, and this time for herself. But that was silly. She didn't have a chance in the world of marrying royalty herself. So what did she care?

"How many eligible royals are there?" she asked.

"Oh, tons. There are all kinds of royals all over."

Marisa raised a skeptical eyebrow, sure she must be overstating the case a bit.

"The trick is to find one who isn't a pampered playboy," Carla said with a sigh, "someone serious and decent, like my brothers."

Marisa nodded at that, helping Carla put her things back on hangers. From what she'd seen, Nico was one hard-working man. Mychale seemed to be another story, but from all accounts Dane was a lot like Nico. Growing up in exile and then fighting to get your country back probably had something to do with producing that sort of man.

"Of course, it would help if I was pretty," Carla said so softly, at first Marisa wasn't sure she'd heard her right.

"What? What are you talking about? You're beautiful!"

"Oh Marisa, don't try to fool me. I've got mirrors."

"You've got mirrors, but no experience," Marisa said firmly. "Just because your style of looks may not be the most popular at the moment, doesn't mean it won't be soon. Style is always in state of flux. The trick is to learn how to use whatever you've got to your own advantage."

"Hmm." Carla looked skeptical. "Be specific."

Marisa was at a loss for a moment, then nodded slowly. "Tell you what. We'll give it our all for the derby. Okay? We'll get your hairstylist in here, and a makeup artist, and see what we can do."

"Really?" Carla looked as though she was hesitant to let herself get too excited. "You promise?"

"I promise." Marisa gave the younger girl a hug. "Time to turn into a butterfly, Carla. You just wait and see."

Nico was quiet at dinner. Carla and the Belgrade cousins did most of the talking, chattering about other derbys they had attended in the past. Marisa tried to join in the general hilarity, but her gaze kept straying to where Nico sat, looking like a man with a lot on his mind. It seemed trivial to talk about pleasure outings when he seemed to be thinking about how to save Carnethian society.

Or was it something more than that? Something more personal? Something more tragic?

Later in the evening, after a game of cards with the others, she was wandering through the house and noticed he'd gone out in the twilight and was sitting at the edge of the grass, staring into the forest, nursing a drink.

"Just leave it alone, Marisa," she told herself fiercely. "He doesn't need you prying into his business. And if he wanted comfort, he wouldn't hesitate to ask for it, would he?"

But she ached inside to see him looking so tormented.

Finally she couldn't stand it any longer. She had to go out.

He looked up as she came near, watching her approach without smiling or making any sign of welcome.

"Nico, what's wrong?" she asked, standing over him.

"Wrong?" He waved his drink in the air. "Why do you ask? Nothing's wrong."

She stared down at him for a moment, then dropped to sit beside him in the grass. "In the evening sometimes you get such a haunted look in your eyes," she said hesitantly, ready to drop this line of conversation if he gave the slightest indication that he hated it. "It looks as though…well, as though you have bad memories."

His head went back and he scowled at her. "Bad memories? Are you kidding? We just went through five years of fighting to restore our monarchy, Marisa. Lots of ugly things happened. Sure I've got bad memories."

She winced. "You have to put them behind you." She hesitated. What was she doing? All things being equal, she ought to know better. Here she was, a nobody with no credentials whatsoever trying to give advice to her country's prince, second in line to the throne. But when she saw him like this, he was just a man. A man she felt a deep connection to, for no logical reason.

"You can't let those bad memories distort the life you have to live now," she added, wishing she could think of some less trite way of putting it.

He stared off at the forest again. "Some things can't be cast off so easily. We can't all have your luck with amnesia."

His tone wasn't friendly, but it wasn't hostile. She took a deep breath and decided to go for broke.

"Is it Andrea?"

He turned quickly, staring at her. "Who told you about Andrea?"

"No one. You called me that name the first night I was here."

A storm was brewing in his blue eyes, but

he didn't say another word. After staring at her for a long moment, he set his glass down in the grass and rose, walking off into the dark forest, leaving her behind.

She stayed where she was, wishing life wasn't so confusing, wishing bad things didn't happen to good people. But they did. All the time.

It was almost a quarter of an hour before he came back. He stopped on the walkway, looking at her, and she was sure he was going to go on in without speaking. But after a moment or two, he turned and walked slowly her way and dropped down onto the grass beside her again.

"Andrea grew up in France," he began without preamble, "like a lot of our exile community. Her father was a big backer of the royal family. Think of your stereotyped picture of a French World-War-Two resistance fighter and you've got a sense of what Andrea looked like."

Despite himself, his voice, which had started out harsh and cold, began to soften with a sense of lost affection.

"She was fearless. Over that last year when the fighting was getting very intense, we lived together in the mountains and fought side by side. We tempted fate and took such chances." He shook his head as though he could hardly believe it now. "We fell in love." His voice broke. "We made a child. I wanted her to go back to Paris where she would be safe, but she wouldn't hear of it. She had to be on the front lines of the rebellion." He half smiled, his eyes on the past, remembering. "In fact, I was furious with her there toward the end. She was carrying our child." His voice rose. "She should have been more careful. It was not just her own life she was risking...."

His voice grew very rough and he stopped for a moment, his eyes closed, composing himself.

"She was hit by a sniper's bullet and then she was dead," he said in a more business-like fashion. "They were both dead. I didn't really have time to grieve at first. We were under attack day and night. I was pretty sure I would be dead, too, before it was all over. It wasn't until we routed the enemy and took over the city that I really had time to sit back and take account of what had been lost. And then I grieved." His voice thickened again. "She was so young, so beautiful, so full of grit and goodness. Our country lost so much when she died. The world lost. For a while, I thought I would go out of my mind with grief."

He paused, closing his eyes and letting the emotion pass. Marisa couldn't know exactly how he felt, but she had a pretty good idea, and she ached for him. Tears welled in her eyes and she bit her lip to keep from letting out a sound.

"But I didn't," he said at last. "I'm still here, still sane. But the pain is always there as well."

"Especially in the evening," she ventured quietly.

"Yes, for some reason." He shrugged. "Especially in the evening."

They were both quiet for a moment, digesting all he'd said. Finally, Marisa said softly, "I'm so sorry."

He turned to her. Reaching up, he soaked up the tears running down her cheeks with his finger.

"I know," he said softly. "I'm sorry too. Everyone's sorry." His hand cupped her chin and he looked down into her warm dark eyes.

"Do you think that you'll ever be able to love that way again?" she asked shakily.

It was a crazy question to ask. Insane. Pathetic. There was no hope for her, no matter how much she might dream. She closed her eyes, wishing she'd kept her emotions to herself. She was only going to drive him away with questions like that.

But he didn't pull away. Though he frowned, he began to trace her lips with his finger.

"I didn't think so. I was sure, in fact. Until…"

She opened her eyes. What was he saying? She could hardly breathe. "Until?" she asked, unable to let it lie there.

Instead of answering, he kissed her gently, tasting her lips as though testing them. Then he leaned back and looked into her face.

"You'd better go in, Marisa," he told her softly. "The night is full of magic and I'm feeling a little crazy."

Looking into his eyes, all she could think of were violins and satin sheets—and a man's hard hand trailing hot excitement down the length of her body. She didn't want to go in. She wanted to hold him with her heart and comfort him with her body. Was it finally time for her to admit it? She was in love with this man.

How had she let this happen? She'd tried to guard against it from the first. She knew there was no future in it. He was royal, for God's sake. And she was not about to let herself be a prince's plaything.

"Tomorrow we are taking you out into the world," he noted, his eyes darkly shadowed in the muted light. "Who knows what will happen? Maybe we'll see someone who remembers you."

She turned to look at him. She knew she could make one simple move and be in his arms. She could feel his desire, could barely conceal her own. He was being a gentleman, but his sensual response lay just beneath the surface and she could coax it out easily. One word, one move, and she could have him. The protection of the forest wasn't far away.

Why not? She wanted to. She ached to feel his strength, to take him in her body and give him all she had to give. If she did it, she would always have a tiny piece of him, a memory.

But that would be all she would ever get. And she knew now how slippery memories could be.

Closing her eyes, she gathered herself together and decided to do what was right. With a sigh, she turned and smiled at him. "Good night," she whispered.

He touched her cheek with his hand, then drew it back and stared past her at the trees. He had a quick fantasy of chucking it all and grabbing Marisa and heading for Tahiti—

never looking back. Could people still hide out in the South Seas? They could live on the beach and go spear-fishing for food. She would look cute in a little grass skirt.

But he knew he wasn't going to do that. He'd spent his life preparing for the restoration of his family to power. Now their dreams had come true and he was going to throw it all away because he had fallen helplessly in love.

Fallen in love. Was that really what he'd done? And if so, who cared? He couldn't do anything about it. He was committed to this job, this country, his family. He couldn't possibly betray them all for a woman. Even a woman like this.

"Tonight may be the last night we have you here," he said softly, his fingers combing through her hair, his hand cupping her head.

"No," she said, a note of near panic in her voice. "Oh no."

"It's possible," he said. "So, just in case…"

He leaned closer and kissed her again. She forgot all about her plans to do the right thing. His kiss was hot and hard and she was dizzy. No room for thought. All she needed to do was feel. She closed her eyes and sank into the kiss, the embrace, the emotion that was building between them. She wanted nothing but him.

"Marisa? Are you out there?" Carla's voice cut through their private moment like a knife.

Nico groaned, pulling back, and Marisa took a deep breath and hoped her voice wouldn't choke in her throat. "Over here, Carla," she called.

"Oh good. Come in quick. The stylists are here. We've got to go over plans for tomorrow."

Nico dropped a quick kiss on her trembling lips and smiled in the darkness. "Good night, Marisa," he said softly. "Dream of me."

CHAPTER NINE

AFTER breakfast the next morning, Marisa wandered into the library, drawn, as usual, to the cookbooks. It would be another hour or so before they left for the races and she had some time to kill. She pulled down a particularly decrepit specimen on yellowed parchment, one of the ones she hadn't looked through before. It was probably the oldest one she'd seen yet. Hundreds of years old. She handled it carefully, afraid to tear the sheets. Studying page after page, she could barely make out the words. In some sections, the symbols didn't even seem to be letters. Could this be a real language? She didn't recognize it as such. In fact, the symbols reminded her of…

Her jaw dropped. She stared at the page for a long, long moment, digesting what this might just mean. Then she grabbed the book to her chest and began to run through the house, searching for Nico.

There didn't seem to be anybody about. She found Chauncy in the butler's pantry, but he was busy on the phone making the weekly grocery order and waved her off. The maids didn't have a clue, but it seemed everyone else was dressing for their outing.

Finally, trepidatious but too full of her news to wait, she ran up the stairs to the prince's suite and knocked on the door. There was no answer. Cautiously, she tried the doorknob. It opened easily to her touch. She stepped inside.

"Nico?" she called, closing the door behind her.

"Marisa?"

His voice came from the bathroom.

"Just a minute."

And then he was walking into the room, clad only in a small white towel he was holding at his waist, water from his shower still glistening on his shoulders.

She gasped and tried to turn away, but just couldn't do it.

He smiled. "This isn't real, is it?" he teased. "You haven't really shown up in my bedroom. I'm dreaming, aren't I?"

She shouldn't have come here. This could take her right down the road she'd vowed not to go on. She started to back away. "Oh, Nico, I'm sorry, I didn't realize…"

"See? My dreams never work out like they should," he said lightly. "And here I thought you'd come to tell me you couldn't live without my gloriously sculpted body any longer."

She was bright red, half-laughing, half-appalled. He was joking but his words were cutting too near the bone for comfort. The cookbook hung forgotten from her fingers. She'd never seen anything more beautiful than this man's body.

"I'd better go," she stuttered out. "I'll come back when you're…"

"Dressed? Turn around. It'll only take a minute."

She turned around, and she closed her eyes for good measure. Not because she was shy. More because she could hardly breathe and was afraid if she saw too much more of him, she might go into an embarrassing swoon. Not to mention lose all ability to resist throwing herself at his feet.

"Okay," he said.

She turned back, then closed her eyes again, scrunching them tightly. "You're going to have to put a shirt on, too," she warned him. "I've got my standards, you know."

He laughed. "Okay, Miss Manners, I'm fully clothed. Your honor is safe, and so is mine."

Opening her eyes, she sighed, thinking of lost opportunities. He still looked good in slacks and a shirt, but something was lost as far as the more carnal senses were concerned.

"Look," she said, remembering what she'd come for. "I was looking through the cookbooks in your library and look what I found."

She spread the book open to the page with the symbols. Nico bent over it and recognized what it was right away.

"It looks like the same style of writing," he said. "Good lord, how old is this thing?"

"Hard to tell. But it looks like something from medieval times, doesn't it?"

"Something very old, dug out of a historical trash heap. Very interesting."

Turning to a tall closet, he opened the door and pulled out a flat drawer, then carefully removed the papers which had been sewn into her skirt.

"Here we go," he said. "Let's compare and contrast, shall we?"

He laid the papers next to the book. They both stared down at the symbols, going from one to the other. Marisa felt prickles on the back of her neck. This was spooky. Raising her head, she met his gaze and they stared at each other.

"They're the same, aren't they?" she said in wonder.

He nodded. "This is the breakthrough we've been waiting for," he said. Reaching over, he picked up his phone. "Get me Trendyce at Intelligence," he said into the receiver. "I've got some new information here."

"Do you think this will help interpret those papers from my skirt?" she asked him.

"No doubt about it." He smiled at her. "You did good, Marisa. This is a great find. I'll give this to Trendyce and he'll get his analysts on it right away."

She nodded, feeling pleased. "I hope it does the trick," she said, glancing back regretfully as she turned to go. "And now, in more than one way, I guess we're off to the races."

Marisa was pretty sure she'd never arrived at an event in a convoy of long black limousines escorted by heavily uniformed men on motorcycles before. That was quite an experience in itself. Colorful banners in blue, yellow and red were flying everywhere. The scene looked as though it was set for a medieval jousting match. People lined the streets and waved little flags, calling out as they passed. She almost felt famous. And that was pretty funny, when she was actually anonymous, even to herself.

The racetrack was in the process of being restored from war damage. There was a new central receiving area with turrets and gold-leaf embellishments on the pillars. They were led in through the main gates, then onto the stand and up the red-carpeted stairs for access to the royal box.

The royal box might have been a confer-ence room in a five-star hotel, with thick carpets and large, plush seating for about twenty people. It also had the best vantage of the field. Waiters stood ready with trays holding glasses of champagne and plates with crudités. The royal party was seated, and they all looked around expectantly. It was all so luxurious, they felt truly pampered.

Visitors came and went, though each went through security first. Carla began to meet some of the young men who had come to pay their respects to the very eligible princess. Marisa looked on happily, feeling just a little smug. Carla looked gorgeous. Instead of wearing her hair in a clump pushed back behind her ears and hanging down her back like a thicket, the way she usually did, Marisa had encouraged the stylist to give her a dramatic cut, even though the princess had squealed in horror at the thought. Now her hair was just below chin length and cut to frame the girl's face in a way that set off her pale eyes and her pretty mouth. A makeup artist had done a little magic to her face. Marisa had helped her choose her outfit for the day, a silky pant suit that hid her tendency toward plumpness. She looked lovely and she was busy developing the kind of confidence that would hold her in good stead in the hunt for a mate suitable for royalty.

That thought gave Marisa a twinge, but she pushed it aside and went on. An employee in tails came into the box with a racing form and everyone placed small bets on their favorites.

"I don't know who any of them are," she told Nico with a frown.

"It's more fun if you place a bet or two," he advised her.

"But how do I choose?"

"You could close your eyes and point," he said. "Or you could look at the names and try to find one you can relate to. Pull something out of your life."

"That's not so easy when your own past is a mystery to you," she reminded him.

"Nothing rang a bell on the drive over?" he asked, looking at her closely and wishing he could nibble on her ear.

"No. Not a thing." They had driven through the city, then along the lake and into the mountains, and nothing had meant a thing to her.

"Then look at the names and just pick something."

She glanced down the list. "Oh, I don't know. Hmm. There's a horse named Piccolo. I had a cat named Piccolo when I was a little girl."

She looked up, realizing what she'd just said. Nico was staring back at her.

"What did you say?" he asked incredulously.

She gasped. "I remembered something from my past," she said, getting excited. "Oh Nico! I remembered something."

He gave her a long, slow smile, enjoying her candid joy. "Great. Now take it easy. Don't try to force anything. Just let it come naturally."

"Okay," she promised, but she was more excited than Christmas morning. Piccolo. She could see that little black cat now. She looked back down at the race list but her mind refused to see it. She was trying hard not to try to remember but she just couldn't help it. The trouble was, nothing else was coming to her. She closed her eyes. Still nothing.

Oh well. She dismissed the whole attempt. She was bound and determined she was going to have a good time today. No disappointing thoughts. She would just try the remembering later on, when the races were over.

The first race was run. Piccolo came in last. Marisa frowned, wondering if that was an omen. But everyone was having a good time, chatting and laughing, and she sat where she could watch Nico and she had to admit she enjoyed that. He was so handsome and gracious to those who came by to talk to him. He seemed to be having fun, too. The worried look was erased for the day, and that was good to see.

Another race was run, and then they were served custard with berry sauce topping, a national dish. Marisa sat beside Carla and watched her begin to try a little flirting with her visitors. Laughing, she egged her on. One handsome swain, introduced as Jans Hunsinger from Amsterdam, a friend of Nadia's, was particularly attentive.

"Princess Carla, your beauty far exceeds all the reports we've had. Why have they been keeping you under wraps?"

Carla blushed under such brutally blunt admiration and looked to Marisa for help.

"The princess has been fully involved in the liberation of Carnethia," Marisa explained. "She hasn't had time for social frivolity. Now that the war is over, she's hoping to have a little fun."

Jans smiled in a practiced sexy way that showed off more guile than sincerity. "Your Highness, I have to admit, fun is practically my middle name. I'd love to show you the highlights in a nighttime tour of the city. Allow me to leave my card with your party. You can call me on a moment's notice. I can personally guarantee that you will have a good time."

"That would be wonderful," Carla said, obviously smitten.

Jans's gaze flickered over Marisa. "And who is this lovely lady accompanying you?"

"Oh, this is my friend Marisa. She's staying with us right now."

He gave her a silky smile and took her hand in his. His gaze traveled down and quickly returned to meet hers, but she knew he had noticed her pregnancy. A scowl from Nico was warning him his visiting time was up. "Lucky girl," he said. "I hope to be allowed to visit you myself one day."

"Oh, I'm sure you will," Carla said. "Maybe Nadia can bring you by."

Nico and Marisa exchanged a look as Jans took his leave. It was evident neither one of them thought much of the young man, but Carla was in ecstasy.

"Wasn't he gorgeous? Oh, Marisa! How can I make sure he's invited to the ball?"

"I guess you can check with the social secretary to see if he's on the list," Marisa said doubtfully.

Another race was about to be run and Aunt Julia had neglected to place a bet.

"I'll do it for you," Marisa offered. She had a yen to walk around a little anyway.

Taking Aunt Julia's pick, she set off to find the betting window. It was exciting being in the crowd, listening to the talk and feeling a part of it all. The line was short and she quickly reached the window and placed the bet. As she was turning back toward the box, she was caught up in a group heading for the railing to watch the race and pushed along like a leaf in the current of the ocean.

Suddenly a rough hand grabbed her arm and pulled her to the side and there was a voice in her ear as a man leaned close from behind.

"Well, Marie, you've certainly landed yourself on a fine perch, haven't you?"

She tried to turn to see who was speaking, but the crowd surged and she was forced to move forward with the man still gripping her arm.

"Let me go," she said loudly, trying to pull away.

The man didn't release her arm. She looked around for help, but no one was paying any attention. Icy fear crept through her. How was she going to get away from this man?

"Listen, Marie," he said, leaning close. "Umberto says all will be forgiven if you just give him a call. Better do it very soon. Bad things will happen if you don't."

She tried again to twist around to see him, and what she saw didn't reassure her. His features were even and not unpleasant, but he had the hardest, coldest eyes she'd ever seen. She didn't have a clue who he might be.

"Take care, my girl," he said. "One day you'll fly alone and we have a nice cage we're saving just for you."

He dropped his grip on her and left as

suddenly as he'd appeared, melting into the crowd. She rubbed her arm where he'd been holding her and pushed her way through the mob to get back to the royal box. For just a moment she wondered if she really wanted to tell Nico what had happened. The man knew her. He was rough and uncouth. What if she was part of a bunch of con artists or something more awful? What would happen if Nico found out she was a crook or some sort of criminal? How long would he still be interested in knowing her?

But she really didn't have any choice in the matter. Looking at him as she entered the box, she felt a flood of emotion—relief, fear, anxiety. He was the one she had to go to.

"What's wrong?" He could see the agitation in her face right away.

She sat down close to him and leaned so only he could hear. "A man accosted me out in the crowd."

He went very still. "Who was he?"

"I don't know, but he called me Marie. He seemed to know me."

Nico rose. "Where did he go?" he asked quickly, looking back the way she'd come.

She shook her head and reached to tug on his sleeve, pulling him back down. "You'll never find him now. He disappeared into the crowd." She licked her dry lips. "He…he gave me a warning."

Nico dropped back down close to her. "What sort of warning?"

She closed her eyes for a few seconds. She hated doing this. For one thing, it put her into a category that wasn't flattering. And she was very much afraid she might just belong there.

Taking a deep breath, she raised her chin and went on. "He said someone named Umberto would make things ugly for me if I didn't contact him very soon."

"Umberto?"

"That's the name he said."

"And you don't know…?"

"No." She shook her head, feeling tragic. "I don't remember that name at all."

He frowned, thinking for a moment. "Don't go out on your own again," he warned her. "Stay near security. And tell me right away if you see him in the crowd."

She nodded. The joy in the day was gone and a sick feeling lay at the pit of her stomach. There were so many questions. Why was she running? What if she was part of some sort of smuggling ring? What if she belonged to a den of thieves, a Mafia family, a gang of grifters? Why did she have coded papers in her clothes? Why did hard-eyed men with rough faces seem to know her?

She did want to find out about her own life. But she was very much afraid that once she knew the truth, once they all knew the truth, she was never going to see Nico again.

She thought about that during the ride back home in the dark that evening. Staring out into the black night, her future was beginning to shape itself from the mist and that future was going to have nothing in common with this royal family. Evidence seemed clear. One way or another, she was involved with some vulgar people. And there was no way she was going to do anything that might tarnish the reputation of this royal family and this royal prince. She felt as though she was back at the beginning again, as she'd been the first night she'd arrived at the palace. She had to get away.

She was up early the next morning, but Nico was up even earlier. By the time she came down to the breakfast room, he was there with a list of all the Umbertos in the kingdom.

"I'm not sure how complete it is," he admitted, handing it to her. "This just goes to prove how important it is to get a modern computer network up and running in this country. Our data banks are so far behind the rest of Europe. They practically had to go out with questionnaires to get this much."

She glanced down the page, pretty sure it wasn't going to help much. Then she looked at Nico sitting nursing a cup of coffee. She loved the way his dark hair fell over his forehead, the way his blue eyes considered something seriously before the flicker of amusement came back into his gaze. If only…

"I have to tell you something," she said quietly. "I think I'm beginning to get my memory back."

His gaze sharpened. "Tell me," he said simply.

"Well, it's not as if I'm getting any sudden revelations or anything like that," she said quickly. "It's more like—I begin to realize that more and more of my background is filling in. Think of one of those paint-by-number canvases where the images come in as you fill in the colors. My canvas is beginning to make sense to me. I'm remembering a childhood that I didn't have a couple of days ago. It's all starting to come back to me." She wrinkled her nose in a sort of smile. "I think."

"You think." He smiled into her eyes. "Let me know everything, okay?"

"Okay." She loved his smile, loved feeling warmed by it. "Let's just hope it's really *my* past, and not someone else's," she added.

He laughed. Rising, he stopped beside her. Her heart began to beat in a crazy pattern in her chest, but all he did was touch her shoulder and then move on, getting ready for his day. She closed her eyes as he left the room. Oh yes, she was going to miss this.

Carla came down for breakfast and they had some fun going over the previous day's events, especially the visit from Jans Hunsinger, which seemed to have left Carla head over heels in infatuation. Marisa had some concerns about that. Something about the young man hadn't sat right with her.

She was coming back from a stroll in the forest around noon when Nico hailed her from the terrace.

"I've got some news for you from Intelligence," he said when she got close enough. "From markings on that cookbook they were able to pinpoint the language of those symbols."

"No kidding." She joined him and they both sat at a little round table with a sweeping view of the palace grounds. "What language is it?"

"It seems to belong to a tiny area in the hill country north of Bennire. It's very remote there and a tribe of ancients set up a protected enclave around a monks' castle where they developed their own language and way of writing. This was all in the thirteenth century."

She frowned. "Well, that's very interesting, but what does it have to do with me?"

He shrugged. "Who knows? This language is so obscure there really isn't much about it in the field. They've sent for an expert who is coming by the end of the week. In the meantime, one thing they can say for sure is that part of the writings on your papers are recipes."

"Recipes?" She gaped at him. "How could recipes be so important I would hide them in the lining of a skirt?"

"That is still a mystery. But it does fit with your obvious talent as a cook, doesn't it?"

She sighed, head in her hands as she leaned on the table.

"So I guess the news is that I'm not a spy after all," she said, feeling a bit sorry to see that go. "It looks like I might be some sort of cook." She looked at him sideways. "I don't know that it's any better that way." What she knew for sure was the fact that cooks and princes did not mix. Not romantically, at any rate.

"Hey, there's nothing better than a sexy cook."

She gave him a look. "How would you know? How many cooks have you dallied with in your time?"

"Hundreds." His eyes warmed her. "But none as sexy as you."

She laughed. "Who else in the world would call a pregnant woman sexy?" she asked, hoping her eyes weren't telegraphing the full affection she was feeling.

"Anyone who took a good look at you."

He wanted to kiss her. The impulse was clear in his eyes. One touch and she would melt. She was so in love with this man. Rising abruptly, she mumbled an excuse, and ran to her room, her heart beating wildly. She wasn't going to be able to resist her feelings much longer. She had to get out of here. She had to do it soon.

Nico sank into a deep chair in the library and stared at a shelf full of books, going into full brooding mode. He didn't want to live without her. That realization was growing stronger and stronger inside him. She was the morning sunlight, the cool caress of moonlight in the evening. He wanted to breathe the air around her. He wanted to see her face when he woke up, feel her body when he lay in bed, hear her soft voice in his ear every day. He needed her. So what was he going to do about it?

Marry her. That was the only way for a man like him. He had to marry her. Just making that decision, just letting himself view it as a possibility, lightened his spirits immensely. He would marry her. They would make a family together.

That was the way it had to be. He had to stay. He had to be a part of the restoration. His whole life was devoted to it. But he had to do it with Marisa by his side. Yes. His mind was made up.

Now, how was he going to convince her of it?

CHAPTER TEN

THE situation seemed to be perfectly timed. Carla and Aunt Julia were on an overnight visit to the Duke of Gevetia's summer estate. The Belgrade cousins, Jan and Jols were at the theater. Prince Nico was at a late meeting at Parliament. Even Chauncy had taken some rare time off. Marisa was going to take this opportunity to make her escape at last.

She had to wear one of Nadia's outfits because she had no choice, but she wasn't packing anything to take along. She agonized over a note to Nico, finally settling on a simple thank you with regrets.

And then she had one thing left to do. She had to get her coded papers back. After all, she'd gone through a lot because of them. They must be important to her real life. She didn't think she ought to try to get away without them.

That meant she had to get into the prince's suite and hope the papers were there. She made sure there was no one to see her, then raced up the stairs and tried the door to his room. It opened without any problem, and she was inside, and suddenly out of breath. She stopped, trying to calm herself. It wasn't that she had run so hard coming up the stairs. It was more because she was scared to death. In some ways, that was a relief. Maybe she wasn't such a bad person after all if she couldn't break into someone's room without feeling awful about it.

She got her breathing under control and opened the tall closet, pulling open the flat drawer. There they were. She was just reaching for them when the door to the room opened and Nico walked in.

She screamed—more evidence that she wasn't used to doing things like this. But Nico nearly jumped out of his skin, then stood staring at her as though she might be a ghost.

"What are you doing here?" he demanded.

She knew what this looked like. After all, he'd thought she was a spy from the beginning. She had a perfectly good explanation—sort of—but she was so unsettled, she couldn't get it out, and instead stood there saying, "I—I—I" over and over again and waving the papers at him.

"You wanted to look at the papers?" he asked skeptically, his face impassive, his eyes cold as steel. "Why didn't you just ask?"

Why not indeed? "Uh…" She licked her lips. "Oh Nico, you've got me so shook up I can't even think straight," she managed at last. "You scared me to death coming in like that. I—I thought you were at Parliament."

The corners of his mouth tweaked and his face began to soften a bit. Obviously, she'd stumbled on to exactly the right tone to lower his suspicions.

"They were all yelling at each other and getting nowhere. I decided to come home and try to get some sleep."

"And I'm in your way." She smiled but knew it must look ghastly. That was certainly the way it felt. "Look, do you mind if I just take these papers back to my room so I can look them over? I—I had some thoughts."

"Sure. Why not?"

He pulled off his tie and draped it across the back of a chair, then began working on the buttons of his shirt. She tried to start gathering up the papers, but somehow she couldn't stop watching him undress.

"You don't have to go right away, do you?" he asked her softly.

She swallowed hard but didn't answer. Not with words, anyway. Her eyes, however, were another story. They were so dark, so huge, so warm, he felt as though he could lose himself in them. There was such sadness there, and yet, there was something so full of a sensual promise, he couldn't turn away.

She knew exactly what she was doing and she knew she shouldn't be. But this was the last time she would ever see him, and it broke her heart. So when he started toward her, she didn't move away or do anything at all to resist or deter him. Instead, she turned into his arms and raised her face for his kiss.

His lips touched hers, then his tongue traced their edges and she moaned, opening her mouth to invite him inside. He filled her with his heat, gathering her up in his arms and pulling her close. She clung to him, luxuriating in his kiss, pressing her breasts against him, feeling the evidence of how much he wanted her and letting the growing excitement in her own body run uncontrolled.

He wanted her and she wanted him and she couldn't think of anything else. He was all she needed. He tasted dark and rich and hot and she wanted all of him with an urgency she couldn't hide.

"Marisa," he whispered close to her ear. "Are you sure?"

She turned her head and caught his mouth with hers in answer, arching her body against him, lifting her arms to encircle his neck and showing him in every way she could how much she needed him. He kissed the tender spot at her ear, kissed his way down her neck, kissed the pulse at the base of her throat, then reached up to tug down the zipper of her top, exposing the swell of her breasts to more kisses.

Her hands slid beneath his shirt and pushed it away from his hot flesh. He felt like liquid gold beneath her touch. She stroked his chest, his back, his sides, her hands sliding all the way down to where his slacks began. She couldn't stop, and when he shuddered under her touch, she felt a power she'd never known she could have.

Somehow they had landed on the bed. Somehow, their limbs were entwined and their bodies were trembling with anticipation. Marisa had never felt so alive. She'd never felt so in love. She'd never felt so ready to make love.

But a sudden sound, like an explosion,

ripped through the house. They both stopped, alert and listening. There was shouting and more banging. Something was going on.

Nico rolled away from her, rose from the bed and went to the door. Opening it, he listened for a moment, then groaned.

"Oh my God. It's Dane."

Nico's brother and the future King of Carnethia could be heard storming through the open areas downstairs like a menacing tornado. There was yelling, there were people scurrying.

"Stay here," Nico advised grimly, putting his shirt on. "I'll go see what the problem is."

Marisa blinked, steadying herself. How could she stay here when all hell seemed to be breaking loose downstairs? Something told her whatever the problem was, it was going to touch her life. She couldn't just wait here and wonder. Pulling her clothing to rights and fluffing her hair, she looked back at the bed with regret, then carefully followed him down the stairs and into the foyer where his brother was holding forth.

Dane was just as handsome as his two brothers, but thicker and fiercer. He'd brought a couple of men with him, and Chauncy had appeared, but Dane was the center of the disturbance. He was waving a newspaper around and speaking emphatically, but she still hadn't caught what he was so upset about. And then he saw her.

"You!" he said, turning to face her, his eyes steely, his tone pure sarcasm. "You're the one. I hear you're carrying my baby."

Her mouth dropped and she turned to look at Nico.

"Don't bully her," Nico said, quickly coming between them protectively. "It's not her fault."

Dane slapped the newspaper he held. "Then tell me, Nico, whose fault is it? I get up this morning and the papers are full of it. Look at this headline—Mother of Future King Hidden in Palace."

He glared at Marisa. "That's you, I take it." He pulled another paper out of a briefcase. "And this one: Found: The Missing Royal Heir. Or how about, Dane's Babe Uncovered."

Nico shook his head, appalled. "Those are just crazy."

"Of course they are. But these people don't care about that. They get a hint of scandal and they run with it." Dane shook his head, looking fierce. "I spend half my time trying to convince you all how detrimental it would be if you get written up in the tabloids, and the next thing I know, out of the blue, *I'm* written about." He waved the papers at Nico again. "I want to know how this happened."

Nico took a paper from him and read the headline for himself. Swearing, he dropped it again. "This was today in Paris? Our local rags will have picked it up by tomorrow, no doubt about it."

"And wait until you read the body of the article. They know things about us I didn't know *we* knew. Now you tell me. How did they get these details?"

Nico stared at him without saying a word. Marisa's heart began to race and her head began to pound.

"I'll tell you how," the crown prince said. "We have only one new element among us."

Everyone turned and stared at Marisa. Shock flashed through her like an electric charge.

"You're blaming me?" she asked in horror. "I didn't have a thing to do with it. I wouldn't even know how to contact this sort of journalist."

Dane gave her a scathing look. "You don't have to worry about that. They'll contact you if they get the idea you might be willing to spill your guts for them. A little information can yield a lot of cash."

"Well, there you go," she said, working hard to hold back any sign of panic. "You can ask Prince Nico. I don't have any money. Case closed."

"No outside bank accounts?" Dane asked, arching a rugged eyebrow.

"Listen, I don't even have a cell phone to use to call the papers with. You may not know this, but I've had amnesia for the last week or so and…"

Dane waved a hand dismissively. "I know all about it—how Nico found you trying to jump off a bridge and all. My family has graciously taken you in while you are recovering, and this is how you repay us."

She felt sick, dizzy, breathless. Her head ached so badly she could hardly stand it. That made it hard to think, hard to figure out a way to defend herself. Prince Dane really seemed to believe that she had done this thing. She looked at Nico. His eyes were unreadable. Her heart sank. He believed it too.

"I didn't do it," she said hoarsely. She put a hand on her rounded belly. "Why would I want anyone to believe this is your child?"

Dane shrugged. "The usual reason, I suppose. Money."

She shook her head, feeling faint.

"These papers are obsessed with our story. They seem to want to write anything about our family, especially if it has to do with the succession." Suddenly, his anger dulling, he mainly looked tired. "The rumor is that the war wounds I sustained or the malaria I had for awhile, or both, have rendered me unable to have children. That I'm sterile."

Without thinking, Marisa asked the unthinkable. "Are you?"

Most in the room gasped, and she winced, wishing she could recall the question, but her head ached so, she hardly knew what she was doing.

Dane looked at her as though she was so outrageous, it was almost amusing. "You'd like to know, wouldn't you? I suppose there would be a nice bonus for that information." He shook his head in disbelief. "Well, I'm not going to talk about that. The people may think they have a right to know everything about me but there are some things I will keep to myself for the moment."

Going into a more philosophical mood, he began to pace the carpet. "Though when you come right down to it, I can hardly blame our people for being concerned. The fact is, after all this war and uncertainty, they want an heir in the pipeline. They want to see a solid line of succession." He stopped before Marisa and looked her over in an assessing way. "So you are Marisa."

She found herself curtsying and her cheeks reddened.

"Yes, I've heard all about you," he said. "Chauncy keeps me informed."

"Chauncy's a snitch?" Nico said, his voice sharp with irony as he looked around to see the butler slinking out of the room.

"Forget it, Nico," Dane responded. "He's known me longer than he's known you. And loves me better, I daresay."

"No doubt."

The two brothers faced each other warily. Marisa could see there was respect between them, but a measure of resentment as well.

"We need to talk," Dane said wearily.

Nico nodded. "Why don't you go on up to your room?" he said quietly to Marisa. "I've got to hash this out with Dane. I'll see you in the morning."

She nodded, then looked into his eyes, wanting to see something that would give her reason to hope. There was no warmth there, and she cringed inside. He believed she was a crook. And why shouldn't he? Every time he turned around, something pointed in that direction, culminating in him finding her rummaging around in his room.

Blinking back tears, she turned and walked sedately to the stairs, even though she wanted to run. She'd never felt so wrongly accused, and there wasn't a thing she could do to prove her innocence.

But hey—it was her own fault. What had she expected? You couldn't play around with royalty and not expect to get burned.

Once in her room, she didn't waste any time. She was ready to go, wasn't she? Why wait around? If only her head would stop pounding. There was the matter of the papers she'd gone to Nico's room for. She still didn't have them. But there was no way to remedy that now. She had to go without them.

Looking out the front, she saw where the guards were. She knew their routine by now and knew she would have to wait a few minutes before she would have the window of opportunity through which she could slip out.

Glancing down, she saw the simple note she'd written to Nico earlier that evening.

Suddenly, she had more to say. Much more. But she had the time. Clearing a place at the vanity table, she sat down, pen in hand, and began to write.

Dane and Nico were squaring off warily as Marisa left for her room. Dane dismissed the others so they could be alone, and once they were, he raised an eyebrow. "Are you and she…?"

"Never mind," Nico responded impatiently. "I can see that you have a plan. Just what is it you want to do to remedy this situation?"

"That's why I came to you," Dane said, running a hand through his thick hair. "You're the idea guy." He swore softly, shaking his head. "Women. Nothing but trouble."

Nico frowned. Something about Dane saying that put his back up, big-time. He thought first of Marisa, and then his mind went back to Andrea charging into danger, risking everything for the cause—the return of the Montenevada family to the throne, the vanquishing of the hateful Acredonnas who had plundered the country and made life miserable for millions. That was what Andrea had given her life for. And what now? Had it all been worth it?

"What did we do this for, Dane?" he asked his brother, a thread of tense emotion in his voice. "In some ways, the country is in worse shape than when we began. Have you seen the statistics, the crime in the streets, the profiteering, the graft? Why aren't we doing anything to stem this filthy tide of corruption?"

"Nico, we are doing something. We have plans…"

"Plans, but no action."

Dane stared at him for a moment, realizing these were more than normal complaints. "Nico," he said at last, "I know you still mourn for Andrea. We all do. But she died doing what she had to do. She wouldn't have had it any other way. She was a born warrior."

"She fought for a better country, not…" He shook his head.

"These things take time."

Nico moved impatiently. "Time you don't seem to have to give them. You're out of the country at these international conferences constantly. When is the hard work going to get done here at home?"

"I have to deal with the international alliances before I can turn my full attention to the local problems."

"That's just wrong, Dane. Our people need you to tend to their needs first and foremost. Let the international world go away for awhile."

"Nico, don't you understand?" Dane responded irritably. "Without international ties, we're alone and defenseless in a dangerous world. Right now we're like a newborn baby. We need help to stay alive. Believe me, there are plenty of bigger powers who would love to snap us up if they saw a hint of weakness on our borders." He scowled. "These tabloid stories help promote weakness."

Nico nodded. He agreed with Dane as far as it went. Still… "So what do you want to do about it?"

Dane's head rose and he met his brother's troubled gaze. "The first thing we have to do is remove that woman from the premises. Put her somewhere out of the public eye, where the press can forget about her—and she can forget about us."

"Sorry," Nico said firmly, returning his brother's gaze with implacable resistance. "We're not going to do that."

Dane's face hardened. "We have to do it. It's the only way." He gestured in the direction Marisa had gone. "She's a traitor. I want her out of here."

Nico stood toe to toe with his older brother. "If she goes, so do I."

Dane frowned, shaking his head as though he couldn't believe what he was hearing. "What are you talking about?"

"It's not all about you, Dane. You may be just a few weeks short of becoming king, but that doesn't make you the most important person on earth. Or even in this country. And right now, as far as I'm concerned, Marisa's feelings are more important than you getting your face out of the tabloids." He shook his head. "She didn't do it. And I won't allow you to persecute her for something that's not her fault."

"Well, if she didn't do it, who did?"

"I don't know. But that's our problem, not hers." His eyes narrowed as he faced the future king. "You can have her expelled from the palace. You're the boss. But if she goes, I go."

Dane stared at his brother for a moment, then abruptly shifted gears. "Calm down, Nico," he said quietly. "I need you by my side. Don't throw up barriers."

"Maybe I've had it," Nico said, though he was talking just as quietly as Dane now. "Maybe it's all gone too far and cost too much. Maybe I should just let you run this damn country by yourself." He shook his head. "I don't even know if it's worth running."

"Oh, it's worth it." The crown prince stared at his brother. "Are you in love with her?"

Nico looked up and saw the humanity in Dane's eyes. "Yes," he said simply. "Yes, I am."

Dane nodded. He took a long, deep breath before he spoke again. "Okay, then. I remember how you were with Andrea. I'll trust your instincts on this, too. I just hope you're right."

Nico's shoulders sagged and all the tension seemed to seep out of him. He took a deep breath of his own and reached out to hug Dane with more awkward affection than grace.

"Thanks," he said, his emotion coloring his voice. "You always were a good guy once you calmed down."

Dane hugged him back roughly. "Hey, it's always been you and me. And it always will be."

CHAPTER ELEVEN

IT wasn't hard to escape from the palace. Marisa had known it wouldn't be. Everything was centered around keeping people out, not locking people in. In no time at all, she was walking quickly down the dark and lonely street. She wasn't as clueless as she'd been the other night. She had a plan this time. She knew where she wanted to go and what she wanted to do.

But she hadn't gone more than two blocks before she knew she wasn't going to be allowed to do things her way. A man was suddenly walking beside her, sliding an arm through hers and sticking something that felt very much like the barrel of a gun in her ribs.

"So there you are, Marie," the cold masculine voice ground out in her ear. "Umberto will be happy to have you home again. He's got plans for you."

She didn't have to turn to know it was the same man who'd accosted her at the races. Closing her eyes, she sighed with resignation.

"It's Tom Verner, isn't it?" she said. "I remember now."

Prince Nico was up early the next morning. He had some work to go over before breakfast, so he was available to take an early phone call from his security staff.

"Good morning, Your Highness. We've got a painter here who claims he's found a suitcase we've been searching for. He was assigned to paint the underside of the Gonglia Bridge and there it was, stuck up under the pilings where it couldn't be seen…"

"I'll be right there," Nico said. He glanced toward the stairway that led to Marisa's room, wondering if he should wake her and take her along, but decided against it. There was plenty of time for her to see the bag later. They had all day.

It certainly looked as if it could be hers. He had it brought into the library and put on the library table, but he didn't want to open it without her. He was surprised she wasn't down yet. She usually showed up before anyone else. He hesitated. He had to remember she was carrying a baby and might need more sleep. He didn't want to disturb her. He waited another half hour, then threw caution to the winds and ran up the stairs and knocked on her door.

When she didn't respond, he knew right away that she was gone. Throwing open the door, he charged inside and cursed loudly. The bed hadn't been slept in. Why hadn't he realized she would finally make good on her need to go? And now, how was he going to find her again?

Just as he turned to leave the room, his eye caught the note on the vanity. He stopped, picked it up, then sank into a chair while he read it.

My dearest Prince Nico,
I didn't tell the tabloids anything. I'm so sorry you think I did.

I've got to go. I'm starting to remember more and more and I think I know why I ran, why I ended up where you found me that night. And why I must go back.

I came to this city hoping to find refuge with a wealthy and influential uncle I hadn't seen for years. I never did contact him. I don't even know if he still lives here in town. I know I was running because of a man named Umberto. He's the father of my baby. He's a criminal. He conned me into a relationship and some financial deals. I know I never married him.

My family has made chocolate for over two hundred years. We make the best gourmet chocolate in this part of Europe. Umberto came to work for me when my father joined the rebel army and disappeared into the mountains. He was charming and smart and handsome. It was amazing how he took to chocolate work. I'd never seen anyone take to it the way he did, so quickly, so expertly. He bowled me over. I'd never known a man, other than my father, who loved it the way I did. Of course, it was all a lie. I found out later when the truth came out that he'd been a chocolatier as long as I had—from birth, and he'd showed up on my doorstep when he did in order to steal my family's recipes. By the time I realized all this, I was pregnant and he had swindled me out of my family's company.

I have to go back and face him and somehow get my company back. And

that is the trajectory of my future life—
so different from yours.

Goodbye, sweet prince. Thank you so
much for all you and your family have
done for me. Tell Carla I love her. May
your family's reign in this country be
long and fruitful. I'll be pulling for you
all the way.

Nico stared at the page. It took a few
minutes to fully digest all that she'd said. But
the reality of her leaving hadn't changed. And
he still didn't know her real name, though the
man at the track had called her Marie. But
where to begin to go to find her. Stuffing the
paper into his pocket, he went back downstairs
and into the library. Taking out a screwdriver,
he began to work on the lock on the suitcase.
In a moment he had it open, and in among the
various clothing and cosmetics he found what
they had been looking for all this time—the
key to the code. The papers were the recipes,
the key would let someone read them. Finally.

But a more important item was missing.
Nowhere did he find a name or an address. He
reached for the telephone. Intelligence was
going to have to try again to come to the rescue.

* * *

An hour later, he was sitting at a conference table working madly at a computer, surrounded by intelligence officers and his brother, Dane. Stacks of paper littered the room, lists of food companies, lists of merchandisers, lists of chocolate makers and chocolate sellers. And everybody seemed to be talking at once.

"Quiet!" Dane thundered at last, running his hands through his thick auburn hair until it stood up like a stand of trees on his head. "I can't hear myself think."

"You're not supposed to be thinking," Nico retorted. "You're supposed to be searching. Come on. We don't have any time."

Dane turned and looked at him in disgust. "Did it ever occur to you that just because the woman thinks her company was the best chocolatier in the country doesn't mean it was actually true?"

"It's true," Nico said calmly. "Keep looking."

Dane frowned at him. "Maybe you should take this as a sign," he said more quietly, meant just for his brother. "Maybe you should let her go. Maybe this was just not meant to be."

The words chilled Nico. A small part of him was saying the same thing. But he wasn't buying it. He was going to find her. He was going to find her and ask her to marry him. And if she said no, he was going to sling her over his shoulder and bring her back here and ply her with food and drink and lots of love until she said yes. She had to marry him. Had to.

"Hey," one of the intelligence officers cried out. "What about this one? Geers chocolates. DuBonnet Chocolatier. It's a really old establishment set in a little town in the Bristol Mountains. They list the owner as Charles DuBonnet."

"Does he have a wife?" Nico asked, his heart beginning to pound in dread of what he might hear.

"Yes."

"What's her name?"

"Uh…wait, I saw it here somewhere."

Nico held his breath. If she turned out to be married after all this…

"Here it is. Her name is Grace."

"Oh." He let the breath out in relief.

"But there seems to be a daughter who has taken over just recently."

"Her name?"

"Marie. Marie DuBonnet."

Nico closed his eyes. That had to be it.

"Chauncy, have them bring the car

around," he called, bolting out of his chair. "I'm going to the Bristol Mountains."

Marisa sat across the table from Umberto. Her memory had been almost completely restored by now. Her real name was Marie DuBonnet, owner and operator of DuBonnet Chocolatier. And she had stupidly allowed this man to take over her company and her life.

She watched as he downed another glass of her vintage wine. Shaking her head, she wondered how she ever could have found him attractive. He was mean and vicious and she had the new bruises to prove it. All she could think of was the contrast to Nico with his intellect and integrity. In her mind the prince had taken on the attributes of the perfect hero. Umberto—not so much.

"Where are the recipes?" he demanded, looking belligerent.

"I told you, I don't have them." She felt calm, serene, sure of herself. That was different and she rather liked it.

"What are you talking about?" he growled at her. "You took them when you left here."

"They're gone. You can search me all you want. They are gone." What luck that she hadn't been able to secrete them out after all.

"You have the translations I made for you. And that's all you're going to get."

"Those translations are no good." He glared at her and then spat. "They're not the same as the originals. They don't come out right and you know it."

She had to smile, because she did know it. That was why she'd written them that way. He had no right to her ancient family recipes and she was going to make sure he never got his hands on them.

If only she'd understood what he wanted from the beginning. But she hadn't known his background then. His family, the Geers, had run a small chocolate company in another region of the country that was almost as old as her family's. Their quality was never top tier and the family had always seemed to operate at the fringe of what was legal and ethical. The DuBonnets had never paid much attention to them. It might have been better if they had, then they might have noticed how much the Geers hated them. For generations, the Geers had built up feelings of being oppressed by Marisa's family operation. Umberto was raised with that. The whole focus of his life was to find a way to get back at the hated DuBonnets and steal the wealth his family felt they'd been cheated out of.

Now here the two of them sat in the outer office of her family company. Plaques and commendations covered the walls and displays of old-fashioned chocolate-making equipment were set out behind glass and on the open counters. Back through the swinging doors, workers who knew and loved her were busy making some of the best chocolate in Europe. But not the specialty items, the twisted bird's nest mocha, the ballerina lace scrollwork, the dark Brazilian corea. They hadn't been able to make those for some time now. They didn't have the recipes.

"I'm not afraid of you anymore, Umberto," she told him, shooting daggers with her eyes. "You can't do anything to hurt me and my chocolate company. You can make faux DuBonnet chocolates all day long. Everyone will know they're fakes. It won't work. You should just go back to your own company and try to work on that quality issue you people seem to have."

She braced herself, ready for him to hit her again. Surprisingly, he held off. Leaning close, he told her through clenched teeth, "I am going to make you sorry, Marie. I am going to take you down to the cellar where no one can see what I do to you. I'll keep you down there as long as it takes. But you are going to give me those damn recipes."

"Never," she said firmly, eyes clear.

He almost hit her then. Holding himself back, he was breathing hard. "I've got my boys, Tom and Willie, to help me. I think we can handle you between us."

Even that didn't frighten her. Funny how she now had the strength to stand up to him on her own. She didn't need the help of her uncle or anyone else. She could tell him straight to his face what she thought.

"I realize something now," she told him, just for his information. "Even if you got hold of the old recipes, it wouldn't help you. Your chocolate will never be the same as ours. Because you don't have the love of chocolate we have always had. You love revenge, not chocolate." She smiled. "I reject you, Umberto. I reject everything about you. I won't be a part of you in any way."

He stared at her in impotent rage. "So you think because you've become the prince's concubine you'll be protected?" he sneered.

That little dart hit its mark, she had to admit, but she tried not to show it. He turned, reaching for the wine bottle. He was still talking, listing all the things he was going to do to her and the way he was going to make her pay if she didn't hand over the real recipes to him. She knew very well he was planning to make her pay even if she did as he demanded.

It was lucky he had no interest in the child, though he knew about her pregnancy. Because of that, he didn't realize how much he could hurt her through her baby. It hadn't occurred to him yet. But that didn't mean it never would. She had to do something but she had a strange calmness about her. She knew she was going to handle this. She had to.

She looked at the display tools sitting on the open counter, the grinders and the sifters and the mallets. The largest mallet was almost within reach and she stared at it, thinking of all the hard chocolate that had been crushed into powder by that mallet over the years. She rather hated to defile it, but there wasn't much choice. Rising smoothly, quietly, she picked it up, took a deep breath, gritted her teeth and swung hard at his head, then watched as he grunted and dropped to the ground. He was out like a light.

"With a swing like that, you should consider trying out for the New York Yankees."